THE COMPLETE TALES OF HENRY JAMES
VOLUME THREE: 1873–1875

The Complete Tales of
HENRY JAMES

THE COMPLETE TALES OF

HENRY JAMES

EDITED WITH AN

INTRODUCTION BY

LEON EDEL

3

1873–1875

RUPERT HART-DAVIS

SOHO SQUARE LONDON

1962

01397284

GARSTANG

PRINTED IN GREAT BRITAIN BY
WESTERN PRINTING SERVICES LTD BRISTOL

CONTENTS

INTRODUCTION: 1873–1875

THE tales Henry James wrote between 1873 and 1875 were the fruit of his second adult encounter with Europe. The first, in 1869–70, he had characterised as a "passionate pilgrimage." The second, which lasted from June 1872 until the autumn of 1874, was a tolerably calculated experiment to discover whether he could support himself—as he travelled—by his writings. During these two years James produced the papers later reprinted in *Transatlantic Sketches* (1875), most of the tales here reprinted, and *Roderick Hudson* (1875). A subsequent winter of work in New York, during which he wrote only one story, "Benvolio," and did considerable hack-work, proved to him that he could more cheaply and profitably practise his art in Europe. I have described the stages by which he reached this decision in the second part of my biography of the novelist, *The Conquest of London*.

The tales of 1873–75 announce certain characteristic, and indeed major, themes while reflecting the writer's personal need to understand his rôle as artist in the two worlds in which he moved: the genteel and parochial life of Boston and Cambridge, and the "international" and cosmopolitan world he was discovering in Paris, Florence and Rome. This is the theme he states in "The Sweetheart of M. Briseux," a tale he never reprinted, and successfully elaborates in "The Madonna of the Future." The latter, one of the most successful tales of this period, contains within it the classic fear of the artist that he may suddenly "run dry" or that—being by his very nature a dreamer—he may dream his life away. American artists, like James, knew then that they risked losing themselves in a dream of the European past. How be a poet, a painter, how indulge in the life of art which is the life of the dream, and be a man of action as well? "The Madonna of the

7

Future," like most of James's stories of artists, seeks the answer to this question: the artist talks brilliantly about his picture—but he cannot paint it; the narrator speaks for the New World and its artistic opportunities; and the debased craftsman makes clever statuettes of animals which look like humans. The tale reflects an old Florentine mood, a memory of his youthful reading of Musset (he incorporates a speech from *Lorenzaccio* at one point), but it contains also a credo which James developed in a rather inflated fashion in the story of M. Briseux. This is that an artist must be hard, un-yielding, resolute, masculine, and if necessary an egotist. The material of these two tales was to be used again, with greater maturity, in the novel of *Roderick Hudson*.

The next four tales (excluding for the moment "Professor Fargo") have similarly congruous themes. "The Last of the Valerii" and "Adina" were both fruit of James's Roman rides and rambles during the winter and spring of 1873. The new Rome of the Risorgimento, in which James was living, was busy excavating its past and modernising itself. The writer looked at statues brought to the surface and ancient artifacts thrown up out of the earth—out of that accretion of pagan and Christian, ancient and medieval, surmounted and gilded by the renaissance, which constituted a kind of mocking pastiche of the centuries. Riding on horseback across the Campagna, James experienced on that rolling terrain, and in the exquisite play of light, the stir of old things; he had a sense of empires that had crumbled; they seemed to lie under the galloping hooves of his horse. Unlike the romantic poets, who had wept for an evanescent and vanished past, James marvelled that so much survived. And yet he was uneasy. He could contemplate the panorama of Rome, and read his Stendhal, de Brosses, or Gregorovius, in a still rustic city; he could see history all round him being turned up by a spade. The ruins were picturesque; yet, like Hawthorne, he felt that they harboured within them memories of the cruel centuries, and some emanation of primordial passion. In "The Last of the Valerii" he wrote a tale which is deceptively Roman surface and sunny warmth, but the substance of which contains the writer's sense of a morbid mouldering antiquity and nightmare evil. The recovered statue threatens the marriage of the American girl and the Italian nobleman (it is one of James's earliest international marriages). The Italian forgets his wife and worships the pagan object; and the solution has to be found by the woman from the New World. She arranges for the past to be recommitted to the past. To disinter it could set the Furies loose again. So, in "Adina," the imperial topaz of Tiberius must be returned to the soft mud of the Tiber. The living jewel—the American girl—triumphs over ancient evil. The implication in these tales is that civilised man must keep the primitive side of his nature properly buried; that it is dangerous to exhume dormant primeval things; that they contain the evil man has eternally sought to master.

By the time he came to the writing of "Madame de Mauves," in the more contemporary setting of an inn in Bad Homburg, James could take a less uneasy view of the marriage of the Old and the New. The reader may feel at first that Euphemia Cleve is a woman wronged by her dissolute husband. He may wonder at a narrator who debates whether it is better to cultivate an art than a passion, as if the two were incompatible. Readers of James's time readily took Euphemia's side against her immoral French husband. But after a while it is impossible not to feel disturbed by Euphemia's smug adherence to a romantic image of love that seems to belong to the romances read by Madame Bovary in her convent. In the end the modern reader may be inclined to join the narrator in the quiet shudder with which the tale ends. Life on Euphemia's terms can be arduous indeed.

"Eugene Pickering," which followed, takes life and love still less strenuously. Eugene's infatuation with a woman older than himself, a Germanic scribbling George Sand character, shows James amusing himself by balancing European sophistication in love against a deadly serious American-adolescent view of it. In these tales—of the buried evils of history, of art *versus* passion, of international marriages and innocent love—James has begun to grasp the fuller meaning of his cosmopolitan theme and the endless pathos and comedy residing in the confrontation of puritan America and "corrupt" Europe.

We need not linger over "Professor Fargo," which is clearly one of James's recurrent potboilers, written for magazines for which he had little respect. Such tales require no critical attention; they are that part of an artist's work in which drudgery makes possible the acts of genius. Nevertheless, in the thematic sequence of James's fiction the writer is telling himself in this tale that there exist already in the New World forms of corruption distinctly American; and this is the first hint of what, in his imaginative fabric, will ultimately be fashioned into his longest American novel, *The Bostonians*.

The last tale in this volume is unique in James's fiction. It is an unashamed personal allegory; and if James, as a realist believed that the allegorical form tends to "spoil" a story, he nevertheless resorted to it on this single occasion to sum up the experience of his two-year exposure to Europe, and his reflections on returning to America. Benvolio is an artistic and pleasure-loving young man, who enjoys both his public and his private life, his monk-like cell on the quiet garden, and his well-furnished room looking out on the large city square. He flirts with a Countess, but he is also devoted to a young woman named Scholastica, daughter of a Philosopher. In this tale James thus faces the duality of his nature and his response to the double environment of his childhood and youth—to the Countess who is Europe, and to Scholastica, who is the very breath of New England. In the tale Scholastica gains the victory, but Benvolio ceases to write verses. In life Henry set sail to live with the Countess—and continued to create.

LEON EDEL

Rome, March 1962

THE MADONNA OF THE FUTURE

WE had been talking about the masters who had achieved but a single masterpiece,—the artists and poets who but once in their lives had known the divine afflatus, and touched the high level of the best. Our host had been showing us a charming little cabinet picture by a painter whose name we had never heard, and who, after this one spasmodic bid for fame, had apparently relapsed into fatal mediocrity. There was some discussion as to the frequency of this phenomenon; during which, I observed, H—— sat silent, finishing his cigar with a meditative air, and looking at the picture, which was being handed round the table. "I don't know how common a case it is," he said at last, "but I've seen it. I've known a poor fellow who painted his one masterpiece, and"—he added with a smile—"he didn't even paint that. He made his bid for fame, and missed it." We all knew H—— for a clever man who had seen much of men and manners, and had a great stock of reminiscences. Some one immediately questioned him further, and while I was engrossed with the raptures of my neighbor over the little picture, he was induced to tell his tale. If I were to doubt whether it would bear repeating, I should only have to remember how that charming woman, our hostess, who had left the table, ventured back in rustling rose-color, to pronounce our lingering a want of gallantry, and, finding us a listening circle, had sunk into her chair in spite of our cigars, and heard the story out so graciously, that when the catastrophe was reached she glanced across at me, and showed me a tender tear in each of her beautiful eyes.

It relates to my youth, and to Italy: two fine things! (H—— began.) I had arrived late in the evening at Florence, and while I finished my bottle of wine at supper, had fancied that, tired traveller though I was, I might pay the city a finer compliment than by going vulgarly to bed. A narrow passage wandered darkly away out of the little square before my hotel, and looked as if it bored into the heart of Florence. I followed it, and at the end of ten minutes emerged upon a great piazza, filled only with the mild autumn moonlight. Opposite rose the Palazzo Vecchio, like some huge civic fortress, with the great bell-tower springing from its embattled verge like a mountain-pine from the edge of a cliff. At its base, in its projected shadow, gleamed certain dim sculptures which I wonderingly approached. One of the images, on the left of the palace door, was a magnificent colossus, shining through the dusky air like some embodied Defiance. In a moment I recognized him as Michael Angelo's David. I turned with a certain relief from his sinister strength to a slender figure in bronze, stationed beneath the high, light loggia, which opposes the free and elegant span of its arches to the dead masonry of the palace; a figure supremely shapely and graceful; gentle, almost, in spite of his holding out with his light nervous arm the snaky head of the slaughtered Gorgon. His name is Perseus, and you may read his story, not in the Greek mythology, but in memoirs of Benvenuto Cellini. Glancing from one of these fine fellows to the other, I probably uttered some irrepressible commonplace of praise, for, as if provoked by my voice, a man rose from the steps of the loggia, where he had been sitting in the shadow, and addressed me in good English,—a small, slim personage, clad in a sort of black velvet tunic (as it seemed), and with a mass of auburn hair, which gleamed in the moonlight, escaping from a little mediæval berretta. In a tone of the most insinuating deference, he asked me for my "impressions." He seemed picturesque, fantastic, slightly unreal. Hovering there in this consecrated neighborhood, he might have passed for the genius of æsthetic hospitality,—if the genius of æsthetic hospitality were not commonly some shabby little custode, flourishing a calico pocket-handkerchief, and openly resentful of the divided franc. This fantasy was made none the less plausible by the brilliant tirade with which he greeted my embarrassed silence.

"I've known Florence long, sir, but I've never known her so lovely as to-night. It's as if the ghosts of her past were abroad in the empty streets. The present is sleeping; the past hovers about us like a dream made visible. Fancy the old Florentines strolling up in couples to pass judgment on the last performance of Michael, of Benvenuto! We should come in for a precious lesson if we might overhear what they say. The plainest burgher of them, in his cap and gown, had a taste in the matter! That was the prime of art, sir. The sun stood high in heaven, and his broad and equal blaze made the darkest places bright and the dullest eyes clear. We live in the evening of time! We grope in the gray dusk, carrying each our poor little taper of selfish and painful wisdom, holding it up to the great models and to the dim idea, and seeing nothing but overwhelming greatness and dimness. The days of illumination are gone! But do you know I fancy—I fancy,"—and he grew suddenly almost familiar in this visionary fervor,—"I fancy the light of that time rests upon us here for an hour! I have never seen the David so grand, the Perseus so fair! Even the inferior productions of John of Bologna and of Baccio Bandinelli seem to realize the artist's dream. I feel as if the moonlit air were charged with the secrets of the masters, and as if, standing here in religious contemplation, we might —we might witness a revelation!" Perceiving at this moment, I suppose, my halting comprehension reflected in my puzzled face, this interesting rhapsodist paused and blushed. Then with a melancholy smile, "You think me a moonstruck charlatan, I suppose. It's not my habit to hang about the piazza and pounce upon innocent tourists. But to-night, I confess,

I'm under the charm. And then, somehow, I fancied you, too, were an artist!"

"I'm not an artist, I'm sorry to say, as you must understand the term. But pray make no apologies. I am also under the charm; your eloquent reflections have only deepened it."

"If you're not an artist, you're worthy to be one!" he rejoined, with a bow. "A young man who arrives at Florence late in the evening, and, instead of going prosaically to bed, or hanging over the travellers' book at his hotel, walks forth without loss of time to pay his devoirs to the beautiful, is a young man after my own heart!"

The mystery was suddenly solved; my friend was an American! He must have been, to take the picturesque so prodigiously to heart. "None the less so, I trust," I answered, "if the young man is a sordid New-Yorker."

"New-Yorkers," he solemnly proclaimed, "have been munificent patrons of art!"

For a moment I was alarmed. Was this midnight revery mere Yankee enterprise, and was he simply a desperate brother of the brush who had posted himself here to extort an "order" from a sauntering tourist? But I was not called to defend myself. A great brazen note broke suddenly from the far-off summit of the bell-tower above us and sounded the first stroke of midnight. My companion started, apologized for detaining me, and prepared to retire. But he seemed to offer so lively a promise of further entertainment, that I was indisposed to part with him, and suggested that we should stroll homeward together. He cordially assented, so we turned out of the Piazza, passed down before the statued arcade of the Uffizi, and came out upon the Arno. What course we took I hardly remember, but we roamed slowly about for an hour, my companion delivering by snatches a sort of moon-touched æsthetic lecture. I listened in puzzled fascination, and wondered who the deuce he was. He confessed with a melancholy but all-respectful head-shake to his American origin. "We are the disinherited of Art!" he cried. "We are condemned to be superficial! We are excluded from the magic circle. The soil of American perception is a poor little barren, artificial deposit. Yes! we are wedded to imperfection. An American, to excel, has just ten times as much to learn as a European. We lack the deeper sense. We have neither taste, not tact, nor force. How should we have them? Our crude and garish climate, our silent past, our deafening present, the constant pressure about us of unlovely circumstance, are as void of all that nourishes and prompts and inspires the artist, as my sad heart is void of bitterness in saying so! We poor aspirants must live in perpetual exile."

"You seem fairly at home in exile," I answered, "and Florence seems to me a very pretty Siberia. But do you know my own thought? Nothing is so idle as to talk about our want of a nutritive soil, of opportunity, of inspiration, and all the rest of it. The worthy part is to do something fine! There's no law in our glorious Constitution against that. Invent, create, achieve! No matter if you've to study fifty times as much as one of these! What else are you an artist for? Be you our Moses," I added, laughing, and laying my hand on his shoulder, "and lead us out of the house of bondage!"

"Golden words,—golden words, young man!" he cried, with a tender smile. " 'Invent, create, achieve!' Yes, that's our business: I know it well. Don't take me, in Heaven's name, for one of your barren complainers,—querulous cynics, who have neither talent nor faith! I'm at work!"—and he glanced about him and lowered his voice as if this were a quite peculiar secret,—"I'm at work night and day. I've undertaken a *creation!* I'm no Moses; I'm only a poor, patient artist; but it would be a fine thing if I were to cause some slender stream of beauty to flow in our thirsty land! Don't think me a monster of conceit," he went on, as he saw me smile at the avidity with which he adopted my fantasy; "I confess that I'm in one of those moods when great things seem possible! This is one of my nervous nights,—I dream waking! When the south-wind blows over Florence at midnight, it seems to coax the soul from all the fair things locked away in her churches and galleries; it comes into my own little studio with the moonlight, and sets my heart beating too deeply for rest. You see I am always adding a thought to my conception! This evening I felt that I couldn't sleep unless I had communed with the genius of Michael!"

He seemed deeply versed in local history and tradition, and he expatiated *con amore* on the charms of Florence. I gathered that he was an old resident, and that he had taken the lovely city into his heart. "I owe her everything," he declared. "It's only since I came here that I have really lived, intellectually. One by one, all profane desires, all mere worldly aims, have dropped away from me, and left me nothing but my pencil, my little note-book" (and he tapped his breast-pocket), "and the worship of the pure masters,—those who were pure because they were innocent, and those who were pure because they were strong!"

"And have you been very productive all this time?" I asked, with amenity.

He was silent awhile before replying. "Not in the vulgar sense!" he said, at last. "I have chosen never to manifest myself by imperfection. The good in every performance I have reabsorbed into the generative force of new creations; the bad—there's always plenty of that—I have religiously destroyed. I may say, with some satisfaction, that I have not added a mite to the rubbish of the world. As a proof of my conscientiousness,"—and he stopped short, and eyed me with extraordinary candor, as if the proof were to be overwhelming,—"I've never sold a picture! 'At least no merchant trafficsi n my heart!' Do you remember the line in Browning? My little studio has never been profaned by superficial, feverish, mercenary work. It's a temple of labor, but of leisure! Art is long. If we work for ourselves, of course we must hurry.

If we work for her, we must often pause. She can wait!"

This had brought us to my hotel door, somewhat to my relief, I confess, for I had begun to feel unequal to the society of a genius of this heroic strain. I left him, however, not without expressing a friendly hope that we should meet again. The next morning my curiosity had not abated; I was anxious to see him by common daylight. I counted upon meeting him in one of the many æsthetic haunts of Florence, and I was gratified without delay. I found him in the course of the morning in the Tribune of the Uffizi,—that little treasure-chamber of perfect works. He had turned his back on the Venus de' Medici, and with his arms resting on the railing which protects the pictures, and his head buried in his hands, he was lost in the contemplation of that superb triptych of Andrea Mantegna,—a work which has neither the material splendor nor the commanding force of some of its neighbors, but which, glowing there with the loveliness of patient labor, suits possibly a more constant need of the soul. I looked at the picture for some time over his shoulder; at last, with a heavy sigh, he turned away and our eyes met. As he recognized me a deep blush rose to his face; he fancied, perhaps, that he had made a fool of himself overnight. But I offered him my hand with a frankness which assured him I was not a scoffer. I knew him by his ardent *chevelure*; otherwise he was much altered. His midnight mood was over, and he looked as haggard as an actor by daylight. He was far older than I had supposed, and he had less bravery of costume and gesture. He seemed the quite poor, patient artist he had proclaimed himself, and the fact that he had never sold a picture was more obvious than glorious. His velvet coat was threadbare, and his short slouched hat, of an antique pattern, revealed a rustiness which marked it an "original," and not one of the picturesque reproductions which brethren of his craft affect. His eye was mild and heavy, and his expression singularly gentle and acquiescent; the more so for a certain pallid leanness of visage which

B

I hardly knew whether to refer to the consuming fire of genius or to a meagre diet. A very little talk, however, cleared his brow and brought back his eloquence.

"And this is your first visit to these enchanted halls?" he cried. "Happy, thrice happy youth!" And taking me by the arm, he prepared to lead me to each of the pre-eminent works in turn and show me the cream of the gallery. But before we left the Mantegna, he pressed my arm and gave it a loving look. "*He* was not in a hurry," he murmured. "He knew nothing of 'raw Haste, half-sister to Delay'!" How sound a critic my friend was I am unable to say, but he was an extremely amusing one; overflowing with opinions, theories, and sympathies, with disquisition and gossip and anecdote. He was a shade too sentimental for my own sympathies, and I fancied he was rather too fond of superfine discriminations and of discovering subtle intentions in the shallow felicities of chance. At moments, too, he plunged into the sea of metaphysics and floundered awhile in waters too deep for intellectual security. But his abounding knowledge and happy judgment told a touching story of long attentive hours in this worshipful company; there was a reproach to my wasteful saunterings in so devoted a culture of opportunity. "There are two moods," I remember his saying, "in which we may walk through galleries,—the critical and the ideal. They seize us at their pleasure, and we can never tell which is to take its turn. The critical mood, oddly, is the genial one, the friendly, the condescending. It relishes the pretty trivialities of art, its vulgar clevernesses, its conscious graces. It has a kindly greeting for anything which looks as if, according to his light, the painter had enjoyed doing it,—for the little Dutch cabbages and kettles, for the taper fingers and breezy mantles of late-coming Madonnas, for the little blue-hilled pastoral, sceptical Italian landscapes. Then there are the days of fierce, fastidious longing,—solemn church-feasts of the intellect,—when all vulgar effort and all petty success is a weariness, and everything but the best—the best of the best—disgusts. In these hours we are relentless aristocrats of taste. We'll not take Michael for granted, we'll not swallow Raphael whole!"

The gallery of the Uffizi is not only rich in its possessions, but peculiarly fortunate in that fine architectural accident, as one may call it, which unites it—with the breadth of river and city between them—to those princely chambers of the Pitti Palace. The Louvre and the Vatican hardly give you such a sense of sustained enclosure as those long passages projected over street and stream to establish a sort of inviolate transition between the two palaces of art. We passed along the gallery in which those precious drawings by eminent hands hang chaste and gray above the swirl and murmur of the yellow Arno, and reached the ducal saloons of the Pitti. Ducal as they are, it must be confessed that they are imperfect as show-rooms, and that with their deep-set windows and their massive mouldings, it is rather a broken light that reaches the pictured walls. But here the masterpieces hang thick, and you seem to see them in a luminous atmosphere of their own. And the great saloons, with their superb dim ceilings, their outer wall in splendid shadow, and the sombre opposite glow of mellow canvas and dusky gilding, make, themselves, almost as fine a picture as the Titians and Raphaels they imperfectly reveal. We lingered briefly before many a Raphael and Titian; but I saw my friend was impatient, and I suffered him at last to lead me directly to the goal of our journey,—the most tenderly fair of Raphael's Virgins, the Madonna in the Chair. Of all the fine pictures of the world, it seemed to me this is the one with which criticism has least to do. None betrays less effort, less of the mechanism of effect and of the irrepressible discord between conception and result, which shows dimly in so many consummate works. Graceful, human, near to our sympathies as it is, it has nothing of manner, of method, nothing, almost, of style; it blooms there in rounded softness, as instinct with harmony as if it were an immediate exhalation of genius. The figure melts away the spectator's mind into a sort of passionate tenderness which he knows not whether he has given to heavenly purity or to earthly charm. He is intoxicated with the fragrance of the tenderest blossom of maternity that ever bloomed on earth.

"That's what I call a fine picture," said my companion, after we had gazed awhile in silence. "I have a right to say so, for I've copied it so often and so carefully that I could repeat it now with my eyes shut. Other works are of Raphael: this *is* Raphael himself. Others you can praise, you can qualify, you can measure, explain, account for: this you can only love and admire. I don't know in what seeming he walked among men, while this divine mood was upon him; but after it, surely, he could do nothing but die; this world had nothing more to teach him. Think of it awhile, my friend, and you'll admit that I'm not raving. Think of his seeing that spotless image, not for a moment, for a day, in a happy dream, as a restless fever-fit, not as a poet in a five minutes' frenzy, time to snatch his phrase and scribble his immortal stanza, but for days together, while the slow labor of the brush went on, while the foul vapors of life interposed, and the fancy ached with tension, fixed, radiant, distinct, as we see it now! What a master, certainly! But ah, what a seer!"

"Don't you imagine," I answered, "that he had a model, and that some pretty young woman—"

"As pretty a young woman as you please! It doesn't diminish the miracle! He took his hint, of course, and the young woman, possibly, sat smiling before his canvas. But, meanwhile, the painter's idea had taken wings. No lovely human outline could charm it to vulgar fact. He saw the fair form made perfect; he rose to the vision without tremor, without effort of wing; he communed with it face to face, and resolved into finer and lovelier truth the purity which completes it as the perfume completes the rose. That's what they call idealism; the word's vastly abused, but the thing is good.

It's my own creed, at any rate. Lovely Madonna, model at once and muse, I call you to witness that I too am an idealist!"

"An idealist, then," I said, half jocosely, wishing to provoke him to further utterance, "is a gentleman who says to Nature in the person of a beautiful girl, 'Go to, you're all wrong! Your fine is coarse, your bright is dim, your grace is *gaucherie*. This is the way you should have done it!' Isn't the chance against him?"

He turned upon me almost angrily, but perceiving the genial flavor of my sarcasm, he smiled gravely. "Look at that picture," he said, "and cease your irreverent mockery! Idealism is *that!* There's no explaining it; one must feel the flame! It says nothing to Nature, or to any beautiful girl, that they'll not both forgive! It says to the fair woman, 'Accept me as your artist-friend, lend me your beautiful face, trust me, help me, and your eyes shall be half my masterpiece!' No one so loves and respects the rich realities of nature as the artist whose imagination caresses and flatters them. He knows what a fact may hold (whether Raphael knew, you may judge by his portrait behind us there, of Tommaso Inghirami); but his fancy hovers above it, as Ariel above the sleeping prince. There is only one Raphael, but an artist may still be an artist. As I said last night, the days of illumination are gone; visions are rare; we have to look long to see them. But in meditation we may still woo the ideal; round it, smooth it, perfect it. The result—the result" (here his voice faltered suddenly, and he fixed his eyes for a moment on the picture; when they met my own again they were full of tears)—"the result may be less than this; but still it may be good, it may be *great!*" he cried with vehemence. "It may hang somewhere, in after years, in goodly company, and keep the artist's memory warm. Think of being known to mankind after some such fashion as this! of hanging here through the slow centuries in the gaze of an altered world, living on and on in the cunning of an eye and hand that are part of the dust of ages, a delight and a law to remote generations; making beauty a force and purity an example!"

"Heaven forbid!" I said, smiling, "that I should take the wind out of your sails; but doesn't it occur to you that beside being strong in his genius, Raphael was happy in a certain good faith of which we have lost the trick? There are people, I know, who deny that his spotless Madonnas are anything more than pretty blondes of that period, enhanced by the Raphaelesque touch, which they declare is a profane touch. Be that as it may, people's religious and æsthetic needs went hand in hand, and there was, as I may say, a demand for the Blessed Virgin, visible and adorable, which must have given firmness to the artist's hand. I'm afraid there is no demand now."

My companion seemed painfully puzzled; he shivered, as it were, in this chilling blast of scepticism. Then shaking his head with sublime confidence: "There is always a demand!" he cried; "that ineffable type is one of the eternal needs of man's heart; but pious souls long for it in silence, almost in shame. Let it appear, and this faith grows brave. How *should* it appear in this corrupt generation? It can't be made to order. It could, indeed, when the order came, trumpet-toned, from the lips of the Church herself, and was addressed to genius panting with inspiration. But it can spring now only from the soil of passionate labor and culture. Do you really fancy that while, from time to time, a man of complete artistic vision is born into the world, that image can perish? The man who paints it has painted everything. The subject admits of every perfection,—form, color, expression, composition. It can be as simple as you please, and yet as rich, as broad and pure, and yet as full of delicate detail. Think of the chance for flesh in the little naked, nestling child, irradiating divinity; of the chance for drapery in the chaste and ample garment of the mother! Think of the great story you compress into that simple theme! Think, above all, of the mother's face and its ineffable suggestiveness, of the mingled burden of joy and trouble, the tenderness turned to worship, and the worship turned to far-seeing pity! Then look at it all in perfect line and lovely color, breathing truth and beauty and mastery!"

"Anch' io son pittore!" I cried. "Unless I'm mistaken, you've a masterpiece on the stocks. If you put all that in, you'll do more than Raphael himself did. Let me know when your picture is finished, and wherever in the wide world I may be, I'll post back to Florence and make my bow to—the *Madonna of the future!*"

He blushed vividly and gave a heavy sigh, half of protest, half of resignation. "I don't often mention my picture, in so many words. I detest this modern custom of premature publicity. A great work needs silence, privacy, mystery even. And then, do you know, people are so cruel, so frivolous, so unable to imagine a man's wishing to paint a Madonna at this time of day, that I've been laughed at,—laughed at, sir!" And his blush deepened to crimson. "I don't know what has prompted me to be so frank and trustful with you. You look as if you wouldn't laugh at me. My dear young man,"—and he laid his hand on my arm,—"I'm worthy of respect. Whatever my talents may be, I'm honest. There's nothing grotesque in a pure ambition, or in a life devoted to it!"

There was something so sternly sincere in his look and tone, that further questions seemed impertinent. I had repeated opportunity to ask them, however; for after this we spent much time together. Daily, for a fortnight, we met by appointment, to see the sights. He knew the city so well, he had strolled and lounged so often through its streets and churches and galleries, he was so deeply versed in its greater and lesser memories, so imbued with the local genius, that he was an altogether ideal *valet de place*, and I was glad enough to leave my Murray at home, and gather facts and opinions alike from his gossiping commentary. He talked of Florence like a lover, and admitted that it was a very old affair; he had lost his heart to her at first sight. "It's the fashion to talk of all cities as feminine," he said, "but, as a rule, it's a monstrous mistake. Is Florence of the same sex as New York, as Chicago? She's the sole true woman of them all; one feels towards her as a lad in his teens feels to some beautiful older woman with a 'history.' It's a sort of aspiring gallantry she creates." This disinterested passion seemed to stand my friend in stead of the common social ties; he led a lonely life, apparently, and cared for nothing but his work. I was duly flattered by his having taken my frivolous self into his favor, and by his generous sacrifice of precious hours, as they must have been, to my society. We spent many of these hours among those early paintings in which Florence is so rich, returning ever and anon with restless sympathies to wonder whether these tender blossoms of art had not a vital fragrance and savor more precious than the full-fruited knowledge of the later works. We lingered often in the sepulchral chapel of San Lorenzo, and watched Michael Angelo's dim-visaged warrior sitting there like some awful Genius of Doubt and brooding behind his eternal mask upon the mysteries of life. We stood more than once in the little convent chambers where Fra Angelico wrought as if an angel indeed had held his hand, and gathered that sense of scattered dews and early bird-notes which makes an hour among his relics seem like a morning stroll in some monkish garden. We did all this and much more,—wandered into dark chapels, damp courts, and dusty palace-rooms, in quest of lingering hints of fresco and lurking treasures of carving.

I was more and more impressed with my companion's prodigious singleness of purpose. Everything was a pretext for some wildly idealistic rhapsody or revery. Nothing could be seen or said that did not end sooner or later in a glowing discourse on the true, the beautiful, and the good. If my friend was not a genius, he was certainly a monomaniac; and I found as great a fascination in watching the odd lights and shades of his character as if he had been a creature from another planet.

He seemed, indeed, to know very little of this one, and lived and moved altogether in his own little province of art. A creature more unsullied by the world it is impossible to conceive, and I often thought it a flaw in his artistic character that he hadn't a harmless vice or two. It amused me vastly at times to think that he was of our shrewd Yankee race; but, after all, there could be no better token of his American origin than this high æsthetic fever. The very heat of his devotion was a sign of conversion; those born to European opportunity manage better to reconcile enthusiasm with comfort. He had, moreover, all our native mistrust for intellectual discretion and our native relish for sonorous superlatives. As a critic he was vastly more generous than just, and his mildest terms of approbation were "stupendous," "transcendent," and "incomparable." The small change of admiration seemed to him no coin for a gentleman to handle; and yet, frank as he was intellectually, he was, personally, altogether a mystery. His professions, somehow, were all half-professions, and his allusions to his work and circumstances left something dimly ambiguous in the background. He was modest and proud, and never spoke of his domestic matters. He was evidently poor; yet he must have had some slender independence, since he could afford to make so merry over the fact that his culture of ideal beauty had never brought him a penny. His poverty, I supposed, was his motive for neither inviting me to his lodging nor mentioning its whereabouts. We met either in some public place or at my hotel, where I entertained him as freely as I might without appearing to be prompted by charity. He seemed always hungry, which was his nearest approach to a "redeeming vice." I made a point of asking no impertinent questions, but, each time we met, I ventured to make some respectful allusion to the *magnum opus*, to inquire, as it were, as to its health and progress. "We're getting on, with the the Lord's help," he would say with a grave smile. "We're doing well. You see I have the grand advantage that I lose no time. These hours I spend with you are pure profit. They're *suggestive!* Just as the truly religious soul is always at worship, the genuine artist is always in labor. He takes his property wherever he finds it, and learns some precious secret from every object that stands up in the light. If you but knew the rapture of observation! I gather with every glance some hint for light, for color or relief! When I get home, I pour out my treasures into the lap of my Madonna. O, I'm not idle! *Nulla dies sine linea.*"

I was introduced in Florence to an American lady whose drawing-room had long formed an attractive place of reunion for the foreign residents. She lived on a fourth floor, and she was not rich; but she offered her visitors very good tea, little cakes at option, and conversation not quite to match. Her conversation had mainly an æsthetic flavor, for Mrs Coventry was famously "artistic." Her apartment was a sort of Pitti Palace *au petit pied.* She possessed "early masters" by the dozen,—a cluster of Peruginos in her dining-room, a Giotto in her boudoir, an Andrea del Sarto over her parlor chimney-piece. Backed by these treasures, and by innumerable bronzes, mosaics, majolica dishes, and little worm-eaten diptychs showing angular saints on gilded panels, our hostess enjoyed the dignity of a sort of high-priestess of the arts. She always wore on her bosom a huge miniature copy of the Madonna della Seggiola. Gaining her ear quietly one evening I asked her whether she knew that remarkable man, Mr Theobald.

"Know him!" she exclaimed; "know poor Theobald! All Florence knows him, his flame-colored locks, his black velvet coat, his interminable harangues on the beautiful, and his wondrous Madonna that mortal eye has never seen, and that mortal patience has quite given up expecting."

"Really," I cried, "you don't believe in his Madonna?"

"My dear ingenuous youth," rejoined my shrewd friend, "has he made a convert of you? Well, we all believed in him once; he came down upon Florence and took the town by storm. Another Raphael, at the very least, had been born among men, and poor, dear America was to have the credit of him. Hadn't he the very hair of Raphael flowing down on his shoulders? The hair, alas, but not the head! We swallowed him whole, however; we hung upon his lips and proclaimed his genius on the house-tops. The women were all dying to sit to him for their portraits and be made immortal, like Leonardo's Joconde. We decided that his manner was a good deal like Leonardo's,—mysterious and inscrutable and fascinating. Mysterious it certainly was; mystery was the beginning and the end of it. The months passed by, and the miracle hung fire; our master never produced his masterpiece. He passed hours in the galleries and churches, posturing, musing, and gazing; he talked more than ever about the beautiful, but he never put brush to canvas. We had all subscribed, as it were, to the great performance; but as it never came off, people began to ask for their money again. I was one of the last of the faithful; I carried devotion so far as to sit to him for my head. If you could have seen the horrible creature he made of me, you would admit that even a woman with no more vanity than will tie her bonnet straight must have cooled off then. The man didn't know the very alphabet of drawing! His strong point, he intimated, was his sentiment; but is it a consolation, when one has been painted a fright, to know it has been done with peculiar gusto? One by one, I confess, we fell away from the faith, and Mr Theobald didn't lift his little finger to preserve us. At the first hint that we were tired of waiting and that we should like the show to begin, he was off in a huff. 'Great work requires time, contemplation, privacy, mystery! O ye of little faith!' We answered that we didn't insist on a great work; that the five-act tragedy might come at his convenience; that we merely asked for something to keep us from yawning, some inexpensive little *lever de rideau*. Hereupon the poor man took his stand as a genius misconceived and persecuted, an *âme méconnue*, and washed his hands of us from that hour! No, I believe he does me the honor to consider me the head and front of the conspiracy formed to nip his glory in the bud,—a bud that has taken twenty years to blossom. Ask him if he knows me, and he'd tell you I'm a horribly ugly old woman who has vowed his destruction because he wouldn't paint her portrait as a pendant to Titian's Flora. I fancy that since then he has had none but chance followers, innocent strangers like yourself, who have taken him at his word. The mountain's still in labor; I've not heard that the mouse has been born. I pass him once in a while in the galleries, and he fixes his great dark eyes on me with a sublimity of indifference, as if I were a bad copy of a Sassoferrato! It is a long time ago now that I heard that he was making studies for a Madonna who was to be a *résumé* of all the other Madonnas of the Italian school,—like that antique Venus who borrowed a nose from one great image and an ankle from another. It's certainly a masterly idea. The parts may be fine, but when I think of my unhappy portrait I tremble for the whole. He has communicated this striking idea under the pledge of solemn secrecy to fifty chosen spirits, to every one he has ever been able to buttonhole for five minutes. I suppose he wants to get an order for it, and he's not to blame; for Heaven knows how he lives. I see by your blush," my hostess frankly continued, "that you have been honored with his confidence. You needn't be ashamed, my dear young man; a man of your age is none the worse for a certain generous credulity. Only allow me to give you a word of advice: keep your credulity out of your pockets! Don't pay for the picture till it's delivered. You've not been treated to a peep at it, I imagine. No more have your fifty predecessors in the faith. There are people who doubt whether there is any picture to be seen. I fancy, myself, that if one were to get into his studio, one would find something very like the picture in that tale of Balzac's,—a mere mass of incoherent scratches and daubs, a jumble of dead paint!"

I listened to this pungent recital in silent wonder. It had a painfully plausible sound, and was not inconsistent with certain shy suspicions of my own. My hostess was a clever woman, and presumably a generous one. I determined to let my judgment wait upon events. Possibly she was right; but if she was wrong, she was cruelly wrong! Her version of my friend's eccentricities made me impatient to see him again and examine him in the light of public opinion. On our next meeting, I immediately asked him if he knew Mrs Coventry. He laid his hand on my arm and gave me a sad smile. "Has she taxed *your* gallantry at last?" he asked. "She's a foolish woman. She's frivolous and heartless, and she pretends to be serious and kind. She prattles about Giotto's second manner and Vittoria Colonna's liaison with 'Michael,'—one would think that Michael lived across the way and was expected in to take a hand at whist,—but she knows as little about art, and about the conditions of production, as I know about Buddhism. She profanes sacred words," he added more vehemently, after a pause. "She cares for you only as some one to hand teacups in that horrible mendacious little parlor of hers, with its trumpery Peruginos! If you can't dash off a new picture every three days, and let her hand it round among her guests, she tells them in plain English you're an impostor!"

This attempt of mine to test Mrs Coventry's accuracy was made in the course of a late afternoon walk to the quiet old church of San Miniato, on one of the hill-tops which directly overlook the city, from whose gate you are guided to it by a stony and cypress-bordered walk, which seems a most fitting avenue to a shrine. No spot is more propitious to lingering repose* than the broad terrace in front of the church, where, lounging against the parapet, you may glance in slow alternation from the black and yellow marbles of the church façade, seamed and cracked with time and wind-sown with a tender flora of its own, down to the full domes and slender towers of

* 1869.

Florence and over to the blue sweep of the wide-mouthed cup
of mountains into whose hollow the little treasure-city has
been dropped. I had proposed, as a diversion from the painful
memories evoked by Mrs Coventry's name, that Theobald
should go with me the next evening to the opera, where some
rarely played work was to be given. He declined, as I had
half expected, for I had observed that he regularly kept his
evenings in reserve, and never alluded to his manner of passing them. "You have reminded me before," I said, smiling,
"of that charming speech of the Florentine painter in Alfred
de Musset's Lorenzaccio: '*I do no harm to any one. I pass my
days in my studio. On Sunday, I go to the Annunziata or to
Santa Maria; the monks think I have a voice; they dress me in a
white gown and a red cap, and I take a share in the choruses,
sometimes I do a little solo: these are the only times I go into
public. In the evening, I visit my sweetheart; when the night is
fine, we pass it on her balcony.*' I don't know whether you have
a sweetheart, or whether she has a balcony. But if you're so
happy, it's certainly better than trying to find a charm in a
third-rate *prima donna*."

He made no immediate response, but at last he turned to
me solemnly. "Can you look upon a beautiful woman with
reverent eyes?"

"Really," I said, "I don't pretend to be sheepish, but I
should be sorry to think I was impudent." And I asked him
what in the world he meant. When at last I had assured him
that I could undertake to temper admiration with respect, he
informed me, with an air of religious mystery, that it was in
his power to introduce me to the most beautiful woman in
Italy. "A beauty with a soul!"

"Upon my word," I cried, "you're extremely fortunate
I shall rejoice to witness the conjunction."

"This woman's beauty," he answered, "is a lesson, a
morality, a poem! It's my daily study."

Of course, after this, I lost no time in reminding him of

what, before we parted, had taken the shape of a promise. "I feel somehow," he had said, "as if it were a sort of violation of that privacy in which I have always contemplated her beauty. This is friendship, my friend. No hint of her existence has ever fallen from my lips. But with too great a familiarity we are apt to lose a sense of the real value of things, and you perhaps will throw some new light upon it and offer a fresher interpretation." We went accordingly by appointment to a certain ancient house in the heart of Florence,—the precinct of the Mercato Vecchio,—and climbed a dark, steep staircase to the very summit of the edifice. Theobald's beauty seemed as jealously exalted above the line of common vision as the Belle aux Cheveux d'Or in her tower-top. He passed without knocking into the dark vestibule of a small apartment, and, flinging open an inner door, ushered me into a small saloon. The room seemed mean and sombre, though I caught a glimpse of white curtains swaying gently at an open window. At a table, near a lamp, sat a woman dressed in black, working at a piece of embroidery. As Theobald entered, she looked up calmly, with a smile; but seeing me, she made a movement of surprise, and rose with a kind of stately grace. Theobald stepped forward, took her hand and kissed it, with an indescribable air of immemorial usage. As he bent his head, she looked at me askance, and I thought she blushed.

"Behold the Serafina!" said Theobald, frankly, waving me forward. "This is a friend, and a lover of the arts," he added, introducing me. I received a smile, a courtesy, and a request to be seated.

The most beautiful woman in Italy was a person of a generous Italian type and of a great simplicity of demeanor. Seated again at her lamp, with her embroidery, she seemed to have nothing whatever to say. Theobald, bending towards her in a sort of Platonic ecstasy, asked her a dozen paternally tender questions as to her health, her state of mind, her occupations, and the progress of her embroidery, which he examined minutely and summoned me to admire. It was some portion of an ecclesiastical vestment,—yellow satin wrought with an elaborate design of silver and gold. She made answer in a full, rich voice, but with a brevity which I hesitated whether to attribute to native reserve or to the profane constraint of my presence. She had been that morning to confession; she had also been to market, and had bought a chicken for dinner. She felt very happy; she had nothing to complain of, except that the people for whom she was making her vestment, and who furnished her materials, should be willing to put such rotten silver thread into the garment, as one might say, of the Lord. From time to time, as she took her slow stitches, she raised her eyes and covered me with a glance which seemed at first to denote a placid curiosity, but in which, as I saw it repeated, I thought I perceived the dim glimmer of an attempt to establish an understanding with me at the expense of our companion. Meanwhile, as mindful as possible of Theobald's injunction of reverence, I considered the lady's personal claims to the fine compliment he had paid her.

That she was indeed a beautiful woman I perceived, after recovering from the surprise of finding her without the freshness of youth. Her beauty was of a sort which, in losing youth, loses little of its essential charm, expressed for the most part as it was in form and structure, and, as Theobald would have said, in "composition." She was broad and ample, lowbrowed and large-eyed, dark and pale. Her thick brown hair hung low beside her cheek and ear, and seemed to drape her head with a covering as chaste and formal as the veil of a nun. The poise and carriage of her head was admirably free and noble, and the more effective that their freedom was at moments discreetly corrected by a little sanctimonious droop, which harmonized admirably with the level gaze of her dark and quiet eye. A strong, serene physical nature and the placid temper which comes of no nerves and no troubles seemed this lady's comfortable portion. She was dressed in plain dull black, save for a sort of dark blue kerchief which was folded across her bosom and exposed a glimpse of her massive throat. Over this kerchief was suspended a little silver cross. I admired her greatly, and yet with a large reserve. A certain mild intellectual apathy belonged properly to her type of beauty, and had always seemed to round and enrich it; but this *bourgeoise* Egeria, if I viewed her right, betrayed a rather vulgar stagnation of mind. There might have been once a dim, spiritual light in her face; but it had long since begun to wane. And furthermore, in plain prose, she was growing stout. My disappointment amounted very nearly to complete disenchantment when Theobald, as if to facilitate my covert inspection, declaring that the lamp was very dim and that she would ruin her eyes without more light, rose and fetched a couple of candles from the mantel-piece, which he placed lighted on the table. In this brighter illumination I perceived that our hostess was decidedly an elderly woman. She was neither haggard nor worn nor gray; she was simply coarse. The "soul" which Theobald had promised seemed scarcely worth making such a point of; it was no deeper mystery than a sort of matronly mildness of lip and brow. I would have been ready even to declare that that sanctified bend of the head was nothing more than the trick of a person constantly working at embroidery. It occurred to me even that it was a trick of a less innocent sort; for, in spite of the mellow quietude of her wits, this stately needlewoman dropped a hint that she took the situation rather less *au sérieux* than her friend. When he rose to light the candles, she looked across at me with a quick, intelligent smile and tapped her forehead with her forefinger; then, as from a sudden feeling of compassionate loyalty to poor Theobald, I preserved a blank face, she gave a little shrug and resumed her work.

What was the relation of this singular couple? Was he the most ardent of friends or the most reverent of lovers? Did she regard him as an eccentric youth whose benevolent admiration

c

of her beauty she was not ill-pleased to humor at this small cost of having him climb into her little parlor and gossip of summer nights? With her decent and sombre dress, her simple gravity, and that fine piece of priestly needlework, she looked like some pious lay-member of a sisterhood, living by special permission outside her convent walls. Or was she maintained here aloft by her friend in comfortable leisure, so that he might have before him the perfect, eternal type, uncorrupted and untarnished by the struggle for existence? Her shapely hands, I observed, were very fair and white; they lacked the traces of what is called "honest toil."

"And the pictures, how do they come on?" she asked of Theobald, after a long pause.

"Finely, finely! I have here a friend whose sympathy and encouragement give me new faith and ardor."

Our hostess turned to me, gazed at me a moment rather inscrutably, and then tapping her forehead with the gesture she had used a minute before, "He has a magnificent genius!" she said, with perfect gravity.

"I'm inclined to think so," I answered, with a smile.

"Eh, why do you smile?" she cried. "If you doubt it, you must see the *bambino!*" And she took the lamp and conducted me to the other side of the room, where on the wall, in a plain black frame, hung a large drawing in red chalk. Beneath it was festooned a little bowl for holy-water. The drawing represented a very young child, entirely naked, half nestling back against his mother's gown, but with his two little arms outstretched, as if in the act of benediction. It was executed with singular freedom and power, and yet seemed vivid with the sacred bloom of infancy. A sort of dimpled elegance and grace, mingled with its boldness, recalled the touch of Correggio. "That's what he can do!" said my hostess. "It's the blessed little boy whom I lost. It's his very image, and the Signor Teobaldo gave it me as a gift. He has given me many things beside!"

I looked at the picture for some time and admired it vastly. Turning back to Theobald, I assured him that if it were hung among the drawings in the Uffizi and labelled with a glorious name, it would hold its own. My praise seemed to give him extreme pleasure; he pressed my hands, and his eyes filled with tears. It moved him apparently with the desire to expatiate on the history of the drawing, for he rose and made his adieux to our companion, kissing her hand with the same mild ardor as before. It occurred to me that the offer of a similar piece of gallantry on my own part might help me to know what manner of woman she was. When she perceived my intention, she withdrew her hand, dropped her eyes solemnly, and made me a severe courtesy. Theobald took my arm and led me rapidly into the street.

"And what do you think of the divine Serafina?" he cried with fervor.

"It's certainly good solid beauty!" I answered.

He eyed me an instant askance, and then seemed hurried along by the current of remembrance. "You should have seen the mother and the child together, seen them as I first saw them,—the mother with her head draped in a shawl, a divine trouble in her face, and the bambino pressed to her bosom. You would have said, I think, that Raphael had found his match in common chance. I was coming in, one summer night, from a long walk in the country, when I met this apparition at the city gate. The woman held out her hand. I hardly knew whether to say, 'What do you want?' or to fall down and worship. She asked for a little money. I saw that she was beautiful and pale. She might have stepped out of the stable of Bethlehem! I gave her money and helped her on her way into the town. I had guessed her story. She, too, was a maiden mother, and she had been turned out into the world in her shame. I felt in all my pulses that here was my subject marvellously realized. I felt like one of the old convent artists who had had a vision. I rescued the poor creatures, cherished them, watched them as I would have done some precious work of art, some lovely fragment of fresco discovered in a mouldering cloister. In a month—as if to deepen and consecrate the pathos of it all—the poor little child died. When she felt that he was going, she held him up to me for ten minutes, and I made that sketch. You saw a feverish haste in it, I suppose; I wanted to spare the poor little mortal the pain of his position. After that, I doubly valued the mother. She is the simplest, sweetest, most natural creature that ever bloomed in this brave old land of Italy. She lives in the memory of her child, in her gratitude for the scanty kindness I have been able to show her, and in her simple religion! She's not even conscious of her beauty; my admiration has never made her vain. Heaven knows I've made no secret of it. You must have observed the singular transparency of her expression, the lovely modesty of her glance. And was there ever such a truly virginal brow, such a natural classic elegance in the wave of the hair and the arch of the forehead? I've studied her; I may say I know her. I've absorbed her little by little; my mind is stamped and imbued, and I have determined now to clinch the impression; I shall at last invite her to sit for me!"

" 'At last,—at last'?" I repeated, in much amazement. "Do you mean that she has never done so yet?"

"I've not really had—a—a sitting," said Theobald, speaking very slowly. "I've taken notes, you know; I've got my grand fundamental impression. That's the great thing! But I've not actually had her as a model, posed and draped and lighted, before my easel."

What had become for the moment of my perception and my tact I am at a loss to say; in their absence, I was unable to repress headlong exclamation. I was destined to regret it. We had stopped at a turning, beneath a lamp. "My poor friend," I exclaimed, laying my hand on his shoulder, "you've *dawdled!* She's an old, old woman—for a Madonna!"

It was as if I had brutally struck him; I shall never forget the long, slow, almost ghastly look of pain with which he answered me. "Dawdled—old, old!" he stammered. "Are you joking?"

"Why, my dear fellow, I suppose you don't take the woman for twenty?"

He drew a long breath and leaned against a house, looking at me with questioning, protesting, reproachful eyes. At last, starting forward, and grasping my arm: "Answer me solemnly: does she seem to you truly old? Is she wrinkled, is she faded, am I blind?"

Then at last I understood the immensity of his illusion; how, one by one, the noiseless years had ebbed away, and left him brooding in charmed inaction, forever preparing for a work forever deferred. It seemed to me almost a kindness now to tell him the plain truth. "I should be sorry to say you're blind," I answered, "but I think you're deceived. You've lost time in effortless contemplation. Your friend was once young and fresh and virginal; but, I protest, that was some years ago. Still, she has *de beaux restes?* By all means make her sit for you!" I broke down; his face was too horribly reproachful.

He took off his hat and stood passing his handkerchief mechanically over his forehead. "*De beaux restes?* I thank you for sparing me the plain English. I must make up my Madonna out of *de beaux restes!* What a masterpiece she'll be! Old— old! Old—old!" he murmured.

"Never mind her age," I cried, revolted at what I had done, "never mind my impression of her! You have your memory, your notes, your genius. Finish your picture in a month. I proclaim it beforehand a masterpiece, and I hereby offer you for it any sum you may choose to ask."

He stared, but he seemed scarcely to understand me. "Old —old!" he kept stupidly repeating. "If she is old, what am I? If her beauty has faded, where—where is my strength? Has life been a dream? Have I worshipped too long,—have I loved too well?" The charm, in truth, was broken. That the chord of illusion should have snapped at my light, accidental touch showed how it had been weakened by excessive tension. The poor fellow's sense of wasted time, of vanished opportunity, seemed to roll in upon his soul in waves of darkness. He suddenly dropped his head and burst into tears.

I led him homeward with all possible tenderness, but I attempted neither to check his grief, to restore his equanimity, nor to unsay the hard truth. When we reached my hotel I tried to induce him to come in. "We'll drink a glass of wine," I said, smiling, "to the completion of the Madonna."

With a violent effort he held up his head, mused for a moment with a formidably sombre frown, and then giving me his hand, "I'll finish it," he cried, "in a month! No, in a fortnight! After all, I have it *here!*" And he tapped his forehead. "Of course she's old! She can afford to have it said of her,— a woman who has made twenty years pass like a twelve-month! Old—old! Why, sir, she shall be eternal!"

I wished to see him safely to his own door, but he waved me back and walked away with an air of resolution, whistling and swinging his cane. I waited a moment, and then followed him at a distance, and saw him proceed to cross the Santa Trinità Bridge. When he reached the middle, he suddenly paused, as if his strength had deserted him, and leaned upon the parapet gazing over into the river. I was careful to keep him in sight; I confess that I passed ten very nervous minutes. He recovered himself at last, and went his way, slowly and with hanging head.

That I should have really startled poor Theobald into a bolder use of his long-garnered stores of knowledge and taste, into the vulgar effort and hazard of production, seemed at first reason enough for his continued silence, and absence; but as day followed day without his either calling or sending me a line, and without my meeting him in his customary haunts, in the galleries, in the chapel at San Lorenzo, or strolling between the Arno-side and the great hedge-screen of verdure which, along the drive of the Cascine, throws the fair occupants of barouche and phaeton into such becoming relief,—as for more than a week I got neither tidings nor sight of him, I began to fear that I had fatally offended him, and that, instead of giving wholesome impetus to his talent, I had brutally paralyzed it. I had a wretched suspicion that I had made him ill. My stay at Florence was drawing to a close, and it was important that, before resuming my journey, I should assure myself of the truth. Theobald, to the last, had kept his lodging a mystery, and I was altogether at a loss where to look for him. The simplest course was to make inquiry of the beauty of the Mercato Vecchio, and I confess that unsatisfied curiosity as to the lady herself counselled it as well. Perhaps I had done her injustice, and she was as immortally fresh and fair as he conceived her. I was, at any rate, anxious to behold once more the ripe enchantress who had made twenty years pass as a twelvemonth. I repaired accordingly, one morning, to her abode, climbed the interminable staircase, and reached her door. It stood ajar, and as I hesitated whether to enter, a little serving-maid came clattering out with an empty kettle, as if she had just performed some savory errand. The inner door, too, was open; so I crossed the little vestibule and entered the room in which I had formerly been received. It had not its evening aspect. The table, or one end of it, was spread for a late breakfast, and before it sat a gentleman,—an individual, at least, of the male sex,—dealing justice upon a beefsteak and onions, and a bottle of wine. At his elbow, in friendly proximity, was placed the lady of the house. Her attitude, as I entered, was not that of an enchantress. With one hand she held in her lap a plate of smoking maccaroni; with the other she had lifted high in air one of the pendulous filaments of this succulent compound, and was in the act of slipping it gently down her throat. On the uncovered end of the table, facing her companion, were ranged half a dozen small statuettes, of some snuff-colored substance resembling terra-cotta. He, brandishing his knife with ardor, was apparently descanting on their merits.

Evidently I darkened the door. My hostess dropped her maccaroni—into her mouth, and rose hastily with a harsh exclamation and a flushed face. I immediately perceived that the Signora Serafina's secret was even better worth knowing than I had supposed, and that the way to learn it was to take it for granted. I summoned my best Italian, I smiled and bowed and apologized for my intrusion; and in a moment, whether or no I had dispelled the lady's irritation, I had, at least, stimulated her prudence. I was welcome, she said; I must take a seat. This was another friend of hers,—also an artist, she declared with a smile which was almost amiable. Her companion wiped his mustache and bowed with great civility. I saw at a glance that he was equal to the situation. He was presumably the author of the statuettes on the table, and he knew a money-spending *forestiere* when he saw one. He was a small, wiry man, with a clever, impudent, tossed-up nose, a sharp little black eye, and waxed ends to his mustache. On the side of his head he wore jauntily a little crimson velvet smoking-cap, and I observed that his feet were encased in brilliant slippers. On Serafina's remarking with dignity that I was the friend of Mr Theobald, he broke out into that fantastic French of which Italians are so insistently lavish, and declared with fervor that Mr Theobald was a magnificent genius.

"I'm sure I don't know," I answered with a shrug. "If you're in a position to affirm it, you have the advantage of me. I've seen nothing from his hand but the bambino yonder, which certainly is fine."

He declared that the bambino was a masterpiece, a pure Correggio. It was only a pity, he added, with a knowing laugh, that the sketch had not been made on some good bit of honeycombed old panel. The stately Serafina hereupon protested that Mr Theobald was the soul of honor, and that he would never lend himself to a deceit. "I'm not a judge of genius," she said, "and I know nothing of pictures. I'm but a poor simple widow; but I know that the Signor Teobaldo has the heart of an angel and the virtue of a saint. He's my bene-factor," she added sententiously. The after-glow of the some-what sinister flush with which she had greeted me still lingered in her cheek, and perhaps did not favor her beauty; I could not but fancy it a wise custom of Theobald's to visit her only by candlelight. She was coarse, and her poor adorer was a poet.

"I have the greatest esteem for him," I said; "it is for this reason that I have been uneasy at not seeing him for ten days. Have you seen him? Is he perhaps ill?"

"Ill! Heaven forbid!" cried Serafina, with genuine vehemence.

Her companion uttered a rapid expletive, and reproached her with not having been to see him. She hesitated a moment; then she simpered the least bit and bridled. "He comes to see me—without reproach! But it would not be the same for me to go to him, though, indeed, you may almost call him a man of holy life."

"He has the greatest admiration for you," I said. "He would have been honored by your visit."

She looked at me a moment sharply. "More admiration than you. Admit that!" Of course I protested with all the eloquence at my command, and my mysterious hostess then confessed that she had taken no fancy to me on my former visit, and that, Theobald not having returned, she believed I had poisoned his mind against her. "It would be no kindness to the poor gentleman, I can tell you that," she said. "He has come to see me every evening for years. It's a long friendship! No one knows him as well as I."

"I don't pretend to know him, or to understand him," I said. "He's a mystery! Nevertheless, he seems to me a little—" And I touched my forehead and waved my hand in the air.

Serafina glanced at her companion a moment, as if for inspiration. He contented himself with shrugging his shoulders, as he filled his glass again. The *padrona* hereupon gave me a more softly insinuating smile than would have seemed likely to bloom on so candid a brow. "It's for that that I love him!" she said. "The world has so little kindness for such persons. It laughs at them, and despises them, and cheats them. He is too good for this wicked life! It's his fancy that he finds a little Paradise up here in my poor apartment. If he thinks so, how can I help it? He has a strange belief—really, I ought to be ashamed to tell you—that I resemble the Blessed Virgin: Heaven forgive me! I let him think what he pleases, so long as it makes him happy. He was very kind to me once, and I am not one that forgets a favor. So I receive him every evening civilly, and ask after his health, and let him look at me on this side and that! For that matter, I may say it without vanity, I was worth looking at once! And he's not always amusing, poor man! He sits sometimes for an hour without speaking a word, or else he talks away, without stopping, on art and nature, and beauty and duty, and fifty fine things that are all so much Latin to me. I beg you to understand that he has never said a word to me that I mightn't decently listen to. He may be a little cracked, but he's one of the saints."

"Eh!" cried the man, "the saints were all a little cracked!"

Serafina, I fancied, left part of her story untold; but she told enough of it to make poor Theobald's own statement seem intensely pathetic in its exalted simplicity. "It's a strange fortune, certainly," she went on, "to have such a friend as this dear man,—a friend who's less than a lover and more than a friend." I glanced at her companion, who preserved an impenetrable smile, twisted the end of his mustache, and disposed of a copious mouthful. Was *he* less than a lover? "But what will you have?" Serafina pursued. "In this hard world one mustn't ask too many questions; one must take what comes and keep what one gets. I've kept my good friend for twenty years, and I do hope that, at this time of day, Signore, you've not come to turn him against me!"

I assured her that I had no such design, and that I should vastly regret disturbing Mr Theobald's habits or convictions. On the contrary, I was alarmed about him, and I should immediately go in search of him. She gave me his address and a florid account of her sufferings at his non-appearance. She had not been to him, for various reasons; chiefly because she was afraid of displeasing him, as he had always made such a mystery of his home. "You might have sent this gentleman!" I ventured to suggest.

"Ah," cried the gentleman, "he admires the Signora Serafina, but he wouldn't admire me." And then, confidentially, with his finger on his nose, "He's a purist!"

I was about to withdraw, on the promise that I would inform the Signora Serafina of my friend's condition, when her companion, who had risen from table and girded his loins apparently for the onset, grasped me gently by the arm, and led me before the row of statuettes. "I perceive by your conversation, signore, that you are a patron of the arts. Allow me to request your honorable attention for these modest products of my own ingenuity. They are brand-new, fresh from my atelier, and have never been exhibited in public. I have brought them here to receive the verdict of this dear lady, who is a good critic, for all she may pretend to the contrary. I am the inventor of this peculiar style of statuette,—of subject, manner, material, everything. Touch them, I pray you; handle them; you needn't fear. Delicate as they look, it is impossible they should break! My various creations have met with great success. They are especially admired by Americans. I have sent them all over Europe,—to London, Paris, Vienna! You may have observed some little specimens in Paris, on the Boulevard, in a shop of which they constitute the specialty. There is always a crowd about the window. They form a very pleasing ornament for the mantel-shelf of a gay young bachelor, for the boudoir of a pretty woman. You couldn't make a prettier present to a person with whom you wished to exchange a harmless joke. It is not classic art, signore, of course; but, between ourselves, isn't classic art sometimes rather a bore? Caricature, burlesque, *la charge*, as the French say, has hitherto been confined to paper, to the pen and pencil. Now, it has been my inspiration to introduce it into statuary. For this purpose I have invented a peculiar plastic compound which you will permit me not to divulge. That's my secret, signore! It's as light, you perceive, as cork, and yet as firm as alabaster! I frankly confess that I really pride myself as much on this little stroke of chemical ingenuity as upon the other element of novelty in my creations,—my types. What do you say to my types, signore? The idea is bold; does it strike you as happy? Cats and monkeys,—monkeys and cats,—all human life is there! Human life, of course, I mean, viewed with the eye of the satirist! To combine sculpture and satire, signore, has been my unprecedented ambition. I flatter myself that I have not egregiously failed."

As this jaunty Juvenal of the chimney-piece delivered himself of his persuasive allocution, he took up his little groups successively from the table, held them aloft, turned them about, rapped them with his knuckles, and gazed at them lovingly with his head on one side. They consisted each of a cat and a monkey, fantastically draped, in some preposterously sentimental conjunction. They exhibited a certain sameness of motive, and illustrated chiefly the different phases of what, in delicate terms, may be called gallantry and coquetry; but they were strikingly clever and expressive, and were at once very perfect cats and monkeys and very natural men and women. I confess, however, that they failed to amuse me. I was doubtless not in a mood to enjoy them, for they seemed to me peculiarly cynical and vulgar. Their imitative felicity was revolting. As I looked askance at the complacent little artist, brandishing them between finger and thumb, and caressing them with an amorous eye, he seemed to me himself little more than an exceptionally intelligent ape. I mustered an admiring grin, however, and he blew another blast. "My figures are studied from life! I have a little menagerie of monkeys whose frolics I contemplate by the hour. As for the cats, one has only to look out of one's back window! Since I have begun to examine these expressive little brutes, I have made many profound observations. Speaking, signore, to a man of imagination, I may say that my little designs are not without a philosophy of their own. Truly, I don't know whether the cats and monkeys imitate us, or whether it's we who imitate them." I congratulated him on his philosophy, and he resumed: "You will do me the honor to admit that I have handled my subjects with delicacy. Eh, it was needed, signore! I have been free, but not too free—eh? Just a hint, you know! You may see as much or as little as you please. These little groups, however, are no measure of my invention. If you will favor me with a call at my studio, I think that you will admit that my combinations are really infinite. I likewise execute figures to command. You have perhaps some little motive,—the fruit of your philosophy of life, signore,—which you would like to have interpreted. I can promise to work it up to your satisfaction; it shall be as malicious as you please! Allow me to present you with my card, and to remind you that my prices are moderate. Only sixty francs for a little group like that. My statuettes are as durable as bronze,—*ære perennius*, signore,—and, between ourselves, I think they are more amusing!"

As I pocketed his card, I glanced at Madonna Serafina, wondering whether she had an eye for contrasts. She had picked up one of the little couples and was tenderly dusting it with a feather broom.

What I had just seen and heard had so deepened my compassionate interest in my deluded friend, that I took a summary leave, and made my way directly to the house designated by this remarkable woman. It was in an obscure corner of the opposite side of the town, and presented a sombre and squalid appearance. An old woman in the doorway, on my inquiring for Theobald, ushered me in with a mumbled blessing and an expression of relief at the poor gentleman having a friend. His lodging seemed to consist of a single room at the top of the house. On getting no answer to my knock, I opened the door, supposing that he was absent; so that it gave me a certain shock to find him sitting there helpless and dumb. He was seated near the single window, facing an easel which supported a large canvas. On my entering, he looked up at me blankly, without changing his position, which was that of absolute lassitude and dejection, his arms loosely folded, his legs stretched before him, his head hanging on his breast. Advancing into the room, I perceived that his face vividly corresponded with his attitude. He was pale, haggard, and unshaven, and his dull and sunken eye gazed at me without a spark of recognition. I had been afraid that he would greet me with fierce reproaches, as the cruelly officious patron who had turned his peace to bitterness, and I was relieved to find that my appearance awakened no visible resentment. "Don't you know me?" I asked, as I put out my hand. "Have you already forgotten me?"

He made no response, kept his position stupidly, and left me staring about the room. It spoke most plaintively for itself. Shabby, sordid, naked, it contained, beyond the wretched bed, but the scantiest provision for personal comfort. It was bed-room at once and studio,—a grim ghost of a studio. A few dusty casts and prints on the walls, three or four old canvases turned face inward, and a rusty-looking color-box formed, with the easel at the window, the sum of its appurtenances. The place savored horribly of poverty. Its only wealth was the picture on the easel, presumably the famous Madonna. Averted as this was from the door, I was unable to see its face; but at last, sickened by the vacant misery of the spot, I passed behind Theobald, eagerly and tenderly. I can hardly say that I was surprised at what I found,—a canvas that was a mere dead blank, cracked and discolored by time. This was his immortal work! Though not surprised, I confess I was powerfully moved, and I think that for five minutes I could not have trusted myself to speak. At last, my silent nearness affected him; he stirred and turned, and then rose and looked at me with a slowly kindling eye. I murmured some kind, ineffective nothings about his being ill and needing advice and care, but he seemed absorbed in the effort to recall distinctly what had last passed between us. "You were right," he said with a pitiful smile, "I'm a dawdler! I'm a failure! I shall do nothing more in this world. You opened my eyes; and, though the truth is bitter, I bear you no grudge. Amen! I've been sitting here for a week, face to face with the truth, with the past, with my weakness and poverty and nullity. I shall never touch a brush! I believe I've neither eaten nor slept. Look at that canvas!" he went on, as I relieved my emotion in the urgent request that he would come home with me and dine. "That was to have contained my masterpiece! Isn't it a promising foundation? The elements of it are all *here*." And he tapped his forehead with that mystic confidence which had marked the gesture before. "If I could only transpose them into some brain that had the hand, the will! Since I've been sitting here taking stock of my intellects, I've come to believe that I have the material for a hundred masterpieces. But my hand is paralyzed now, and they'll never be painted. I never began! I waited and waited to be worthier to begin, and wasted my life in preparation. While I fancied my creation was growing, it was dying. I've taken it all too hard! Michael Angelo didn't when he went at the Lorenzo! He did his best at a venture, and his venture is immortal. *That*'s mine!" And he pointed with a gesture I shall never forget at the empty canvas. "I suppose we're a genus by ourselves in the providential scheme,—we talents that can't act, that can't do nor dare! We take it out in talk, in plans and promises, in study, in visions! But our visions, let me tell you," he cried, with a toss of his head, "have a way of being brilliant, and a man hasn't lived in vain who has seen the things I have! Of course you'll not believe in them when that bit of worm-eaten cloth is all I have to show for them; but to convince you, to enchant and astound the world, I need only the hand of Raphael. I have his brain. A pity, you'll say, I haven't his modesty! Ah, let me babble now; it's all I have left! I'm the half of a genius! Where in the wide world is my other half? Lodged perhaps in the vulgar soul, the cunning, ready fingers of some dull copyist or some trivial artisan who turns out by the dozen his easy prodigies of touch! But it's not for me to sneer at him; he at least does something. He's not a dawdler! Well for me if I had been vulgar and clever and reckless, if I could have shut my eyes and dealt my stroke!"

What to say to the poor fellow, what to do for him, seemed hard to determine; I chiefly felt that I must break the spell of his present inaction, and remove him from the haunted atmosphere of the little room it seemed such cruel irony to call a studio. I cannot say I persuaded him to come out with me; he simply suffered himself to be led, and when we began to walk in the open air I was able to measure his pitifully weakened condition. Nevertheless, he seemed in a certain way to revive, and murmured at last that he would like to go to the Pitti Gallery. I shall never forget our melancholy stroll through those gorgeous halls, every picture on whose walls seemed, even to my own sympathetic vision, to glow with a sort of insolent renewal of strength and lustre. The eyes and lips of the great portraits seemed to smile in ineffable scorn of the dejected pretender who had dreamed of competing with their triumphant authors; the celestial candor, even, of the Maddonna in the Chair, as we paused in perfect silence before her, was tinged with the sinister irony of the women of Leonardo. Perfect silence indeed marked our whole progress,

—the silence of a deep farewell; for I felt in all my pulses, as Theobald, leaning on my arm, dragged one heavy foot after the other, that he was looking his last. When we came out, he was so exhausted that, instead of taking him to my hotel to dine, I called a carriage and drove him straight to his own poor lodging. He had sunk into an extraordinary lethargy; he lay back in the carriage, with his eyes closed, as pale as death, his faint breathing interrupted at intervals by a sudden gasp, like a smothered sob or a vain attempt to speak. With the help of the old woman who had admitted me before, and who emerged from a dark back court, I contrived to lead him up the long steep staircase and lay him on his wretched bed. To her I gave him in charge, while I prepared in all haste to seek a physician. But she followed me out of the room with a pitiful clasping of her hands.

"Poor, dear, blessed gentleman," she murmured; "is he dying?"

"Possibly. How long has he been thus?"

"Since a night he passed ten days ago. I came up in the morning to make his poor bed, and found him sitting up in his clothes before that great canvas he keeps there. Poor, dear, strange man, he says his prayers to it! He had not been to bed, nor since then properly! What has happened to him? Has he found out about the Serafina?" she whispered with a glittering eye and a toothless grin.

"Prove at least that one old woman can be faithful," I said, "and watch him well till I come back." My return was delayed, through the absence of the English physician on a round of visits, and my vainly pursuing him from house to house before I overtook him. I brought him to Theobald's bedside none too soon. A violent fever had seized our patient, and the case was evidently grave. A couple of hours later I knew that he had brain-fever. From this moment I was with him constantly, but I am far from wishing to describe his illness. Excessively painful to witness, it was happily brief. Life burned out in delirium.

D

A certain night that I passed at his pillow, listening to his wild snatches of regret, of aspiration, of rapture and awe at the phantasmal pictures with which his brain seemed to swarm, recurs to my memory now like some stray page from a lost masterpiece of tragedy. Before a week was over we had buried him in the little Protestant cemetery on the way to Fiesole. The Signora Serafina, whom I had caused to be informed of his illness, had come in person, I was told, to inquire about its progress; but she was absent from his funeral, which was attended by but a scanty concourse of mourners. Half a dozen old Florentine sojourners, in spite of the prolonged estrangement which had preceded his death, had felt the kindly impulse to honor his grave. Among them was my friend Mrs Coventry, whom I found, on my departure, waiting at her carriage door at the gate of the cemetery.

"Well," she said, relieving at last with a significant smile the solemnity of our immediate greeting, "and the great Madonna? Have you seen her, after all?"

"I've seen her," I said; "she's mine,—by request. But I shall never show her to you."

"And why not, pray?"

"My dear Mrs Coventry, you'd not understand her!"

"Upon my word, you're polite."

"Excuse me; I'm sad and vexed and bitter." And with reprehensible rudeness, I marched away. I was excessively impatient to leave Florence; my friend's dark spirit seemed diffused through all things. I had packed my trunk to start for Rome that night, and meanwhile, to beguile my unrest, I aimlessly paced the streets. Chance led me at last to the church of San Lorenzo. Remembering poor Theobald's phrase about Michael Angelo,—"He did his best at a venture,"—I went in and turned my steps to the chapel of the tombs. Viewing in sadness the sadness of its immortal treasures, I fancied, while I stood there, that the scene demanded no ampler commentary. As I passed through the church again to depart, a woman, turning away from one of the side-altars, met me face to face. The black shawl depending from her head draped picturesquely the handsome visage of Madonna Serafina. She stopped as she recognized me, and I saw that she wished to speak. Her eye was bright and her ample bosom heaved in a way that seemed to portend a certain sharpness of reproach. But the expression of my own face, apparently, drew the sting from her resentment, and she addressed me in a tone in which bitterness was tempered by a sort of dogged resignation. "I know it was you, now, that separated us," she said. "It was a pity he ever brought you to see me! Of course, you couldn't think of me as he did. Well, the Lord gave him, the Lord has taken him. I've just paid for a nine days' mass for his soul. And I can tell you this, signore, I never deceived him. Who put it into his head that I was made to live on holy thoughts and fine phrases? It was his own fancy, and it pleased him to think so. Did he suffer much?" she added more softly, after a pause.

"His sufferings were great, but they were short."

"And did he speak of me?" She had hesitated and dropped her eyes; she raised them with her question, and revealed in their sombre stillness a gleam of feminine confidence which, for the moment, revived and illumined her beauty. Poor Theobald! Whatever name he had given his passion, it was still her fine eyes that had charmed him.

"Be contented, madam," I answered, gravely.

She dropped her eyes again and was silent. Then exhaling a full, rich sigh, as she gathered her shawl together: "He was a magnificent genius!"

I bowed, and we separated.

Passing through a narrow side-street on my way back to my hotel, I perceived above a doorway a sign which it seemed to me I had read before. I suddenly remembered that it was identical with the superscription of a card that I had carried for an hour in my waistcoat-pocket. On the threshold stood the ingenious artist whose claims to public favor were thus distinctly signalized, smoking a pipe in the evening air, and giving the finishing polish with a bit of rag to one of his inimitable "combinations." I caught the expressive curl of a couple of tails. He recognized me, removed his little red cap with a most obsequious bow, and motioned me to enter his studio. I returned his bow and passed on, vexed with the apparition. For a week afterwards, whenever I was seized among the ruins of triumphant Rome with some peculiarly poignant memory of Theobald's transcendent illusions and deplorable failure, I seemed to hear a fantastic, impertinent murmur, "Cats and monkeys, monkeys and cats; all human life is there!"

THE SWEETHEART OF M. BRISEUX

THE little picture gallery at M—— is a typical *musée de province*—cold, musty, unvisited, and enriched chiefly with miniature works by painters whose maturity was not to be powerful. The floors are tiled in brick, and the windows draped in faded moreen; the very light seems pale and neutral, as if the dismal lack-lustre atmosphere of the pictures were contagious. The subjects represented are of course of the familiar academic sort—the Wisdom of Solomon and the Fureurs d'Oreste; together with a few elegant landscapes exhibiting the last century view of nature, and half a dozen neat portraits of French gentlefolks of that period, in the act, as one may say, of taking the view in question. To me, I confess, the place had a melancholy charm, and I found none of the absurd old paintings too absurd to enjoy. There is always an agreeable finish in the French touch, even when the hand is not a master's. The catalogue, too, was prodigiously queer; a bit of very ancient literature, with comments, in the manner of the celebrated M. La Harpe. I wondered, as I turned its pages, into what measure of reprobation pictures and catalogue together had been compressed by that sole son of M——, who has achieved more than local renown in the arts. Conjecture was pertinent, for it was in these crepuscular halls that this deeply original artist must have heard the first early bird-notes of awakening genius: first, half credulously, as we may suppose, on festal Sundays, with his hand in his father's, gazing rosy and wide-eyed at the classical wrath of Achilles and the sallow flesh-tints of Dido; and later, with his hands in his pockets, an incipient critical frown and the mental vision

53

of an Achilles somehow more in earnest and a Dido more deeply desirable. It was indeed doubly pertinent, for the little Musée had at last, after much watching and waiting and bargaining, become possessor of one of Briseux's pictures. I was promptly informed of the fact by the *concierge*, a person much reduced by years and chronic catarrh, but still robust enough to display his æsthetic culture to a foreigner presumably of distinction. He led me solemnly into the presence of the great work, and placed a chair for me in the proper light. The famous painter had left his native town early in life, before making his mark, and an inappreciative family—his father was a small apothecary with a proper admiration of the arts, but a horror of artists—had been at no pains to preserve his boyish sketches. The more fools they! The merest scrawl with his signature now brought hundreds of francs, and there were those of his blood still in the town with whom the francs were scarce enough. To obtain a serious picture had of course been no small affair, and little M——, though with the yearning heart of a mother, happened to have no scanty maternal savings. Yet the thing had been managed by subscription, and the picture paid for. To make the triumph complete, a fortnight after it had been hung on its nail, M. Briseux succumbs to a fever in Rome and his pictures rise to the most fantastic prices! This was the very work which had made the painter famous. The portrait of a Lady in a Yellow Shawl in the Salon of 1836 had *fait époque*. Every one had heard of the Yellow Shawl; people talked of it as they did of the Chapeau de Paille of Rubens, or the "Torn Glove" of Titian; or if they didn't, posterity would! Such was the discursive murmur of the concierge as I examined this precious specimen of Briseux's first manner; and there was a plaintive cadence in this last assurance, which seemed to denote a too vivid prevision of the harvest of tributary francs to be reaped by his successors in office. It would be graceless praise to say that a glimpse of the picture is worth your franc. It is a superb performance, and I spent half an hour before it in such serene enjoyment that I forgot the concierge was a bore.

It is a half-length portrait representing a young woman, not exactly beautiful, yet very far from plain, draped with a singularly simple elegance in a shawl of yellow silk embroidered with fantastic arabesque. She is dark and grave, her dress is dark, the background is of a sober tone, and this brilliant scarf glows splendidly by contrast. It seems indeed to irradiate luminous color, and makes the picture brilliant in spite of its sombre accessories; and yet it leaves their full value to the tenderly glowing flesh portions. The portrait lacks a certain harmonious finish, that masterly interfusion of parts which the painter afterwards practised; the touch is hasty, and here and there a little heavy; but its splendid vivacity and energy, and the almost boyish good faith of some of its more venturesome strokes, make it a capital example of that momentous point in the history of genius when still tender promise blooms—in a night, as it were—into perfect force. It was little wonder that the picture had made a noise: judges of the more penetrating sort must have felt that it contained that invaluable something which an artist gives but once—the prime outgush of his effort—the flower of his originality. As I continued to look, however, I began to wonder whether it did not contain something better still—the reflection of a countenance very nearly as deep and ardent as the artist's talent. In spite of the expressive repose of the figure the brow and mouth wore a look of smothered agitation, the dark gray eye almost glittered, and the flash in the cheek burned ominously. Evidently this was the picture of something more than a yellow shawl. To the analytic eye it was the picture of a mind, or at least of a mood. "Who was the lady?" I asked of my companion.

He shrugged his shoulders, and for an instant looked uncertain. But, as a Frenchman, he produced his hypothesis as follows: "Mon Dieu! a sweetheart of M. Briseux!—*Ces artistes!*"

I left my place and passed into the adjoining rooms, where, as I have said, I found half an hour's diversion. On my return, my chair was occupied by a lady, apparently my only fellow-visitor. I noticed her no further than to see that, though comely, she was no longer young, that she was dressed in black, and that she was looking intently at the picture. Her intentness indeed at last attracted me, and while I lingered to gather a final impression, I covertly glanced at her. She was so far from being young that her hair was white, but with that charming and often premature brilliancy which belongs to fine brunettes. The concierge hovered near, narrating and expounding, and I fancied that her brief responses (for she asked no questions) betrayed an English accent. But I had doubtless no business to fancy anything, for my companion, as if with a sudden embarrassing sense of being watched, gathered her shawl about her, rose, and prepared to turn away. I should have immediately retreated, but that with this movement of hers our eyes met, and in the light of her rapid, just slightly deprecating glance, I read something which helped curiosity to get the better of politeness. She walked away, and I stood staring; and as she averted her head it seemed to me that my rather too manifest surprise had made her blush. I watched her slowly cross the room and pass into the next one, looking very vaguely at the pictures; and then addressed a keenly questioning glance at the Lady with the Yellow Shawl. Her startlingly vivid eyes answered my question most distinctly. I was satisfied, and I left the Musée.

It would perhaps be more correct to say that I was wholly unsatisfied. I strolled at haphazard through the little town, and emerged, as a matter of course, on the local promenade. The promenade at M—— is a most agreeable spot. It stretches along the top of the old town wall, over whose sturdy parapet, polished by the peaceful showers of many generations, you enjoy a view of the pale-hued but charming Provencal landscape. The middle of the rampart is adorned with a row of close-clipped lime-trees, with benches in the spaces between them; and, as you sit in the shade, the prospect is framed to your vision by the level parapet and the even limit of the far-projecting branches. What you see is therefore a long horizontal strip of landscape—a radiant stretch of white rocks and vaporous olives, scintillating in the southern light. Except a *bonne* or two, with a couple of children grubbing in the gravel, an idle apprentice in a blouse dozing on a bench, and a couple of red-legged soldiers leaning on the wall, I was the only lounger on the rampart, and this was a place to relish solitude. By nature a very sentimental traveller, there is nothing I like better than to light a cigar and lose myself in a meditative perception of local color. I love to ruminate the picturesque, and the scene before me was redolent of it. On this occasion however, the shady rampart and the shining distance were less interesting than a figure, disembodied but distinct, which soon obtruded itself on my attention. The mute assurance gathered before leaving the Musée had done as much to puzzle as to enlighten me. Was that modest and venerable person, then, the sweetheart of the illustrious Briseux? one of *ces artistes*, as rumor loudly proclaimed him, in the invidious as well as in the most honorable sense of the term. Plainly, she was the original of the portrait. In the days when her complexion would bear it, she had worn the yellow shawl. Time had changed, but not transformed her, as she must have fancied it had, to come and contemplate thus frankly this monument of her early charms. Why had she come? Was it accident, or was it vanity? How did it seem to her to find herself so strangely lifted out of her own possession and made a helpless spectator of her survival to posterity? The more I consulted my impression of her, the more certain I felt that she was no French-woman, but a modest spinster of my own transatlantic race, on whom posterity had as little claim as this musty Musée, which indeed possessed much of that sepulchral chill which clings to such knowledge of us as posterity enjoys. I found it hard to reconcile the lady with herself, and it was with the restlessness of conjecture that I left my place and strolled to the further end of the rampart. Here conjecture paused, amazed at its opportunities; for M. Briseux's sweetheart was seated on a bench under the lime-trees. She was gazing almost as thoughtfully on the distant view as she had done on her portrait; but as I passed, she gave me a glance from which embarrassment seemed to have vanished. I slowly walked the length of the rampart again, and as I went an impulse, born somehow of the delicious mild air, the light-bathed landscape of rock and olive, and of the sense of a sort of fellowship in isolation in the midst of these deeply foreign influences, as well as of a curiosity which was after all but the frank recognition of an obvious fact, was transmuted into a decision sufficiently remarkable in a bashful man. I proceeded gravely to carry it out. I approached my companion and bowed. She acknowledged my bow with a look which, though not exactly mistrustful, seemed to demand an explanation. To give it, I seated myself beside her. Something in her face made explanation easy. I was sure that she was an old maid, and gently but frankly eccentric. Her age left her at liberty to be as frank as she chose, and though I was somewhat her junior, I had gray hairs enough in my moustache to warrant her in smiling at my almost ardent impatience. Her smile, when she perceived that my direct appeal was deeply respectful, broke into a genial laugh which completed our introduction. To her inner sense, as well, evidently, the gray indifference of the historic rampart, the olive-sown landscape, the sweet foreign climate, left the law very much in our own hands; and then moreover, as something in her eyes proclaimed, the well of memory in her soul had been so strongly stirred that it naturally overflowed. I fancy that she looked more like her portrait for that hour or two than she had done in twenty years. At any rate, it had come to seem, before many minutes, a delightful matter of course that I should sit there—a perfect stranger—listening to the story into which her broken responses to my first questions gradually shaped themselves. I should add that I had made a point of appearing a zealous student of the lamented Briseux. This was no more than the truth, and I proved categorically that I knew his works. We were thus pilgrims in the same faith, and licensed to discuss its mysteries. I repeat her story literally, and I surely don't transgress the proper limits of editorial zeal in supplying a single absent clause: she must in those days have been a wonderfully charming girl.

I have been spending the winter (she said) with my niece at Cannes, where I accidentally heard from an English gentleman interested in such matters, that Briseux's "Yellow Shawl" had been purchased by this little Musée. He had stopped to see it on his way from Paris, and, though a famous *connoisseur*, poor man, do you know he never discovered what it took you but a moment to perceive? I didn't enlighten him, in spite of his kindness in explaining, "Bradshaw" in hand, just how I might manage to diverge on my way to Paris and give a day to M——. I contented myself with telling him that I had known M. Briseux thirty years ago, and had chanced to have the first glimpse of his first masterpiece. Even this suggested nothing. But in fact, why should it have suggested anything? As I sat before the picture just now, I felt in all my pulses that I am *not* the person who stands masquerading there with that strangely cynical smile. That poor girl is dead and buried; I should tell no falsehood in saying I'm not she. Yet as I looked at her, time seemed to roll backward and experience to repeat itself. Before me stood a pale young man in a ragged coat, with glowing dark eyes, brushing away at a great canvas, with gestures more like those of inspiration than any I have ever seen. I seemed to see myself—to *be* myself—muffled in that famous shawl, *posing* there for hours in a sort of fever that made me unconscious of fatigue. I've often wondered whether, during those memorable hours, I was more or less myself than usual, and whether the singular episode they brought forth was an act of folly or of transcendent reason. Perhaps you can tell me.

It was in Paris, in my twenty-first year. I had come abroad with Mrs Staines, an old and valued friend of my mother's, who during the last days of her life, a year before, had consigned me appealingly to this lady's protection. But for Mrs Staines, indeed, I should have been homeless. My brother had recently married, but not happily, and experiment had shown me that under his roof I was an indifferent peacemaker. Mrs Staines was what is called a very superior person—a person with an aquiline nose, who wore gloves in the house, and gave you her ear to kiss. My mother, who considered her the wisest of women, had written her every week since their schooldays a crossed letter beginning "My dearest Lucretia"; but it was my poor mother's nature to like being patronized and bullied. Mrs Staines would send her by return of mail a budget of advice adapted to her "station"—this being a considerate mode of allusion to the fact that she had married a very poor clergyman. Mrs Staines received me, however, with such substantial kindness, that I should have had little grace to complain that the manner of it was frigid. When I knew her better I forgave her frigidity, for it was that of a disappointed woman. She was ambitious, and her ambitions had failed. She had married a very clever man, a rising young lawyer, of political tendencies, who promised to become famous. She would have enjoyed above all things being the wife of a legal luminary, and she would have insisted on his expanding to the first magnitude. She believed herself born, I think, to be the lawful Egeria of a cabinet minister. A cabinet minister poor Mr Staines might have become if he had lived; but he broke down at thirty-five from overwork, and a year later his wife had to do double mourning. As time went on she transferred her hopes to her only boy; but here her disappointment lay the heavier on her heart that maternal pride had bidden it be forever dumb. He would never tread in his father's steps, nor redeem his father's pledges. His genius—if genius it was —was bent in quite another way, and he was to be, not a useful, but an ornamental member of society. Extremely ornamental he seemed likely to become, and his mother found partial comfort as he grew older. He did his duty apparently in growing up so very handsome that, whatever else he might do, he would be praised less for that than for his good looks. They were those of a decorous young Apollo. When I first saw him, as he was leaving college, he might well have passed for an incipient great man. He had in perfection the *air* of distinction, and he carried it out in gesture and manner. Never was a handsomer, graver, better-bred young man. He was tall, slender, and fair, with the finest blonde hair curling close about his shapely head; a blue eye, as clear and cold as a winter's morning; a set of teeth so handsome that his infrequent smile might have seemed almost a matter of modesty; and a general expression of discretion and maturity which seemed to protest against the imputation of foppishness. After a while, probably, you would have found him too imperturbably neat and polite, and have liked him better if his manner had been sometimes at fault and his cravat occasionally awry. Me, I confess, he vastly impressed from the first, and I secretly worshipped him. I had never seen so fine a gentleman, and I doubted if the world contained such another. My experience of the world was small, and I had lived among what Harold Staines would have considered very shabby people—several of whom wore ill-brushed hats. I was, therefore, not sorry to find that I appreciated merit of the most refined sort; and in fact, ignorant though I was, my judgment was not at fault. Harold was perfectly honorable and amiable, and his only fault was that he looked wiser than he could reasonably be expected to be. In the evening especially, in a white cravat, leaning in a doorway, and overtopping the crowd by his whole handsome head, he seemed some inscrutable young diplomatist whose skepticism hadn't undermined his courtesy.

He had, through his mother, expectation of property sufficient to support him in ample ease; but though he had elegant tastes, idleness was not one of them, and he agreed with his mother that he ought to choose a profession. Then it was that she fully measured her disappointment. There had been nothing in her family but judges and bishops, and anything else was of questionable respectability. There was a great deal of talk on the matter between them; for superficially at least they were a most united pair, and if Harold had not asked her opinion from conviction he would have done so from politeness. In reality, I believe, there was but one person in the world whose opinion he greatly cared for—and that person was not Mrs Staines; nor had it yet come to pass that he pretended for a while it was I. It was so far from being Mrs Staines that one day, after a long talk, I found her leaving him in tears; and tears with this superior woman were an event of portentous rarity. Harold on the same day was not at home at dinner, and I thought the next day held his handsome head even higher than usual. I asked no questions, but a little later my curiosity was satisfied. Mrs Staines informed me, with an air of dignity which evidently cost her some effort and seemed intended to deprecate criticism, that Harold had determined to be an—artist. "It's not the career I should have preferred," she said, "but my son has talent—and respectability—which will make it honorable." That Harold would do anything more for the profession of the brush than Raphael and Rembrandt had done, I was perhaps not prepared to affirm; but I answered that I was very glad, and that I wished him all success. Indeed, I was not surprised, for Mrs Staines had what in any one else would have been called a mania for pictures and bronzes, old snuff-boxes and candlesticks. He had not apparently used his pencil very freely; but he had recently procured—indeed, I think he had himself designed—a "sketching apparatus" of the most lavish ingenuity. He was now going to use it in earnest, and I remember reflecting with a good deal of satisfaction that the great white umbrella which formed its principal feature was large enough to protect his handsome complexion from the sun.

It was at this time I came to Mrs Staines to stay indefinitely —with doubts and fears so few that I must have been either very ignorant or very confident. I had indeed an ample measure of the blessed simplicity of youth; but if I judged my situation imperfectly, I did so at any rate with a conscience. I was stoutly determined to receive no favors that I couldn't repay, and to be as quietly useful and gracefully agreeable as I could modestly devise occasion for. I was a homeless girl, but I was not a poor relation. My fortune was slender, but I was ready to go out into the world and seek a better, rather than fall into an attitude of irresponsive dependence. Mrs Staines thought at first that I was dull and amiable, and that as a companion I would do no great credit to anything but her benevolence. Later, for a time, as I gave proofs of some sagacity and perhaps of some decision, I think she fancied me a schemer and—Heaven forgive her!—a hypocrite. But at last, evidently—although to the end, I believe, she continued to compliment my shrewdness at the expense of that feminine sweetness by which I should have preferred to commend myself—she decided that I was a person of the best intentions, and—here comes my story—that I would make a suitable wife for her son.

To this unexpectedly flattering conclusion, of course, she was slow in coming; it was the result of the winter we passed together after Harold had "turned his attention," as his mother always publicly phrased it, "to art." He had declared that we must immediately go abroad that he might study the works of the masters. His mother, I believe, suggested that he might begin with the rudiments nearer home. But apparently he had mastered the rudiments, for she was overruled and we went to Rome. I don't know how many of the secrets of the masters Harold learned; but we passed a delightful winter. He began his studies with the solemn promptitude which he used in all things, and devoted a great deal of time to copying from the antique in the Vatican and the Capitol. He worked slowly, but with extraordinary precision and neatness, and finished his drawings with exquisite care. He was openly very little of a dogmatist, but on coming to know him you found that he had various principles of which he was extremely tenacious. Several of these related to the proportions of the human body, as ascertained by himself. They constituted, he affirmed, an infallible method for learning to draw. If other artists didn't know it, so much the worse for them. He applied this rare method persistently all winter, and carried away from Rome a huge portfolio full of neatly shaded statues and statuesque *contadini*. At first he had gone into a painter's studio with several other pupils, but he took no fancy to either his teacher or his companions, and came home one day in disgust, declaring that he had washed his hands of them. As he never talked about disagreeable things, he said nothing as to what had vexed him; but I guessed that he had received some mortal offence, and I was not surprised that he shouldn't care to fraternize with the common herd of art-students. They had long, untidy hair, and smoked bad tobacco; they lay no one knew where, and borrowed money and took liberties. Mr Staines certainly was not a man to refuse a needy friend a napoleon, but he couldn't forgive a liberty. He took none with himself! We became very good friends, and it was especially for this that I liked him. Nothing is truer than that in the long run we like our opposites; they're a change and a rest from ourselves. I confess that my good intentions sometimes clashed with a fatal light-headedness, of which a fair share of trouble had not cured me. In moments of irritation I had a trick of giving the reins to my "sarcasm;" so at least my partners in quadrilles had often called it. At my leisure I was sure to repent, and frank public amends followed fast on the heels of offence. Then I believe I was called generous—not only by my partners in quadrilles. But I had a secret admiration for people who were just, from the first and always, and whose demeanor seemed to shape itself with a sort of harmonious unity, like the outline of a beautiful statue. Harold Staines was a finished gentleman, as we used to say in those days, and I admired him the more that I still had ringing in my ears that eternal refrain of my schoolroom days—"My child, my child, when will you ever learn to be a lady?" He seemed to me an embodiment of the serene amenities of life, and I didn't know how very great a personage I thought him until I once over-heard a young man in a crowd at St Peter's call him *that con-founded prig*. Then I came to the conclusion that it was a very coarse and vulgar world, and that Mr Staines was too good for it.

This impression was not removed by—I hardly know what to call it—the gallant propriety of his conduct toward me. He had treated me at first with polite condescension, as a very young and rather humble person, whose presence in the house rested on his mother's somewhat eccentric benevolence, rather than on any very obvious merits of her own. But later, as my native merit, whatever it was, got the better of my shy-ness, he approached me, especially in company, with a sort of ceremonious consideration which seemed to give notice to the world that if his mother and he treated me as their equal—why, I *was* their equal. At last, one fine day in Rome, I learned that I had the honor to please him. It had seemed to me so little of a matter of course that I should captivate Mr Staines, that for a moment I was actually disappointed, and felt disposed to tell him that I had expected more of his taste. But as I grew used to the idea, I found no fault with it, and I felt prodigi-ously honored. I didn't take him for a man of genius, but his admiration pleased me more than if it had come in chorus from a dozen of the men of genius whom I had had pointed out to me at archæological picnics. They somehow were covered

E

with the world's rust and haunted with the world's errors, and certainly on any vital question could not be trusted to make their poor wives the same answers two days running. Besides, they were dreadfully ugly. Harold was consistency itself, and his superior manner and fine blond beauty seemed a natural result of his spiritual serenity. The way he declared himself was very characteristic, and to some girls might have seemed prosaic. To my mind it had a peculiar dignity. I had asked him, a week before, as we stood on the platform before the Lateran, some question about the Claudian aqueduct, which he had been unable to answer at the moment, although on coming to Rome he had laid in a huge provision of books of reference which he consulted with unfailing diligence. "I'll look it up," he said gravely; but I thought no more about it, and a few days afterwards, when he asked me to ride with him on the Campagna, I never supposed I was to be treated to an archæological lecture. It was worthy of a wiser listener. He led the way to a swelling mound, overlooking the long stretch of the aqueduct, and poured forth the result of his researches. This was surely not a trivial compliment; and it seemed to me a finer sort of homage than if he had offered me a fifty-franc bouquet or put his horse at a six-foot wall. He told me the number of the arches, and very possibly of the stones; his story bristled with learning. I listened respectfully and stared hard at the long ragged ruin, as if it had suddenly become intensely interesting. But it was Mr Staines who was interesting: all honor to the man who kept his polite promises so handsomely! I said nothing when he paused, and after a few minutes was going to turn away my horse. Then he laid his hand on the bridle, and, in the same tone, as if he were still talking of the aqueduct, informed me of the state of his affections. I, in my unsuspectingness, had enslaved them, and it was proper that I should know he adored me. Proper! I have always remembered the word, though I was far from thinking then that it clashed with his eloquence. It often occurred to me afterwards as the key-note of his character. In a moment more, he formally offered himself.

Don't be surprised at these details: to be just I must be perfectly frank, and if I consented to tell you my story, it is because I fancied I should find profit in hearing it myself. As I speak my words come back to me. I left Rome engaged to Mr Staines, subject to his mother's approval. He might dispense with it, I told him, but I could not, and as yet I had no reason to expect it. She would, of course, wish him to marry a woman of more consequence. Mine of late had risen in her eyes, but she could hardly regard me as yet as a possible daughter-in-law. With time I hoped to satisfy her and to receive her blessing. Then I would ask for no further delay. We journeyed slowly up from Rome along the Mediterranean, stopping often for several days to allow Harold to sketch. He depicted mountains and villages with the same diligence as the statues in the Vatican, and presumably with the same success. As his winter's practice had given him great facility, he would dash off a magnificent landscape in a single morning. I always thought it strange that, being very sober in his speech and manner, he should be extremely fond of color in art. Such at least was the fact, and these rapid water-colors were a wonderful medley. Crimson and azure, orange and emerald—nothing less would satisfy him. But, for that matter, nature in those regions has a dazzling brightness. So at least it had for a lively girl of twenty, just engaged. So it had for a certain time afterwards. I'll not deny, the lustrous sea and sky began vaguely to reflect my own occasionally sombre mood. How to explain to you the process of my feeling at this time is more than I can say; how especially to make you believe that I was neither perverse nor capricious. I give it up; I can only assure you that I observed my emotions, even before I understood them, with painful surprise. I was not disillusioned, but an end had suddenly come to my elation. It was as if my heart had had wings, which had been suddenly clipped. I have never been especially fond of my own possessions, and I have learned that if I wish to admire a thing in peace, I must remain at a respectful distance. My happiness in Harold's affection reached its climax too suddenly, and before I knew it I found myself wondering, questioning, and doubting. It was no fault of his, certainly, and he had promised me nothing that he was not ready to bestow. He was all attention and decorous devotion. If there was a fault, it was mine, for having judged like the very young and uninformed person I was. Since my engagement I felt five years older, and the first use I made of my maturity—cruel as it may seem—was to turn round and look keenly at my lover and revise my judgment. His rigid urbanity was still extremely impressive, but at times I could have fancied that I was listening to a musical symphony, of which only certain brief, unresonant notes were audible. Was this all, and were there no others? It occurred to me more than once, with a kind of dull dismay, in the midst of my placid expectancy, that Harold's grave notes were the beginning and the end of his character. If the human heart were a less incurable skeptic, I might have been divinely happy. I sat by my lover's side while he worked, gazing at the loveliest landscape in the world, and admiring the imperturbable audacity with which he attacked it. Sooner than I expected, these rather silent interviews, as romantic certainly as scenery could make them, received Mrs Staines's sanction. She had guessed our secret, and disapproved of nothing but its secrecy. She was satisfied with her son's choice, and declared with great emphasis that she was not ambitious. She was kindness itself (though, as you see, she indulged in no needless flattery), and I wondered that I could ever have thought her stern. From this time forward she talked to me a great deal about her son; too much, I might have thought, if I had cared less for the theme. I have said I was not perverse. Do I judge myself too tenderly? Before long I found something oppressive—something almost irritating—in the frequency and complacency of Mrs Staines's maternal disquisitions. One day, when she had been reminding me at greater length than usual of what a prize I had drawn, I abruptly changed the subject in the midst of a sentence, and left her staring at my petulance. She was on the point, I think, of administering a reprimand, but she suppressed it and contented herself with approaching the topic more cautiously in future. Here is another reminiscence. One morning (it was near Spezia, I think) Harold had been sketching under a tree, not far from the inn, and I sitting by and reading aloud from Shelley, whom one might feel a kindness for there if nowhere else. We had had a little difference of opinion about one of the poems—the beautiful "Stanzas written in Dejection near Naples," which you probably remember. Harold pronounced them childish. I thought the term ill-chosen, and remember saying, to reinforce my opinion, that though I was no judge of painting, I pretended to be of poetry. He told me (I have not forgotten his words) that "I lacked cultivation in each department," and I believe I replied that I would rather lack cultivation than imagination. For a pair of lovers it was a very pretty quarrel as it stood. Shortly afterwards he discovered that he had left one of his brushes at the inn, and went off in search of it. He had trouble in finding it, and was absent for some time. His verdict on poor Shelley rang in my ears as I sat looking out on the blue iridescence of the sea, and murmuring the lines in which the poet has so wonderfully suggested it. Then I went and sat down on Harold's stool to see how he had rendered this enchanting effect. The picture was nearly finished, but unfortunately I had too little cultivation to enjoy it. The blue sea, however, seemed in all conscience blue enough. While I was comparing it with the far-fading azure of the original, I heard a voice behind me, and turning, saw two gentlemen from the inn, one of whom had been my neighbor the evening before at dinner. He was a foreigner, but he spoke English. On recognizing me he advanced gallantly, ushering his companion, and immediately fell into ecstasies over my picture. I informed him without delay that the picture was not mine; it was the work of Mr Staines. Nothing daunted, he declared that it was pretty enough to be mine, and that I must have given suggestions; but his companion, a less superficial character apparently, and extremely near-sighted, after examining it minutely with his nose close to the paper, exclaimed with an annoying smile, "Monsieur Staines? Surprising! I should have sworn it was the work of a *jeune fille*."

The compliment was doubtful, and not calculated to restore my equanimity. As a *jeune fille* I suppose I ought to have been gratified, but as a betrothed I should have preferred Harold to paint like a man. I don't know how long after this it was that I allowed myself to wonder, by way of harmless conjecture, how a woman might feel who should find herself married to an ineffective mediocrity. Then I remembered—as if the case were my own—that I had never heard any one talk about his pictures, and that when I had seen them handed about before company by his mother, the buzz of admiration usual on such occasions seemed rather heavy-winged. But I quickly reminded myself that it was not because he painted better or worse that I cared for him, but because personally and morally he was the pink of perfection. This being settled, I fell to wondering whether one mightn't grow weary of perfection—whether (Heaven forgive me!) I was not already the least bit out of patience with Harold's. I could fancy him a trifle too absolute, too imperturbable, too prolific in cut-and-dried opinions. Had he settled everything, then, in his mind? Yes, he had certainly made the most of his time, and I could only admire his diligence. From the moment that I observed that he wasted no time in moods, or reveries, or intellectual pleasantry of any sort, I decided without appeal that he was not a man of genius; and yet, to listen to him at times, you would have vowed at least that he might be. He dealt out his opinions as if they were celestial manna, and nothing was more common than for him to say, "You remember, a month ago, I told you so-and-so;" meaning that he had laid down the law on some point and expected me to engrave it on my heart. It often happened that I had forgotten the lesson, and was obliged to ask him to repeat it; but it left me more unsatisfied than before. Harold would settle his shirt collar as if he considered that he had exhausted the subject, and I would take refuge in a silence which from day to day covered more treacherous conjectures. Nevertheless (strange as you may think it), I believe I should have decided that, Harold being a paragon, my doubts were immoral, if Mrs Staines, after his cause might have been supposed to be gained, had not persisted in pleading it in season and out. I don't know whether she suspected my secret falterings, but she seemed to wish to secure me beyond relapse. I was so very modest a match for her son, that if I had been more worldly-wise, her enthusiasm might have alarmed me. Later I understood it; then I only understood that there was a general flavor of insinuation in her talk which made me vaguely uneasy. I did the poor lady injustice, and if I had been quicker-witted (and possibly harder-hearted) we might have become sworn allies. She judged her son less with a mother's tenderness than with a mother's zeal, and foresaw the world's verdict—which I won't anticipate! She perceived that he must depend upon a clever wife to float him into success; he would never prosper on his own merits. She did me the honor to believe me socially a sufficiently buoyant body for this arduous purpose, and must have felt it a thousand pities that she couldn't directly speak her mind. A thousand pities indeed! My answer would have been to the point, and would have saved us all a vast deal of pain. Meanwhile, trying half to convince and half to entangle me, she did everything to hasten our marriage.

If there had been anything less than the happiness of a life-time at stake, I think I should have felt that I owed Harold a sort of reparation for thinking him too great a man, and

should still have offered him an affection none the less genuine
for being transposed into a minor key. But it was hard for a
girl who had dreamed blissfully of a grandly sentimental
union, to find herself suddenly face to face with a sternly
rational one. When, therefore, Harold mentioned a certain
day as the latest for which he thought it proper to wait, I
found it impossible to assent, and asked for another month's
delay. What I wished to wait for I could hardly have told.
Possibly for the first glow of illusion to return; possibly for
the last uneasy throb which told that illusion was ebbing
away. Harold received this request very gravely, and inquired
whether I doubted of his affection.

"No," I said, "I believe it's greater than I deserve."

"Why then," he asked, "should you wait?"

"Suppose I were to doubt of my own?"

He looked as if I had said something in very bad taste, and
I was almost frightened at his sense of security. But he at last
consented to the delay. Perhaps on reflection he was alarmed,
for the grave politeness with which he discharged his attentions took a still more formal turn, as if to remind me at
every hour of the day that his was not a sentiment to be trifled
with. To trifle, Heaven knows, was far enough from my
thoughts; for I was fast losing my spirits, and I woke up one
morning with the conviction that I was decidedly not happy.

We were to be married in Paris, where Harold had determined to spend six months in order that he might try his
fortune again in the studio of a painter whom he especially
esteemed—a certain Monsieur Martinet, an old man, and be-
longing, I believe, to a rather antiquated school of art. During
our first days in Paris I went with Harold a great deal to the
Louvre, where he was a very profitable companion. He had
the history of the schools at his fingers' ends, and, as the
phrase is, he knew what he liked. We had a fatal habit of
not liking the same things; but I pretended to no critical
insight, and desired nothing better than to agree with him.

I listened devoutly to everything that could be said for Guido and Caravaggio. One day we were standing before the inscrutable "Joconde" of Leonardo, a picture disagreeable to most women. I had been expressing my great aversion to the lady's countenance, which Harold on this occasion seemed to share. I was surprised therefore, when, after a pause, he said quietly, "I believe I'll copy her."

I hardly knew why I should have smiled, but I did, apparently to his annoyance. "She must be very difficult," I said. "Try something easier."

"I want something difficult," he answered sternly.

"Truly?" I said. "You mean what you say?"

"Why not?"

"Why then copy a portrait when you can copy an original?"

"What original?"

"Your betrothed! Paint my portrait. I promise to be difficult enough. Indeed, I'm surprised you should never have proposed it." In fact the idea had just occurred to me; but I embraced it with a sort of relief. It seemed to me that it would somehow test my lover, and that if he succeeded, I might believe in him irremissibly. He stared a moment as if he had hardly understood me, and I completed my thought. "Paint my portrait, and the day you finish it I'll fix our wedding day."

The proposal was after all not very terrible, and before long he seemed to relish it. The next day he told me that he had composed his figure mentally, and that we might begin immediately. Circumstances favored us, for he had for the time undisturbed all of M. Martinet's studio. This gentleman had gone into the country to paint a portrait, and Harold just then was his only pupil. Our first sitting took place without delay. At his request I brought with me a number of draperies among which was the yellow shawl you have just been admiring. We wore such things then, just as we played on the harp and read "Corinne." I tried on my scarfs and veils, one after the other, but Harold was satisfied with none. The yellow shawl, in especial, he pronounced a meretricious ornament, and decided that I should be represented in a plain dark dress, with as few accessories as possible. He quoted with a bow the verse about beauty when unadorned, and began his work.

After the first day or two it progressed slowly, and I felt at moments as if I had saddled him with a cruel burden. He expressed no irritation, but he often looked puzzled and wearied, and sometimes would lay aside his brushes, fold his arms, and stand gazing at his work with a sort of vacant scowl which tried my patience. "Frown at me," I said more than once; "don't frown at that blameless sheet of canvas. Don't spare me, though I confess it's not my fault if I'm hard to paint." Thus admonished, he would turn toward me without smiling, often shading his eyes with his hand, and would walk slowly round the room, examining me at a distance. Then coming back to his easel, he would make half a dozen strokes and pause again, as if his impetus had already expired. For some time I was miserable; it seemed to me that I had been wonderfully wise to withhold my hand till the picture was finished. He begged I would not look at it, but I knew it was standing still. At last, one morning, after gazing at his work for some time in silence, he laid down his palette gravely, but with no further sign of discomposure than that he gently wiped his forehead with his pocket-handkerchief. "You make me nervous," he suddenly declared.

I fancied there was a tremor in his voice, and I began to pity him. I left my place and laid my hand on his arm. "If it wearies you," I said, "give it up."

He turned away and for some time made no answer. I knew what he was thinking about, and I suppose he knew that I knew it, and was hesitating to ask me seriously whether in giving up his picture he gave up something more. He decided apparently to give up nothing, but grasped his palette, and, with the short incisive gesture habitual to him, motioned me back to my seat. "I'll bother no longer over the drawing," he said; "I'll begin to paint." With his colors he was more prosperous, for the next day he told me that we were progressing fast.

We generally went together to the studio, but it happened one day that he was to be occupied during the early morning at the other end of Paris, and he arranged to meet me there. I was punctual, but he had not arrived, and I found myself face to face with my reluctant image. Opportunity served too well, and I looked at it in spite of his prohibition, meaning of course to confess my fault. It brought me less pleasure than faults are reputed to bring. The picture, as yet very slight and crude, was unpromising and unflattering. I chiefly distinguished a long white face with staring black eyes, and a terribly angular pair of arms. Was it in this unlovely form that I had impressed myself on Harold's vision? Absorbed by the question, it was some moments before I perceived that I was not alone. I heard a sound, looked round, and discovered a stranger, a young man, gazing over my shoulder at Harold's canvas. His gaze was intense and not expressive of pleasure, and some moments passed before he perceived that I had noticed him. He reminded me strongly of certain dishevelled copyists whom I had seen at work in the Louvre, and as I supposed he had some lawful errand in the studio, I contented myself with thinking that he hadn't the best manners in the world, and walked to the other end of the room. At last, as he continued to betray no definite intentions, I ventured to look at him again. He was young—twenty-five at most—and excessively shabby. I remember, among other details, that he had a black cravat wound two or three times round his neck without any visible linen. He was short, thin, pale, and hungry-looking. As I turned toward him, he passed his hand through his hair, as if to do what he could to make himself presentable, and called my attention to his prodigious shock of thick black curls—a real *coiffure de rapin*. His face would have been meagre and vulgar, if from beneath their umbrageous locks there had not glanced an extraordinary pair of eyes—eyes really of fire. They were not tender nor appealing, but they glittered with a sort of feverish intelligence and penetration, and stamped their possessor not, as the French say, the first comer. He almost glared at me and stopped my words short.

"That's your portrait?" he asked, with a toss of his head.

I assented with dignity.

"It's bad, bad, bad!" he cried. "Excuse my frankness, but it's really too bad. It's a waste of colors, of money, of time."

His frankness certainly was extreme; but his words had an accent of ardent conviction which doesn't belong to commonplace impertinence. "I don't know who you are that I should value your opinion," I said.

"Who I am? I'm an artist, mademoiselle. If I had money to buy visiting-cards, I would present you with one. But I haven't even money to buy colors—hardly to buy bread. I've talent—I've imagination—too much!—I've ideas—I've promise—I've a future; and yet the machine won't work—for want of fuel! I have to roam about with my hands in my pockets—to keep them warm—for want of the very tools of my trade. I've been a fool—an ignoble fool; I've thrown precious hours to the dogs and made enemies of precious friends. Six months ago I quarrelled with the père Martinet, who believed in me and would have been glad to keep me. *Il faut que jeunesse se passe!* Mine has passed at a rattling pace, ill-mounted though it was; we have parted company forever. Now I only ask to do a man's work with a man's will. Meanwhile the père Martinet, justly provoked, has used his tongue so well that not a colorman in Paris will trust me. There's a situation! And yet what could I do with ten francs' worth of paint? I want a room and light and a model, and a dozen yards of satin tumbling about her feet. Bah! I shall have to want! There are things I want more. Behold the force of circumstances. I've come back with my pride in my pocket to make it up with the venerable author of the 'Apotheosis of Molière,' and ask him to lend me a louis."

I arrested this vehement effusion by informing him that M. Martinet was out of town, and that for the present the studio was—private. But he seemed too much irritated to take my hint. "That's not his work?" he went on, turning to the portrait. "Martinet is bad, but is not as bad as that. *Quel genre!* You deserve, mademoiselle, to be better treated; you're an excellent model. Excuse me, once for all; I know I'm atrociously impudent. But I'm an artist, and I find it pitiful to see a fine great canvas besmeared in such a fashion as that! There ought to be a society for the protection of such things."

I was at loss what to reply to this extraordinary explosion of contempt. Strange to say—it's the literal truth—I was neither annoyed nor disgusted; I simply felt myself growing extremely curious. This impudent little Bohemian was forcing me somehow to respect his opinion; he spoke with penetrating authority. Don't say that I was willing to be convinced; if you had been there, you would have let him speak. It would have been, of course, the part of propriety to request him in a chilling voice to leave the room, or to ring for the concierge, or to flee in horror. I did none of these things: I went back to the picture, and tried hard to see something in it which would make me passionately contradict him. But it seemed to exhale a mortal chill, and all I could say was: "Bad—bad? How bad?"

"Ridiculously bad; impossibly bad! You're an angel of charity, mademoiselle, not to see it!"

"Is it weak—cold—ignorant?"

"Weak, cold, ignorant, stiff, empty, hopeless! And, on top of all, pretentious—oh, pretentious as the *façade* of the Madeleine!"

I endeavored to force a skeptical smile. "After all, monsieur, I'm not bound to believe you."

"Evidently!" And he rubbed his forehead and looked

gloomily round the room. "But one thing I can tell you"—fixing me suddenly with his extraordinary eyes, which seemed to expand and glow with the vividness of prevision—"the day will come when people will fight for the honor of having believed me, and of having been the first. 'I discovered him—I always said so. But for me you'd have let the poor devil starve!' You'll hear the chorus! So now's your chance, mademoiselle! Here I stand, a man of genius if there ever was one, without a sou, without a friend, without a ray of reputation. Believe in me now, and you'll be the first, by many a day. You'd find it easier, you'll say, if I had a little more modesty. I assure you I don't go about blowing my trumpet in this fashion every day. This morning I'm in a kind of fever, and I've reached a crisis. I must do something—even make an ass of myself! I can't go on devouring my own heart. You see for these three months I've been *à sec*. I haven't dined every day. Perhaps a sinking at the stomach is propitious to inspiration: certainly, week by week, my brain has grown clearer, my imagination more restless, my desires more boundless, my visions more splendid! Within the last fortnight my last doubt has vanished, and I feel as strong as the sun in heaven! I roam about the streets and lounge in the public gardens for want of a better refuge, and everything I look at—the very sunshine in the gutter, the chimney-pots against the sky—seems a picture, a subject, an opportunity! I hang over the balustrade that runs before the pictures at the Louvre, and Titian and Correggio seem to turn pale, like people when you've guessed their secret. I don't know who the author of this masterpiece may be, but I fancy he would have more talent if he weren't so sure of his dinner. Do you know how I learned to look at things and use my eyes? By staring at the *charcutier's* windows when my pockets were empty. It's a great lesson to learn even the shape of a sausage and the color of a ham. This gentleman, it's easy to see, hasn't noticed such matters. He goes by the sense of taste. *Voilà le monde!* I—I—I—"—and he slapped his forehead with a kind of dramatic fury—"here as you see me—ragged, helpless, hopeless, with my soul aching with ambition and my fingers itching for a brush—and *he*, standing up here after a good breakfast, in this perfect light, among pictures and tapestries and carvings, with you in your blooming beauty for a model, and painting that—sign-board."

His violence was startling; I didn't know what might come next, and I took up my bonnet and mantle. He immediately protested with ardor. "A moment's reflection, mademoiselle, will tell you that, with the appearance I present, I don't talk about your beauty *pour vous faire la cour*. I repeat with all respect, you're a model to make a painter's fortune. I doubt if you've many attitudes or much flexibility; but for once— the portrait of Mlle X.—you're perfect."

"I'm obliged to you for your—information," I answered gravely. "You see my artist is chosen. I expect him here at any moment, and I won't answer for his listening to you as patiently as I have done."

"He's coming?" cried my visitor. "*Quelle chance!* I shall be charmed to meet him. I shall vastly enjoy seeing the human head from which that conception issued. I see him already: I construct the author from the work. He's tall and blond, with eyes very much the color of his own china-blue there. He wears straw-colored whiskers, and doubtless he paints in straw-colored gloves. In short, he's *un homme magnifique!*"

This was sarcasm run mad; but I listened to it and resented it as little as I enjoyed it. My companion seemed to possess a sort of demonic veracity of which the influence was irresistible. I questioned his sincerity so little that, if I offered him charity, it was with no intention of testing it. "I dare say you've im- mense talent," I said, "but you've horrible manners. Never- theless, I believe you will perceive that there is no reason why our conversation should continue; and I should pay you a poor compliment in thinking that you need to be bribed to withdraw. But since M. Martinet isn't here to lend you a louis, let me act for him." And I laid the piece of gold on the table.

He looked at it hard for a moment and then at me, and I wondered whether he thought the gift too meagre. "I won't go so far as to say that I'm proud," he answered at last. "But from a lady, *ma foi!* it's beggarly—it's humiliating. Excuse me then if I refuse; I mean to ask for something else. To do me justice, remember that I speak to you not as a man, but as an artist. Bestow your charity on the artist, and if it costs you an effort, remember that that is the charity which is of most account with heaven. Keep your louis; go and stand as you've been standing for this picture, in the same light and the same attitude, and then let me look at you for three little minutes." As he spoke he drew from his pocket a ragged note-book and the stump of a pencil. "The few scrawls I shall make here will be your alms."

He spoke of effort, but it is a fact that I made little to comply. While I resumed my familiar attitude in front of Harold's canvas, he walked rapidly across the room and stooped over a chair upon which a mass of draperies had been carelessly tossed. In a moment I saw what had attracted him. He had caught a glimpse of the famous yellow scarf, glowing splendidly beneath a pile of darker stuffs. He pulled out the beautiful golden-hued tissue with furious alacrity, held it up before him and broke into an ecstasy of admiration. "What a tone—what a glow—what a texture! In Heaven's name, put it on!" And without further ceremony he tossed it over my shoulders. I need hardly tell you that I obeyed but a natural instinct in gathering it into picturesque folds. He rushed away, and stood gazing and clapping his hands. "The harmony is perfect—the effect sublime! You possess that thing and you bury it out of sight? Wear it, wear it, I entreat you—and your portrait—but ah!" and he glared angrily askance at the picture: "you'll never wear it there!"

"We thought of using it, but it was given up."

"Given up? *Quelle horreur!* He hadn't the pluck to attack it! Oh, if I could just take a brush at it and rub it in for him!" And, as if possessed by an uncontrollable impulse, he seized poor Harold's palette. But I made haste to stop his hand. He flung down the brushes, buried his face in his hands, and pressed back, I could fancy, the tears of baffled eagerness. "You'll think me crazy!" he cried.

He was not crazy, to my sense; but he was a raging, aimless force, which I suddenly comprehended that I might use. I seemed to measure the full proportions of Harold's inefficiency and to foresee the pitiful result of his undertaking. He wouldn't succumb, but he would doggedly finish his task and present me, in evidence of his claim, with a dreadful monument of his pretentious incapacity. Twenty strokes from this master-hand would make a difference; ten minutes' work would carry the picture forward. I thrust the palette into the young man's grasp again and looked at him solemnly. "Paint away for your life," I said; "but promise me this: to succeed!"

He waved his hand in the air, despatched me with a glance to my place, and let himself loose on the canvas; there are no other words for his tremulous eagerness. A quarter of an hour passed in silence. As I watched his motions grow every moment broader and more sweeping, I could fancy myself listening to some ardent pianist, plunging deeper into a passionate symphony and devouring the key-board with out-stretched arms. Flushed and dishevelled, consuming me al-most with his ardent stare, daubing, murmuring, panting, he seemed indeed to be painting for life.

At last I heard a tread in the vestibule. I knew it was Harold's, and I hurried to look at the picture. How would he take it? I confess I was prepared for the worst. The picture spoke for itself. Harold's work had disappeared with magical rapidity, and even my unskilled eye perceived that a graceful and expressive figure had been powerfully sketched in. As

F

Harold appeared, I turned to meet him. He seemed surprised at not finding me alone, and I laid my finger gravely on my lips and led him to the front of the canvas. The position of things was so singular that for some moments it baffled his comprehension. My companion finished what he was immediately concerned with; then with an obsequious bow laid down his brushes. "It was a loan, monsieur," he said. "I return it with interest."

Harold flushed to his eyes, and sat down in silence. I had expected him to be irritated; but this was more than irritation. At last: "Explain this extraordinary performance," he said in a low voice.

I felt pain, and yet somehow I felt no regret. The situation was tense, as the phrase is, and yet I almost relished it. "This gentleman is a great artist," I said boldly. "Look for yourself. Your picture was lost; he has redeemed it."

Harold looked at the intruder slowly from head to foot. "Who is this person?" he demanded, as if he had not heard me.

The young man understood no English, but he apparently guessed at the question. "My name is Pierre Briseux; let *that*" (pointing to his work) "denote my profession. If you're affronted, monsieur, don't visit your displeasure on mademoiselle; I alone am responsible. You had got into a tight place; I wished to help you out of it; *sympathie de confrère!* I've done you no injury. I've made you a present of half a masterpiece. If I could only trust you not to spoil it!"

Harold's face betrayed his invincible disgust, and I saw that my offence was mortal. He had been wounded in his tenderest part, and his self-control was rapidly ebbing. His lips trembled, but he was too angry even to speak. Suddenly he seized a heavy brush which stood in a pot of dusky varnish, and I thought for a moment he was going to fling it at Briseux. He balanced it an instant, and then tossed it full in the face of the picture. I raised my hands to my face as if I felt the blow. Briseux, at least, felt it sorely.

"*Malheureux!*" he cried. "Are you blind as well? Don't
you know a good thing when you see it? That's what I call a
waste of material. *Allons*, you're very angry; let me explain. In
meddling with your picture I certainly took a great liberty.
My misery is my excuse. You have money, materials, models
—everything but talent. No, no, you're no painter; it's impossible! There isn't an intelligent line on your canvas. I, on
the other hand, am a born painter. I've talent and nothing
more. I came here to see M. Martinet; learning he was absent,
I staid for very envy! I looked at your work, and found it a
botch; at your empty stool and idle palette, and found them an
immense temptation; at mademoiselle, and found her a perfect model. I persuaded, frightened, convinced her, and out of
charity she gave me a five minutes' sitting. Once the brush in
my hand, I felt the divine afflatus; I hoped for a miracle—
that you'd never come back, that you'd be run over in the
street, or have an attack of apoplexy. If you had only let me
go on, I should have served you up a great work, monsieur—
a work to which, in spite of your natural irritation, you
wouldn't have dared to do a violence. You'd have been afraid
of it. That's the sort of thing I meant to paint. If you could
only believe me, you'd not regret it. Give me a start, and ten
years hence I shall see you buying my pictures, and not thinking them dear. Oh, I thought I had my foot in the stirrup; I
dreamed I was in the saddle and riding hard. But I've turned
a somersault!"

I doubt that Harold, in his resentment, either understood
M. Briseux's words or appreciated his sketch. He simply felt
that he had been the victim of a monstrous aggression, in
which I, in some painfully inexplicable way, had been half
dupe and half accomplice. I was watching his anger and
weighing its ominous significance. His cold fury, and the
expression it threw into his face and gestures, told me more
about him than weeks of placid love-making had done, and,
following close upon my vivid sense of his incapacity, seemed

suddenly to cut the knot that bound us together, and over which my timid fingers had been fumbling. "Put on your bonnet," he said to me; "get a carriage and go home."

I can't describe his tone. It contained an assumption of my confusion and compliance, which made me feel that I ought to lose no time in undeceiving him. Nevertheless I felt cruelly perplexed, and almost afraid of his displeasure. Mechanically I took up my bonnet. As I held it in my hand, my eyes met those of our terrible companion, who was evidently trying to read the riddle of my relations with Harold. Planted there with his trembling lips, his glittering, searching eyes, an indefinable something in his whole person that told of joyous impulse arrested, but pausing only for a more triumphant effort, he seemed a strangely eloquent embodiment of youthful genius. I don't know whether he read in my glance a ray of sympathy, but his lips formed a soundless "*Restez, madame,*" which quickened the beating of my heart. The feeling that then invaded it I despair of making you understand; yet it must help in your eyes to excuse me, and it was so profound that often in memory it seems more real and poignant than the things of the present. Poor little Briseux, ugly, shabby, disreputable, seemed to me some appealing messenger from the mysterious immensity of life; and Harold, beside him, comely, elegant, imposing, justly indignant, seemed to me simply his narrow, personal, ineffectual self. This was a wider generalization than the feminine heart is used to. I flung my bonnet on the floor and burst into tears.

"This is not an exhibition for a stranger," said Harold grimly. "Be so good as to follow me."

"You must excuse me; I can't follow you; I can't explain. I have something more to say to M. Briseux. He's less of a stranger than you think."

"I'm to leave you here?" stammered Harold.

"It's the simplest way."

"With that dirty little Frenchman?"

"What should I care for his being clean? It's his genius that interests me."

Harold stared in dark amazement. "Are you insane? Do you know what you're doing?"

"An act, I believe, of real charity."

"Charity begins at home. It's an act of desperate folly. Must I *command* you to leave?"

"You've done that already. I can't obey you. If I were to do so, I should pretend what isn't true; and, let me say it, it's to undeceive you that I refuse."

"I don't understand you," cried Harold, "nor to what spell this meddlesome little beggar has subjected you! But I'm not a man to be trifled with, you know, and this is my last request; my last, do you understand? If you prefer the society of this abandoned person, you're welcome, but you forfeit mine forever. It's a choice! You give up the man who has offered you an honorable affection, a name, a fortune, who has trusted and cherished you, who stands ready to make you a devoted husband. What you get the Lord knows!"

I had sunk into a chair. I listened in silence, and for some time answered nothing. His words were vividly true. He offered me much, and I gave up everything. He had played an honorable part, and I was playing a very strange one. I asked myself sternly whether I was ready to rise and take his arm and let him lead me blindfold through life. When I raised my eyes Briseux stood before me, and from the expression of his face I could have fancied he had guessed at the meaning of Harold's words. "I'll make you immortal," he murmured; "I'll delight mankind—and I'll begin my own career!"

An ineffable prevision of the truth which after the lapse of years has brought about our meeting here seemed to raise me as if on wings, and made decision easy. We women are so habitually condemned by fate to act simply in what is called the domestic sphere, that there is something intoxicating in the opportunity to exert a far-reaching influence outside of it.

To feel the charms of such an opportunity, one must perhaps be of a reprehensibly fanciful turn. Such at any rate was my mood for that hour. I seemed to be the end of an electric chain, of which the rest was throbbing away through time. I seemed to hold in my hand an immeasurable gift. "We had better part on the spot," I said to Harold. "I've foreseen our parting for weeks, only it has come more abruptly. Forgive the abruptness. To myself the pretext seems better than to you; perhaps some day you'll appreciate it. A single question," I added. "Could you ever have finished my portrait?"

He looked at me askance for some moments, with a strange mistrust, as if I had suddenly developed some monstrous and sinister slyness; then catching his breath with a little groan—almost a shudder—he marched out of the room.

Briseux clasped his hands in ecstasy. "You're magnificent!" he cried. "If you could only look so for three hours!"

"To business," I said sternly. "If you don't paint a perfect picture, you're the most shameless of impostors."

He had but a single sitting, but it was a long one; though how many hours it lasted, I doubt that either of us could have told. He painted till dusk, and then we had lamps. Before I left him I looked at the picture for the last and only time before seeing it to-day. It seemed to me as perfect as it seemed this morning, and I felt that my choice was justified and that Briseux's fortune was made. It gave me all the strength I needed for the immediate future. He was evidently of the same opinion and profoundly absorbed in it. When I bade him farewell, in very few words, he answered me almost absently. I had served his purpose and had already passed into that dusky limbo of unhonored victims, the experience—intellectual and other—of genius. I left him the yellow shawl, that he might finish this part of his work at his leisure, and, as for the picture, I told him to keep it, for that I should have little pleasure in seeing it again. Then he stared a moment, but the next he was painting hard.

I had the next morning what under other circumstances I might call an explanation with Mr Staines, an explanation in which I explained nothing to his satisfaction but that he had been hideously wronged, and that I was a demon of inconstancy. He wrapped himself in an icy silence, and, I think, expected some graceful effusion of humility. I may not have been humble, but I was considerate, and I perceived, for my reward, that the sore point with him was not that he had lost me, but that I had ventured to judge him. Mrs Staines's manner, on the other hand, puzzled me, so strange a mixture was it of half-disguised elation and undisguised sarcasm. At last I guessed her meaning. Harold, after all, had had an escape; instead of being the shrewd, practical girl she had thought me, I was a terribly romantic one! Perhaps she was right; I was romantic enough to make no further claim on her hospitality, and with as little delay as possible I returned home. A month later I received an enclosure of half a dozen cuttings from newspapers, scrawled boldly across with the signature of Pierre Briseux. The Paris *salon* had opened and the critics had spoken. They had not neglected the portrait of Mademoiselle X——. The picture was an immense success, and M. Briseux was famous. There were a few protesting voices, but it was evident that his career had begun. For Mademoiselle X—— herself, I believe, there were none but compliments, several of which took the form of gallant conjecture as to her real identity. Mademoiselle X—— was an assumed name, and according to more than one voice the lady was an imperious Russian princess with a distaste for vulgar publicity. You know the rest of M. Briseux's history. Since then he has painted real princesses by the dozen. He has delighted mankind rarely. As for his having made me immortal, I feel as if it were almost true. It must be an eternity since the thing happened—so very unreservedly I've described it!

THE LAST OF THE VALERII

I HAD had occasion to declare more than once that if my god-daughter married a foreigner I should refuse to give her away. And yet when the young Conte Valerio was presented to me, in Rome, as her accepted and plighted lover, I found myself looking at the happy fellow, after a momentary stare of amazement, with a certain paternal benevolence; thinking, indeed, that from the picturesque point of view (she with her yellow locks and he with his dusky ones), they were a strikingly well-assorted pair. She brought him up to me half proudly, half timidly, pushing him before her, and begging me with one of her dovelike glances to be very polite. I don't know that I am particularly addicted to rudeness; but she was so deeply impressed with his grandeur that she thought it impossible to do him honor enough. The Conte Valerio's grandeur was doubtless nothing for a young American girl, who had the air and almost the habits of a princess, to sound her trumpet about; but she was desperately in love with him, and not only her heart, but her imagination, was touched. He was extremely handsome, and with a more significant sort of beauty than is common in the handsome Roman race. He had a sort of sunken depth of expression, and a grave, slow smile, suggesting no great quickness of wit, but an unimpassioned intensity of feeling which promised well for Martha's happiness. He had little of the light, inexpensive urbanity of his countrymen, and more of a sort of heavy sincerity in his gaze which seemed to suspend response until he was sure he understood you. He was perhaps a little stupid, and I fancied that to a political or æsthetic question the response would be particularly slow.

89

"He is good, and strong, and brave," the young girl however assured me; and I easily believed her. Strong the Conte Valerio certainly was; he had a head and throat like some of the busts in the Vatican. To my eye, which has looked at things now so long with the painter's purpose, it was a real perplexity to see such a throat rising out of the white cravat of the period. It sustained a head as massively round as that of the familiar bust of the Emperor Caracalla, and covered with the same dense sculptural crop of curls. The young man's hair grew superbly; it was such hair as the old Romans must have had when they walked bareheaded and bronzed about the world. It made a perfect arch over his low, clear forehead, and prolonged itself on cheek and chin in a close, crisp beard, strong with its own strength and unstiffened by the razor. Neither his nose nor his mouth was delicate; but they were powerful, shapely, and manly. His complexion was of a deep glowing brown which no emotion would alter, and his large, lucid eyes seemed to stare at you like a pair of polished agates. He was of middle stature, and his chest was of so generous a girth that you half expected to hear his linen crack with its even respirations. And yet, with his simple human smile, he looked neither like a young bullock nor a gladiator. His powerful voice was the least bit harsh, and his large, ceremonious reply to my compliment had the massive sonority with which civil speeches must have been uttered in the age of Augustus. I had always considered my god-daughter a very American little person, in all delightful meanings of the word, and I doubted if this sturdy young Latin would understand the transatlantic element in her nature; but, evidently, he would make her a loyal and ardent lover. She seemed to me, in her blond prettiness, so tender, so appealing, so bewitching, that it was impossible to believe he had not more thoughts for all this than for the pretty fortune which it yet bothered me to believe that he must, like a good Italian, have taken the exact measure of. His own worldly goods consisted of the paternal estate, a villa within the walls of Rome, which his scanty funds had suffered to fall into sombre disrepair. "It's the Villa she's in love with, quite as much as the Count," said her mother. "She dreams of converting the Count; that's all very well. But she dreams of refurnishing the Villa!"

The upholsterers were turned into it, I believe, before the wedding, and there was a great scrubbing and sweeping of saloons and raking and weeding of alleys and avenues. Martha made frequent visits of inspection while these ceremonies were taking place; but one day, on her return, she came into my little studio with an air of amusing horror. She had found them *scraping* the sarcophagus in the great ilex-walk; divesting it of its mossy coat, disincrusting it of the sacred green mould of the ages! This was their idea of making the Villa comfortable. She had made them transport it to the dampest place they could find; for, next after that slow-coming, slow-going smile of her lover, it was the rusty complexion of his patrimonial marbles that she most prized. The young Count's conversion proceeded less rapidly, and indeed I believe that his betrothed brought little zeal to the affair. She loved him so devoutly that she believed no change of faith could better him, and she would have been willing for his sake to say her prayers to the sacred Bambino at Epiphany. But he had the good taste to demand no such sacrifice, and I was struck with the happy promise of a scene of which I was an accidental observer. It was at St Peter's, one Friday afternoon, during the vesper service which takes place in the chapel of the Choir. I met my god-daughter wandering happily on her lover's arm, her mother being established on her camp-stool near the chapel door. The crowd was collected thereabouts, and the body of the church was empty. Now and then the high voices of the singers escaped into the outer vastness and melted slowly away in the incense-thickened air. Something in the young girl's step and the clasp of her arm in her lover's told me that her contentment was perfect. As she threw back her head and gazed into the magnificent immensity of vault and dome, I felt that she was in that enviable mood in which all consciousness revolves on a single centre, and that her sense of the splendors around her was one with the ecstasy of her trust. They stopped before that sombre group of confessionals which proclaims so portentously the world's sinfulness, and Martha seemed to make some almost passionate protestation. A few minutes later I overtook them.

"Don't you agree with me, dear friend," said the Count, who always addressed me with the most affectionate deference, "that before I marry so pure and sweet a creature as this, I ought to go into one of those places and confess every sin I ever was guilty of,—every evil thought and impulse and desire of my grossly evil nature?"

Martha looked at him, half in deprecation, half in homage, with a look which seemed at once to insist that her lover could have no vices, and to plead that, if he had, there would be something magnificent in them. "Listen to him!" she said, smiling. "The list would be long, and if you waited to finish it, you would be late for the wedding! But if you confess your sins for me, it's only fair I should confess mine for you. Do you know what I have been saying to Camillo?" she added, turning to me with the half-filial confidence she had always shown me and with a rosy glow in her cheeks; "that I want to do something more for him than girls commonly do for their lovers,—to take some step, to run some risk, to break some law, even! I'm willing to change my religion, if he bids me. There are moments when I'm terribly tired of simply staring at Catholicism; it will be a relief to come into a church to kneel. That's, after all, what they are meant for! Therefore, Camillo mio, if it casts a shade across your heart to think that I'm a heretic, I'll go and kneel down to that good old priest who has just entered the confessional yonder and say to him, 'My father, I repent, I abjure, I believe. Baptize me in the only faith.'"

"If it's as a compliment to the Count," I said, "it seems to me he ought to anticipate it by turning Protestant."

She had spoken lightly and with a smile, and yet with an undertone of girlish ardor. The young man looked at her with a solemn, puzzled face and shook his head. "Keep your religion," he said. "Every one his own. If you should attempt to embrace mine, I'm afraid you would close your arms about a shadow. I'm a poor Catholic! I don't understand all these chants and ceremonies and splendors. When I was a child I never could learn my catechism. My poor old confessor long ago gave me up; he told me I was a good boy but a *pagan!* You must not be a better Catholic than your husband. I don't understand your religion any better, but I beg you not to change it for mine. If it has helped to make you what you are, it must be good." And taking the young girl's hand, he was about to raise it affectionately to his lips; but suddenly remembering that they were in a place unaccordant with profane passions, he lowered it with a comical smile. "Let us go!" he murmured, passing his hand over his forehead. "This heavy atmosphere of St Peter's always stupefies me."

They were married in the month of May, and we separated for the summer, the Contessa's mamma going to illuminate the domestic circle in New York with her reflected dignity. When I returned to Rome in the autumn, I found the young couple established at the Villa Valerio, which was being gradually reclaimed from its antique decay. I begged that the hand of improvement might be lightly laid on it, for as an unscrupulous old *genre* painter, with an eye to "subjects," I preferred that ruin should accumulate. My god-daughter was quite of my way of thinking, and she had a capital sense of the picturesque. Advising with me often as to projected changes, she was sometimes more conservative than myself; and I more than once smiled at her archæological zeal, and declared that I believed she had married the Count because he was like a statue of the Decadence. I had a constant invitation to spend my days at the Villa, and my easel was always planted in one of the garden-walks. I grew to have a painter's passion for the place, and to be intimate with every tangled shrub and twisted tree, every moss-coated vase and mouldy sarcophagus and sad, disfeatured bust of those grim old Romans who could so ill afford to become more meagre-visaged. The place was of small extent; but though there were many other villas more pretentious and splendid, none seemed to me more deeply picturesque, more romantically idle and untrimmed, more encumbered with precious antique rubbish, and haunted with half-historic echoes. It contained an old ilex-walk in which I used religiously to spend half an hour every day,—half an hour being, I confess, just as long as I could stay without beginning to sneeze. The trees arched and intertwisted here along their dusky vista in the quaintest symmetry; and as it was exposed uninterruptedly to the west, the low evening sun used to transfuse it with a sort of golden mist and play through it—over leaves and knotty boughs and mossy marbles—with a thousand crimson fingers. It was filled with disinterred fragments of sculpture,—nameless statues and noseless heads and rough-hewn sarcophagi, which made it deliciously solemn. The statues used to stand there in the perpetual twilight like conscious things, brooding on their gathered memories. I used to linger about them, half expecting they would speak and tell me their stony secrets,—whisper heavily the whereabouts of their mouldering fellows, still unrecovered from the soil.

My god-daughter was idyllically happy and absolutely in love. I was obliged to confess that even rigid rules have their exceptions, and that now and then an Italian count is an honest fellow. Camillo was one to the core, and seemed quite content to be adored. Their life was a childlike interchange of caresses, as candid and unmeasured as those of a shepherd and shepherdess in a bucolic poem. To stroll in the ilex-walk and feel her husband's arm about her waist and his shoulder against her cheek; to roll cigarettes for him while he puffed them in the great marble-paved rotunda in the centre of the house; to fill his glass from an old rusty red amphora,—these graceful occupations satisfied the young Countess.

She rode with him sometimes in the grassy shadow of aqueducts and tombs, and sometimes suffered him to show his beautiful wife at Roman dinners and balls. She played dominos with him after dinner, and carried out in a desultory way a daily scheme of reading him the newspapers. This observance was subject to fluctuations caused by the Count's invincible tendency to go to sleep,—a failing his wife never attempted to disguise or palliate. She would sit and brush the flies from him while he lay picturesquely snoozing, and, if I ventured near him, would place her finger on her lips and whisper that she thought her husband was as handsome asleep as awake. I confess I often felt tempted to reply to her that he was at least as entertaining, for the young man's happiness had not multiplied the topics on which he readily conversed. He had plenty of good sense, and his opinions on practical matters were always worth having. He would often come and sit near me while I worked at my easel and offer a friendly criticism. His taste was a little crude, but his eye was excellent, and his measurement of the resemblance between some point of my copy and the original as trustworthy as that of a mathematical instrument. But he seemed to me to have either a strange reserve or a strange simplicity; to be fundamentally unfurnished with "ideas." He had no beliefs nor hopes nor fears,—nothing but senses, appetites, and serenely luxurious tastes. As I watched him strolling about looking at his finger-nails, I often wondered whether he had anything that could properly be termed a soul, and whether good health and good-nature were not the sum of his advantages. "It's lucky he's good-natured," I used to say to myself; "for if he were not, there is nothing in his conscience to keep him in order. If he had irritable nerves instead of quiet ones, he would strangle us as the infant Hercules strangled the poor little snakes. He's the natural man!

Happily, his nature is gentle; I can mix my colors at my ease."
I wondered what he thought about and what passed through
his mind in the sunny leisure which seemed to shut him in
from that modern work-a-day world of which, in spite of my
passion for bedaubing old panels with ineffective portraiture
of mouldy statues against screens of box, I still flattered myself I was a member. I went so far as to believe that he sometimes withdrew from the world altogether. He had moods in
which his consciousness seemed so remote and his mind so
irresponsive and dumb, that nothing but a powerful caress or a
sudden violence was likely to arouse him. Even his lavish
tenderness for his wife had a quality which I but half relished.
Whether or no he had a soul himself, he seemed not to suspect
that she had one. I took a godfatherly interest in what it had
not always seemed to me crabbed and pedantic to talk of as
her moral development. I fondly believed her to be a creature
susceptible of the finer spiritual emotions. But what was becoming of her spiritual life in this interminable heathenish
honeymoon? Some fine day she would find herself tired of the
Count's *beaux yeux* and make an appeal to his mind. She had,
to my knowledge, plans of study, of charity, of worthily playing her part as a Contessa Valerio,—a position as to which the
family records furnished the most inspiring examples. But if
the Count found the newspapers soporific, I doubted if he
would turn Dante's pages very fast for his wife, or smile with
much zest at the anecdotes of Vasari. How could he advise her,
instruct her, sustain her? And if she became a mother, how
could he share her responsibilities? He doubtless would assure
his little son and heir a stout pair of arms and legs and a magnificent crop of curls, and sometimes remove his cigarette to
kiss a dimpled spot; but I found it hard to picture him lending
his voice to teach the lusty urchin his alphabet or his prayers,
or the rudiments of infant virtue. One accomplishment indeed
the Count possessed which would make him an agreeable
playfellow: he carried in his pocket a collection of precious

fragments of antique pavement,—bits of porphyry and mala-
chite and lapis and basalt,—disinterred on his own soil and
brilliantly polished by use. With these you might see him
occupied by the half-hour, playing the simple game of catch-
and-toss, ranging them in a circle, tossing them in rotation,
and catching them on the back of his hand. His skill was remarkable; he would send a stone five feet into the air, and
pitch and catch and transpose the rest before he received it
again. I watched with affectionate jealousy for the signs of a
dawning sense, on Martha's part, that she was the least bit
strangely mated. Once or twice, as the weeks went by, I
fancied I read them, and that she looked at me with eyes which
seemed to remember certain old talks of mine in which I had
declared—with such verity as you please—that a Frenchman,
an Italian, a Spaniard, might be a very good fellow, but that
he never really respected the woman he pretended to love. For
the most part, however, these dusky broodings of mine spent
themselves easily in the charmed atmosphere of our romantic
home. We were out of the modern world and had no business
with modern scruples. The place was so bright, so still, so
sacred to the silent, imperturbable past, that drowsy contentment seemed a natural law; and sometimes when, as I sat at
my work, I saw my companions passing arm-in-arm across
the end of one of the long-drawn vistas, and, turning back to
my palette, found my colors dimmer for the radiant vision, I
could easily believe that I was some loyal old chronicler of a
perfectly poetical legend.

It was a help to ungrudging feelings that the Count, yielding to his wife's urgency, had undertaken a series of system-
atic excavations. To excavate is an expensive luxury, and
neither Camillo nor his latter forefathers had possessed the
means for a disinterested pursuit of archæology. But his young
wife had persuaded herself that the much-trodden soil of the
Villa was as full of buried treasures as a bride-cake of plums,
and that it would be a pretty compliment to the ancient house

G

which had accepted her as mistress, to devote a portion of her dowry to bringing its mouldy honors to the light. I think she was not without a fancy that this liberal process would help to disinfect her Yankee dollars of the impertinent odor of trade. She took learned advice on the subject, and was soon ready to swear to you, proceeding from irrefutable premises, that a colossal gilt-bronze Minerva mentioned by Strabo was placidly awaiting resurrection at a point twenty rods from the north-west angle of the house. She had a couple of grotesque old antiquaries to lunch, whom having plied with unwonted pota-tions, she walked off their legs in the grounds; and though they agreed on nothing else in the world, they individually assured her that properly conducted researches would prob-ably yield an unequalled harvest of discoveries. The Count had been not only indifferent, but even averse, to the scheme, and had more than once arrested his wife's complacent allu-sions to it by an unaccustomed acerbity of tone. "Let them lie, the poor disinherited gods, the Minerva, the Apollo, the Ceres you are so sure of finding," he said, "and don't break their rest. What do you want of them? We can't worship them. Would you put them on pedestals to stare and mock at them? If you can't believe in them, don't disturb them. Peace be with them!" I remember being a good deal impressed by a vigorous confession drawn from him by his wife's playfully declaring in answer to some remonstrances in this strain that he was absolutely superstitious. "Yes, by Bacchus, I am super-stitious!" he cried. "Too much so, perhaps! But I'm an old Italian, and you must take me as you find me. There have been things seen and done here which leave strange influences behind! They don't touch you, doubtless, who come of another race. But they touch me, often, in the whisper of the leaves and the odor of the mouldy soil and the blank eyes of the old statues. I can't bear to look the statues in the face. I seem to see other strange eyes in the empty sockets, and I hardly know what they say to me. I call the poor old statues ghosts. In conscience, we've enough on the place already, lurking and peering in every shady nook. Don't dig up any more, or I won't answer for my wits!"

This account of Camillo's sensibilities was too fantastic not to seem to his wife almost a joke; and though I imagined there was more in it, he made a joke so seldom that I should have been sorry to cut short the poor girl's smile. With her smile she carried her point, and in a few days arrived a kind of archæological detective, with a dozen workmen armed with pickaxes and spades. For myself, I was secretly vexed at these energetic measures; for, though fond of disinterred statues, I disliked the disinterment, and deplored the profane sounds which were henceforth to jar upon the sleepy stillness of the gardens. I especially objected to the personage who conducted the operations; an ugly little dwarfish man who seemed altogether a subterranean genius, an earthy gnome of the underworld, and went prying about the grounds with a malicious smile which suggested more delight in the money the Signor Conte was going to bury than in the expected marbles and bronzes. When the first sod had been turned, the Count's mood seemed to alter, and his curiosity got the better of his scruples. He sniffed delightedly the odor of the humid earth, and stood watching the workmen, as they struck constantly deeper, with a kindling wonder in his eyes. Whenever a pickaxe rang against a stone he would utter a sharp cry, and be deterred from jumping into the trench only by the little explorer's assurance that it was a false alarm. The near prospect of discoveries seemed to act upon his nerves, and I met him more than once strolling restlessly among his cedarn alleys, as if at last he had fallen a thinking. He took me by the arm and made me walk with him, and discoursed ardently of the chance of a "find." I rather marvelled at his sudden zeal, and wondered whether he had an eye to the past or to the future,— to the beauty of possible Minervas and Apollos or to their market value. Whenever the Count would come and denounce his little army of spadesmen for a set of loitering vagabonds, the little explorer would glance at me with a sarcastic twinkle which seemed to hint that excavations were a snare. We were kept some time in suspense, for several false beginnings were made. The earth was probed in the wrong places. The Count began to be discouraged and to prolong his abbreviated siesta. But the little expert, who had his own ideas, shrewdly continued his labors; and as I sat at my easel I heard the spades ringing against the dislodged stones. Now and then I would pause, with an uncontrollable acceleration of my heart-beats. "It *may* be," I would say, "that some marble masterpiece is stirring there beneath its lightening weight of earth! There are as good fish in the sea . . .! I *may* be summoned to welcome another Antinous back to fame,—a Venus, a Faun, an Augustus!"

One morning it seemed to me that I had been hearing for half an hour a livelier movement of voices than usual; but as I was preoccupied with a puzzling bit of work, I made no inquiries. Suddenly a shadow fell across my canvas, and I turned round. The little explorer stood beside me, with a glittering eye, cap in hand, his forehead bathed in perspiration. Resting in the hollow of his arm was an earth-stained fragment of marble. In answer to my questioning glance he held it up to me, and I saw it was a woman's shapely hand. "Come!" he simply said, and led the way to the excavation. The workmen were so closely gathered round the open trench that I saw nothing till he made them divide. Then, full in the sun and flashing it back, almost, in spite of her dusky incrustations, I beheld, propped up with stones against a heap of earth, a majestic marble image. She seemed to me almost colossal, though I afterwards perceived that she was of perfect human proportions. My pulses began to throb, for I felt she was something great, and that it was great to be among the first to know her. Her marvellous beauty gave her an almost human look, and her absent eyes seemed to wonder back at us. She was amply draped, so that I saw that she was not a Venus. "She's a Juno," said the excavator, decisively; and she seemed indeed an embodiment of celestial supremacy and repose. Her beautiful head, bound with a single band, could have bent only to give the nod of command; her eyes looked straight before her; her mouth was implacably grave; one hand, outstretched, appeared to have held a kind of imperial wand, the arm from which the other had been broken hung at her side with the most classical majesty. The workmanship was of the rarest finish; and though perhaps there was a sort of vaguely modern attempt at character in her expression, she was wrought, as a whole, in the large and simple manner of the great Greek period. She was a masterpiece of skill and a marvel of preservation. "Does the Count know?" I soon asked, for I had a guilty sense that our eyes were taking something from her.

"The Signor Conte is at his siesta," said the explorer, with his sceptical grin. "We don't like to disturb him."

"Here he comes!" cried one of the workmen, and we made way for him. His siesta had evidently been suddenly broken, for his face was flushed and his hair disordered.

"Ah, my dream—my dream was right, then!" he cried, and stood staring at the image.

"What was your dream?" I asked, as his face seemed to betray more dismay than delight.

"That they'd found a Juno; and that she rose and came and laid her marble hand on mine. Eh?" said the Count excitedly.

A kind of awe-struck, guttural *a-ah!* burst from the listening workmen.

"This is the hand!" said the little explorer, holding up his perfect fragment. "I've had it this half-hour, so it can't have touched you."

"But you're apparently right as to her being a Juno," I said. "Admire her at your leisure." And I turned away; for if the Count was superstitious, I wished to leave him free to relieve himself. I repaired to the house to carry the news to my god-daughter, whom I found slumbering—dreamlessly, it appeared—over a great archæological octavo. "They've touched bottom," I said. "They've found a Juno of Praxiteles at the very least!" She dropped her octavo, and rang for a parasol. I described the statue, but not graphically, I presume, for Martha gave a little sarcastic grimace.

"A long, fluted *peplum?*" she said. "How very odd! I don't believe she's beautiful."

"She's beautiful enough, *figlioccia mia*," I answered, "to make you jealous."

We found the Count standing before the resurgent goddess in fixed contemplation, with folded arms. He seemed to have recovered from the irritation of his dream, but I thought his face betrayed a still deeper emotion. He was pale, and gave no response as his wife caressingly clasped his arm. I'm not sure, however, that his wife's attitude was not a livelier tribute to the perfection of the image. She had been laughing at my rhapsody as we walked from the house, and I had bethought myself of a statement I had somewhere seen, that women lacked the perception of the purest beauty. Martha, however, seemed slowly to measure our Juno's infinite stateliness. She gazed a long time silently, leaning against her husband, and then stepped half timidly down on the stones which formed a rough base for the figure. She laid her two rosy, ungloved hands upon the stony fingers of the goddess, and remained for some moments pressing them in her warm grasp, and fixing her living eyes upon the inexpressive brow. When she turned round her eyes were bright with an admiring tear,—a tear which her husband was too deeply absorbed to notice. He had apparently given orders that the workmen should be treated to a cask of wine, in honor of their discovery. It was now brought and opened on the spot, and the little explorer, having drawn the first glass, stepped forward, hat in hand, and obsequiously presented it to the Countess. She only moistened her lips with it and passed it to her husband. He raised it mechanically to his own; then suddenly he stopped, held it a moment aloft, and poured it out slowly and solemnly at the feet of the Juno.

"Why, it's a libation!" I cried. He made no answer, and walked slowly away.

There was no more work done that day. The laborers lay on the grass, gazing with the native Roman relish of a fine piece of sculpture, but wasting no wine in pagan ceremonies. In the evening the Count paid the Juno another visit, and gave orders that on the morrow she should be transferred to the Casino. The Casino was a deserted garden-house, built in not ungraceful imitation of an Ionic temple, in which Camillo's ancestors must often have assembled to drink cool syrups from Venetian glasses, and listen to learned madrigals. It contained several dusty fragments of antique sculpture, and it was spacious enough to enclose that richer collection of which I began fondly to regard the Juno as but the nucleus. Here, with short delay, this fine creature was placed, serenely upright, a reversed funereal *cippus* forming a sufficiently solid pedestal. The little explorer, who seemed an expert in all the offices of restoration, rubbed her and scraped her with mysterious art, removed her earthy stains, and doubled the lustre of her beauty. Her mellow substance seemed to glow with a kind of renascent purity and bloom, and, but for her broken hand, you might have fancied she had just received the last stroke of the chisel. Her fame remained no secret. Within two or three days half a dozen inquisitive *conoscenti* posted out to obtain sight of her. I happened to be present when the first of these gentlemen (a German in blue spectacles, with a portfolio under his arm) presented himself at the Villa. The Count, hearing his voice at the door, came forward and eyed him coldly from head to foot.

"Your new Juno, Signor Conte," began the German, "is, in my opinion, much more likely to be a certain Proserpine—"

"I've neither a Juno nor a Proserpine to discuss with you," said the Count, curtly. "You're misinformed."

"You've dug up no statue?" cried the German. "What a scandalous hoax!"

"None worthy of your learned attention. I'm sorry you should have the trouble of carrying your little note-book so far." The Count had suddenly become witty!

"But you've something, surely. The rumor is running through Rome."

"The rumor be damned!" cried the Count, savagely. "I've *nothing*,—do you understand? Be so good as to say so to your friends."

The answer was explicit, and the poor archæologist departed, tossing his flaxen mane. But I pitied him, and ventured to remonstrate with the Count. "She might as well be still in the earth, if no one is to see her," I said.

"*I*'m to see her: that's enough!" he answered with the same unnatural harshness. Then, in a moment, as he caught me eying him askance in troubled surprise, "I hated his great portfolio. He was going to make some hideous drawing of her."

"Ah, that touches me," I said. "I too have been planning to make a little sketch."

He was silent for some moments, after which he turned and grasped my arm, with less irritation, but with extraordinary gravity. "Go in there towards twilight," he said, "and sit for an hour and look at her. I think you'll give up your sketch. If you don't, my good old friend,—you're welcome!"

I followed his advice, and, as a friend, I gave up my sketch. But an artist is an artist, and I secretly longed to attempt one. Orders strictly in accordance with the Count's reply to our German friend were given to the servants, who, with an easy Italian conscience and a gracious Italian persuasiveness, assured all subsequent inquirers that they had been regrettably misinformed. I have no doubt, indeed, that, in default of larger opportunity, they made condolence remunerative. Further excavation was, for the present, suspended, as implying an affront to the incomparable Juno. The workmen departed, but the little explorer still haunted the premises and sounded the soil for his own entertainment. One day he came to me with his usual ambiguous grimace. "The beautiful hand of the Juno," he murmured; "what has become of it?"

"I've not seen it since you called me to look at her. I remember when I went away it was lying on the grass near the excavation."

"Where I placed it myself! After that it disappeared. Ecco!"

"Do you suspect one of your workmen? Such a fragment as that would bring more scudi than most of them ever looked at."

"Some, perhaps, are greater thieves than the others. But if I were to call up the worst of them and accuse him, the Count would interfere."

"He must value that beautiful hand, nevertheless."

The little expert in disinterment looked about him and winked. "He values it so much that he himself purloined it. That's my belief, and I think that the less we say about it the better."

"Purloined it, my dear sir? After all, it's his own property."

"Not so much as that comes to! So beautiful a creature is more or less the property of every one; we've all a right to look at her. But the Count treats her as if she were a sacrosanct image of the Madonna. He keeps her under lock and key, and pays her solitary visits. What does he do, after all? When a beautiful woman is in stone, all he can do is to look at her. And what does he do with that precious hand? He keeps it in a silver box; he has made a relic of it!" And this cynical personage began to chuckle grotesquely and walked away.

He left me musing uncomfortably, and wondering what the deuce he meant. The Count certainly chose to make a mystery of the Juno, but this seemed a natural incident of the first rapture of possession. I was willing to wait for a free access to her, and in the mean time I was glad to find that there was a limit to his constitutional apathy. But as the days elapsed I began to be conscious that his enjoyment was not communicative, but strangely cold and shy and sombre. That he should admire a marble goddess was no reason for his despising mankind; yet he really seemed to be making invidious comparisons between us. From this untender proscription his charming wife was not excepted. At moments when I tried to persuade myself that he was neither worse nor better company than usual, her face condemned my optimism. She said nothing, but she wore a constant look of pathetic perplexity. She sat at times with her eyes fixed on him with a kind of imploring curiosity, as if pitying surprise held resentment yet awhile in check. What passed between them in private, I had, of course, no warrant to inquire. Nothing, I imagined,—and that was the misery! It was part of the misery, too, that he seemed impenetrable to these mute glances, and looked over her head with an air of superb abstraction. Occasionally he noticed me looking at him in urgent deprecation, and then for a moment his heavy eye would sparkle, half, it as seemed, in defiant irony and half with a strangely stifled impulse to justify himself. But from his wife he kept his face inexorably averted; and when she approached him with some persuasive caress, he received it with an ill-concealed shudder. I inwardly protested and raged. I grew to hate the Count and everything that belonged to him. "I was a thousand times right," I cried; "an Italian count may be mighty fine, but he won't *wear!* Give us some wholesome young fellow of our own blood, who'll play us none of these dusky old-world tricks. Painter as I am, I'll never recommend a picturesque husband!" I lost my pleasure in the Villa, in the purple shadows and glowing lights, the mossy marbles and the long-trailing profile of the Alban Hills. My painting stood still; everything looked ugly. I sat and fumbled with my palette, and seemed to be mixing mud with my colors. My head was stuffed with dismal thoughts; an intolerable weight seemed to lie upon my heart. The Count became, to my imagination, a dark efflorescence of the evil germs which history had implanted in his line. No wonder he was foredoomed to be cruel. Was not cruelty a tradition in his race, and crime an example? The unholy passions of his forefathers stirred blindly in his untaught nature and clamored dumbly for an issue. What a heavy heritage it seemed to me, as I reckoned it up in my melancholy musings, the Count's interminable ancestry! Back to the profligate revival of arts and vices,— back to the bloody medley of mediæval wars,—back through the long, fitfully glaring dusk of the early ages to its ponderous origin in the solid Roman state,—back through all the darkness of history it seemed to stretch, losing every feeblest claim on my sympathies as it went. Such a record was in itself a curse; and my poor girl had expected it to sit as lightly and gratefully on her consciousness as her feather on her hat! I have little idea how long this painful situation lasted. It seemed the longer from my god-daughter's continued reserve, and my inability to offer her a word of consolation. A sensitive woman, disappointed in marriage, exhausts her own ingenuity before she takes counsel. The Count's preoccupations, whatever they were, made him increasingly restless; he came and went at random, with nervous abruptness; he took long rides alone, and, as I inferred, rarely went through the form of excusing himself to his wife; and still, as time went on, he came no nearer explaining his mystery. With the lapse of time, however, I confess that my apprehensions began to be tempered with pity. If I had expected to see him propitiate his urgent ancestry by a crime, now that his native rectitude seemed resolute to deny them this satisfaction, I felt a sort of grudging gratitude. A man couldn't be so gratuitously sombre without being unhappy. He had always treated me with that antique deference to a grizzled beard for which elderly men

reserve the flower of their general tenderness for waning
fashions, and I thought it possible he might suffer me to lay
a healing hand upon his trouble. One evening, when I had
taken leave of my god-daughter and given her my useless
blessing in a silent kiss, I came out and found the Count sitting in the garden in the mild starlight, and staring at a mouldy
Hermes, nestling in a clump of oleander. I sat down by him
and informed him roundly that his conduct needed an explanation. He half turned his head, and his dark pupil gleamed an
instant.

"I understand," he said, "you think me crazy!" And he
tapped his forehead.

"No, not crazy, but unhappy. And if unhappiness runs its
course too freely, of course, our poor wits are sorely tried."

He was silent awhile, and then, "I'm not unhappy!" he
cried abruptly. "I'm prodigiously happy. You wouldn't
believe the satisfaction I take in sitting here and staring at that
old weather-worn Hermes. Formerly I used to be afraid of
him: his frown used to remind me of a little bushy-browed old
priest who taught me Latin and looked at me terribly over the
book when I stumbled in my Virgil. But now it seems to me
the friendliest, jolliest thing in the world, and suggests the
most delightful images. He stood pouting his great lips in
some old Roman's garden two thousand years ago. He saw
the sandalled feet treading the alleys and the rose-crowned
heads bending over the wine; he knew the old feasts and the
old worship, the old Romans and the old gods. As I sit here
he speaks to me, in his own dumb way, and describes it all!
No, no, my friend, I'm the happiest of men!"

I had denied that I thought he was crazy, but I suddenly
began to suspect it, for I found nothing reassuring in this
singular rhapsody. The Hermes, for a wonder, had kept his
nose; and when I reflected that my dear Countess was being
neglected for this senseless pagan block, I secretly promised
myself to come the next day with a hammer and deal him such

a lusty blow as would make him too ridiculous for a sentimental tête-à-tête. Meanwhile, however, the Count's infatuation was no laughing matter, and I expressed my sincerest
conviction when I said, after a pause, that I should recommend him to see either a priest or a physician.

He burst into uproarious laughter. "A priest! What should
I do with a priest, or he with me? I never loved them, and I
feel less like beginning than ever. A priest, my dear friend,"
he repeated, laying his hand on my arm, "don't set a priest at
me, if you value *his* sanity! My confession would frighten the
poor man out of his wits. As for a doctor, I never was better
in my life; and unless," he added abruptly, rising, and eying
me askance, "you want to poison me, in Christian charity I
advise you to leave me alone."

Decidedly, the Count *was* unsound, and I had no heart, for
some days, to go back to the Villa. How should I treat him,
what stand should I take, what course did Martha's happiness
and dignity demand? I wandered about Rome, revolving these
questions, and one afternoon found myself in the Pantheon.
A light spring shower had begun to fall, and I hurried for
refuge into the great temple which its Christian altars have but
half converted into a church. No Roman monument retains a
deeper impress of ancient life, or verifies more forcibly those
prodigious beliefs which we are apt to regard as dim fables.
The huge dusky dome seems to the spiritual ear to hold a
vague reverberation of pagan worship, as a gathered shell
holds the rumor of the sea. Three or four persons were scattered before the various altars; another stood near the centre,
beneath the aperture in the dome. As I drew near I perceived
this was the Count. He was planted with his hands behind
him, looking up first at the heavy rain-clouds, as they crossed
the great bull's-eye, and then down at the besprinkled circle
on the pavement. In those days the pavement was rugged and
cracked and magnificently old, and this ample space, in free
communion with the weather, had become as mouldy and

mossy and verdant as a strip of garden soil. A tender herbage had sprung up in the crevices of the slabs, and the little microscopic shoots were twinkling in the rain. This great weather-current, through the uncapped vault, deadens most effectively the customary odors of incense and tallow, and transports one to a faith that was on friendly terms with nature. It seemed to have performed this office for the Count; his face wore an indefinable expression of ecstasy, and he was so rapt in contemplation that it was some time before he noticed me. The sun was struggling through the clouds without, and yet a thin rain continued to fall and came drifting down into our gloomy enclosure in a sort of illuminated drizzle. The Count watched it with the fascinated stare of a child watching a fountain, and then turned away, pressing his hand to his brow, and walked over to one of the ornamental altars. Here he again stood staring, but in a moment wheeled about and returned to his former place. Just then he recognized me, and perceived, I suppose, the puzzled gaze I must have fixed on him. He saluted me frankly with his hand, and at last came toward me. I fancied that he was in a kind of nervous tremor and was trying to appear calm.

"This is the best place in Rome," he murmured. "It's worth fifty St Peters'. But do you know I never came here till the other day? I left it to the *forestieri*. They go about with their red books, and read about this and that, and think they know it. Ah! you must *feel* it,—feel the beauty and fitness of that great open skylight. Now, only the wind and the rain, the sun and the cold, come down; but of old—of old"—and he touched my arm and gave me a strange smile—"the pagan gods and goddesses used to come sailing through it and take their places at their altars. What a procession, when the eyes of faith could see it! Those are the things they have given us instead!" And he gave a pitiful shrug. "I should like to pull down their pictures, overturn their candlesticks, and poison their holy-water!"

"My dear Count," I said gently, "you should tolerate people's honest beliefs. Would you renew the Inquisition, and in the interest of Jupiter and Mercury?"

"People wouldn't tolerate my belief, if they guessed it!" he cried. "There's been a great talk about the pagan persecutions; but the Christians persecuted as well, and the old gods were worshipped in caves and woods as well as the new. And none the worse for that! It was in caves and woods and streams, in earth and air and water, they dwelt. And there— and here, too, in spite of all your Christian lustrations—a son of old Italy may find them still!"

He had said more than he meant, and his mask had fallen. I looked at him hard, and felt a sudden outgush of the compassion we always feel for a creature irresponsibly excited. I seemed to touch the source of his trouble, and my relief was great, for my discovery made me feel like bursting into laughter. But I contented myself with smiling benignantly. He looked back at me suspiciously, as if to judge how far he had betrayed himself; and in his glance I read, somehow, that he had a conscience we could take hold of. In my gratitude, I was ready to thank any gods he pleased. "Take care, take care," I said, "you're saying things which if the sacristan there were to hear and report—!" And I passed my hand through his arm and led him away.

I was startled and shocked, but I was also amused and comforted. The Count had suddenly become for me a delightfully curious phenomenon, and I passed the rest of the day in meditating on the strange ineffaceability of race-characteristics. A sturdy young Latin I had called Camillo; sturdier, indeed, than I had dreamed him! Discretion was now misplaced, and on the morrow I spoke to my god-daughter. She had lately been hoping, I think, that I would help her to unburden her heart, for she immediately gave way to tears and confessed that she was miserable. "At first," she said, "I thought it was all fancy, and not his tenderness that was growing less, but my exactions that were growing greater. But suddenly it settled upon me like a mortal chill,—the conviction that he had ceased to care for me, that something had come between us. And the puzzling thing has been the want of possible cause in my own conduct, or of any sign that there is another woman in the case. I have racked my brain to discover what I had said or done or thought to displease him! And yet he goes about like a man too deeply injured to complain. He has never uttered a harsh word or given me a reproachful look. He has simply renounced me. I have dropped out of his life."

She spoke with such an appealing tremor in her voice that I was on the point of telling her that I had guessed the riddle, and that this was half the battle. But I was afraid of her incredulity. My solution was so fantastic, so apparently far-fetched, so absurd, that I resolved to wait for convincing evidence. To obtain it, I continued to watch the Count, covertly and cautiously, but with a vigilance which disinterested curiosity now made intensely keen. I returned to my painting, and neglected no pretext for hovering about the gardens and the neighborhood of the Casino. The Count, I think, suspected my designs, or at least my suspicions, and would have been glad to remember just what he had suffered himself to say to me in the Pantheon. But it deepened my interest in his extraordinary situation that, in so far as I could read his deeply brooding face, he seemed to have grudgingly pardoned me. He gave me a glance occasionally, as he passed me, in which a sort of dumb desire for help appeared to struggle with the instinct of mistrust. I was willing enough to help him, but the case was prodigiously delicate, and I wished to master the symptoms. Meanwhile I worked and waited and wondered. Ah! I wondered, you may be sure, with an interminable wonder; and, turn it over as I would, I couldn't get used to my idea. Sometimes it offered itself to me with a perverse fascination which deprived me of all wish to interfere. The Count took the form of a precious psychological study, and refined feeling seemed to dictate a tender respect for his delusion. I envied him the force of his imagination, and I used sometimes to close my eyes with a vague desire that when I opened them I might find Apollo under the opposite tree, lazily kissing his flute, or see Diana hurrying with long steps down the ilex-walk. But for the most part my host seemed to me simply an unhappy young man, with an unwholesome mental twist which should be smoothed away as speedily as possible. If the remedy was to match the disease, however, it would have to be an ingenious compound!

One evening, having bidden my god-daughter good night, I had started on my usual walk to my lodgings in Rome. Five minutes after leaving the villa-gate I discovered that I had left my eye-glass—an object in constant use—behind me. I immediately remembered that, while painting, I had broken the string which fastened it round my neck, and had hooked it provisionally upon a twig of a flowering-almond tree within arm's reach. Shortly afterwards I had gathered up my things and retired, unmindful of the glass; and now, as I needed it to read the evening paper at the Caffè Greco, there was no alternative but to retrace my steps and detach it from its twig. I easily found it, and lingered awhile to note the curious night-aspect of the spot I had been studying by daylight. The night was magnificent, and full-charged with the breath of the early Roman spring. The moon was rising fast and flinging her silver checkers into the heavy masses of shadow. Watching her at play, I strolled farther and suddenly came in sight of the Casino.

Just then the moon, which for a moment had been concealed, touched with a white ray a small marble figure which adorned the pediment of this rather factitious little structure. Its sudden illumination suggested that a rarer spectacle was at hand, and that the same influence must be vastly becoming to the imprisoned Juno. The door of the Casino was, as usual, locked, but the moonlight was flooding the high-placed windows so generously that my curiosity became obstinate—and

H

inventive. I dragged a garden-seat round from the portico, placed it on end, and succeeded in climbing to the top of it and bringing myself abreast of one of the windows. The casement yielded to my pressure, turned on its hinges, and showed me what I had been looking for,—Juno visited by Diana. The beautiful image stood bathed in the radiant flood and shining with a purity which made her most persuasively divine. If by day her mellow complexion suggested faded gold, her substance now might have passed for polished silver. The effect was almost terrible; beauty so eloquent could hardly be inanimate. This was my foremost observation. I leave you to fancy whether my next was less interesting. At some distance from the foot of the statue, just out of the light, I perceived a figure lying flat on the pavement, prostrate apparently with devotion. I can hardly tell you how it completed the impressiveness of the scene. It marked the shining image as a goddess indeed, and seemed to throw a sort of conscious pride into her stony mask. I of course immediately recognized this recumbent worshipper as the Count, and while I stood gazing, as if to help me to read the full meaning of his attitude, the moonlight travelled forward and covered his breast and face. Then I saw that his eyes were closed, and that he was either asleep or swooning. Watching him attentively, I detected his even respirations, and judged there was no reason for alarm. The moonlight blanched his face, which seemed already pale with weariness. He had come into the presence of the Juno in obedience to that fabulous passion of which the symptoms had so wofully perplexed us, and, exhausted either by compliance or resistance, he had sunk down at her feet in a stupid sleep. The bright moonshine soon aroused him, however; he muttered something and raised himself, vaguely staring. Then recognizing his situation, he rose and stood for some time gazing fixedly at the glowing image with an expression which I fancied was not that of wholly unprotesting devotion. He uttered a string of broken words of which I was unable to catch the meaning, and then, after another pause and a long, melancholy moan, he turned slowly to the door. As rapidly and noiselessly as possible I descended from my post of vigilance and passed behind the Casino, and in a moment I heard the sound of the closing lock and of his departing footsteps.

The next day, meeting the little antiquarian in the grounds, I shook my finger at him with what I meant he should consider portentous gravity. But he only grinned like the malicious earth-gnome to which I had always compared him, and twisted his mustache as if my menace was a capital joke. "If you dig any more holes here," I said, "you shall be thrust into the deepest of them, and have the earth packed down on top of you. We have made enough discoveries, and we want no more statues. Your Juno has almost ruined us."

He burst out laughing. "I expected as much," he cried; "I had my notions!"

"What did you expect?"

"That the Signor Conte would begin and say his prayers to her."

"Good heavens! Is the case so common? Why did you expect it?"

"On the contrary, the case is rare. But I've fumbled so long in the monstrous heritage of antiquity, that I have learned a multitude of secrets; learned that ancient relics may work modern miracles. There's a pagan element in all of us,—I don't speak for you, *illustrissimi forestieri*,—and the old gods have still their worshippers. The old spirit still throbs here and there, and the Signor Conte has his share of it. He's a good fellow, but, between ourselves, he's an impossible Christian!" And this singular personage resumed his impertinent hilarity.

"If your previsions were so distinct," I said, "you ought to have given me a hint of them. I should have sent your spadesmen walking."

"Ah, but the Juno is so beautiful!"

"Her beauty be blasted! Can you tell me what has become of the Contessa's? To rival the Juno, she's turning to marble herself."

He shrugged his shoulders. "Ah, but the Juno is worth fifty thousand scudi!"

"I'd give a hundred thousand," I said, "to have her annihilated. Perhaps, after all, I shall want you to dig another hole."

"At your service!" he answered, with a flourish; and we separated.

A couple of days later I dined, as I often did, with my host and hostess, and met the Count face to face for the first time since his prostration in the Casino. He bore the traces of it, and sat plunged in sombre distraction. I fancied that the path of the antique faith was not strewn with flowers, and that the Juno was becoming daily a harder mistress to serve. Dinner was scarcely over before he rose from table and took up his hat. As he did so, passing near his wife, he faltered a moment, stopped and gave her—for the first time, I imagine—that vaguely imploring look which I had often caught. She moved her lips in inarticulate sympathy and put out her hands. He drew her towards him, kissed her with a kind of angry ardor, and strode away. The occasion was propitious, and further delay unnecessary.

"What I have to tell you is very strange," I said to the Countess, "very fantastic, very incredible. But perhaps you'll not find it so bad as you feared. There *is* a woman in the case! Your enemy is the Juno. The Count—how shall I say it?— the Count takes her *au sérieux*." She was silent; but after a moment she touched my arm with her hand, and I knew she meant that I had spoken her own belief. "You admired his antique simplicity: you see how far it goes. He has reverted to the faith of his fathers. Dormant through the ages, that imperious statue has silently aroused it. He believes in the pedigrees you used to dog's-ear your School Mythology with trying to get by heart. In a word, dear child, Camillo is a pagan!"

"I suppose you'll be terribly shocked," she answered, "if I say that he's welcome to any faith, if he will only share it with me. I'll believe in Jupiter, if he'll bid me! My sorrow's not for that: let my husband be himself! My sorrow is for the gulf of silence and indifference that has burst open between us. His Juno's the reality; I'm the fiction!"

"I've lately become reconciled to this gulf of silence, and to your fading for a while into a fiction. After the fable, the moral! The poor fellow has but half succumbed: the other half protests. The modern man is shut out in the darkness with his incomparable wife. How can he have failed to feel— vaguely and grossly if it must have been, but in every throb of his heart—that you are a more perfect experiment of nature, a riper fruit of time, than those primitive persons for whom Juno was a terror and Venus an example? He pays you the compliment of believing you an inconvertible modern. He has crossed the Acheron, but he has left you behind, as a pledge to the present. We'll bring him back to redeem it. The old ancestral ghosts ought to be propitiated when a pretty creature like you has sacrificed the fragrance of her life. He has proved himself one of the Valerii; we shall see to it that he is the last, and yet that his decease shall leave the Conte Camillo in excellent health."

I spoke with confidence which I had partly felt, for it seemed to me that if the Count was to be touched, it must be by the sense that his strange spiritual excursion had not made his wife detest him. We talked long and to a hopeful end, for before I went away my god-daughter expressed the desire to go out and look at the Juno. "I was afraid of her almost from the first," she said, "and have hardly seen her since she was set up in the Casino. Perhaps I can learn a lesson from her,— perhaps I can guess how she charms him!"

For a moment I hesitated, with the fear that we might intrude upon the Count's devotions. Then, as something in the poor girl's face suggested that she had thought of this and felt a sudden impulse to pluck victory from the heart of danger, I bravely offered her my arm. The night was cloudy, and on this occasion, apparently, the triumphant goddess was to depend upon her own lustre. But as we approached the Casino I saw that the door was ajar, and that there was lamplight within. The lamp was suspended in front of the image, and it showed us that the place was empty. But the Count had lately been there. Before the statue stood a roughly extemporized altar, composed of a nameless fragment of antique marble, engraved with an illegible Greek inscription. We seemed really to stand in a pagan temple, and we gazed at the serene divinity with an impulse of spiritual reverence. It ought to have been deepened, I suppose, but it was rudely checked, by our observing a curious glitter on the face of the low altar. A second glance showed us it was blood!

My companion looked at me in pale horror, and turned away with a cry. A swarm of hideous conjectures pressed into my mind, and for a moment I was sickened. But at last I remembered that there is blood and blood, and the Latins were posterior to the cannibals.

"Be sure it's very innocent," I said; "a lamb, a kid, or a sucking calf!" But it was enough for her nerves and her conscience that it was a crimson trickle, and she returned to the house in sad agitation. The rest of the night was not passed in a way to restore her to calmness. The Count had not come in, and she sat up for him from hour to hour. I remained with her and smoked my cigar as composedly as I might; but internally I wondered what in horror's name had become of him. Gradually, as the hours wore away, I shaped a vague interpretation of these dusky portents,—an interpretation none the less valid and devoutly desired for its being tolerably cheerful. The blood-drops on the altar, I mused, were the last instalment of his debt and the end of his delusion. They had been a happy necessity, for he was, after all, too gentle a creature not to hate himself for having shed them, not to abhor so cruelly insistent an idol. He had wandered away to recover himself in solitude, and he would come back to us with a repentant heart and an inquiring mind! I should certainly have believed all this more easily, however, if I could have heard his footstep in the hall. Toward dawn, scepticism threatened to creep in with the gray light, and I restlessly betook myself to the portico. Here in a few moments I saw him cross the grass, heavy-footed, splashed with mud, and evidently excessively tired. He must have been walking all night, and his face denoted that his spirit had been as restless as his body. He paused near me, and before he entered the house he stopped, looked at me a moment, and then held out his hand. I grasped it warmly, and it seemed to me to throb with all that he could not utter.

"Will you see your wife?" I asked.

He passed his hand over his eyes and shook his head. "Not now—not yet—some time!" he answered.

I was disappointed, but I convinced her, I think, that he had cast out the devil. She felt, poor girl, a pardonable desire to celebrate the event. I returned to my lodging, spent the day in Rome, and came back to the Villa toward dusk. I was told that the Countess was in the grounds. I looked for her cautiously at first, for I thought it just possible I might interrupt the natural consequences of a reconciliation; but failing to meet her, I turned toward the Casino, and found myself face to face with the little explorer.

"Does your excellency happen to have twenty yards of stout rope about him?" he asked gravely.

"Do you want to hang yourself for the trouble you've stood sponsor to?" I answered.

"It's a hanging matter, I promise you. The Countess has given orders. You'll find her in the Casino. Sweet-voiced as she is, she knows how to make her orders understood."

At the door of the Casino stood half a dozen of the laborers on the place, looking vaguely solemn, like outstanding dependants at a superior funeral. The Countess was within, in a position which was an answer to the surveyor's riddle. She stood with her eyes fixed on the Juno, who had been removed from her pedestal and lay stretched in her magnificent length upon a rude litter.

"Do you understand?" she said. "She's beautiful, she's noble, she's precious, but she must go back!" And, with a passionate gesture, she seemed to indicate an open grave.

I was hugely delighted, but I thought it discreet to stroke my chin and look sober. "She's worth fifty thousand scudi."

She shook her head sadly. "If we were to sell her to the Pope and give the money to the poor, it wouldn't profit us. She must go back,—she must go back! We must smother her beauty in the dreadful earth. It makes me feel almost as if she were alive; but it came to me last night with overwhelming force, when my husband came in and refused to see me, that he'll not be himself as long as she is above ground. To cut the knot we must bury her! If I had only thought of it before!"

"Not before!" I said, shaking my head in turn. "Heaven reward our sacrifice now!"

The little surveyor, when he reappeared, seemed hardly like an agent of the celestial influences, but he was deft and active, which was more to the point. Every now and then he uttered some half-articulate lament, by way of protest against the Countess's cruelty; but I saw him privately scanning the recumbent image with an eye which seemed to foresee a malicious glee in standing on a certain unmarked spot on the turf and grinning till people stared. He had brought back an abundance of rope, and having summoned his assistants, who vigorously lifted the litter, he led the way to the original excavation, which had been left unclosed with the project of further researches. By the time we reached the edge of the grave the evening had fallen, and the beauty of our marble victim was shrouded in a dusky veil. No one spoke,—if not exactly for shame, at least for regret. Whatever our plea, our performance looked, at least, monstrously profane. The ropes were adjusted and the Juno was slowly lowered into her earthy bed. The Countess took a handful of earth and dropped it solemnly on her breast. "May it lie lightly, but forever!" she said.

"Amen!" cried the little surveyor with a strange mocking inflection; and he gave us a bow, as he departed, which betrayed an agreeable consciousness of knowing where fifty thousand scudi were buried. His underlings had another cask of wine, the result of which, for them, was a suspension of all consciousness, and a subsequent irreparable confusion of memory as to where they had plied their spades.

The Countess had not yet seen her husband, who had again apparently betaken himself to communion with the great god Pan. I was of course unwilling to leave her to encounter alone the results of her momentous deed. She wandered into the drawing-room and pretended to occupy herself with a bit of embroidery, but in reality she was bravely composing herself for an "explanation." I took up a book, but it held my attention as feebly. As the evening wore away I heard a movement on the threshold and saw the Count lifting the tapestried curtain which masked the door, and looking silently at his wife. His eyes were brilliant, but not angry. He had missed the Juno—and drawn a long breath! The Countess kept her eyes fixed on her work, and drew her silken stitches like an image of wifely contentment. The image seemed to fascinate him: he came in slowly, almost on tiptoe, walked to the chimney-piece, and stood there in a sort of rapt contemplation. What had passed, what was passing, in his mind, I leave to your own apprehension. My god-daughter's hand trembled as it rose and fell, and the color came into her cheek. At last she raised her eyes and sustained the gaze in which all his returning faith seemed concentrated. He hesitated a moment, as if her very forgiveness kept the gulf open between them, and then he strode forward, fell on his two knees and buried his head in her lap. I departed as the Count had come in, on tiptoe.

He never became, if you will, a thoroughly modern man; but one day, years after, when a visitor to whom he was showing his cabinet became inquisitive as to a marble hand, suspended in one of its inner recesses, he looked grave and turned the lock on it. "It is the hand of a beautiful creature," he said, "whom I once greatly admired."

"Ah,—a Roman?" said the gentleman, with a smirk.

"A Greek," said the Count, with a frown.

MADAME DE MAUVES

I

THE view from the terrace at Saint-Germain-en-Laye is immense and famous. Paris lies spread before you in dusky vastness, domed and fortified, glittering here and there through her light vapors, and girdled with her silver Seine. Behind you is a park of stately symmetry, and behind that a forest, where you may lounge through turfy avenues and light-checkered glades, and quite forget that you are within half an hour of the boulevards. One afternoon, however, in mid-spring, some five years ago, a young man seated on the terrace had chosen not to forget this. His eyes were fixed in idle wistfulness on the mighty human hive before him. He was fond of rural things, and he had come to Saint-Germain a week before to meet the spring half-way; but though he could boast of a six months' acquaintance with the great city, he never looked at it from his present standpoint without a feeling of painfully unsatisfied curiosity. There were moments when it seemed to him that not to be there just then was to miss some thrilling chapter of experience. And yet his winter's experience had been rather fruitless, and he had closed the book almost with a yawn. Though not in the least a cynic, he was what one may call a disappointed observer; and he never chose the right-hand road without beginning to suspect after an hour's wayfaring that the left would have been the interesting one. He now had a dozen minds to go to Paris for the evening, to dine at the Café Brébant, and to repair afterwards to the Gymnase and listen to the latest exposition of the duties of the injured husband. He would probably have risen to execute this project, if he had not observed a little girl who, wandering along the terrace, had suddenly stopped short and begun to gaze at him with round-eyed frankness. For a moment he was simply amused, for the child's face denoted helpless wonderment; the next he was agreeably surprised. "Why, this is my friend Maggie," he said; "I see you have not forgotten me."

Maggie, after a short parley, was induced to seal her remembrance with a kiss. Invited then to explain her appearance at Saint-Germain, she embarked on a recital in which the general, according to the infantine method, was so fatally sacrificed to the particular, that Longmore looked about him for a superior source of information. He found it in Maggie's mamma, who was seated with another lady at the opposite end of the terrace; so, taking the child by the hand, he led her back to her companions.

Maggie's mamma was a young American lady, as you would immediately have perceived, with a pretty and friendly face and an expensive spring toilet. She greeted Longmore with surprised cordiality, mentioned his name to her friend, and bade him bring a chair and sit with them. The other lady, who, though equally young and perhaps even prettier, was dressed more soberly, remained silent, stroking the hair of the little girl, whom she had drawn against her knee. She had never heard of Longmore, but she now perceived that her companion had crossed the ocean with him, had met him afterwards in travelling, and (having left her husband in Wall Street) was indebted to him for various small services.

Maggie's mamma turned from time to time and smiled at her friend with an air of invitation; the latter smiled back, and continued gracefully to say nothing.

For ten minutes Longmore felt a revival of interest in his interlocutress; then (as riddles are more amusing than commonplaces) it gave way to curiosity about her friend. His eyes wandered; her volubility was less suggestive than the latter's silence.

The stranger was perhaps not obviously a beauty nor obviously an American, but essentially both, on a closer scrutiny. She was slight and fair, and, though naturally pale, delicately flushed, apparently with recent excitement. What chiefly struck Longmore in her face was the union of a pair of beautifully gentle, almost languid gray eyes, with a mouth peculiarly expressive and firm. Her forehead was a trifle more expansive than belongs to classic types, and her thick brown hair was dressed out of the fashion, which was just then very ugly. Her throat and bust were slender, but all the more in harmony with certain rapid, charming movements of the head, which she had a way of throwing back every now and then, with an air of attention and a sidelong glance from her dove-like eyes. She seemed at once alert and indifferent, contemplative and restless; and Longmore very soon discovered that if she was not a brilliant beauty, she was at least an extremely interesting one. This very impression made him magnanimous. He perceived that he had interrupted a confidential conversation, and he judged it discreet to withdraw, having first learned from Maggie's mamma—Mrs Draper—that she was to take the six-o'clock train back to Paris. He promised to meet her at the station.

He kept his appointment, and Mrs Draper arrived betimes, accompanied by her friend. The latter, however, made her farewells at the door and drove away again, giving Longmore time only to raise his hat. "Who is she?" he asked with visible ardor, as he brought Mrs Draper her tickets.

"Come and see me to-morrow at the Hôtel de l'Empire," she answered, "and I will tell you all about her." The force of this offer in making him punctual at the Hôtel de l'Empire Longmore doubtless never exactly measured; and it was perhaps well that he did not, for he found his friend, who was on the point of leaving Paris, so distracted by procrastinating milliners and perjured lingères that she had no wits left for disinterested narrative. "You must find Saint-Germain dreadfully

dull," she said, as he was going. "Why won't you come with
me to London?"

"Introduce me to Madame de Mauves," he answered, "and
Saint-Germain will satisfy me." All he had learned was the
lady's name and residence.

"Ah! she, poor woman, will not make Saint-Germain
cheerful for you. She's very unhappy."

Longmore's further inquiries were arrested by the arrival
of a young lady with a bandbox; but he went away with the
promise of a note of introduction, to be immediately despatched to him at Saint-Germain.

He waited a week, but the note never came; and he declared that it was not for Mrs Draper to complain of her
milliner's treachery. He lounged on the terrace and walked in
the forest, studied suburban street life, and made a languid
attempt to investigate the records of the court of the exiled
Stuarts; but he spent most of his time in wondering where
Madame de Mauves lived, and whether she never walked on
the terrace. Sometimes, he finally discovered; for one afternoon toward dusk he perceived her leaning against the parapet,
alone. In his momentary hesitation to approach her, it seemed
to him that there was almost a shade of trepidation; but his
curiosity was not diminished by the consciousness of this
result of a quarter of an hour's acquaintance. She immediately
recognized him on his drawing near, with the manner of a
person unaccustomed to encounter a confusing variety of
faces. Her dress, her expression, were the same as before; her
charm was there, like that of sweet music on a second hearing.
She soon made conversation easy by asking him for news of
Mrs Draper. Longmore told her that he was daily expecting
news, and, after a pause, mentioned the promised note of
introduction.

"It seems less necessary now," he said—"for me, at least.
But for you—I should have liked you to know the flattering
things Mrs Draper would probably have said about me."

"If it arrives at last," she answered, "you must come and see me and bring it. If it doesn't, you must come without it."

Then, as she continued to linger in spite of the thickening twilight, she explained that she was waiting for her husband, who was to arrive in the train from Paris, and who often passed along the terrace on his way home. Longmore well remembered that Mrs Draper had pronounced her unhappy, and he found it convenient to suppose that this same husband made her so. Edified by his six months in Paris—"What else is possible," he asked himself, "for a sweet American girl who marries an unclean Frenchman?"

But this tender expectancy of her lord's return undermined his hypothesis, and it received a further check from the gentle eagerness with which she turned and greeted an approaching figure. Longmore beheld in the fading light a stoutish gentleman, on the fair side of forty, in a high light hat, whose countenance, indistinct against the sky, was adorned by a fantastically pointed mustache. M. de Mauves saluted his wife with punctilious gallantry, and having bowed to Longmore, asked her several questions in French. Before taking his proffered arm to walk to their carriage, which was in waiting at the terrace gate, she introduced our hero as a friend of Mrs Draper, and a fellow-countryman, whom she hoped to see at home. M. de Mauves responded briefly, but civilly, in very fair English, and led his wife away.

Longmore watched him as he went, twisting his picturesque mustache, with a feeling of irritation which he certainly would have been at a loss to account for. The only conceivable cause was the light which M. de Mauves's good English cast upon his own bad French. For reasons involved apparently in the very structure of his being, Longmore found himself unable to speak the language tolerably. He admired and enjoyed it, but the very genius of awkwardness controlled his phraseology. But he reflected with satisfaction that Madame de

Mauves and he had a common idiom, and his vexation was effectually dispelled by his finding on his table that evening a letter from Mrs Draper. It enclosed a short, formal missive to Madame de Mauves, but the epistle itself was copious and confidential. She had deferred writing till she reached London, where for a week, of course, she had found other amusements.

"I think it is these distracting Englishwomen," she wrote, "with their green barege gowns and their white-stitched boots, who have reminded me in self-defence of my graceful friend at Saint-Germain and my promise to introduce you to her. I believe I told you that she was unhappy, and I wondered afterwards whether I had not been guilty of a breach of confidence. But you would have found it out for yourself, and besides, she told me no secrets. She declared she was the happiest creature in the world, and then, poor thing, she burst into tears, and I prayed to be delivered from such happiness. It's the miserable story of an American girl, born to be neither a slave nor a toy, marrying a profligate Frenchman, who believes that a woman must be one or the other. The silliest American woman is too good for the best foreigner, and the poorest of us have moral needs a Frenchman can't appreciate. She was romantic and wilful, and thought Americans were vulgar. Matrimonial felicity perhaps *is* vulgar; but I think nowadays she wishes she were a little less elegant. M. de Mauves cared, of course, for nothing but her money, which he's spending royally on his *menus plaisirs*. I hope you appreciate the compliment I pay you when I recommend you to go and console an unhappy wife. I have never given a man such a proof of esteem, and if you were to disappoint me I should renounce the world. Prove to Madame de Mauves that an American friend may mingle admiration and respect better than a French husband. She avoids society and lives quite alone, seeing no one but a horrible French sister-in-law. Do let me hear that you have drawn some of the sadness from that desperate smile of hers. Make her smile with a good conscience."

These zealous admonitions left Longmore slightly disturbed. He found himself on the edge of a domestic tragedy from which he instinctively recoiled. To call upon Madame de Mauves with his present knowledge seemed a sort of fishing in troubled waters. He was a modest man, and yet he asked himself whether the effect of his attentions might not be to add to her tribulation. A flattering sense of unwonted opportunity, however, made him, with the lapse of time, more confident,—possibly more reckless. It seemed a very inspiring idea to draw the sadness from his fair countrywoman's smile, and at least he hoped to persuade her that there was such a thing as an agreeable American. He immediately called upon her.

II

She had been placed for her education, fourteen years before, in a Parisian convent, by a widowed mamma, fonder of Homburg and Nice than of letting out tucks in the frocks of a vigorously growing daughter. Here, besides various elegant accomplishments,—the art of wearing a train, of composing a bouquet, of presenting a cup of tea,—she acquired a certain turn of the imagination which might have passed for a sign of precocious worldliness. She dreamed of marrying a title,— not for the pleasure of hearing herself called Mme la Vicomtesse (for which it seemed to her that she should never greatly care), but because she had a romantic belief that the best birth is the guaranty of an ideal delicacy of feeling. Romances are rarely shaped in such perfect good faith, and Euphemia's excuse was in the radical purity of her imagination. She was profoundly incorruptible, and she cherished this pernicious conceit as if it had been a dogma revealed by a white-winged angel. Even after experience had given her a hundred rude

I

hints, she found it easier to believe in fables, when they had a certain nobleness of meaning, than in well-attested but sordid facts. She believed that a gentleman with a long pedigree must be of necessity a very fine fellow, and that the consciousness of a picturesque family tradition imparts an exquisite tone to the character. *Noblesse oblige*, she thought, as regards yourself, and insures, as regards your wife. She had never spoken to a nobleman in her life, and these convictions were but a matter of transcendent theory. They were the fruit, in part, of the perusal of various ultramontane works of fiction—the only ones admitted to the convent library—in which the hero was always a legitimist vicomte who fought duels by the dozen, but went twice a month to confession; and in part of the perfumed gossip of her companions, many of them *filles de haut lieu,* who in the convent garden, after Sundays at home, depicted their brothers and cousins as Prince Charmings and young Paladins. Euphemia listened and said nothing; she shrouded her visions of matrimony under a coronet in religious mystery. She was not of that type of young lady who is easily induced to declare that her husband must be six feet high and a little near-sighted, part his hair in the middle, and have amber lights in his beard. To her companions she seemed to have a very pallid fancy; and even the fact that she was a sprig of the transatlantic democracy never sufficiently explained her apathy on social questions. She had a mental image of that son of the Crusaders who was to suffer her to adore him, but like many an artist who has produced a masterpiece of idealization, she shrank from exposing it to public criticism. It was the portrait of a gentleman rather ugly than handsome, and rather poor than rich. But his ugliness was to be nobly expressive, and his poverty delicately proud. Euphemia had a fortune of her own, which, at the proper time, after fixing on her in eloquent silence those fine eyes which were to soften the feudal severity of his visage, he was to accept with a world of stifled protestations. One condition alone she was to make,—that his blood should be of the very finest strain. On this she would stake her happiness.

It so chanced that circumstances were to give convincing color to this primitive logic.

Though little of a talker, Euphemia was an ardent listener, and there were moments when she fairly hung upon the lips of Mademoiselle Marie de Mauves. Her intimacy with this chosen schoolmate was, like most intimacies, based on their points of difference. Mademoiselle de Mauves was very positive, very shrewd, very ironical, very French,—everything that Euphemia felt herself unpardonable in not being. During her Sundays *en ville* she had examined the world and judged it, and she imparted her impressions to our attentive heroine with an agreeable mixture of enthusiasm and scepticism. She was moreover a handsome and well-grown person, on whom Euphemia's ribbons and trinkets had a trick of looking better than on their slender proprietress. She had, finally, the supreme merit of being a rigorous example of the virtue of exalted birth, having, as she did, ancestors honorably mentioned by Joinville and Commines, and a stately grandmother with a hooked nose, who came up with her after the holidays from a veritable *castel* in Auvergne. It seemed to Euphemia that these attributes made her friend more at home in the world than if she had been the daughter of even the most prosperous grocer. A certain aristocratic impudence Mademoiselle de Mauves abundantly possessed, and her raids among her friend's finery were quite in the spirit of her baronial ancestors in the twelfth century,—a spirit which Euphemia considered but a large way of understanding friendship,—a freedom from small deference to the world's opinions which would sooner or later justify itself in acts of surprising magnanimity. Mademoiselle de Mauves perhaps enjoyed but slightly that easy attitude toward society which Euphemia envied her. She proved herself later in life such an accomplished schemer that her sense of having further heights to scale must have awakened early.

Our heroine's ribbons and trinkets had much to do with the other's sisterly patronage, and her appealing pliancy of character even more; but the concluding motive of Marie's writing to her grandmamma to invite Euphemia for a three weeks' holiday to the *castel* in Auvergne, involved altogether superior considerations. Mademoiselle de Mauves was indeed at this time seventeen years of age, and presumably capable of general views; and Euphemia, who was hardly less, was a very well-grown subject for experiment, besides being pretty enough almost to pre-assure success. It is a proof of the sincerity of Euphemia's aspirations that the *castel* was not a shock to her faith. It was neither a cheerful nor a luxurious abode, but the young girl found it as delightful as a play. It had battered towers and an empty moat, a rusty drawbridge and a court paved with crooked, grass-grown slabs, over which the antique coach-wheels of the old lady with the hooked nose seemed to awaken the echoes of the seventeenth century. Euphemia was not frightened out of her dream; she had the pleasure of seeing it assume the consistency of a flattering pre-sentiment. She had a taste for old servants, old anecdotes, old furniture, faded household colors, and sweetly stale odors,— musty treasures in which the Château de Mauves abounded. She made a dozen sketches in water-colors, after her conventual pattern; but sentimentally, as one may say, she was forever sketching with a freer hand.

Old Madame de Mauves had nothing severe but her nose, and she seemed to Euphemia, as indeed she was, a graciously venerable relic of a historic order of things. She took a great fancy to the young American, who was ready to sit all day at her feet and listen to anecdotes of the *bon temps* and quotations from the family chronicles. Madame de Mauves was a very honest old woman, and uttered her thoughts with antique plainness. One day, after pushing back Euphemia's shining locks and blinking at her with some tenderness from under her spectacles, she declared, with an energetic shake of the head,

that she didn't know what to make of her. And in answer to
the young girl's startled blush,—"I should like to advise
you," she said, "but you seem to me so all of a piece that I am
afraid that if I advise you, I shall spoil you. It's easy to see
that you're not one of us. I don't know whether you're better,
but you seem to me to listen to the murmur of your own
young spirit, rather than to the voice from behind the confessional or to the whisper of opportunity. Young girls, in my
day, when they were stupid, were very docile, but when they
were clever, were very sly. You're clever enough, I imagine,
and yet if I guessed all your secrets at this moment, is there
one I should have to frown at? I can tell you a wickeder one
than any you have discovered for yourself. If you expect
to live in France, and you want to be happy, don't listen too
hard to that little voice I just spoke of,—the voice that is
neither the curé's nor the world's. You'll fancy it saying things
that it won't help your case to hear. They'll make you sad,
and when you're sad you'll grow plain, and when you're plain
you'll grow bitter, and when you're bitter you'll be very disagreeable. I was brought up to think that a woman's first duty
was to please, and the happiest women I've known have been
the ones who performed this duty faithfully. As you're not a
Catholic, I suppose you can't be a dévote; and if you don't
take life as a fifty years' mass, the only way to take it is as a
game of skill. Listen: not to lose, you must,—I don't say
cheat; but don't be too sure your neighbor won't, and don't
be shocked out of your self-possession if he does. Don't lose,
my dear; I beseech you, don't lose. Be neither suspicious nor
credulous; but if you find your neighbor peeping, don't cry
out, but very politely wait your own chance. I've had my
revanche more than once in my day, but I'm not sure that the
sweetest I could take against life as a whole would be to have
your blessed innocence profit by my experience."

This was rather awful advice, but Euphemia understood it
too little to be either edified or frightened. She sat listening to

it very much as she would have listened to the speeches of an old lady in a comedy, whose diction should picturesquely correspond to the pattern of her mantilla and the fashion of her head-dress. Her indifference was doubly dangerous, for Madame de Mauves spoke at the prompting of coming events, and her words were the result of a somewhat troubled conscience,—a conscience which told her at once that Euphemia was too tender a victim to be sacrificed to an ambition, and that the prosperity of her house was too precious a heritage to be sacrificed to a scruple. The prosperity in question had suffered repeated and grievous breaches, and the house of De Mauves had been pervaded by the cold comfort of an establishment in which people were obliged to balance dinner-table allusions to feudal ancestors against the absence of side dishes; a state of things the more regrettable as the family was now mainly represented by a gentleman whose appetite was large, and who justly maintained that its historic glories were not established by underfed heroes.

Three days after Euphemia's arrival, Richard de Mauves came down from Paris to pay his respects to his grandmother, and treated our heroine to her first encounter with a gentilhomme in the flesh. On coming in he kissed his grandmother's hand, with a smile which caused her to draw it away with dignity, and set Euphemia, who was standing by, wondering what had happened between them. Her unanswered wonder was but the beginning of a life of bitter perplexity, but the reader is free to know that the smile of M. de Mauves was a reply to a certain postscript affixed by the old lady to a letter promptly addressed to him by her granddaughter, after Euphemia had been admitted to justify the latter's promises. Mademoiselle de Mauves brought her letter to her grandmother for approval, but obtained no more than was expressed in a frigid nod. The old lady watched her with a sombre glance as she proceeded to seal the letter, and suddenly bade her open it again and bring her a pen.

"Your sister's flatteries are all nonsense," she wrote; "the young lady is far too good for you, *mauvais sujet*. If you have a conscience you'll not come and take possession of an angel of innocence."

The young girl, who had read these lines, made up a little face as she redirected the letter; but she laid down her pen with a confident nod, which might have seemed to mean that, to the best of her belief, her brother had not a conscience.

"If you meant what you said," the young man whispered to his grandmother on the first opportunity, "it would have been simpler not to let her send the letter!"

It was perhaps because she was wounded by this cynical insinuation, that Madame de Mauves remained in her own apartment during a greater part of Euphemia's stay, so that the latter's angelic innocence was left entirely to the Baron's mercy. It suffered no worse mischance, however, than to be prompted to intenser communion with itself. M. de Mauves was the hero of the young girl's romance made real, and so completely accordant with this creature of her imagination, that she felt afraid of him, very much as she would have been of a supernatural apparition. He was thirty-five years old,— young enough to suggest possibilities of ardent activity, and old enough to have formed opinions which a simple woman might deem it an intellectual privilege to listen to. He was perhaps a trifle handsomer than Euphemia's rather grim, Quixotic ideal, but a very few days reconciled her to his good looks, as they would have reconciled her to his ugliness. He was quiet, grave, and eminently distinguished. He spoke little, but his speeches, without being sententious, had a certain nobleness of tone which caused them to re-echo in the young girl's ears at the end of the day. He paid her very little direct attention, but his chance words—if he only asked her if she objected to his cigarette—were accompanied by a smile of extraordinary kindness.

It happened that shortly after his arrival, riding an unruly horse, which Euphemia with shy admiration had watched him mount in the castle yard, he was thrown with a violence which, without disparaging his skill, made him for a fortnight an interesting invalid, lounging in the library with a bandaged knee. To beguile his confinement, Euphemia was repeatedly induced to sing to him, which she did with a little natural tremor in her voice, which might have passed for an exquisite refinement of art. He never overwhelmed her with compliments, but he listened with unwandering attention, remembered all her melodies, and sat humming them to himself. While his imprisonment lasted, indeed, he passed hours in her company, and made her feel not unlike some unfriended artist who has suddenly gained the opportunity to devote a fortnight to the study of a great model. Euphemia studied with noiseless diligence what she supposed to be the "character" of M. de Mauves, and the more she looked the more fine lights and shades she seemed to behold in this masterpiece of nature. M. de Mauves's character indeed, whether from a sense of being generously scrutinized, or for reasons which bid graceful defiance to analysis, had never been so amiable; it seemed really to reflect the purity of Euphemia's interpretation of it. There had been nothing especially to admire in the state of mind in which he left Paris,—a hard determination to marry a young girl whose charms might or might not justify his sister's account of them, but who was mistress, at the worst, of a couple of hundred thousand francs a year. He had not counted out sentiment; if she pleased him, so much the better; but he had left a meagre margin for it, and he would hardly have admitted that so excellent a match could be improved by it. He was a placid sceptic, and it was a singular fate for a man who believed in nothing to be so tenderly believed in. What his original faith had been he could hardly have told you; for as he came back to his childhood's home to mend his fortunes by pretending to fall in love, he was a thoroughly perverted creature, and overlaid with more corruptions than a summer day's questioning of his conscience would have released him from. Ten years' pursuit of pleasure, which a bureau full of unpaid bills was all he had to show for, had pretty well stifled the natural lad, whose violent will and generous temper might have been shaped by other circumstances to a result which a romantic imagination might fairly accept as a late-blooming flower of hereditary honor. The Baron's violence had been subdued, and he had learned to be irreproachably polite; but he had lost the edge of his generosity, and his politeness, which in the long run society paid for, was hardly more than a form of luxurious egotism, like his fondness for cambric handkerchiefs, lavender gloves, and other fopperies by which shopkeepers remained out of pocket. In after years he was terribly polite to his wife. He had formed himself, as the phrase was, and the form prescribed to him by the society into which his birth and his tastes introduced him was marked by some peculiar features. That which mainly concerns us is its classification of the fairer half of humanity as objects not essentially different—say from the light gloves one soils in an evening and throws away. To do M. de Mauves justice, he had in the course of time encountered such plentiful evidence of this pliant, glove-like quality in the feminine character, that idealism naturally seemed to him a losing game.

Euphemia, as he lay on his sofa, seemed by no means a refutation; she simply reminded him that very young women are generally innocent, and that this, on the whole, was the most charming stage of their development. Her innocence inspired him with profound respect, and it seemed to him that if he shortly became her husband it would be exposed to a danger the less. Old Madame de Mauves, who flattered herself that in this whole matter she was being laudably rigid, might have learned a lesson from his gallant consideration. For a fortnight the Baron was almost a blushing boy again. He watched from behind the "Figaro," and admired, and held his tongue. He was not in the least disposed toward a flirtation; he had no desire to trouble the waters he proposed to transfuse into the golden cup of matrimony. Sometimes a word, a look, a movement of Euphemia's, gave him the oddest sense of being, or of seeming at least, almost bashful; for she had a way of not dropping her eyes, according to the mysterious virginal mechanism, of not fluttering out of the room when she found him there alone, of treating him rather as a benignant than as a pernicious influence,—a radiant frankness of demeanor, in fine, in spite of an evident natural reserve, which it seemed equally graceless not to make the subject of a compliment and indelicate not to take for granted. In this way there was wrought in the Baron's mind a vague, unwonted resonance of soft impressions, as we may call it, which indicated the transmutation of "sentiment" from a contingency into a fact. His imagination enjoyed it; he was very fond of music, and this reminded him of some of the best he had ever heard. In spite of the bore of being laid up with a lame knee, he was in a better humor than he had known for months; he lay smoking cigarettes and listening to the nightingales, with the comfortable smile of one of his country neighbors whose big ox should have taken the prize at a fair. Every now and then, with an impatient suspicion of the resemblance, he declared that he was pitifully *bête*; but he was under a charm which braved even the supreme penalty of seeming ridiculous. One morning he had half an hour's tête-à-tête with his grandmother's confessor, a soft-voiced old abbé, whom, for reasons of her own, Madame de Mauves had suddenly summoned, and had left waiting in the drawing-room while she rearranged her curls. His reverence, going up to the old lady, assured her that M. le Baron was in a most edifying state of mind, and a promising subject for the operation of grace. This was a pious interpretation of the Baron's momentary good-humor. He had always lazily wondered what priests were good for, and he now remembered, with a sense of especial obligation to the abbé, that they were excellent for marrying people.

A day or two after this he left off his bandages, and tried to walk. He made his way into the garden and hobbled successfully along one of the alleys; but in the midst of his progress he was seized with a spasm of pain which forced him to stop and call for help. In an instant Euphemia came tripping along the path and offered him her arm with the frankest solicitude.

"Not to the house," he said, taking it; "farther on, to the bosquet." This choice was prompted by her having immediately confessed that she had seen him leave the house, had feared an accident, and had followed him on tiptoe.

"Why didn't you join me?" he had asked, giving her a look in which admiration was no longer disguised, and yet felt itself half at the mercy of her replying that a *jeune fille* should not be seen following a gentleman. But it drew a breath which filled its lungs for a long time afterward, when she replied simply that if she had overtaken him he might have accepted her arm out of politeness, whereas she wished to have the pleasure of seeing him walk alone.

The bosquet was covered with an odorous tangle of blossoming vines, and a nightingale overhead was shaking out love-notes with a profuseness which made the Baron consider his own conduct the perfection of propriety,

"In America," he said, "I have always heard that when a man wishes to marry a young girl, he offers himself simply, face to face, without any ceremony,—without parents, and uncles, and cousins sitting round in a circle."

"Why, I believe so," said Euphemia, staring, and too surprised to be alarmed.

"Very well, then," said the Baron, "suppose our bosquet here to be America. I offer you my hand, à l'Américaine. It will make me intensely happy to have you accept it."

Whether Euphemia's acceptance was in the American

manner is more than I can say; I incline to think that for
fluttering, grateful, trustful, softly-amazed young hearts, there
is only one manner all over the world.

That evening, in the little turret chamber which it was her
happiness to inhabit, she wrote a dutiful letter to her mamma,
and had just sealed it when she was sent for by Madame de
Mauves. She found this ancient lady seated in her boudoir, in a
lavender satin gown, with all her candles lighted, as if to
celebrate her grandson's betrothal. "Are you very happy?"
Madame de Mauves demanded, making Euphemia sit down
before her.

"I'm almost afraid to say so," said the young girl, "lest I
should wake myself up,"

"May you never wake up, *belle enfant*," said the old lady,
solemnly. "This is the first marriage ever made in our family
in this way,—by a Baron de Mauves proposing to a young girl
in an arbor, like Jeannot and Jeannette. It has not been our
way of doing things, and people may say it wants frankness.
My grandson tells me he considers it the perfection of frankness. Very good. I'm a very old woman, and if your differ-
ences should ever be as frank as your agreement, I shouldn't
like to see them. But I should be sorry to die and think you
were going to be unhappy. You can't be, beyond a certain
point; because, though in this world the Lord sometimes
makes light of our expectations, he never altogether ignores
our deserts. But you're very young and innocent, and easy to
deceive. There never was a man in the world—among the
saints themselves—as good as you believe the Baron. But he's
a *galant homme* and a gentleman, and I've been talking to him
to-night. To you I want to say this,—that you're to forget the
worldly rubbish I talked the other day about frivolous women
being happy. It's not the kind of happiness that would suit
you. Whatever befalls you, promise me this: to be yourself.
The Baronne de Mauves will be none the worse for it. Yourself, understand, in spite of everything,—bad precepts and

bad examples, bad usage even. Be persistently and patiently yourself, and a De Mauves will do you justice!"

Euphemia remembered this speech in after years, and more than once, wearily closing her eyes, she seemed to see the old woman sitting upright in her faded finery and smiling grimly, like one of the Fates who sees the wheel of fortune turning up her favorite event. But at the moment it seemed to her simply to have the proper gravity of the occasion; this was the way, she supposed, in which lucky young girls were addressed on their engagement by wise old women of quality.

At her convent, to which she immediately returned, she found a letter from her mother, which shocked her far more than the remarks of Madame de Mauves. Who were these people, Mrs Cleve demanded, who had presumed to talk to her daughter of marriage without asking her leave? Questionable gentlefolk, plainly; the best French people never did such things. Euphemia would return straightway to her convent, shut herself up, and await her own arrival.

It took Mrs Cleve three weeks to travel from Nice to Paris, and during this time the young girl had no communication with her lover beyond accepting a bouquet of violets, marked with his initials and left by a female friend. "I've not brought you up with such devoted care," she declared to her daughter at their first interview, "to marry a penniless Frenchman. I will take you straight home, and you will please to forget M. de Mauves."

Mrs Cleve received that evening at her hotel a visit from the Baron which mitigated her wrath, but failed to modify her decision. He had very good manners, but she was sure he had horrible morals; and Mrs Cleve, who had been a very good-natured censor on her own account, felt a genuine spiritual need to sacrifice her daughter to propriety. She belonged to that large class of Americans who make light of America in familiar discourse, but are startled back into a sense of moral responsibility when they find Europeans taking them at their word. "I know the type, my dear," she said to her daughter with a sagacious nod. "He'll not beat you; sometimes you'll wish he would."

Euphemia remained solemnly silent; for the only answer she felt capable of making her mother was that her mind was too small a measure of things, and that the Baron's "type" was one which it took some mystical illumination to appreciate. A person who confounded him with the common throng of her watering-place acquaintance was not a person to argue with. It seemed to Euphemia that she had no cause to plead; her cause was in the Lord's hands and her lover's.

M. de Mauves had been irritated and mortified by Mrs Cleve's opposition, and hardly knew how to handle an adversary who failed to perceive that a De Mauves of necessity gave more than he received. But he had obtained information on his return to Paris which exalted the uses of humility. Euphemia's fortune, wonderful to say, was greater than its fame, and in view of such a prize, even a De Mauves could afford to take a snubbing.

The young man's tact, his deference, his urbane insistence, won a concession from Mrs Cleve. The engagement was to be suspended and her daughter was to return home, be brought out and receive the homage she was entitled to, and which would but too surely take a form dangerous to the Baron's suit. They were to exchange neither letters, nor mementos, nor messages; but if at the end of two years Euphemia had refused offers enough to attest the permanence of her attachment, he should receive an invitation to address her again.

This decision was promulgated in the presence of the parties interested. The Baron bore himself gallantly, and looked at the young girl, expecting some tender protestation. But she only looked at him silently in return, neither weeping, nor smiling, nor putting out her hand. On this they separated; but as the Baron walked away, he declared to himself that, in spite of the confounded two years, he was a very happy fellow,—to have a fiancée who, to several millions of francs, added such strangely beautiful eyes.

How many offers Euphemia refused but scantily concerns us,—and how the Baron wore his two years away. He found that he needed pastimes, and, as pastimes were expensive, he added heavily to the list of debts to be cancelled by Euphemia's millions. Sometimes, in the thick of what he had once called pleasure with a keener conviction than now, he put to himself the case of their failing him after all; and then he remembered that last mute assurance of her eyes, and drew a long breath of such confidence as he felt in nothing else in the world save his own punctuality in an affair of honor.

At last, one morning, he took the express to Havre with a letter of Mrs Cleve's in his pocket, and ten days later made his bow to mother and daughter in New York. His stay was brief, and he was apparently unable to bring himself to view what Euphemia's uncle, Mr Butterworth, who gave her away at the altar, called our great experiment in democratic self-government in a serious light. He smiled at everything, and seemed to regard the New World as a colossal *plaisanterie*. It is true that a perpetual smile was the most natural expression of countenance for a man about to marry Euphemia Cleve.

III

LONGMORE'S first visit seemed to open to him so large an opportunity for tranquil enjoyment, that he very soon paid a second, and, at the end of a fortnight, had spent a great many hours in the little drawing-room which Madame de Mauves rarely quitted except to drive or walk in the forest. She lived in an old-fashioned pavilion, between a high-walled court and an excessively artificial garden, beyond whose enclosure you saw a long line of tree-tops. Longmore liked the garden, and in the mild afternoons used to move his chair through the open window to the little terrace which overlooked it, while his hostess sat just within. After a while she came out and wandered through the narrow alleys and beside the thin-spouting fountain, and last introduced him to a little gate in the garden wall, opening upon a lane which led into the forest. Hitherward, more than once, she wandered with him, bare-headed and meaning to go but twenty rods, but always strolling good-naturedly farther, and often taking a generous walk. They discovered a vast deal to talk about, and to the pleasure of finding the hours tread inaudibly away, Longmore was able to add the satisfaction of suspecting that he was a "resource" for Madame de Mauves. He had made her acquaintance with the sense, not altogether comfortable, that she was a woman with a painful secret, and that seeking her acquaintance would be like visiting at a house where there was an invalid who could bear no noise. But he very soon perceived that her sorrow, since sorrow it was, was not an aggressive one; that it was not fond of attitudes and ceremonies, and that her earnest wish was to forget it. He felt that even if Mrs Draper had not told him she was unhappy, he would have guessed it; and yet he could hardly have pointed to his evidence. It was chiefly negative,—she never alluded to her husband. Beyond this it seemed to him simply that her whole being was pitched on a lower key than harmonious Nature meant; she was like a powerful singer who had lost her high notes. She never drooped nor sighed nor looked unutterable things; she indulged in no dusky sarcasms against fate; she had, in short, none of the coquetry of unhappiness. But Longmore was sure that her gentle gayety was the result of strenuous effort, and that she was trying to interest herself in his thoughts to escape from her own. If she had wished to irritate his curiosity and lead him to take her confidence by storm, nothing could have served her purpose better than this ingenuous reserve. He declared to himself that there was a rare magnanimity in such ardent self-effacement, and that but one woman in ten thousand was capable of merging an intensely personal grief in thankless outward contemplation. Madame de Mauves, he instinctively felt, was not sweeping the horizon for a compensation or a consoler; she had suffered a personal deception which had disgusted her with persons. She was not striving to balance her sorrow with some strongly flavored joy; for the present, she was trying to live with it, peaceably, reputably, and without scandal,—turning the key on it occasionally, as you would on a companion liable to attacks of insanity. Longmore was a man of fine senses and of an active imagination, whose leading-strings had never been slipped. He began to regard his hostess as a figure haunted by a shadow which was somehow her intenser, more authentic self. This hovering mystery came to have for him an extraordinary charm. Her delicate beauty acquired to his eye the serious cast of certain blank-browed Greek statues, and sometimes, when his imagination, more than his ear, detected a vague tremor in the tone in which she attempted to make a friendly question seem to have behind it none of the hollow resonance of absent-mindedness, his marvelling eyes gave her an answer more eloquent, though much less to the point, than the one she demanded.

She gave him indeed much to wonder about, and, in his ignorance, he formed a dozen experimental theories upon the history of her marriage. She had married for love and staked her whole soul on it; of that he was convinced. She had not married a Frenchman to be near Paris and her base of supplies of millinery; he was sure she had seen conjugal happiness in a light of which her present life, with its conveniences for shopping and its moral aridity, was the absolute negation. But by what extraordinary process of the heart—through what mysterious intermission of that moral instinct which may keep pace with the heart, even when that organ is making unprecedented time—had she fixed her affections on an arrogantly

K

frivolous Frenchman? Longmore needed no telling; he knew
M. de Mauves was frivolous; it was stamped on his eyes, his
nose, his mouth, his carriage. For French women Longmore
had but a scanty kindness, or at least (what with him was very
much the same thing) but a scanty gallantry; they all seemed to
belong to the type of a certain fine lady to whom he had ventured to present a letter of introduction, and whom, directly
after his first visit to her, he had set down in his note-book as
"metallic." Why should Madame de Mauves have chosen a
French woman's lot,—she whose character had a perfume
which doesn't belong to even the brightest metals? He asked
her one day frankly if it had cost her nothing to transplant
herself,—if she was not oppressed with a sense of irreconcilable difference from "all these people." She was silent
awhile, and he fancied that she was hesitating as to whether
she should resent so unceremonious an allusion to her husband. He almost wished she would; it would seem a proof that
her deep reserve of sorrow had a limit.

"I almost grew up here," she said at last, "and it was here
for me that those dreams of the future took shape that we all
have when we cease to be very young. As matters stand, one
may be very American and yet arrange it with one's conscience to live in Europe. My imagination perhaps—I had a
little when I was younger—helped me to think I should find
happiness here. And after all, for a woman, what does it sig-
nify? This is not America, perhaps, about me, but it's quite
as little France. France is out there, beyond the garden, in the
town, in the forest; but here, close about me, in my room
and"—she paused a moment—"in my mind, it's a nameless
country of my own. It's not her country," she added, "that
makes a woman happy or unhappy."

Madame Clairin, Euphemia's sister-in-law, might have been
supposed to have undertaken the graceful task of making
Longmore ashamed of his uncivil jottings about her sex and
nation. Mademoiselle de Mauves, bringing example to the

confirmation of precept, had made a remunerative match and sacrificed her name to the millions of a prosperous and aspiring wholesale druggist,—a gentleman liberal enough to consider his fortune a moderate price for being towed into circles unpervaded by pharmaceutic odors. His system, possibly, was sound, but his own application of it was unfortunate. M. Clairin's head was turned by his good luck. Having secured an aristocratic wife, he adopted an aristocratic vice and began to gamble at the Bourse. In an evil hour he lost heavily and staked heavily to recover himself. But he overtook his loss only by a greater one. Then he let everything go,—his wits, his courage, his probity,—everything that had made him what his ridiculous marriage had so promptly unmade. He walked up the Rue Vivienne one day with his hands in his empty pockets, and stood for half an hour staring confusedly up and down the glittering boulevard. People brushed against him, and half a dozen carriages almost ran over him, until at last a policeman, who had been watching him for some time, took him by the arm and led him gently away. He looked at the man's cocked hat and sword with tears in his eyes; he hoped he was going to interpret to him the wrath of Heaven,—to execute the penalty of his dead-weight of self-abhorrence. But the sergent de ville only stationed him in the embrasure of a door, out of harm's way, and walked away to supervise a financial contest between an old lady and a cabman. Poor M. Clairin had only been married a year, but he had had time to measure the lofty spirit of a De Mauves. When night had fallen, he repaired to the house of a friend and asked for a night's lodging; and as his friend, who was simply his old head book-keeper and lived in a small way, was put to some trouble to accommodate him,—"You must excuse me," Clairin said, "but I can't go home. I'm afraid of my wife!" Toward morning he blew his brains out. His widow turned the remnants of his property to better account than could have been expected, and wore the very handsomest mourning. It was for this latter reason, perhaps, that she was obliged to retrench at other points and accept a temporary home under her brother's roof.

Fortune had played Madame Clairin a terrible trick, but had found an adversary and not a victim. Though quite without beauty, she had always had what is called the grand air, and her air from this time forward was grander than ever. As she trailed about in her sable furbelows, tossing back her well-dressed head, and holding up her vigilant eye-glass, she seemed to be sweeping the whole field of society and asking herself where she should pluck her revenge. Suddenly she espied it, ready made to her hand, in poor Longmore's wealth and amiability. American dollars and American complaisance had made her brother's fortune; why shouldn't they make hers? She overestimated Longmore's wealth and misinterpreted his amiability; for she was sure that a man could not be so contented without being rich, nor so unassuming without being weak. He encountered her advances with a formal politeness which covered a great deal of unflattering discomposure. She made him feel acutely uncomfortable; and though he was at a loss to conceive how he could be an object of interest to a shrewd Parisienne, he had an indefinable sense of being enclosed in a magnetic circle, like the victim of an incantation. If Madame Clairin could have fathomed his Puritanic soul, she would have laid by her wand and her book and admitted that he was an impossible subject. She gave him a kind of moral chill, and he never mentally alluded to her save as that dreadful woman,—that terrible woman. He did justice to her grand air, but for his pleasure he preferred the small air of Madame de Mauves; and he never made her his bow, after standing frigidly passive for five minutes to one of her gracious overtures to intimacy, without feeling a peculiar desire to ramble away into the forest, fling himself down on the warm grass, and, staring up at the blue sky, forget that there were any women in nature who didn't please like the swaying tree-tops. One day, on his arrival, she met him in the court and told him that her sister-in-law was shut up with a headache, and that his visit must be for her. He followed her into the drawing-room with the best grace at his command, and sat twirling his hat for half an hour. Suddenly he understood her; the caressing cadence of her voice was a distinct invitation to solicit the incomparable honor of her hand. He blushed to the roots of his hair and jumped up with uncontrollable alacrity; then, dropping a glance at Madame Clairin, who sat watching him with hard eyes over the edge of her smile, as it were, perceived on her brow a flash of unforgiving wrath. It was not becoming, but his eyes lingered a moment, for it seemed to illuminate her character. What he saw there frightened him, and he felt himself murmuring, "Poor Madame de Mauves!" His departure was abrupt, and this time he really went into the forest and lay down on the grass.

After this he admired Madame de Mauves more than ever; she seemed a brighter figure, dogged by a darker shadow. At the end of a month he received a letter from a friend with whom he had arranged a tour through the Low Countries, reminding him of his promise to meet him promptly at Brussels. It was only after his answer was posted that he fully measured the zeal with which he had declared that the journey must either be deferred or abandoned,—that he could not possibly leave Saint-Germain. He took a walk in the forest, and asked himself if this was irrevocably true. If it was, surely his duty was to march straight home and pack his trunk. Poor Webster, who, he knew, had counted ardently on this excursion, was an excellent fellow; six weeks ago he would have gone through fire and water to join Webster. It had never been in his books to throw overboard a friend whom he had loved for ten years for a married woman whom for six weeks he had—admired. It was certainly beyond question that he was lingering at Saint-Germain because this admirable married woman was there; but in the midst of all this admiration what had become of prudence? This was the conduct of a man prepared to fall utterly in love. If she was as unhappy as he believed, the love of such a man would help her very little more than his indifference; if she was less so, she needed no help and could dispense with his friendly offices. He was sure, moreover, that if she knew he was staying on her account, she would be extremely annoyed. But this very feeling had much to do with making it hard to go; her displeasure would only enhance the gentle stoicism which touched him to the heart. At moments, indeed, he assured himself that to linger was simply impertinent; it was indelicate to make a daily study of such a shrinking grief. But inclination answered that some day her self-support would fail, and he had a vision of this admirable creature calling vainly for help. He would be her friend, to any length; it was unworthy of both of them to think about consequences. But he was a friend who carried about with him a muttering resentment that he had not known her five years earlier, and a brooding hostility to those who had anticipated him. It seemed one of fortune's most mocking strokes, that she should be surrounded by persons whose only merit was that they threw the charm of her character into radiant relief.

Longmore's growing irritation made it more and more difficult for him to see any other merit than this in the Baron de Mauves. And yet, disinterestedly, it would have been hard to give a name to the portentous vices which such an estimate implied, and there were times when our hero was almost persuaded against his finer judgment that he was really the most considerate of husbands, and that his wife liked melancholy for melancholy's sake. His manners were perfect, his urbanity was unbounded, and he seemed never to address her but, sentimentally speaking, hat in hand. His tone to Longmore (as the latter was perfectly aware) was that of a man of the world to a man not quite of the world; but what it lacked in deference it made up in easy friendliness. "I can't thank you enough for having overcome my wife's shyness," he more than once declared. "If we left her to do as she pleased, she would bury herself alive. Come often, and bring some one else. She'll have nothing to do with my friends, but perhaps she'll accept yours."

The Baron made these speeches with a remorseless placidity very amazing to our hero, who had an innocent belief that a man's head may point out to him the shortcomings of his heart and make him ashamed of them. He could not fancy him capable both of neglecting his wife and taking an almost humorous view of her suffering. Longmore had, at any rate, an exasperating sense that the Baron thought rather less of his wife than more, for that very same fine difference of nature which so deeply stirred his own sympathies. He was rarely present during Longmore's visits, and made a daily journey to Paris, where he had "business," as he once mentioned,— not in the least with a tone of apology. When he appeared, it was late in the evening, and with an imperturbable air of being on the best of terms with every one and everything, which was peculiarly annoying if you happened to have a tacit quarrel with him. If he was a good fellow, he was surely a good fellow spoiled. Something he had, however, which Longmore vaguely envied—a kind of superb positiveness—a manner rounded and polished by the traditions of centuries—an amenity exercised for his own sake and not his neighbors'—which seemed the result of something better than a good conscience —of a vigorous and unscrupulous temperament. The Baron was plainly not a moral man, and poor Longmore, who was, would have been glad to learn the secret of his luxurious serenity. What was it that enabled him, without being a monster with visibly cloven feet, exhaling brimstone, to misprize so cruelly a lovely wife, and to walk about the world with a smile under his mustache? It was the essential grossness of his imagination, which had nevertheless helped him to turn so many neat compliments. He could be very polite, and he could doubtless be supremely impertinent; but he was as unable to draw a moral inference of the finer strain, as a school-boy who has been playing truant for a week to solve a problem in algebra. It was ten to one he didn't know his wife was unhappy; he and his brilliant sister had doubtless agreed to consider their companion a Puritanical little person, of meagre aspirations and slender accomplishments, contented with looking at Paris from the terrace, and, as an especial treat, having a countryman very much like herself to supply her with homely transatlantic gossip. M. de Mauves was tired of his companion: he relished a higher flavor in female society. She was too modest, too simple, too delicate; she had too few arts, too little coquetry, too much charity. M. de Mauves, some day, lighting a cigar, had probably decided she was stupid. It was the same sort of taste, Longmore moralized, as the taste for Gérôme in painting, and for M. Gustave Flaubert in literature. The Baron was a pagan and his wife was a Christian, and between them, accordingly, was a gulf. He was by race and instinct a *grand seigneur*. Longmore had often heard of this distinguished social type, and was properly grateful for an opportunity to examine it closely. It had certainly a picturesque boldness of outline, but it was fed from spiritual sources so remote from those of which he felt the living gush in his own soul, that he found himself gazing at it, in irreconcilable antipathy, across a dim historic mist. "I'm a modern *bourgeois*," he said, "and not perhaps so good a judge of how far a pretty woman's tongue may go at supper without prejudice to her reputation. But I've not met one of the sweetest of women without recognizing her and discovering that a certain sort of character offers better entertainment than Thérésa's songs, sung by a dissipated duchess. Wit for wit, I think mine carries me further." It was easy indeed to perceive that, as became a *grand seigneur*, M. de Mauves had a stock of rigid notions. He would not especially have desired, perhaps, that his wife should compete in amateur operettas with the duchesses in question, chiefly of recent origin; but he held that a gentleman may take his amusement where he finds it, that he is quite at liberty not to find it at home; and that the wife of a De Mauves who should hang her head and have red eyes, and allow herself to make any other response to officious condolence than that her husband's amusements were his own affair, would have forfeited every claim to having her finger-tips bowed over and kissed. And yet in spite of these sound principles, Longmore fancied that the Baron was more irritated than gratified by his wife's irreproachable reserve. Did it dimly occur to him that it was self-control and not self-effacement? She was a model to all the inferior matrons of his line, past and to come, and an occasional "scene" from her at a convenient moment would have something reassuring,—would attest her stupidity a trifle more forcibly than her inscrutable tranquillity.

Longmore would have given much to know the principle of her submissiveness, and he tried more than once, but with rather awkward timidity, to sound the mystery. She seemed to him to have been long resisting the force of cruel evidence, and, though she had succumbed to it at last, to have denied herself the right to complain, because if faith was gone her heroic generosity remained. He believed even that she was capable of reproaching herself with having expected too much, and of trying to persuade herself out of her bitterness by saying that her hopes had been illusions and that this was simply —life. "I hate tragedy," she once said to him; "I have a really pusillanimous dread of moral suffering. I believe that—without base concessions—there is always some way of escaping from it. I had almost rather never smile all my life than have a single violent explosion of grief." She lived evidently in nervous apprehension of being fatally convinced,—of seeing to the end of her deception. Longmore, when he thought of this, felt an immense longing to offer her something of which she could be as sure as of the sun in heaven.

IV

His friend Webster lost no time in accusing him of the basest infidelity, and asking him what he found at Saint-Germain to prefer to Van Eyck and Memling, Rubens and Rembrandt. A day or two after the receipt of Webster's letter, he took a walk with Madame de Mauves in the forest. They sat down on a fallen log, and she began to arrange into a bouquet the anemones and violets she had gathered. "I have a letter," he said at last, "from a friend whom I some time ago promised to join at Brussels. The time has come,—it has passed. It finds me terribly unwilling to leave Saint-Germain."

She looked up with the candid interest which she always displayed in his affairs, but with no disposition, apparently, to make a personal application of his words. "Saint-Germain is pleasant enough," she said; "but are you doing yourself justice? Won't you regret in future days that instead of travelling and seeing cities and monuments and museums and improving your mind, you sat here—for instance—on a log, pulling my flowers to pieces?"

"What I shall regret in future days," he answered after some hesitation, "is that I should have sat here and not spoken the truth on the matter. I am fond of museums and monuments and of improving my mind, and I'm particularly fond of my friend Webster. But I can't bring myself to leave Saint-Germain without asking you a question. You must forgive me if it's unfortunate, and be assured that curiosity was never more respectful. Are you really as unhappy as I imagine you to be?"

She had evidently not expected his question, and she greeted it with a startled blush. "If I strike you as unhappy," she said, "I have been a poorer friend to you than I wished to be."

"I, perhaps, have been a better friend of yours than you have supposed. I've admired your reserve, your courage, your studied gayety. But I have felt the existence of something beneath them that was more *you*—more you as I wished to know you—than they were; something that I have believed to be a constant sorrow."

She listened with great gravity, but without an air of offence, and he felt that while he had been timorously calculating the last consequences of friendship, she had placidly accepted them. "You surprise me," she said slowly, and her blush still lingered. "But to refuse to answer you would confirm an impression which is evidently already too strong. An unhappiness that one can sit comfortably talking about, is an unhappiness with distinct limitations. If I were examined before a board of commissioners for investigating the felicity of mankind, I'm sure I should be pronounced a very fortunate woman."

There was something delightfully gentle to him in her tone, and its softness seemed to deepen as she continued: "But let me add, with all gratitude for your sympathy, that it's my own affair altogether. It needn't disturb you, Mr Longmore, for I have often found myself in your company a very contented person."

"You're a wonderful woman," he said, "and I admire you as I never have admired any one. You're wiser than anything I, for one, can say to you; and what I ask of you is not to let me advise or console you, but simply thank you for letting me know you." He had intended no such outburst as this, but his voice rang loud, and he felt a kind of unfamiliar joy as he uttered it.

She shook her head with some impatience. "Let us be friends,—as I supposed we were going to be,—without protestations and fine words. To have you making bows to my wisdom,—that would be real wretchedness. I can dispense with your admiration better than the Flemish painters can,—

better than Van Eyck and Rubens, in spite of all their worshippers. Go join your friend,—see everything, enjoy everything, learn everything, and write me an excellent letter,
brimming over with your impressions. I'm extremely fond of
the Dutch painters," she added with a slight faltering of the
voice, which Longmore had noticed once before, and which
he had interpreted as the sudden weariness of a spirit self-
condemned to play a part.

"I don't believe you care about the Dutch painters at all,"
he said with an unhesitating laugh. "But I shall certainly write
you a letter."

She rose and turned homeward, thoughtfully rearranging
her flowers as she walked. Little was said; Longmore was
asking himself, with a tremor in the unspoken words, whether
all this meant simply that he was in love. He looked at the
rooks wheeling against the golden-hued sky, between the
tree-tops, but not at his companion, whose personal presence
seemed lost in the felicity she had created. Madame de Mauves
was silent and grave, because she was painfully disappointed.
A sentimental friendship she had not desired; her scheme
had been to pass with Longmore as a placid creature with a
good deal of leisure, which she was disposed to devote to
profitable conversation of an impersonal sort. She liked him
extremely, and felt that there was something in him to which,
when she made up her girlish mind, that a needy French baron
was the ripest fruit of time, she had done very scanty justice.
They went through the little gate in the garden wall and
approached the house. On the terrace Madame Clairin was
entertaining a friend,—a little elderly gentleman with a white
mustache, and an order in his button-hole. Madame de Mauves
chose to pass round the house into the court; whereupon her
sister-in-law, greeting Longmore with a commanding nod,
lifted her eye-glass and stared at them as they went by. Longmore heard the little old gentleman uttering some old-
fashioned epigram about "la vieille galanterie Française," and

then, by a sudden impulse, he looked at Madame de Mauves and wondered what she was doing in such a world. She stopped before the house, without asking him to come in. "I hope," she said, "you'll consider my advice, and waste no more time at Saint-Germain."

For an instant there rose to his lips some faded compliment about his time not being wasted, but it expired before the simple sincerity of her look. She stood there as gently serious as the angel of disinterestedness, and Longmore felt as if he should insult her by treating her words as a bait for flattery. "I shall start in a day or two," he answered, "but I won't promise you not to come back."

"I hope not," she said simply. "I expect to be here a long time."

"I shall come and say good by," he rejoined; on which she nodded with a smile, and went in.

He turned away, and walked slowly homeward by the terrace. It seemed to him that to leave her thus, for a gain on which she herself insisted, was to know her better and admire her more. But he was in a vague ferment of feeling which her evasion of his question half an hour before had done more to deepen than to allay. Suddenly, on the terrace, he encountered M. de Mauves, who was leaning against the parapet finishing a cigar. The Baron, who, he fancied, had an air of peculiar affability, offered him his fair, plump hand. Longmore stopped; he felt a sudden angry desire to cry out to him that he had the loveliest wife in the world; that he ought to be ashamed of himself not to know it; and that for all his shrewdness he had never looked into the depths of her eyes. The Baron, we know, considered that he had; but there was something in Euphemia's eyes now that was not there five years before. They talked for a while about various things, and M. de Mauves gave a humorous account of his visit to America. His tone was not soothing to Longmore's excited sensibilities. He seemed to consider the country a gigantic joke, and his urbanity only went so far as to admit that it was not a bad one. Longmore was not, by habit, an aggressive apologist for our institutions; but the Baron's narrative confirmed his worst impressions of French superficiality. He had understood nothing, he had felt nothing, he had learned nothing; and our hero, glancing askance at his aristocratic profile, declared that if the chief merit of a long pedigree was to leave one so vaingloriously stupid, he thanked his stars that the Longmores had emerged from obscurity in the present century, in the person of an enterprising lumber merchant. M. de Mauves dwelt of course on that prime oddity of ours,—the liberty allowed to young girls; and related the history of his researches into the "opportunities" it presented to French noblemen,—researches in which, during a fortnight's stay, he seemed to have spent many agreeable hours. "I am bound to admit," he said, "that in every case I was disarmed by the extreme candor of the young lady, and that they took care of themselves to better purpose than I have seen some mammas in France take care of them." Longmore greeted this handsome concession with the grimmest of smiles, and damned his impertinent patronage.

Mentioning at last that he was about to leave Saint-Germain, he was surprised, without exactly being flattered, by the Baron's quickened attention. "I'm very sorry," the latter cried. "I hoped we had you for the summer." Longmore murmured something civil, and wondered why M. de Mauves should care whether he stayed or went. "You were a diversion to Madame de Mauves," the Baron added. "I assure you I mentally blessed your visits."

"They were a great pleasure to me," Longmore said gravely. "Some day I expect to come back."

"Pray do," and the Baron laid his hand urgently on his arm. "You see I have confidence in you!" Longmore was silent for a moment, and the Baron puffed his cigar reflectively and watched the smoke. "Madame de Mauves," he said at last, "is a rather singular person."

Longmore shifted his position, and wondered whether he was going to "explain" Madame de Mauves.

"Being as you are her fellow-countryman," the Baron went on, "I don't mind speaking frankly. She's just a little morbid, —the most charming woman in the world, as you see, but a little fanciful,—a little *exaltée*. Now you see she has taken this extraordinary fancy for solitude. I can't get her to go any-where,—to see any one. When my friends present themselves she's polite, but she's freezing. She doesn't do herself justice, and I expect every day to hear two or three of them say to me, 'Your wife's *jolie à croquer:* what a pity she hasn't a little *esprit*.' You must have found out that she has really a great deal. But to tell the whole truth, what she needs is to forget herself. She sits alone for hours poring over her English books and looking at life through that terrible brown fog which they always seem to me to fling over the world. I doubt if your English authors," the Baron continued, with a serenity which Longmore afterwards characterized as sublime, "are very sound reading for young married women. I don't pretend to know much about them; but I remember that, not long after our marriage, Madame de Mauves undertook to read me one day a certain Wordsworth,—a poet highly esteemed, it appears, *chez vous*. It seemed to me that she took me by the nape of the neck and forced my head for half an hour over a basin of *soupe aux choux*, and that one ought to ventilate the drawing-room before any one called. But I suppose you know him,—*ce génie là*. I think my wife never forgave me, and that it was a real shock to her to find she had married a man who had very much the same taste in literature as in cookery. But you're a man of general culture," said the Baron, turning to Longmore and fixing his eyes on the seal on his watch-guard. "You can talk about everything, and I'm sure you like Alfred de Musset as well as Wordsworth. Talk to her about every-thing, Alfred de Musset included. Bah! I forgot you're going. Come back then as soon as possible and talk about your travels. If Madame de Mauves too would travel for a couple of months, it would do her good. It would enlarge her horizon," —and M. de Mauves made a series of short nervous jerks with his stick in the air,—"it would wake up her imagination. She's too rigid, you know,—it would show her that one may bend a trifle without breaking." He paused a moment and gave two or three vigorous puffs. Then turning to his companion again, with a little nod and a confidential smile:—"I hope you admire my candor. I wouldn't say all this to one of *us*."

Evening was coming on, and the lingering light seemed to float in the air in faintly golden motes. Longmore stood gazing at these luminous particles; he could almost have fancied them a swarm of humming insects, murmuring as a refrain, "She has a great deal of *esprit*,—she has a great deal of *esprit*." "Yes, she has a great deal," he said mechanically, turning to the Baron. M. de Mauves glanced at him sharply, as if to ask what the deuce he was talking about. "She has a great deal of intelligence," said Longmore, deliberately, "a great deal of beauty, a great many virtues."

M. de Mauves busied himself for a moment in lighting another cigar, and when he had finished, with a return of his confidential smile, "I suspect you of thinking," he said, "that I don't do my wife justice. Take care,—take care, young man; that's a dangerous assumption. In general, a man always does his wife justice. More than justice," cried the Baron with a laugh,—"that we keep for the wives of other men!"

Longmore afterwards remembered it in favor of the Baron's grace of address that he had not measured at this moment the dusky abyss over which it hovered. But a sort of deepening subterranean echo lingered on his spiritual ear. For the present his keenest sensation was a desire to get away and cry aloud that M. de Mauves was an arrogant fool. He bade him an abrupt good-night, which must serve also, he said, as goodby.

"Decidedly, then, you go?" said M. de Mauves, almost peremptorily.

"Decidedly."

"Of course you'll come and say good by to Madame de Mauves." His tone implied that the omission would be most uncivil; but there seemed to Longmore something so ludicrous in his taking a lesson in consideration from M. de Mauves, that he burst into a laugh. The Baron frowned, like a man for whom it was a new and most unpleasant sensation to be perplexed. "You're a queer fellow," he murmured, as Longmore turned away, not forseeing that he would think him a very queer fellow indeed before he had done with him.

Longmore sat down to dinner at his hotel with his usual good intentions; but as he was lifting his first glass of wine to his lips, he suddenly fell to musing and set down his wine untasted. His revery lasted long, and when he emerged from it, his fish was cold; but this mattered little, for his appetite was gone. That evening he packed his trunk with a kind of indignant energy. This was so effective that the operation was accomplished before bedtime, and as he was not in the least sleepy, he devoted the interval to writing two letters; one was a short note to Madame de Mauves, which he intrusted to a servant, to be delivered the next morning. He had found it best, he said, to leave Saint-Germain immediately, but he expected to be back in Paris in the early autumn. The other letter was the result of his having remembered a day or two before that he had not yet complied with Mrs Draper's injunction to give her an account of his impressions of her friend. The present occasion seemed propitious, and he wrote half a dozen pages. His tone, however, was grave, and Mrs Draper, on receiving them, was slightly disappointed,—she would have preferred a stronger flavor of rhapsody. But what chiefly concerns us is the concluding sentences.

"The only time she ever spoke to me of her marriage," he wrote, "she intimated that it had been a perfect love-match. With all abatements, I suppose most marriages are; but in her case this would mean more, I think, than in that of most

L

women; for her love was an absolute idealization. She believed her husband was a hero of rose-colored romance, and he turns out to be not even a hero of very sad-colored reality. For some time now she has been sounding her mistake, but I don't believe she has touched the bottom of it yet. She strikes me as a person who is begging off from full knowledge,—who has struck a truce with painful truth, and is trying awhile the experiment of living with closed eyes. In the dark she tries to see again the gilding on her idol. Illusion of course is illusion, and one must always pay for it; but there is something truly tragical in seeing an earthly penalty levied on such divine folly as this. As for M. de Mauves, he's a Frenchman to his fingers' ends; and I confess I should dislike him for this if he were a much better man. He can't forgive his wife for having married him too sentimentally and loved him too well; for in some uncorrupted corner of his being he feels, I suppose, that as she saw him, so he ought to have been. It's a perpetual vexation to him that a little American bourgeoise should have fancied him a finer fellow than he is, or than he at all wants to be. He hasn't a glimmering of real acquaintance with his wife; he can't understand the stream of passion flowing so clear and still. To tell the truth, I hardly can myself; but when I see the spectacle I can admire it furiously. M. de Mauves, at any rate, would like to have the comfort of feeling that his wife was as corruptible as himself; and you'll hardly believe me when I tell you that he goes about intimating to gentlemen whom he deems worthy of the knowledge, that it would be a convenience to him to have them make love to her."

V

ON reaching Paris, Longmore straightway purchased a Murray's "Belgium," to help himself to believe that he would start on the morrow for Brussels; but when the morrow came, it occurred to him that, by way of preparation, he ought to acquaint himself more intimately with the Flemish painters in the Louvre. This took a whole morning, but it did little to hasten his departure. He had abruptly left Saint-Germain, because it seemed to him that respect for Madame de Mauves demanded that he should allow her husband no reason to suppose that he had understood him; but now that he had satisfied this immediate need of delicacy, he found himself thinking more and more ardently of Euphemia. It was a poor expression of ardor to be lingering irresolutely on the deserted boulevards, but he detested the idea of leaving Saint-Germain five hundred miles behind him. He felt very foolish, nevertheless, and wandered about nervously, promising himself to take the next train; but a dozen trains started, and Longmore was still in Paris. This sentimental tumult was more than he had bargained for, and, as he looked in the shop windows, he wondered whether it was a "passion." He had never been fond of the word, and had grown up with a kind of horror of what it represented. He had hoped that when he fell in love, he should do it with an excellent conscience, with no greater agitation than a mild general glow of satisfaction. But here was a sentiment compounded of pity and anger, as well as admiration, and bristling with scruples and doubts. He had come abroad to enjoy the Flemish painters and all others; but what fair-tressed saint of Van Eyck or Memling was so appealing a figure as Madame de Mauves? His restless steps carried him at last out of the long villa-bordered avenue which leads to the Bois de Boulogne.

Summer had fairly begun, and the drive beside the lake was empty, but there were various loungers on the benches and chairs, and the great café had an air of animation. Longmore's walk had given him an appetite, and he went into the establishment and demanded a dinner, remarking for the hundredth time, as he observed the smart little tables disposed in the open air, how much better they ordered this matter in France.

"Will monsieur dine in the garden, or in the salon?" asked the waiter. Longmore chose the garden; and observing that a great vine of June roses was trained over the wall of the house, placed himself at a table near by, where the best of dinners was served him on the whitest of linen, in the most shining of porcelain. It so happened that his table was near a window, and that as he sat he could look into a corner of the salon. So it was that his attention rested on a lady seated just within the window, which was open, face to face apparently to a companion who was concealed by the curtain. She was a very pretty woman, and Longmore looked at her as often as was consistent with good manners. After a while he even began to wonder who she was, and to suspect that she was one of those ladies whom it is no breach of good manners to look at as often as you like. Longmore, too, if he had been so disposed, would have been the more free to give her all his attention, that her own was fixed upon the person opposite to her. She was what the French call a *belle brune*, and though our hero, who had rather a conservative taste in such matters, had no great relish for her bold outlines and even bolder coloring, he could not help admiring her expression of basking contentment.

She was evidently very happy, and her happiness gave her an air of innocence. The talk of her friend, whoever he was, abundantly suited her humor, for she sat listening to him with a broad, lazy smile, and interrupted him occasionally, while she crunched her bon-bons, with a murmured response, presumably as broad, which seemed to deepen his eloquence. She drank a great deal of champagne and ate an immense number of strawberries, and was plainly altogether a person with an impartial relish for strawberries, champagne, and what she would have called *bêtises*.

They had half finished dinner when Longmore sat down, and he was still in his place when they rose. She had hung her bonnet on a nail above her chair, and her companion passed round the table to take it down for her. As he did so, she bent her head to look at a wine stain on her dress, and in the movement exposed the greater part of the back of a very handsome neck. The gentleman observed it, and observed also, apparently, that the room beyond them was empty; that he stood within eyeshot of Longmore, he failed to observe. He stooped suddenly and imprinted a gallant kiss on the fair expanse. Longmore then recognized M. de Mauves. The recipient of this vigorous tribute put on her bonnet, using his flushed smile as a mirror, and in a moment they passed through the garden on their way to their carriage.

Then, for the first time, M. de Mauves perceived Longmore. He measured with a rapid glance the young man's relation to the open window, and checked himself in the impulse to stop and speak to him. He contented himself with bowing with great gravity as he opened the gate for his companion.

That evening Longmore made a railway journey, but not to Brussels. He had effectually ceased to care about Brussels; the only thing he now cared about was Madame de Mauves. The atmosphere of his mind had had a sudden clearing up; pity and anger were still throbbing there, but they had space to rage at their pleasure, for doubts and scruples had abruptly departed. It was little, he felt, that he could interpose between her resignation and the unsparing harshness of her position; but that little, if it involved the sacrifice of everything that bound him to the tranquil past, it seemed to him that he could offer her with a rapture which at last made reflection a wofully halting substitute for faith. Nothing in his tranquil past had given such a zest to consciousness as the sense of tending with all his being to a single aim which bore him company on his journey to Saint-Germain. How to justify his return, how to explain his ardor, troubled him little. He was not sure, even, that he wished to be understood; he wished only to feel that it was by no fault of his that Madame de Mauves was alone with the ugliness of fate. He was conscious of no distinct desire to "make love" to her; if he could have uttered the essence of his longing, he would have said that he wished her to remember that in a world colored gray to her vision by disappointment, there was one vividly honest man. She might certainly have remembered it, however, without his coming back to remind her; and it is not to be denied that, as he packed his valise that evening, he wished immensely to hear the sound of her voice.

He waited the next day till his usual hour of calling,—the late afternoon; but he learned at the door that Madame de Mauves was not at home. The servant offered the information that she was walking in the forest. Longmore went through the garden and out of the little door into the lane, and, after half an hour's vain exploration, saw her coming toward him at the end of a green by-path. As he appeared, she stopped for a moment, as if to turn aside; then recognizing him, she slowly advanced, and he was soon shaking hands with her.

"Nothing has happened," she said, looking at him fixedly. "You're not ill?"

"Nothing, except that when I got to Paris I found how fond I had grown of Saint-Germain."

She neither smiled nor looked flattered; it seemed indeed to Longmore that she was annoyed. But he was uncertain, for he immediately perceived that in his absence the whole character of her face had altered. It told him that something momentous had happened. It was no longer self-contained melancholy that he read in her eyes, but grief and agitation which had lately struggled with that passionate love of peace of which she had spoken to him, and forced it to know that deep experience is never peaceful. She was pale, and she had evidently been shedding tears. He felt his heart beating hard; he seemed now to know her secrets. She continued to look at him with a contracted brow, as if his return had given her a sense of responsibility too great to be disguised by a commonplace welcome. For some moments, as he turned and walked beside her, neither spoke; then abruptly,—"Tell me truly, Mr Longmore," she said, "why you have come back."

He turned and looked at her with an air which startled her into a certainty of what she had feared. "Because I've learned the real answer to the question I asked you the other day. You're not happy,—you're too good to be happy on the terms offered you. Madame de Mauves," he went on with a gesture which protested against a gesture of her own, "I can't be happy if you're not. I don't care for anything so long as I see such a depth of unconquerable sadness in your eyes. I found during three dreary days in Paris that the thing in the world I most care for is this daily privilege of seeing you. I know it's absolutely brutal to tell you I admire you; it's an insult to you to treat you as if you had complained to me or appealed to me. But such a friendship as I waked up to there," —and he tossed his head toward the distant city—"is a potent force, I assure you; and when forces are compressed they explode. But if you had told me every trouble in your heart, it would have mattered little; I couldn't say more than I must say now,—that if that in life from which you've hoped most has given you least, *my* devoted respect will refuse no service and betray no trust."

She had begun to make marks in the earth with the point of her parasol; but she stopped and listened to him in perfect immobility. Rather, her immobility was not perfect; for when he stopped speaking a faint flush had stolen into her cheek. It told Longmore that she was moved, and his first perceiving it was the happiest instant of his life. She raised her eyes at last, and looked at him with what at first seemed a pleading dread of excessive emotion.

"Thank you—thank you!" she said, calmly enough; but the next moment her own emotion overcame her calmness, and she burst into tears. Her tears vanished as quickly as they came, but they did Longmore a world of good. He had always felt indefinably afraid of her; her being had somehow seemed fed by a deeper faith and a stronger will than his own; but her half-dozen smothered sobs showed him the bottom of her heart, and assured him that she was weak enough to be grateful.

"Excuse me," she said; "I'm too nervous to listen to you. I believe I could have faced an enemy to-day, but I can't endure a friend."

"You're killing yourself with stoicism,—that's my belief," he cried. "Listen to a friend for his own sake, if not for yours. I have never ventured to offer you an atom of compassion, and you can't accuse yourself of an abuse of charity."

She looked about her with a kind of weary confusion which promised a reluctant attention. But suddenly perceiving by the wayside the fallen log on which they had rested a few evenings before, she went and sat down on it in impatient resignation, and looked at Longmore, as he stood silent, watching her, with a glance which seemed to urge that, if she was charitable now, he must be very wise.

"Something came to my knowledge yesterday," he said as he sat down beside her, "which gave me a supreme sense of your moral isolation. You are truth itself, and there is no truth about you. You believe in purity and duty and dignity, and you live in a world in which they are daily belied. I some-times ask myself with a kind of rage how you ever came into such a world,—and why the perversity of fate never let me know you before."

"I like my 'world' no better than you do, and it was not for its own sake I came into it. But what particular group of

people is worth pinning one's faith upon? I confess it sometimes seems to me that men and women are very poor
creatures. I suppose I'm romantic. I have a most unfortunate
taste for poetic fitness. Life is hard prose, which one must
learn to read contentedly. I believe I once thought that all the
prose was in America, which was very foolish. What I thought,
what I believed, what I expected, when I was an ignorant girl,
fatally addicted to falling in love with my own theories, is
more than I can begin to tell you now. Sometimes, when I
remember certain impulses, certain illusions of those days,
they take away my breath, and I wonder my bedazzled
visions didn't lead me into troubles greater than any I have
now to lament. I had a conviction which you would probably
smile at if I were to attempt to express it to you. It was a
singular form for passionate faith to take, but it had all of the
sweetness and the ardor of passionate faith. It led me to take
a great step, and it lies behind me now in the distance like a
a shadow melting slowly in the light of experience. It has
faded, but it has not vanished. Some feelings, I am sure, die
only with ourselves; some illusions are as much the condition
of our life as our heart-beats. They say that life itself is an
illusion,—that this world is a shadow of which the reality is
yet to come. Life is all of a piece, then, and there is no shame in
being miserably human. As for my 'isolation,' it doesn't
greatly matter; it's the fault, in part, of my obstinacy. There
have been times when I have been frantically distressed, and,
to tell you the truth, wretchedly homesick, because my maid
—a jewel of a maid—lied to me with every second breath.
There have been moments when I have wished I was the
daughter of a poor New England minister, living in a little white
house under a couple of elms, and doing all the housework."

She had begun to speak slowly, with an air of effort; but
she went on quickly, as if talking were a relief. "My marriage
introduced me to people and things which seemed to me at
first very strange and then very horrible, and then, to tell the

truth, very contemptible. At first I expended a great deal of sorrow and dismay and pity on it all; but there soon came a time when I began to wonder whether it was worth one's tears. If I could tell you the eternal friendships I've seen broken, the inconsolable woes consoled, the jealousies and vanities leading off the dance, you would agree with me that tempers like yours and mine can understand neither such losses nor such compensations. A year ago, while I was in the country, a friend of mine was in despair at the infidelity of her husband; she wrote me a most tragical letter, and on my return to Paris I went immediately to see her. A week had elapsed, and, as I had seen stranger things, I thought she might have recovered her spirits. Not at all; she was still in despair,—but at what? At the conduct, the abandoned, shameless conduct of Mme de T. You'll imagine, of course, that Mme de T. was the lady whom my friend's husband preferred to his wife. Far from it; he had never seen her. Who, then, was Mme de T.? Mme de T. was cruelly devoted to M. de V. And who was M. de V.? M. de V.—in two words, my friend was cultivating two jealousies at once. I hardly know what I said to her; something, at any rate, that she found unpardonable, for she quite gave me up. Shortly afterward my husband proposed we should cease to live in Paris, and I gladly assented, for I believe I was falling into a state of mind that made me a detestable companion. I should have preferred to go quite into the country, into Auvergne, where my husband has a place. But to him Paris, in some degree, is necessary, and Saint-Germain has been a sort of compromise."

"A sort of compromise!" Longmore repeated. "That's your whole life."

"It's the life of many people, of most people of quiet tastes, and it is certainly better than acute distress. One is at loss theoretically to defend a compromise; but if I found a poor creature clinging to one from day to day, I should think it poor friendship to make him lose his hold." Madame de

Mauves had no sooner uttered these words than she smiled faintly, as if to mitigate their personal application.

"Heaven forbid," said Longmore, "that one should do that unless one has something better to offer. And yet I am haunted by a vision of a life in which you should have found no compromises, for they are a perversion of natures that tend only to goodness and rectitude. As I see it, you should have found happiness serene, profound, complete; a *femme de chambre* not a jewel perhaps, but warranted to tell but one fib a day; a society possibly rather provincial, but (in spite of your poor opinion of mankind) a good deal of solid virtue; jealousies and vanities very tame, and no particular iniquities and adulteries. A husband," he added after a moment,—"a husband of your own faith and race and spiritual substance, who would have loved you well."

She rose to her feet, shaking her head. "You are very kind to go to the expense of visions for me. Visions are vain things; we must make the best of the reality."

"And yet," said Longmore, provoked by what seemed the very wantonness of her patience, "the reality, if I'm not mistaken, has very recently taken a shape that keenly tests your philosophy."

She seemed on the point of replying that his sympathy was too zealous; but a couple of impatient tears in his eyes proved that it was founded on a devotion to which it was impossible not to defer. "Philosophy?" she said. "I have none. Thank Heaven!" she cried, with vehemence, "I have none. I believe, Mr Longmore," she added in a moment, "that I have nothing on earth but a conscience,—it's a good time to tell you so,—nothing but a dogged, clinging, inexpugnable conscience. Does that prove me to be indeed of your faith and race, and have you one for which you can say as much? I don't say it in vanity, for I believe that if my conscience will prevent me from doing anything very base, it will effectually prevent me from doing anything very fine."

"I am delighted to hear it," cried Longmore. "We are made for each other. It's very certain I too shall never do anything fine. And yet I have fancied that in my case this inexpugnable organ you so eloquently describe might be blinded and gagged awhile, in a fine cause, if not turned out of doors. In yours," he went on with the same appealing irony, "is it absolutely invincible?"

But her fancy made no concession to his sarcasm. "Don't laugh at your conscience," she answered gravely; "that's the only blasphemy I know."

She had hardly spoken when she turned suddenly at an unexpected sound, and at the same moment Longmore heard a footstep in an adjacent by-path which crossed their own at a short distance from where they stood.

"It's M. de Mauves," said Euphemia directly, and moved slowly forward. Longmore, wondering how she knew it, had overtaken her by the time her husband advanced into sight. A solitary walk in the forest was a pastime to which M. de Mauves was not addicted, but he seemed on this occasion to have resorted to it with some equanimity. He was smoking a fragrant cigar, and his thumb was thrust into the armhole of his waistcoat, with an air of contemplative serenity. He stopped short with surprise on seeing his wife and her companion, and Longmore considered his surprise impertinent. He glanced rapidly from one to the other, fixed Longmore's eye sharply for a single instant, and then lifted his hat with formal politeness.

"I was not aware," he said, turning to Madame de Mauves, "that I might congratulate you on the return of monsieur."

"You should have known it," she answered gravely, "if I had expected Mr Longmore's return."

She had become very pale, and Longmore felt that this was a first meeting after a stormy parting. "My return was unexpected to myself," he said. "I came last evening."

M. de Mauves smiled with extreme urbanity. "It's needless

for me to welcome you. Madame de Mauves knows the duties
of hospitality." And with another bow he continued his walk.

Madame de Mauves and her companion returned slowly
home, with few words, but, on Longmore's part at least, many
thoughts. The Baron's appearance had given him an angry
chill; it was a dusky cloud reabsorbing the light which had
begun to shine between himself and his companion.

He watched Euphemia narrowly as they went, and wondered what she had last had to suffer. Her husband's presence
had checked her frankness, but nothing indicated that she had
accepted the insulting meaning of his words. Matters were
evidently at a crisis between them, and Longmore wondered
vainly what it was on Euphemia's part that prevented an
absolute rupture. What did she suspect?—how much did she
know? To what was she resigned?—how much had she for-
given? How, above all, did she reconcile with knowledge, or
with suspicion, that ineradicable tenderness of which she had
just now all but assured him? "She has loved him once,"
Longmore said with a sinking of the heart, "and with her to
love once is to commit one's being forever. Her husband
thinks her too rigid! What would a poet call it?"

He relapsed with a kind of aching impotence into the sense
of her being somehow beyond him, unattainable, immeasurable by his own fretful spirit. Suddenly he gave three passionate switches in the air with his cane, which made Madame de
Mauves look round. She could hardly have guessed that they
meant that where ambition was so vain, it was an innocent
compensation to plunge into worship.

Madame de Mauves found in her drawing-room the little
elderly Frenchman, M. de Chalumeau, whom Longmore had
observed a few days before on the terrace. On this occasion,
too, Madame Clairin was entertaining him, but as his sister-in-
law came in she surrendered her post and addressed herself to
our hero. Longmore, at thirty, was still an ingenuous youth,
and there was something in this lady's large coquetry which

had the power of making him blush. He was surprised at finding he had not absolutely forfeited her favor by his deportment at their last interview, and a suspicion of her meaning to approach him on another line completed his uneasiness.

"So you've returned from Brussels," she said, "by way of the forest."

"I've not been to Brussels. I returned yesterday from Paris by the only way,—by the train."

Madame Clairin stared and laughed. "I've never known a young man to be so fond of Saint-Germain. They generally declare it's horribly dull."

"That's not very polite to you," said Longmore, who was vexed at his blushes, and determined not to be abashed.

"Ah, what am I?" demanded Madame Clairin, swinging open her fan. "I'm the dullest thing here. They've not had your success with my sister-in-law."

"It would have been very easy to have it. Madame de Mauves is kindness itself."

"To her own countrymen!"

Longmore remained silent; he hated the talk. Madame Clairin looked at him a moment, and then turned her head and surveyed Euphemia, to whom M. de Chalumeau was serving up another epigram, which she was receiving with a slight droop of the head and her eyes absently wandering through the window. "Don't pretend to tell me," she murmured suddenly, "that you're not in love with that pretty woman."

"*Allons donc!*" cried Longmore, in the best French he had ever uttered. He rose the next minute, and took a hasty farewell.

VI

HE allowed several days to pass without going back; it seemed delicate not to appear to regard his friend's frankness during their last interview as a general invitation. This cost him a great effort, for hopeless passions are not the most deferential; and he had, moreover, a constant fear, that if, as he believed, the hour of supreme "explanations" had come, the magic of her magnanimity might convert M. de Mauves. Vicious men, it was abundantly recorded, had been so converted as to be acceptable to God, and the something divine in Euphemia's temper would sanctify any means she should choose to employ. Her means, he kept repeating, were no business of his, and the essence of his admiration ought to be to respect her freedom; but he felt as if he should turn away into a world out of which most of the joy had departed, if her freedom, after all, should spare him only a murmured "Thank you."

When he called again he found to his vexation that he was to run the gantlet of Madame Clairin's officious hospitality. It was one of the first mornings of perfect summer, and the drawing-room, through the open windows, was flooded with a sweet confusion of odors and bird-notes which filled him with the hope that Madame de Mauves would come out and spend half the day in the forest. But Madame Clairin, with her hair not yet dressed, emerged like a brassy discord in a maze of melody.

At the same moment the servant returned with Euphemia's regrets; she was indisposed and unable to see Mr Longmore. The young man knew that he looked disappointed, and that Madame Clairin was observing him, and this consciousness impelled her to give him a glance of almost aggressive frigidity. This was apparently what she desired. She wished to throw him him off his balance, and, if he was not mistaken, she had the means.

"Put down your hat, Mr Longmore," she said, "and be polite for once. You were not at all polite the other day when I asked you that friendly question about the state of your heart."

"I have no heart—to talk about," said Longmore, uncompromisingly.

"As well say you've none at all. I advise you to cultivate a little eloquence; you may have use for it. That was not an idle question of mine; I don't ask idle questions. For a couple of months now that you've been coming and going among us, it seems to me that you have had very few to answer of any sort."

"I have certainly been very well treated," said Longmore.

Madame Clairin was silent a moment, and then—"Have you never felt disposed to ask any?" she demanded.

Her look, her tone, were so charged with roundabout meanings that it seemed to Longmore as if even to understand her would savor of dishonest complicity. "What is it you have to tell me?" he asked, frowning and blushing.

Madame Clairin flushed. It is rather hard, when you come bearing yourself very much as the sibyl when she came to the Roman king, to be treated as something worse than a vulgar gossip. "I might tell you, Mr Longmore," she said, "that you have as bad a *ton* as any young man I ever met. Where have you lived,—what are your ideas? I wish to call your attention to a fact which it takes some delicacy to touch upon. You have noticed, I supposed, that my sister-in-law is not the happiest woman in the world."

Longmore assented with a gesture.

Madame Clairin looked slightly disappointed at his want of enthusiasm. Nevertheless—"You have formed, I suppose," she continued, "your conjectures on the causes of her—dissatisfaction."

"Conjecture has been superfluous. I have seen the causes—or at least a specimen of them—with my own eyes."

"I know perfectly what you mean. My brother, in a single word, is in love with another woman. I don't judge him; I don't judge my sister-in-law. I permit myself to say that in her position I would have managed otherwise. I would have kept my husband's affection, or I would have frankly done without it, before this. But my sister is an odd compound; I don't profess to understand her. Therefore it is, in a measure, that I appeal to you, her fellow-countryman. Of course you'll be surprised at my way of looking at the matter, and I admit that it's a way in use only among people whose family traditions compel them to take a superior view of things." Madame Clairin paused, and Longmore wondered where her family traditions were going to lead her.

"Listen," she went on. "There has never been a De Mauves who has not given his wife the right to be jealous. We know our history for ages back, and the fact is established. It's a shame if you like, but it's something to have a shame with such a pedigree. The De Mauves are real Frenchmen, and their wives—I may say it—have been worthy of them. You may see all their portraits in our Château de Mauves; every one of them an 'injured' beauty, but not one of them hanging her head. Not one of them had the bad taste to be jealous, and yet not one in a dozen was guilty of an escapade,—not one of them was talked about. There's good sense for you! How they managed—go and look at the dusky, faded canvases and pastels, and ask. They were femmes d'esprit. When they had a headache, they put on a little rouge and came to supper as usual; and when they had a heart-ache, they put a little rouge on their hearts. These are fine traditions, and it doesn't seem to me fair that a little American bourgeoise should come in and interrupt them, and should hang her photograph, with her obstinate little *air penché*, in the gallery of our shrewd fine ladies. A De Mauves must be a De Mauves. When she married

M

my brother, I don't suppose she took him for a member of a *societé de bonnes œuvres*. I don't say we're right; who is right? But we're as history has made us, and if any one is to change, it had better be Madame de Mauves herself."Again Madame Clairin paused and opened and closed her fan. "Let her conform!" she said, with amazing audacity.

Longmore's reply was ambiguous; he simply said, "Ah!"

Madame Clairin's pious retrospect had apparently imparted an honest zeal to her indignation. "For a long time," she continued, "my sister has been taking the attitude of an injured woman, affecting a disgust with the world, and shutting herself up to read the 'Imitation.' I've never remarked on her conduct, but I've quite lost patience with it. When a woman with her prettiness lets her husband wander, she deserves her fate. I don't wish you to agree with me—on the contrary; but I call such a woman a goose. She must have bored him to death. What has passed between them for many months needn't concern us; what provocation my sister has had—monstrous, if you wish—what ennui my brother has suffered. It's enough that a week ago, just after you had ostensibly gone to Brussels, something happened to produce an explosion. She found a letter in his pocket—a photograph —a trinket—*que sais-je?* At any rate, the scene was terrible. I didn't listen at the keyhole, and I don't know what was said; but I have reason to believe that my brother was called to account as I fancy none of his ancestors have ever been,— even by injured sweethearts."

Longmore had leaned forward in silent attention with his elbows on his knees, and instinctively he dropped his face into his hands. "Ah, poor woman!" he groaned.

"Voilà!" said Madame Clairin. "You pity her."

"Pity her?" cried Longmore, looking up with ardent eyes and forgetting the spirit of Madame Clairin's narrative in the miserable facts. "Don't you?"

"A little. But I'm not acting sentimentally; I'm acting politically. I wish to arrange things,—to see my brother free to do as he chooses,—to see Euphemia contented. Do you understand me?"

"Very well, I think. You're the most immoral person I've lately had the privilege of conversing with."

Madame Clairin shrugged her shoulders. "Possibly. When was there a great politician who was not immoral?"

"Nay," said Longmore in the same tone. "You're too superficial to be a great politician. You don't begin to know anything about Madame de Mauves."

Madame Clairin inclined her head to one side, eyed Longmore sharply, mused a moment, and then smiled with an excellent imitation of intelligent compassion. "It's not in my interest to contradict you."

"It would be in your interest to learn, Madame Clairin," the young man went on with unceremonious candor, "what honest men most admire in a woman,—and to recognize it when you see it."

Longmore certainly did injustice to her talents for diplomacy, for she covered her natural annoyance at this sally with a pretty piece of irony. "So you *are* in love!" she quietly exclaimed.

Longmore was silent awhile. "I wonder if you would understand me," he said at last, "if I were to tell you that I have for Madame de Mauves the most devoted friendship?"

"You underrate my intelligence. But in that case you ought to exert your influence to put an end to these painful domestic scenes."

"Do you suppose," cried Longmore, "that she talks to me about her domestic scenes?"

Madame Clairin stared. "Then your friendship isn't returned?" And as Longmore turned away, shaking his head,— "Now, at least," she added, "she will have something to tell you. I happen to know the upshot of my brother's last interview with his wife." Longmore rose to his feet as a sort of protest against the indelicacy of the position into which he was being forced; but all that made him tender made him curious, and she caught in his averted eyes an expression which prompted her to strike her blow. "My brother is monstrously in love with a certain person in Paris; of course he ought not to be; but he wouldn't be a De Mauves if he were not. It was this unsanctified passion that spoke. 'Listen, madam,' he cried at last: 'let us live like people who understand life! It's unpleasant to be forced to say such things outright, but you have a way of bringing one down to the rudiments. I'm faithless, I'm heartless, I'm brutal, I'm everything horrible,—it's understood. Take your revenge, console yourself; you're too pretty a woman to have anything to complain of. Here's a handsome young man sighing himself into a consumption for you. Listen to the poor fellow, and you'll find that virtue is none the less becoming for being goodnatured. You'll see that it's not after all such a doleful world, and that there is even an advantage in having the most impudent of husbands.' " Madame Clairin paused; Longmore had turned very pale. "You may believe it," she said; "the speech took place in my presence; things were done in order. And now, Mr Longmore,"—this with a smile which he was too troubled at the moment to appreciate, but which he remembered later with a kind of awe,—"we count upon you!"

"He said this to her, face to face, as you say it to me now?" Longmore asked slowly, after a silence.

"Word for word, and with the greatest politeness."

"And Madame de Mauves—what did she say?"

Madame Clairin smiled again. "To such a speech as that a woman says—nothing. She had been sitting with a piece of needlework, and I think she had not seen her husband since their quarrel the day before. He came in with the gravity of an ambassador, and I'm sure that when he made his *demande en mariage* his manner was not more respectful. He only wanted white gloves!" said Madame Clairin. "Euphemia sat silent a few moments drawing her stitches, and then without a word, without a glance, she walked out of the room. It was just what she should have done!"

"Yes," Longmore repeated, "it was just what she should have done."

"And I, left alone with my brother, do you know what I said?"

Longmore shook his head. "*Mauvais sujet!*" he suggested.

" 'You've done me the honor,' I said, 'to take this step in my presence. I don't pretend to qualify it. You know what you're about, and it's your own affair. But you may confide in my discretion.' Do you think he has had reason to complain of it?" She received no answer; Longmore was slowly turning away and passing his gloves mechanically round the band of his hat. "I hope," she cried, "you're not going to start for Brussels!"

Plainly, Longmore was deeply disturbed, and Madame Clairin might flatter herself on the success of her plea for old-fashioned manners. And yet there was something that left her more puzzled than satisfied in the reflective tone with which he answered, "No, I shall remain here for the present," The processes of his mind seemed provokingly subterranean, and she would have fancied for a moment that he was linked with her sister in some monstrous conspiracy of asceticism.

"Come this evening," she boldly resumed. "The rest will take care of itself. Meanwhile I shall take the liberty of telling my sister-in-law that I have repeated—in short, that I have put you *au fait*."

Longmore started and colored, and she hardly knew whether he was going to assent or demur. "Tell her what you please. Nothing you can tell her will affect her conduct."

"Voyons! Do you mean to tell me that a woman, young, pretty, sentimental, neglected—insulted, if you will— ? I see you don't believe it. Believe simply in your own opportunity! But for heaven's sake, if it's to lead anywhere, don't come back with that *visage de croquemort*. You look as if you were going to bury your heart,—not to offer it to a pretty woman. You're much better when you smile. Come, do yourself justice."

"Yes," he said, "I must do myself justice." And abruptly, with a bow, he took his departure.

VII

HE felt, when he found himself unobserved, in the open air, that he must plunge into violent action, walk fast and far, and defer the opportunity for thought. He strode away into the forest, swinging his cane, throwing back his head, gazing away into the verdurous vistas, and following the road without a purpose. He felt immensely excited, but he could hardly have said whether his emotion was a pain or a joy. It was joyous as all increase of freedom is joyous; something seemed to have been knocked down across his path; his destiny appeared to have rounded a cape and brought him into sight of an open sea. But his freedom resolved itself somehow into the need of despising all mankind, with a single exception; and the fact of Madame de Mauves inhabiting a planet contaminated by the presence of this baser multitude kept his elation from seeming a pledge of ideal bliss.

But she was there, and circumstance now forced them to be intimate. She had ceased to have what men call a secret for him, and this fact itself brought with it a sort of rapture. He had no prevision that he should "profit," in the vulgar sense, by the extraordinary position into which they had been thrown; it might be but a cruel trick of destiny to make hope a harsher mockery and renunciation a keener suffering. But above all this rose the conviction that she could do nothing that would not deepen his admiration.

It was this feeling that circumstance—unlovely as it was

in itself—was to force the beauty of her character into more perfect relief, that made him stride along as if he were celebrating a kind of spiritual festival He rambled at random for a couple of hours, and found at last that he had left the forest behind him and had wandered into an unfamiliar region. It was a perfectly rural scene, and the still summer day gave it a charm for which its meagre elements but half accounted.

Longmore thought he had never seen anything so characteristically French; all the French novels seemed to have described it, all the French landscapists to have painted it. The fields and trees were of a cool metallic green; the grass looked as if it might stain your trousers, and the foliage your hands. The clear light had a sort of mild grayness; the sunbeams were of silver rather than gold. A great red-roofed, high-stacked farm-house, with whitewashed walls and a straggling yard, surveyed the high road, on one side, from behind a transparent curtain of poplars. A narrow stream, half choked with emerald rushes and edged with gray aspens, occupied the opposite quarter. The meadows rolled and sloped away gently to the low horizon, which was barely concealed by the continuous line of clipped and marshalled trees. The prospect was not rich, but it had a frank homeliness which touched the young man's fancy. It was full of light atmosphere and diffused sunshine, and if it was prosaic, it was soothing.

Longmore was disposed to walk further, and he advanced along the road beneath the poplars. In twenty minutes he came to a village which straggled away to the right, among orchards and *potagers*. On the left, at a stone's throw from the road, stood a little pink-faced inn, which reminded him that he had not breakfasted, having left home with a prevision of hospitality from Madame de Mauves. In the inn he found a brick-tiled parlor and a hostess in sabots and a white cap, whom, over the omelette she speedily served him,—borrowing license from the bottle of sound red wine which accompanied it,—he assured that she was a true artist. To reward his compliment, she invited him to smoke his cigar in her little garden behind the house.

Here he found a *tonnelle* and a view of ripening crops, stretching down to the stream. The tonnelle was rather close, and he preferred to lounge on a bench against the pink wall, in the sun, which was not too hot. Here, as he rested and gazed and mused, he fell into a train of thought which, in an indefinable fashion, was a soft influence from the scene about him. His heart, which had been beating fast for the past three hours, gradually checked its pulses and left him looking at life with a rather more level gaze. The homely tavern sounds coming out through the open windows, the sunny stillness of the fields and crops, which covered so much vigorous natural life, suggested very little that was transcendental, had very little to say about renunciation,—nothing at all about spiritual zeal. They seemed to utter a message from plain ripe nature, to express the unperverted reality of things, to say that the common lot is not brilliantly amusing, and that the part of wisdom is to grasp frankly at experience, lest you miss it altogether. What reason there was for his falling a-wondering after this whether a deeply wounded heart might be soothed and healed by such a scene, it would be difficult to explain; certain it is that, as he sat there, he had a waking dream of an unhappy woman strolling by the slow-flowing stream before him, and pulling down the blossoming boughs in the orchards. He mused and mused, and at last found himself feeling angry that he could not somehow think worse of Madame de Mauves,— or at any rate think otherwise. He could fairly claim that in a sentimental way he asked very little of life,—he made modest demands on passion; why then should his only passion be born to ill-fortune? why should his first—his last—glimpse of positive happiness be so indissolubly linked with renunciation?

It is perhaps because, like many spirits of the same stock, he had in his composition a lurking principle of asceticism to whose authority he had ever paid an unquestioning respect, that he now felt all the vehemence of rebellion. To renounce—to renounce again—to renounce forever—was this all that youth and longing and resolve were meant for? Was experience to be muffled and mutilated, like an indecent picture? Was a man to sit and deliberately condemn his future to be the blank memory of a regret, rather than the long reverberation of a joy? Sacrifice? The word was a trap for minds muddled by fear, an ignoble refuge of weakness. To insist now seemed not to dare, but simply to be, to live on possible terms.

His hostess came out to hang a cloth to dry on the hedge, and, though her guest was sitting quietly enough, she seemed to see in his kindled eyes a flattering testimony to the quality of her wine.

As she turned back into the house, she was met by a young man whom Longmore observed in spite of his preoccupation. He was evidently a member of that jovial fraternity of artists whose very shabbiness has an affinity with the element of picturesqueness and unexpectedness in life which provokes a great deal of unformulated envy among people foredoomed to be respectable.

Longmore was struck first with his looking like a very clever man, and then with his looking like a very happy one. The combination, as it was expressed in his face, might have arrested the attention of even a less cynical philosopher. He had a slouched hat and a blond beard, a light easel under one arm, and an unfinished sketch in oils under the other.

He stopped and stood talking for some moments to the landlady with a peculiarly good-humored smile. They were discussing the possibilities of dinner; the hostess enumerated some very savory ones, and he nodded briskly, assenting to everything. It couldn't be, Longmore thought, that he found such soft contentment in the prospect of lamb chops and spinach and a *tarte à la crême*. When the dinner had been ordered, he turned up his sketch, and the good woman fell a-wondering and looking off at the spot by the stream-side where he had made it.

Was it his work, Longmore wondered, that made him so happy? Was a strong talent the best thing in the world? The landlady went back to her kitchen, and the young painter stood as if he were waiting for something, beside the gate which opened upon the path across the fields. Longmore sat brooding and asking himself whether it was better to cultivate an art than to cultivate a passion. Before he had answered the question the painter had grown tired of waiting. He picked up a pebble, tossed it lightly into an upper window, and called, "Claudine!"

Claudine appeared; Longmore heard her at the window, bidding the young man to have patience. "But I'm losing my light," he said; "I must have my shadows in the same place as yesterday."

"Go without me, then," Claudine answered; "I will join you in ten minutes." Her voice was fresh and young; it seemed to say to Longmore that she was as happy as her companion.

"Don't forget the Chénier," cried the young man; and turning away, he passed out of the gate and followed the path across the fields until he disappeared among the trees by the side of the stream. Who was Claudine? Longmore vaguely wondered; and was she as pretty as her voice? Before long he had a chance to satisfy himself; she came out of the house with her hat and parasol, prepared to follow her companion. She had on a pink muslin dress and a little white hat, and she was as pretty as a Frenchwoman needs to be to be pleasing. She had a clear brown skin and a bright dark eye, and a step which seemed to keep time to some slow music, heard only by herself. Her hands were encumbered with various articles which she seemed to intend to carry with her. In one arm she held her parasol and a large roll of needlework, and in the other a shawl and a heavy white umbrella, such as painters use for sketching. Meanwhile she was trying to thrust into her pocket a paper-covered volume which Longmore saw to be the Poems of André Chénier; but in the effort she dropped the large umbrella, and uttered a half-smiling exclamation of disgust. Longmore stepped forward with a bow and picked up the umbrella, and as she, protesting her gratitude, put out her hand to take it, it seemed to him that she was unbecomingly overburdened.

"You have too much to carry," he said; "you must let me help you."

"You're very good, monsieur," she answered. "My husband always forgets something. He can do nothing without his umbrella. He is *d'une étourderie*—"

"You must allow me to carry the umbrella," Longmore said. "It's too heavy for a lady."

She assented, after many compliments to his politeness; and he walked by her side into the meadow. She went lightly and rapidly, picking her steps and glancing forward to catch a glimpse of her husband. She was graceful, she was charming, she had an air of decision and yet of sweetness, and it seemed to Longmore that a young artist would work none the worse for having her seated at his side, reading Chénier's iambics. They were newly married, he supposed, and evidently their path of life had none of the mocking crookedness of some others. They asked little; but what need one ask more than such quiet summer days, with the creature one loves, by a shady stream, with art and books and a wide, unshadowed horizon? To spend such a morning, to stroll back to dinner in the red-tiled parlor of the inn, to ramble away again as the sun got low,—all this was a vision of bliss which floated before him, only to torture him with a sense of the impossible. All Frenchwomen are not coquettes, he remarked, as he kept pace with his companion. She uttered a word now and then, for politeness' sake, but she never looked at him, and seemed not in the least to care that he was a well-favored young man.

She cared for nothing but the young artist in the shabby coat and the slouched hat, and for discovering where he had set up his easel.

This was soon done. He was encamped under the trees, close to the stream, and, in the diffused green shade of the little wood, seemed to be in no immediate need of his umbrella. He received a vivacious rebuke, however, for forgetting it, and was informed of what he owed to Longmore's complaisance. He was duly grateful; he thanked our hero warmly, and offered him a seat on the grass. But Longmore felt like a marplot, and lingered only long enough to glance at the young man's sketch, and to see it was a very clever rendering of the silvery stream and the vivid green rushes. The young wife had spread her shawl on the grass at the base of a tree, and meant to seat herself when Longmore had gone, and murmur Chénier's verses to the music of the gurgling river. Longmore looked awhile from one to the other, barely stifled a sigh, bade them good morning, and took his departure.

He knew neither where to go nor what to do; he seemed afloat on the sea of ineffectual longing. He strolled slowly back to the inn, and in the doorway met the landlady coming back from the butcher's with the lamb chops for the dinner of her lodgers.

"Monsieur has made the acquaintance of the *dame* of our young painter," she said with a broad smile,—a smile too broad for malicious meanings. "Monsieur has perhaps seen the young man's picture. It appears that he has a great deal of talent."

"His picture was very pretty," said Longmore, "but his *dame* was prettier still."

"She's a very nice little woman; but I pity her all the more."

"I don't see why she's to be pitied," said Longmore; "they seem a very happy couple."

The landlady gave a knowing nod.

"Don't trust to it, monsieur! Those artists,—*ça n'a pas de principes!* From one day to another he can plant her there! I know them, *allez*. I've had them here very often; one year with one, another year with another."

Longmore was puzzled for a moment. Then, "You mean she's not his wife?" he asked.

She shrugged her shoulders. "What shall I tell you? They are not *des hommes sérieux*, those gentlemen! They don't engage themselves for an eternity. It's none of my business, and I've no wish to speak ill of madame. She's a very nice little woman, and she loves her *jeune homme* to distraction."

"Who is she?" asked Longmore. "What do you know about her?"

"Nothing for certain; but it's my belief that she's better than he. I've even gone so far as to believe that she's a lady,— a true lady,—and that she has given up a great many things for him. I do the best I can for them, but I don't believe she's been obliged all her life to content herself with a dinner of two courses." And she turned over her lamb chops tenderly, as if to say that though a good cook could imagine better things, yet if you could have but one course, lamb chops had much in their favor. "I shall cook them with bread crumbs. *Voilà les femmes, monsieur!*"

Longmore turned away with the feeling that women were indeed a measureless mystery, and that it was hard to say whether there was greater beauty in their strength or in their weakness. He walked back to Saint-Germain, more slowly than he had come, with less philosophic resignation to any event, and more of the urgent egotism of the passion which philosophers call the supremely selfish one. Every now and then the episode of the happy young painter and the charming woman who had given up a great many things for him rose vividly in his mind, and seemed to mock his moral unrest like some obtrusive vision of unattainable bliss.

The landlady's gossip cast no shadow on its brightness; her

voice seemed that of the vulgar chorus of the uninitiated, which stands always ready with its gross prose rendering of the inspired passages in human action. Was it possible a man could take *that* from a woman,—take all that lent lightness to that other woman's footstep and intensity to her glance,—and not give her the absolute certainty of a devotion as unalterable as the process of the sun? Was it possible that such a rapturous union had the seeds of trouble,—that the charm of such a perfect accord could be broken by anything but death? Longmore felt an immense desire to cry out a thousand times "No!" for it seemed to him at last that he was somehow spiritually the same as the young painter, and that the latter's companion had the soul of Euphemia de Mauves.

The heat of the sun, as he walked along, became oppressive and when he re-entered the forest he turned aside into the deepest shade he could find, and stretched himself on the mossy ground at the foot of a great beech. He lay for a while staring up into the verdurous dusk overhead, and trying to conceive Madame de Mauves hastening toward some quiet stream-side where he waited, as he had seen that trusting creature do an hour before. It would be hard to say how well he succeeded; but the effort soothed him rather than excited him, and as he had had a good deal both of moral and physical fatigue, he sank at last into a quiet sleep.

While he slept he had a strange, vivid dream. He seemed to be in a wood, very much like the one on which his eyes had lately closed; but the wood was divided by the murmuring stream he had left an hour before. He was walking up and down, he thought, restlessly and in intense expectation of some momentous event. Suddenly, at a distance, through the trees, he saw the gleam of a woman's dress, and hurried forward to meet her. As he advanced he recognized her, but he saw at the same time that she was on the opposite bank of the river. She seemed at first not to notice him, but when they were opposite each other she stopped and looked at him very gravely and pityingly. She made him no motion that he should cross the stream, but he wished greatly to stand by her side. He knew the water was deep, and it seemed to him that he knew that he should have to plunge, and that he feared that when he rose to the surface she would have disappeared. Nevertheless, he was going to plunge, when a boat turned into the current from above and came swiftly toward them, guided by an oarsman, who was sitting so that they could not see his face. He brought the boat to the bank where Longmore stood; the latter stepped in, and with a few strokes they touched the opposite shore. Longmore got out, and, though he was sure he had crossed the stream, Madame de Mauves was not there. He turned with a kind of agony and saw that now she was on the other bank,—the one he had left. She gave him a grave, silent glance, and walked away up the stream. The boat and the boatman resumed their course, but after going a short distance they stopped, and the boatman turned back and looked at the still divided couple. Then Longmore recognized him,—just as he had recognized him a few days before at the café in the Bois de Boulogne.

VIII

HE must have slept some time after he ceased dreaming, for he had no immediate memory of his dream. It came back to him later, after he had roused himself and had walked nearly home. No great ingenuity was needed to make it seem a rather striking allegory, and it haunted and oppressed him for the rest of the day. He took refuge, however, in his quickened conviction that the only sound policy in life is to grasp unsparingly at happiness; and it seemed no more than one of the vigorous measures dictated by such a policy, to return that evening to Madame de Mauves. And yet when he had decided

to do so, and had carefully dressed himself, he felt an irresistible nervous tremor which made it easier to linger at his open
window, wondering, with a strange mixture of dread and
desire, whether Madame Clairin had told her sister-in-law that
she had told him. . . . His presence now might be simply a
gratuitous cause of suffering; and yet his absence might seem
to imply that it was in the power of circumstances to make
them ashamed to meet each other's eyes. He sat a long time
with his head in his hands, lost in a painful confusion of hopes
and questionings. He felt at moments as if he could throttle
Madame Clairin, and yet he could not help asking himself
whether it was not possible that she might have done him a
service. It was late when he left the hotel, and as he entered the
gate of the other house his heart was beating so that he was
sure his voice would show it.

The servant ushered him into the drawing-room, which
was empty, with the lamp burning low. But the long windows
were open, and their light curtains swaying in a soft, warm
wind, and Longmore stepped out upon the terrace. There he
found Madame de Mauves alone, slowly pacing up and down.
She was dressed in white, very simply, and her hair was
arranged, not as she usually wore it, but in a single loose coil,
like that of a person unprepared for company.

She stopped when she saw Longmore, seemed slightly
startled, uttered an exclamation, and stood waiting for him to
speak. He looked at her, tried to say something, but found no
words. He knew it was awkward, it was offensive, to stand
silent, gazing; but he could not say what was suitable, and
he dared not say what he wished.

Her face was indistinct in the dim light, but he could see
that her eyes were fixed on him, and he wondered what they
expressed. Did they warn him, did they plead or did they confess to a sense of provocation? For an instant his head swam;
he felt as if it would make all things clear to stride forward
and fold her in his arms. But a moment later he was still

standing looking at her; he had not moved; he knew that she had spoken, but he had not understood her.

"You were here this morning," she continued, and now, slowly, the meaning of her words came to him. "I had a bad headache and had to shut myself up." She spoke in her usual voice.

Longmore mastered his agitation and answered her without betraying himself: "I hope you are better now."

"Yes, thank you, I'm better—much better."

He was silent a moment, and she moved away to a chair and seated herself. After a pause he followed her and stood before her, leaning against the balustrade of the terrace. "I hoped you might have been able to come out for the morning into the forest. I went alone; it was a lovely day, and I took a long walk."

"It was a lovely day," she said absently, and sat with her eyes lowered, slowly opening and closing her fan. Longmore, as he watched her, felt more and more sure that her sister-in-law had seen her since her interview with him; that her attitude toward him was changed. It was this same something that chilled the ardor with which he had come, or at least converted the dozen passionate speeches which kept rising to his lips into a kind of reverential silence. No, certainly, he could not clasp her to his arms now, any more than some early worshipper could have clasped the marble statue in his temple. But Longmore's statue spoke at last, with a full human voice, and even with a shade of human hesitation. She looked up, and it seemed to him that her eyes shone through the dusk.

"I'm very glad you came this evening," she said. "I have a particular reason for being glad. I half expected you, and yet I thought it possible you might not come."

"As I have been feeling all day," Longmore answered, "it was impossible I should not come. I have spent the day in thinking of you."

She made no immediate reply, but continued to open and

N

close her fan thoughtfully. At last,—"I have something to say to you," she said abruptly. "I want you to know to a certainty that I have a very high opinion of you." Longmore started and shifted his position. To what was she coming? But he said nothing, and she went on.

"I take a great interest in you; there's no reason why I should not say it,—I have a great friendship for you."

He began to laugh; he hardly knew why, unless that this seemed the very mockery of coldness. But she continued without heeding him.

"You know, I suppose, that a great disappointment always implies a great confidence—a great hope?"

"I have hoped," he said, "hoped strongly; but doubtless never rationally enough to have a right to bemoan my disappointment."

"You do yourself injustice. I have such confidence in your reason, that I should be greatly disappointed if I were to find it wanting."

"I really almost believe that you are amusing yourself at my expense," cried Longmore. "My reason? Reason is a mere word! The only reality in the world is *feeling!*"

She rose to her feet and looked at him gravely. His eyes by this time were accustomed to the imperfect light, and he could see that her look was reproachful, and yet that it was beseechingly kind. She shook her head impatiently, and laid her fan upon his arm with a strong pressure.

"If that were so, it would be a weary world. I know your feeling, however, nearly enough. You needn't try to express it. It's enough that it gives me the right to ask a favor of you, —to make an urgent, a solemn request."

"Make it; I listen."

"*Don't disappoint me.* If you don't understand me now, you will to-morrow, or very soon. When I said just now that I had a very high opinion of you, I meant it very seriously. It was not a vain compliment. I believe that there is no appeal one

may make to your generosity which can remain long unanswered. If this were to happen,—if I were to find you selfish
where I thought you generous, narrow where I thought you
large,"—and she spoke slowly, with her voice lingering with
emphasis on each of these words,—"vulgar where I thought
you rare,—I should think worse of human nature. I should
suffer,—I should suffer keenly. I should say to myself in the
dull days of the future, 'There was one man who might have
done so and so; and he, too, failed.' But this shall not be.
You have made too good an impression on me not to make
the very best. If you wish to please me forever, there's a
way."

She was standing close to him, with her dress touching
him, her eyes fixed on his. As she went on her manner grew
strangely intense, and she had the singular appearance of a
woman preaching reason with a kind of passion. Longmore
was confused, dazzled, almost bewildered. The intention of
her words was all remonstrance, refusal, dismissal; but her
presence there, so close, so urgent, so personal, seemed a distracting contradiction of it. She had never been so lovely. In
her white dress, with her pale face and deeply lighted eyes, she
seemed the very spirit of the summer night. When she had
ceased speaking, she drew a long breath; Longmore felt it on
his cheek, and it stirred in his whole being a sudden, rapturous conjecture. Were her words in their soft severity a
mere delusive spell, meant to throw into relief her almost
ghostly beauty, and was this the only truth, the only reality,
the only law?

He closed his eyes and felt that she was watching him, not
without pain and perplexity herself. He looked at her again,
met her own eyes, and saw a tear in each of them. Then this
last suggestion of his desire seemed to die away with a stifled
murmur, and her beauty, more and more radiant in the darkness, rose before him as a symbol of something vague which
was yet more beautiful than itself.

"I may understand you to-morrow," he said, "but I don't understand you now."

"And yet I took counsel with myself to-day and asked myself how I had best speak to you. On one side, I might have refused to see you at all." Longmore made a violent movement, and she added: "In that case I should have written to you. I might see you, I thought, and simply say to you that there were excellent reasons why we should part, and that I begged this visit should be your last. This I inclined to do; what made me decide otherwise was—simply friendship! I said to myself that I should be glad to remember in future days, not that I had dismissed you, but that you had gone away out of the fulness of your own wisdom."

"The fulness—the fulness!" cried Longmore.

"I'm prepared, if necessary," Madame de Mauves continued after a pause, "to fall back upon my strict right. But, as I said before, I shall be greatly disappointed, if I am obliged to."

"When I hear you say that," Longmore answered, "I feel so angry, so horribly irritated, that I wonder it is not easy to leave you without more words."

"If you should go away in anger, this idea of mine about our parting would be but half realized. No, I don't want to think of you as angry; I don't want even to think of you as making a serious sacrifice. I want to think of you as—"

"As a creature who never has existed,—who never can exist! A creature who knew you without loving you,—who left you without regretting you!"

She turned impatiently away and walked to the other end of the terrace. When she came back, he saw that her impatience had become a cold sternness. She stood before him again, looking at him from head to foot, in deep reproachfulness, almost in scorn. Beneath her glance he felt a kind of shame. He colored; she observed it and withheld something she was about to say. She turned away again, walked to the other end of the terrace, and stood there looking away into the garden.

It seemed to him that she had guessed he understood her, and slowly—slowly—half as the fruit of his vague self-reproach, —he did understand her. She was giving him a chance to do gallantly what it seemed unworthy of both of them he should do meanly.

She liked him, she must have liked him greatly, to wish so to spare him, to go to the trouble of conceiving an ideal of conduct for him. With this sense of her friendship,—her strong friendship she had just called it,—Longmore's soul rose with a new flight, and suddenly felt itself breathing a clearer air. The words ceased to seem a mere bribe to his ardor; they were charged with ardor themselves; they were a present happiness. He moved rapidly toward her with a feeling that this was something he might immediately enjoy.

They were separated by two thirds of the length of the terrace, and he had to pass the drawing-room window. As he did so he started with an exclamation. Madame Clairin stood posted there, watching him. Conscious, apparently, that she might be suspected of eavesdropping, she stepped forward with a smile and looked from Longmore to his hostess.

"Such a tête-à-tête as that," she said, "one owes no apology for interrupting. One ought to come in for good manners."

Madame de Mauves turned round, but she answered nothing. She looked straight at Longmore, and her eyes had extraordinary eloquence. He was not exactly sure, indeed, what she meant them to say; but they seemed to say plainly something of this kind; "Call it what you will, what you have to urge upon me is the thing which this woman can best conceive. What I ask of you is something she can't!" They seemed, somehow, to beg him to suffer her to be herself, and to intimate that that self was as little as possible like Madame Clairin. He felt an immense answering desire not to do anything which would seem natural to this lady. He had laid his hat and cane on the parapet of the terrace. He took them up, offered his hand to Madame de Mauves with a simple good night, bowed silently to Madame Clairin, and departed.

IX

HE went home and without lighting his candle flung himself on his bed. But he got no sleep till morning; he lay hour after hour tossing, thinking, wondering; his mind had never been so active. It seemed to him that Euphemia had laid on him in those last moments an inspiring commission, and that she had expressed herself almost as largely as if she had listened assentingly to an assurance of his love. It was neither easy nor delightful thoroughly to understand her; but little by little her perfect meaning sank into his mind and soothed it with a sense of opportunity, which somehow stifled his sense of loss. For, to begin with, she meant that she could love him in no degree nor contingency, in no imaginable future. This was absolute; he felt that he could alter it no more than he could transpose the constellations he lay gazing at through his open window. He wondered what it was, in the background of her life, that she grasped so closely: a sense of duty, unquenchable to the end? a love that no offence could trample out? "Good heavens!" he thought, "is the world so rich in the purest pearls of passion, that such tenderness as that can be wasted forever,—poured away without a sigh into bottomless darkness?" Had she, in spite of the detestable present, some precious memory which contained the germ of a shrinking hope? Was she prepared to submit to everything and yet to believe? Was it strength, was it weakness, was it a vulgar fear, was it conviction, conscience, constancy?

Longmore sank back with a sigh and an oppressive feeling that it was vain to guess at such a woman's motives. He only felt that those of Madame de Mauves were buried deep in her soul, and that they must be of some fine temper, not of a base one. He had a dim, overwhelming sense of a sort of invulnerable constancy being the supreme law of her character,—a constancy which still found a foothold among crumbling ruins. "She has loved once," he said to himself as he rose and wandered to his window; "that's forever. Yes, yes,—if she loved again she would be *common*." He stood for a long time looking out into the starlit silence of the town and the forest, and thinking of what life would have been if *his* constancy had met hers unpledged. But life was this, now, and he must live. It was living keenly to stand there with a petition from such a woman to revolve. He was not to disappoint her, he was to justify a conception which it had beguiled her weariness to shape. Longmore's imagination swelled; he threw back his head and seemed to be looking for Madame de Mauves's conception among the blinking, mocking stars. But it came to him rather on the mild night-wind, as it wandered in over the house-tops which covered the rest of so many heavy human hearts. What she asked he felt that she was asking, not for her own sake (she feared nothing, she needed nothing), but for that of his own happiness and his own character. He must assent to destiny. Why else was he young and strong, intelligent and resolute? He must not give it to her to reproach him with thinking that she had a moment's attention for his love, —to plead, to argue, to break off in bitterness; he must see everything from above, her indifference and his own ardor; he must prove his strength, he must do the handsome thing; he must decide that the handsome thing was to submit to the inevitable, to be supremely delicate, to spare her all pain, to stifle his passion, to ask no compensation, to depart without delay and try to believe that wisdom is its own reward. All this, neither more nor less, it was a matter of friendship with Madame de Mauves to expect of him. And what should he gain by it? He should have pleased her! . . . He flung himself on his bed again, fell asleep at last, and slept till morning.

Before noon the next day he had made up his mind that he would leave Saint-Germain at once. It seemed easier to leave without seeing her, and yet if he might ask a grain of "compensation," it would be five minutes face to face with her. He passed a restless day. Wherever he went he seemed to see her standing before him in the dusky halo of evening, and looking at him with an air of still negation more intoxicating than the most passionate self-surrender. He must certainly go, and yet it was hideously hard. He compromised and went to Paris to spend the rest of the day. He strolled along the boulevards and looked at the shops, sat awhile in the Tuileries gardens and looked at the shabby unfortunates for whom this only was nature and summer; but simply felt, as a result of it all, that it was a very dusty, dreary, lonely world into which Madame de Mauves was turning him away.

In a sombre mood he made his way back to the boulevards and sat down at a table on the great plain of hot asphalt, before a café. Night came on, the lamps were lighted, the tables near him found occupants, and Paris began to wear that peculiar evening look of hers which seems to say, in the flare of windows and theatre doors, and the muffled rumble of swift-rolling carriages, that this is no world for you unless you have your pockets lined and your scruples drugged. Longmore, however, had neither scruples nor desires; he looked at the swarming city for the first time with an easy sense of repaying its indifference. Before long a carriage drove up to the pavement directly in front of him, and remained standing for several minutes without its occupant getting out. It was one of those neat, plain coupés, drawn by a single powerful horse, in which one is apt to imagine a pale, handsome woman, buried among silk cushions, and yawning as she sees the gas-lamps glittering in the gutters. At last the door opened and out stepped M. de Mauves. He stopped and leaned on the window for some time, talking in an excited manner to a person within. At last he gave a nod and the carriage rolled away. He stood swinging his cane and looking up and down the boulevard, with the air of a man fumbling, as one may say, with the loose change of time. He turned toward the café and was apparently, for want of anything better worth his attention, about to seat himself at one of the tables, when he perceived Longmore. He wavered an instant, and then, without a change in his nonchalant gait, strolled toward him with a bow and a vague smile.

It was the first time they had met since their encounter in the forest after Longmore's false start for Brussels. Madame Clairin's revelations, as we may call them, had not made the Baron especially present to his mind; he had another office for his emotions than disgust. But as M. de Mauves came toward him he felt deep in his heart that he abhorred him. He noticed, however, for the first time, a shadow upon the Baron's cool placidity, and his delight at finding that somewhere at last the shoe pinched *him*, mingled with his impulse to be as exasperatingly impenetrable as possible, enabled him to return the other's greeting with all his own self-possession.

M. de Mauves sat down, and the two men looked at each other across the table, exchanging formal greetings which did little to make their mutual scrutiny seem gracious. Longmore had no reason to suppose that the Baron knew of his sister's revelations. He was sure that M. de Mauves cared very little about his opinions, and yet he had a sense that there was that in his eyes which would have made the Baron change color if keener suspicion had helped him to read it. M. de Mauves did not change color, but he looked at Longmore with a half-defiant intentness, which betrayed at once an irritating memory of the episode in the Bois de Boulogne, and such vigilant curiosity as was natural to a gentleman who had intrusted his "honor" to another gentleman's magnanimity,—or to his artlessness. It would appear that Longmore seemed to the Baron to possess these virtues in rather scantier measure than a few days before; for the cloud deepened on his face, and he turned away and frowned as he lighted a cigar.

The person in the coupé, Longmore thought, whether or no the same person as the heroine of the episode of the Bois de Boulogne, was not a source of unalloyed delight. Longmore had dark blue eyes, of admirable lucidity,—truth-telling eyes which had in his childhood always made his harshest taskmasters smile at his nursery fibs. An observer watching the two men, and knowing something of their relations, would certainly have said that what he saw in those eyes must not a little have puzzled and tormented M. de Mauves. They judged him, they mocked him, they eluded him, they threatened him, they triumphed over him, they treated him as no pair of eyes had ever treated him. The Baron's scheme had been to make no one happy but himself, and here was Longmore already, if looks were to be trusted, primed for an enterprise more inspiring than the finest of his own achievements. Was this candid young barbarian but a *faux bonhomme* after all? He had puzzled the Baron before, and this was once too often.

M. de Mauves hated to seem preoccupied, and he took up the evening paper to help himself to look indifferent. As he glanced over it he uttered some cold commonplace on the political situation, which gave Longmore an easy opportunity of replying by an ironical sally which made him seem for the moment aggressively at his ease. And yet our hero was far from being master of the situaion. The Baron's ill-humor did him good, so far as it pointed to a want of harmony with the lady in the coupé; but it disturbed him sorely as he began to suspect that it possibly meant jealousy of himself. It passed through his mind that jealousy is a passion with a double face, and that in some of its moods it bears a plausible likeness to affection. It recurred to him painfully that the Baron might grow ashamed of his political compact with his wife, and he felt that it would be far more tolerable in the future to think of his continued turpitude than of his repentance. The two men

sat for half an hour exchanging stinted small-talk, the Baron
feeling a nervous need of playing the spy, and Longmore in-
dulging a ferocious relish of his discomfort. These rigid cour-
tesies were interrupted however by the arrival of a friend of
M. de Mauves,—a tall, pale, consumptive-looking dandy,
who filled the air with the odor of heliotrope. He looked up
and down the boulevard wearily, examined the Baron's toilet
from head to foot, then surveyed his own in the same fashion,
and at last announced languidly that the Duchess was in
town! M. de Mauves must come with him to call; she had
abused him dreadfully a couple of evenings before,—a sure
sign she wanted to see him.

"I depend upon you," said M. de Mauves's friend with an
infantine drawl, "to put her *en train.*"

M. de Mauves resisted, and protested that he was *d'une
humeur massacrante;* but at last he allowed himself to be
drawn to his feet, and stood looking awkwardly—awkwardly
for M. de Mauves—at Longmore. "You'll excuse me," he said
dryly; "you, too, probably, have occupation for the evening?"

"None but to catch my train," Longmore answered, looking at his watch.

"Ah, you go back to Saint-Germain?"

"In half an hour."

M. de Mauves seemed on the point of disengaging himself
from his companion's arm, which was locked in his own; but
on the latter uttering some persuasive murmur, he lifted his
hat stiffly and turned away.

Longmore packed his trunk the next day with dogged
heroism and wandered off to the terrace, to try and beguile
the restlessness with which he waited for evening; for he
wished to see Madame de Mauves for the last time at the hour
of long shadows and pale pink-reflected lights, as he had
almost always seen her. Destiny, however, took no account of
this humble plea for poetic justice; it was his fortune to meet
her on the terrace sitting under a tree, alone. It was an hour

when the place was almost empty; the day was warm, but as he took his place beside her a light breeze stirred the leafy edges on the broad circle of shadow in which she sat. She looked at him with candid anxiety, and he immediately told her that he should leave Saint-Germain that evening,—that he must bid her farewell. Her eye expanded and brightened for a moment as he spoke; but she said nothing and turned her glance away toward distant Paris, as it lay twinkling and flashing through its hot exhalations. "I have a request to make of you," he added. "That you think of me as a man who has felt much and claimed little."

She drew a long breath, which almost suggested pain. "I can't think of you as unhappy. It's impossible. You have a life to lead, you have duties, talents, and interests. I shall hear of your career. And then," she continued after a pause and with the deepest seriousness, "one can't be unhappy through having a better opinion of a friend, instead of a worse."

For a moment he failed to understand her. "Do you mean that there can be varying degrees in my opinion of you?"

She rose and pushed away her chair. "I mean," she said quickly, "that it's better to have done nothing in bitterness,— nothing in passion," And she began to walk.

Longmore followed her, without answering. But he took off his hat and with his pocket-handkerchief wiped his forehead. "Where shall you go? what shall you do?" he asked at last, abruptly.

"Do? I shall do as I've always done,—except perhaps that I shall go for a while to Auvergne."

"I shall go to America. I have done with Europe for the present."

She glanced at him as he walked beside her after he had spoken these words, and then bent her eyes for a long time on the ground. At last, seeing that she was going far, she stopped and put out her hand. "Good by," she said; "may you have all the happiness you deserve!"

He took her hand and looked at her, but something was passing in him that made it impossible to return her hand's light pressure. Something of infinite value was floating past him, and he had taken an oath not to raise a finger to stop it. It was borne by the strong current of the world's great life and not of his own small one. Madame de Mauves disengaged her hand, gathered her shawl, and smiled at him almost as you would do at a child you should wish to encourage. Several moments later he was still standing watching her receding figure. When it had disappeared, he shook himself, walked rapidly back to his hotel, and without waiting for the evening train paid his bill and departed.

Later in the day M. de Mauves came into his wife's drawing-room, where she sat waiting to be summoned to dinner. He was dressed with a scrupulous freshness which seemed to indicate an intention of dining out. He walked up and down for some moments in silence, then rang the bell for a servant, and went out into the hall to meet him. He ordered the carriage to take him to the station, paused a moment with his hand on the knob of the door, dismissed the servant angrily as the latter lingered observing him, re-entered the drawing-room, resumed his restless walk, and at last stepped abruptly before his wife, who had taken up a book. "May I ask the favor," he said with evident effort, in spite of a forced smile of easy courtesy, "of having a question answered?"

"It's a favor I never refused," Madame de Mauves replied.

"Very true. Do you expect this evening a visit from Mr Longmore?"

"Mr Longmore," said his wife, "has left Saint-Germain." M. de Mauve started and his smile expired. "Mr Longmore," his wife continued, "has gone to America."

M. de Mauves stared a moment, flushed deeply, and turned away. Then recovering himself,—"Had anything happened?" he asked, "Had he a sudden call?"

But his question received no answer. At the same moment

the servant threw open the door and announced dinner; Madame Clairin rustled in, rubbing her white hands, Madame de Mauves passed silently into the dining-room, and he stood frowning and wondering. Before long he went out upon the terrace and continued his uneasy walk. At the end of a quarter of an hour the servant came to inform him that the carriage was at the door. "Send it away," he said curtly. "I shall not use it." When the ladies had half finished dinner he went in and joined them, with a formal apology to his wife for his tardiness.

The dishes were brought back, but he hardly tasted them; on the other hand, he drank a great deal of wine. There was little talk; what there was, was supplied by Madame Clairin. Twice she saw her brother's eyes fixed on her own, over his wineglass, with a piercing, questioning glance. She replied by an elevation of the eyebrows, which did the office of a shrug of the shoulders. M. de Mauves was left alone to finish his wine; he sat over it for more than an hour, and let the darkness gather about him. At last the servant came in with a letter and lighted a candle. The letter was a telegram, which M. de Mauves, when he had read it, burnt at the candle. After five minutes' meditation, he wrote a message on the back of a visiting-card and gave it to the servant to carry to the office. The man knew quite as much as his master suspected about the lady to whom the telegram was addressed; but its contents puzzled him; they consisted of the single word, "*Impossible.*" As the evening passed without her brother reappearing in the drawing-room, Madame Clairin came to him where he sat, by his solitary candle. He took no notice of her presence for some time; but he was the one person to whom she allowed this license. At last, speaking in a peremptory tone, "The American has gone home at an hour's notice," he said. "What does it mean?"

Madame Clairin now gave free play to the shrug she had been obliged to suppress at the table. "It means that I have a sister-in-law whom I haven't the honor to understand."

He said nothing more, and silently allowed her to depart, as if it had been her duty to provide him with an explanation and he was disgusted with her levity. When she had gone, he went into the garden and walked up and down, smoking. He saw his wife sitting alone on the terrace, but remained below strolling along the narrow paths. He remained a long time. It became late and Madame de Mauves disappeared. Toward midnight he dropped upon a bench, tired, with a kind of angry sigh. It was sinking into his mind that he, too, did not understand Madame Clairin's sister-in-law.

Longmore was obliged to wait a week in London for a ship. It was very hot, and he went out for a day to Richmond. In the garden of the hotel at which he dined he met his friend Mrs Draper, who was staying there. She made eager inquiry about Madame de Mauves, but Longmore at first, as they sat looking out at the famous view of the Thames, parried her questions and confined himself to small-talk. At last she said she was afraid he had something to conceal; whereupon, after a pause, he asked her if she remembered recommending him, in the letter she sent to him at Saint-Germain, to draw the sadness from her friend's smile. "The last I saw of her was her smile," said he,—"when I bade her good by."

"I remember urging you to 'console' her," Mrs Draper answered, "and I wondered afterwards whether—a model of discretion as you are—I hadn't given you rather foolish advice."

"She has her consolation in herself," he said; "she needs none that any one else can offer her. That's for troubles for which—be it more, be it less—our own folly has to answer. Madame de Mauves has not a grain of folly left."

"Ah, don't say that!" murmured Mrs Draper. "Just a little folly is very graceful."

Longmore rose to go, with a quick nervous movement. "Don't talk of grace," he said, "till you have measured her reason."

For two years after his return to America he heard nothing
of Madame de Mauves. That he thought of her intently, constantly, I need hardly say: most people wondered why such
a clever young man should not "devote" himself to something; but to himself he seemed absorbingly occupied. He
never wrote to her; he believed that she preferred it. At last he
heard that Mrs Draper, had come home, and he immediately
called on her. "Of course," she said after the first greetings,
"you are dying for news of Madame de Mauves. Prepare
yourself for something strange. I heard from her two or three
times during the year after your return. She left Saint-
Germain and went to live in the country, on some old property of her husband's. She wrote me very kind little notes,
but I felt somehow that—in spite of what you said about 'consolation'—they were the notes of a very sad woman. The only
advice I could have given her was to leave her wretch of a
husband and come back to her own land and her own people.
But this I didn't feel free to do, and yet it made me so miserable not to be able to help her that I preferred to let our correspondence die a natural death. I had no news of her for a
year. Last summer, however, I met at Vichy a clever young
Frenchman whom I accidentally learned to be a friend of
Euphemia's lovely sister-in-law, Madame Clairin. I lost no
time in asking him what he knew about Madame de Mauves,—
a countrywoman of mine and an old friend. 'I congratulate
you on possessing her friendship,' he answered. 'That's the
charming little woman who killed her husband.' You may
imagine that I promptly asked for an explanation, and he proceeded to relate to me what he called the whole story. M. de
Mauves had *fait quelques folies*, which his wife had taken
absurdly to heart. He had repented and asked her forgiveness,
which she had inexorably refused. She was very pretty, and
severity, apparently, suited her style; for whether or no her
husband had been in love with her before, he fell madly in love
with her now. He was the proudest man in France, but he had

begged her on his knees to be readmitted to favor. All in vain! She was stone, she was ice, she was outraged virtue. People noticed a great change in him: he gave up society, ceased to care for anything, looked shockingly. One fine day they learned that he had blown out his brains. My friend had the story of course from Madame Clairin."

Longmore was strongly moved, and his first impulse after he had recovered his composure was to return immediately to Europe. But several years have passed, and he still lingers at home. The truth is, that in the midst of all the ardent tenderness of his memory of Madame de Mauves, he has become conscious of a singular feeling,—a feeling for which awe would be hardly too strong a name.

O

ADINA

I

WE had been talking of Sam Scrope round the fire—mindful, such of us, of the rule *de mortuis*. Our host, however, had said nothing; rather to my surprise, as I knew he had been particularly intimate with our friend. But when our group had dispersed, and I remained alone with him, he brightened the fire, offered me another cigar, puffed his own awhile with a retrospective air, and told me the following tale:

Eighteen years ago Scrope and I were together in Rome. It was the beginning of my acquaintance with him, and I had grown fond of him, as a mild, meditative youth often does of an active, irreverent, caustic one. He had in those days the germs of the eccentricities,—not to call them by a hard name, —which made him afterwards the most intolerable of the friends we did not absolutely break with; he was already, as they say, a crooked stick. He was cynical, perverse, conceited, obstinate, brilliantly clever. But he was young, and youth, happily, makes many of our vices innocent. Scrope had his merits, or our friendship would not have ripened. He was not an amiable man, but he was an honest one—in spite of the odd caprice I have to relate; and half my kindness for him was based in a feeling that at bottom, in spite of his vanity, he enjoyed his own irritability as little as other people. It was his fancy to pretend that he enjoyed nothing, and that what sentimental travelers call picturesqueness was a weariness to his spirit; but the world was new to him and the charm of fine things often took him by surprise and stole a march on his premature cynicism. He was an observer in spite of himself, and in his happy moods, thanks to his capital memory and ample information, an excellent critic and most profitable companion. He was a punctilious classical scholar. My boyish journal, kept in those days, is stuffed with learned allusions; they are all Scrope's. I brought to the service of my Roman experience much more loose sentiment than rigid science. It was indeed a jocular bargain between us that in our wanderings, picturesque and archæological, I should undertake the sentimental business—the raptures, the reflections, the sketching, the quoting from Byron. He considered me absurdly Byronic, and when, in the manner of tourists at that period, I breathed poetic sighs over the subjection of Italy to the foreign foe, he used to swear that Italy had got no more than she deserved, that she was a land of vagabonds and declaimers, and that he had yet to see an Italian whom he would call a man. I quoted to him from Alfieri that the "human plant" grew stronger in Italy than anywhere else, and he retorted, that nothing grew strong there but lying and cheating, laziness, beggary and vermin. Of course we each said more than we believed. If we met a shepherd on the Campagna, leaning on his crook and gazing at us darkly from under the shadow of his matted locks, I would proclaim that he was the handsomest fellow in the world, and demand of Scrope to stop and let me sketch him. Scrope would confound him for a filthy scarecrow and me for a drivelling album-poet. When I stopped in the street to stare up at some mouldering *palazzo* with a patched petticoat hanging to dry from the drawing-room window, and assured him that its haunted disrepair was dearer to my soul than the neat barred front of my Aunt Esther's model mansion in Mount Vernon street, he would seize me by the arm and march me off, pinching me till I shook myself free, and whelming me, my soul and my *palazzo* in a ludicrous torrent of abuse. The truth was that the picturesque of Italy, both in man and in nature, fretted him, depressed him strangely. He was consciously a harsh note in the midst of so many mellow harmonies; every thing seemed to say to him—"Don't you wish you were as easy, as loveable, as carelessly beautiful as we?" In the bottom of his heart he did wish it. To appreciate the bitterness of this dumb disrelish of the Italian atmosphere, you must remember how very ugly the poor fellow was. He was uglier at twenty than at forty, for as he grew older it became the fashion to say that his crooked features were "distinguished." But twenty years ago, in the infancy of modern æsthetics, he could not have passed for even a bizarre form of ornament. In a single word, poor Scrope looked *common:* that was where the shoe pinched. Now you know that in Italy almost everything has, to the outer sense, what artists call style.

In spite of our clashing theories, our friendship *did* ripen, and we spent together many hours, deeply seasoned with the sense of youth and freedom. The best of these, perhaps, were those we passed on horseback, on the Campagna; you remember such hours; you remember those days of early winter, when the sun is as strong as that of a New England June, and the bare, purple-drawn slopes and hollows lie bathed in the yellow light of Italy. On such a day, Scrope and I mounted our horses in the grassy terrace before St John Lateran, and rode away across the broad meadows over which the Claudian Aqueduct drags its slow length—stumbling and lapsing here and there, as it goes, beneath the burden of the centuries. We rode a long distance—well towards Albano, and at last stopped near a low fragment of ruin, which seemed to be all that was left of an ancient tower. Was it indeed ancient, or was it a relic of one of the numerous mediæval fortresses, with which the grassy desert of the Campagna is studded? This was one of the questions which Scrope, as a competent classicist, liked to ponder; though when I called his attention to the picturesque effect of the fringe of wild plants which crowned the ruin, and detached their clear filaments in the deep blue air, he shrugged his shoulders, and said they only helped the brick-work to crumble. We tethered our horses to a wild fig tree hard by, and strolled around the tower. Suddenly, on the sunny side of it, we came upon a figure asleep on the grass. A young man lay there, all unconscious, with his head upon a pile of weed-smothered stones. A rusty gun was on the ground beside him, and an empty game-bag, lying near it, told of his being an unlucky sportsman. His heavy sleep seemed to point to a long morning's fruitless tramp. And yet he must have been either very unskilled, or very little in earnest, for the Campagna is alive with small game, every month in the year— or was, at least, twenty years ago. It was no more than I owed to my reputation for Byronism, to discover a careless, youthful grace in the young fellow's attitude. One of his legs was flung over the other; one of his arms was thrust back under his head, and the other resting loosely on the grass; his head drooped backward, and exposed a strong, young throat; his hat was pulled over his eyes, so that we could see nothing but his mouth and chin. "An American rustic asleep is an ugly fellow," said I; "but this young Roman clodhopper, as he lies snoring there, is really statuesque;" "clodhopper," was for argument, for our rustic Endymion, judging by his garments, was something better than a mere peasant. He turned uneasily, as we stood above him, and muttered something. "It's not fair to wake him," I said, and passed my arm into Scrope's, to lead him away; but he resisted, and I saw that something had struck him.

In his change of position, our picturesque friend had opened the hand which was resting on the grass. The palm, turned upward, contained a dull-colored oval object, of the size of a small snuff-box. "What has he got there?" I said to Scrope; but Scrope only answered by bending over and looking at it. "Really, we are taking great liberties with the poor fellow," I said. "Let him finish his nap in peace." And I was on the point of walking away. But my voice had aroused him; he lifted his hand, and, with the movement, the object I have compared to a snuff-box caught the light, and emitted a dull flash.

"It's a gem," said Scrope, "recently disinterred and encrusted with dirt."

The young man awoke in earnest, pushed back his hat, stared at us, and slowly sat up. He rubbed his eyes, to see if he were not still dreaming, then glanced at the gem, if gem it was, thrust his hand mechanically into his pocket, and gave us a broad smile. "Gentle, serene Italian nature!" I exclaimed. "A young New England farmer, whom we should have disturbed in this fashion, would wake up with an oath and a kick."

"I mean to test his gentleness," said Scrope. "I'm determined to see what he has got there." Scrope was very fond of small *bric-a-brac*, and had ransacked every curiosity shop in Rome. It was an oddity among his many oddities, but it agreed well enough with the rest of them. What he looked for and relished in old prints and old china was not, generally, beauty of form nor romantic association; it was elaborate and patient workmanship, fine engraving, skillful method.

"Good day," I said to our young man; "we didn't mean to interrupt you."

He shook himself, got up, and stood before us, looking out from under his thick curls, and still frankly smiling. There was something very simple,—a trifle silly,—in his smile, and I wondered whether he was not under-witted. He was young, but he was not a mere lad. His eyes were dark and heavy, but they gleamed with a friendly light, and his parted lips showed the glitter of his strong, white teeth. His complexion was of a fine, deep brown, just removed from coarseness by that vague suffused pallor common among Italians. He had the frame of a young Hercules; he was altogether as handsome a vagabond as you could wish for the foreground of a pastoral landscape.

"You've not earned your rest," said Scrope, pointing to his empty game-bag; "you've got no birds."

He looked at the bag and at Scrope, and then scratched his

head and laughed. "I don't want to kill them," he said. "I bring out my gun because it's stupid to walk about pulling a straw! And then my uncle is always grumbling at me for not doing something. When he sees me leave the house with my gun, he thinks I may, at least, get my dinner. He didn't know the lock's broke; even if I had powder and shot, the old blunderbuss wouldn't go off. When I'm hungry I go to sleep." And he glanced, with his handsome grin, at his recent couch. "The birds might come and perch on my nose, and not wake me up. My uncle never thinks of asking me what I have brought home for supper. He is a holy man, and lives on black bread and beans.

"Who is your uncle?" I inquired.

"The Padre Girolamo at Lariccia."

He looked at our hats and whips, asked us a dozen questions about our ride, our horses, and what we paid for them, our nationality, and our way of life in Rome, and at last walked away to caress our browsing animals and scratch their noses. "He has got something precious there," Scrope said, as we strolled after him. "He has evidently found it in the ground. The Campagna is full of treasures yet." As we overtook our new acquaintance he thrust his indistinguishable prize behind him, and gave a foolish laugh, which tried my companion's patience. "The fellow's an idiot!" he cried. "Does he think I want to snatch the thing?"

"What is it you've got there?" I asked kindly.

"Which hand will you have?" he said, still laughing.

"The right."

"The left," said Scrope, as he hesitated.

He fumbled behind him a moment more, and then produced his treasure with a flourish. Scrope took it, wiped it off carefully with his handkerchief, and bent his near-sighted eyes over it. I left him to examine it. I was more interested in watching the Padre Girolamo's nephew. The latter stood looking at my friend gravely, while Scrope rubbed and scratched the little black stone, breathed upon it and held it up to the light. He frowned and scratched his head; he was evidently trying to concentrate his wits on the fine account he expected Scrope to give of it. When I glanced towards Scrope, I found he had flushed excitedly, and I immediately bent my nose over it too. It was of about the size of a small hen's-egg, of a dull brown color, stained and encrusted by long burial, and deeply corrugated on one surface. Scrope paid no heed to my questions, but continued to scrape and polish. At last—"How did you come by this thing?" he asked dryly.

"I found it in the earth, a couple of miles from here, this morning." And the young fellow put out his hand nervously, to take it back. Scrope resisted a moment, but thought better, and surrendered it. As an old mouser, he began instinctively to play at indifference. Our companion looked hard at the little stone, turned it over and over, then thrust it behind him again, with his simple-souled laugh.

"Here's a precious chance," murmured Scrope.

"But in Heaven's name, what is it," I demanded, impatiently.

"Don't ask me. I don't care to phrase the conjecture audibly—it's immense—if it's what I think it is; and here stands this giggling lout with a prior claim to it. What shall I do with him? I should like to knock him in the head with the butt end of his blunderbuss."

"I suppose he'll sell you the thing, if you offer him enough."

"Enough? What does he know about enough? He don't know a topaz from a turnip."

"Is it a topaz, then?"

"Hold your tongue, and don't mention names. He must sell it as a turnip. Make him tell you just where he found it."

He told us very frankly, still smiling from ear to ear. He had observed in a solitary ilex-tree, of great age, the traces of a recent lightning-stroke. (A week of unseasonably sultry weather had, in fact some days before, culminated in a terrific thunder-storm.) The tree had been shivered and killed, and the earth turned up at its foot. The bolt, burying itself, had dug a deep, straight hole, in which one might have planted a stake. "I don't know why," said our friend, "but as I stood looking at it, I thrust the muzzle of my old gun into the aperture. It descended for some distance and stopped with a strange noise, as if it were striking a metallic surface. I rammed it up and down, and heard the same noise. Then I said to myself—'Something is hidden there—*quattrini*, perhaps; let us see.' I made a spade of one of the shivered ilex-boughs, dug, and scraped and scratched; and, in twenty minutes, fished up a little, rotten, iron box. It was so rotten that the lid and sides were as thin as letter-paper. When I gave them a knock, they crumbled. It was filled with other bits of iron of the same sort, which seemed to have formed the compartments of a case; and with the damp earth, which had oozed in through the holes and crevices. In the middle lay this stone, embedded in earth and mold. There was nothing else. I broke the box to pieces and kept the stone. *Ecco!*"

Scrope, with a shrug, repossessed himself of the moldy treasure, and our friend, as he gave it up, declared it was a thousand years old. Julius Cæsar had worn it in his crown!

"Julius Cæsar wore no crown, my dear friend," said Scrope urbanely. "It may be a thousand years old, and it may be ten. It may be an—agate, and it may be a flint! I don't know. But if you will sell it on the chance?——" And he tossed it three times high into the air, and caught it as it fell.

"I have my idea it's precious," said the young man. "Precious things are found here every day—why shouldn't I stumble on something as well as another? Why should the lightning strike just that spot, and no other? It was sent there by my patron, the blessed Saint Angelo!"

He was not such a simpleton, after all; or rather he was a puzzling mixture of simplicity and sense. "If you really want the thing," I said to Scrope, "make him an offer, and have done with it."

" 'Have done with it,' is easily said. How little do you suppose he will take?"

"I haven't the smallest idea of its value."

"It's value has nothng to do with the matter. Estimate it at its value and we may as well put it back into its hole—of its probable value, he knows nothing; he need never know," and Scrope, musing an instant, counted, and flung them down on the grass, ten silver *scudi*—the same number of dollars. Angelo,—he virtually told us his name,—watched them fall, one by one, but made no movement to pick them up. But his eyes brightened; his simplicity and his shrewdness were debating the question. The little heap of silver was most agreeable; to make a poor bargain, on the other hand, was not. He looked at Scrope with a dumb appeal to his fairness which quite touched me. It touched Scrope, too, a trifle; for, after a moment's hesitation, he flung down another *scudi*. Angelo gave a puzzled sigh, and Scrope turned short about and began to mount. In another moment we were both in the saddle. Angelo stood looking at his money. "Are you satisfied?" said my companion, curtly.

The young fellow gave a strange smile. "Have *you* a good conscience?" he demanded.

"Hang your impudence!" cried Scrope, very red. "What's my conscience to you?" And he thrust in his spurs and galloped away. I waved my hand to our friend and followed more slowly. Before long I turned in the saddle and looked back. Angelo was standing as we had left him, staring after us, with his money evidently yet untouched. But, of course, he would pick it up!

I rode along with my friend in silence; I was wondering over his off-hand justice. I was youthful enough to shrink from being thought a Puritan or a casuist, but it seemed to me that I scented sophistry in Scrope's double valuation of

Angelo's treasure. If it was a prize for him, it was a prize for Angelo, and ten *scudi*,—and one over,—was meager payment for a prize. It cost me some discomfort to find rigid Sam Scrope, of all men, capable of a piece of bargaining which needed to be ingeniously explained. Such as it was, he offered his explanation at last—half angrily, as if he knew his logic was rather grotesque. "Say it out; say it, for Heaven's sake!" he cried. "I know what you're thinking—I've played that pretty-faced simpleton a trick, eh?—and I'm no better than a swindler, evidently! Let me tell you, once for all, that I'm not ashamed of having got my prize cheap. It was ten *scudi* or nothing! If I had offered a farthing more I should have opened those sleepy eyes of his. It was a case to pocket one's scruples and *act*. That silly boy was not to be trusted with the keeping of such a prize for another half hour; the deuce knows what might have become of it. I rescued it in the interest of art, of science, of taste. The proper price of the thing I couldn't have dreamed of offering; where was I to raise ten thousand dollars to buy a bauble? Say I had offered a hundred—forthwith our picturesque friend, thick-witted though he is, would have pricked up his ears and held fast! He would have asked time to reflect and take advice, and he would have hurried back to his village and to his uncle, the shrewd old priest, Padre Girolamo. The wise-heads of the place would have held a conclave, and decided—I don't know what; that they must go up to Rome and see Signor Castillani, or the director of the Papal excavations. Some knowing person would have got wind of the affair, and whispered to the Padre Girolamo that his handsome nephew had been guided by a miracle to a fortune, and might marry a *contessina*. And when all was done, where should I be for my pains? As it is, I discriminate; I look at the matter all round, and I decide. I get my prize; the ingenious Angelo gets a month's carouse,—he'll enjoy it,—and goes to sleep again. Pleasant dreams to him! What does he want of money? Money would have corrupted him! I've saved the *contessina*, too; I'm sure he would have beaten her. So, if we're all satisfied, is it for you to look black? My mind's at ease; I'm neither richer nor poorer. I'm not poorer, because against my eleven *scudi* may stand the sense of having given a harmless treat to an innocent lad; I'm not richer, because,—I hope you understand,—I mean never to turn my stone into money. There it is that delicacy comes in. It's a stone and nothing more; and all the income I shall derive from it will be enjoying the way people open their eyes and hold their breath when I make it sparkle under the lamp, and tell them just what stone it is."

"What stone is it, then, in the name of all that's demoralizing?" I asked, with ardor.

Scrope broke into a gleeful chuckle, and patted me on the arm. "*Pazienza!* Wait till we get under the lamp, some evening, and then I'll make it sparkle and tell you. I must be sure first," he added, with sudden gravity.

But it was the feverish elation of his tone, and not its gravity, that struck me. I began to hate the stone; it seemed to have corrupted him. His ingenious account of his motives left something vaguely unexplained—almost inexplicable. There are dusky corners in the simplest natures; strange, moral involutions in the healthiest. Scrope was not simple, and, in virtue of his defiant self-consciousness, he might have been called morbid; so that I came to consider his injustice in this particular case as the fruit of a vicious seed which I find it hard to name. Everything in Italy seemed mutely to reproach him with his meager faculty of pleasing; the indefinable gracefulness of nature and man murmured forever in his ears that he was an angular cynic. This was the real motive of his intolerance of my sympathetic rhapsodies, and it prompted him now to regale himself, once for all, with the sense of an advantage wrested, if not by fair means, then by foul, from some sentient form of irritating Italian felicity. This is a rather metaphysical account of the matter; at the time I guessed the secret, without phrasing it.

Scrope carried his stone to no appraiser, and asked no archæological advice about it. He quietly informed himself, as if from general curiosity, as to the best methods of cleansing, polishing, and restoring antique gems, laid in a provision of delicate tools and acids, turned the key in his door, and took the measure of his prize. I asked him no questions, but I saw that he was intensely preoccupied, and was becoming daily better convinced that it was a rare one. He went about whistling and humming odd scraps of song, like a lover freshly accepted. Whenever I heard him I had a sudden vision of our friend Angelo staring blankly after us, as we rode away like a pair of ravishers in a German ballad. Scrope and I lodged in the same house, and one evening, at the end of a week, after I had gone to bed, he made his way into my room, and shook me out of my slumbers as if the house were on fire. I guessed his errand before he had told it, shuffled on my dressing-gown, and hurried to his own apartment. "I couldn't wait till morning," he said, "I've just given it the last touch; there it lies in its imperial beauty!"

There it lay, indeed, under the lamp, flashing back the light from its glowing heart—a splendid golden topaz on a cushion of white velvet. He thrust a magnifying glass into my hand, and pushed me into a chair by the table. I saw the surface of the stone was worked in elaborate intaglio, but I was not prepared for the portentous character of image and legend. In the center was a full-length naked figure, which I supposed at first to be a pagan deity. Then I saw the orb of sovereignty in one outstretched hand, the chiselled imperial scepter in the other, and the laurel-crown on the low-browed head. All round the face of the stone, near the edges, ran a chain of carven figures—warriors, and horses, and chariots, and young men and women interlaced in elaborate confusion. Over the head of the image, within this concave frieze, stood the inscription:

DIVUS TIBERIUS CÆSAR TOTIUS ORBIS IMPERATOR

The workmanship was extraordinarily delicate; beneath the powerful glass I held in my hand, the figures revealed the perfection and finish of the most renowned of antique marbles. The color of the stone was superb, and, now that its purity had been restored, its size seemed prodigious. It was in every way a gem among gems, a priceless treasure.

"Don't you think it was worth while getting up to shake hands with the Emperor Tiberius?" cried Scrope, after observing my surprise. "Shabby Nineteenth Century Yankees, as we are, we are having our audience. Down on your knees, barbarian, we're in a tremendous presence! Haven't I worked all these days and nights, with my little rags and files, to some purpose? I've annulled the centuries—I've resuscitated a *totius orbis imperator*. Do you conceive, do you apprehend, does your heart thump against your ribs? Not as it should, evidently. This is where Cæsar wore it, dull modern—here, on his breast, near the shoulder, framed in chiselled gold, circled about with pearls as big as plums, clasping together the two sides of his gold-stiffened mantle. It was the agraffe of the imperial purple. Tremble, sir!" and he took up the splendid jewel, and held it against my breast. "No doubts—no objections—no reflections—or we're mortal enemies. How do I know it—where's my warrant? It simply must be! It's too precious to have been anything else. It's the finest intaglio in the world. It has told me its secret; it has lain whispering classic Latin to me by the hour all this week past."

"And has it told you how it came to be buried in its iron box?"

"It has told me everything—more than I can tell you now. Content yourself for the present with admiring it."

Admire it I did for a long time. Certainly, if Scrope's hypothesis was not sound, it ought to have been, and if the Emperor Tiberius had never worn the topaz in his mantle, he was by so much the less imperial. But the design, the legend, the shape of the stone, were all very cogent evidence that the gem had played a great part. "Yes, surely," I said, "it's the finest of known intaglios."

Scrope was silent a while. "Say of unknown," he answered at last. "No one shall ever know it. You I hereby hold pledged to secrecy. I shall show it to no one else—except to my mistress, if I ever have one. I paid for the chance of its turning out something great. I couldn't pay for the renown of possessing it. That only a princely fortune could have purchased. To be known as the owner of the finest intaglio in the world would make a great man of me, and that would hardly be fair to our friend Angelo. I shall sink the glory, and cherish my treasure for its simple artistic worth."

"And how would you express that simple artistic worth in Roman *scudi?*"

"It's impossible. Fix upon any sum you please."

I looked again at the golden topaz, gleaming in its velvet nest; and I felt that there could be no successful effort to conceal such a magnificent negation of obscurity. "I recommend you," I said at last, "to think twice before showing it to your mistress."

I had no idea, when I spoke, that my words were timely; for I had vaguely taken for granted that my friend was foredoomed to dispense with this graceful appendage, very much as Peter Schlemihl, in the tale, was condemned to have no shadow. Nevertheless, before a month had passed, he was in a fair way to become engaged to a charming girl. "Juxtaposition is much," says Clough; especially juxtaposition, he implies, in foreign countries; and in Scrope's case it had been particularly close. His cousin, Mrs Waddington, arrived in Rome, and with her a young girl who, though really no relative, offered him all the opportunities of cousinship, added to the remoter charm of a young lady to whom he had to be introduced. Adina Waddington was her companion's stepdaughter, the elder lady having, some eight years before, married a widower

with a little girl. Mr Waddington had recently died, and the
two ladies were just emerging from their deep mourning.
These dusky emblems of a common grief helped them to seem
united, as indeed they really were, although Mrs Waddington was but ten years older than her stepdaughter. She was an
excellent woman, without a fault that I know of, but that of
thinking all the world as good as herself and keeping dinner
waiting sometimes while she sketched the sunset. She was
stout and fresh-colored, she laughed and talked rather loud,
and generally, in galleries and temples, caused a good many
stiff British necks to turn round.

She had a mania for excursions, and at Frascati and Tivoli
she inflicted her good-humored ponderosity on diminutive
donkeys with a relish which seemed to prove that a passion
for scenery, like all our passions, is capable of making the best
of us pitiless. I had often heard Scrope say that he detested
boisterous women, but he forgave his cousin her fine spirits,
and stepped into his place as her natural escort and adviser. In
the vulgar sense he was not selfish; he had a very definite
theory as to the sacrifices a gentleman should make to formal
courtesy; but I was nevertheless surprised at the easy terms on
which the two ladies secured his services. The key to the mystery was the one which fits so many locks; he was in love with
Miss Waddington. There was a sweet stillness about her
which balanced the widow's exuberance. Her pretty name of
Adina seemed to me to have somehow a mystic fitness to her
personality. She was short and slight and blonde, and her
black dress gave a sort of infantine bloom to her fairness.
She wore her auburn hair twisted into a thousand fantastic
braids, like a coiffure in a Renaissance drawing, and she looked
out at you from grave blue eyes, in which, behind a cold shy-
ness, there seemed to lurk a tremulous promise to be franker
when she knew you better. She never consented to know me
well enough to be very frank; she talked very little, and we
hardly exchanged a dozen words a day; but I confess that I

P

found a perturbing charm in those eyes. As it was all in silence, though, there was no harm.

Scrope, however, ventured to tell his love—or, at least, to hint at it eloquently enough. I was not so deeply smitten as to be jealous, and I drew a breath of relief when I guessed his secret. It made me think better of him again. The stand he had taken about poor Angelo's gem, in spite of my efforts to account for it philosophically, had given an uncomfortable twist to our friendship. I asked myself if he really had no heart; I even wondered whether there was not a screw loose in his intellect. But here was a hearty, healthy, natural passion, such as only an honest man could feel—such as no man could feel without being the better for it. I began to hope that the sunshine of his fine sentiment would melt away his aversion to giving Angelo his dues. He was charmed, soul and sense, and for a couple of months he really forgot himself, and ceased to send forth his unsweetened wit to do battle for his ugly face. His happiness rarely made him "gush," as they say; but I could see that he was vastly contented with his prospects. More than once, when we were together, he broke into a kind of nervous, fantastic laugh, over his own thoughts; and on his refusal to part with them for the penny which one offers under those circumstances, I said to myself, that this was humorous surprise at his good luck. How had *he* come to please that exquisite creature? Of course, I learned even less from the young girl about her own view of the case; but Mrs Waddington and I, not being in love with each other, had nothing to do but to gossip about our companions whenever (which was very often) they consigned us to a *tête-à-tête*.

"She tells me nothing," the good-humored widow said; "and if I'm to know the answer to a riddle, I must have it in black and white. My cousin is not what is called 'attractive,' but I think Adina, nevertheless, is interested in him. How do you and I know how passion may transfigure and exalt him? And who shall say beforehand what a fanciful young girl shall do with that terrible little piece of machinery she calls her heart? Adina is a strange child; she is fanciful without being capricious. For all I know, she may admire my cousin for his very ugliness and queerness. She has decided, very likely, that she wants an 'intellectual' husband, and if Mr Scrope is not handsome, nor frivolous, nor over-polite, there's a greater chance of his being wise." Why Adina should have listened to my friend, however, was her own business. Listen to him she did, and with a sweet attentiveness which may well have flattered and charmed him.

We rarely spoke of the imperial topaz; it seemed not a subject for light allusions. It might properly make a man feel solemn to possess it; the mere memory of its luster lay like a weight on my own conscience. I had felt, as we lost sight of our friend Angelo that, in one way or another, we should hear of him again; but the weeks passed by without his re-appearing, and my conjectures as to the sequel, on his side, of his remarkable bargain remained quite unanswered. Christmas arrived, and with it the usual ceremonies. Scrope and I took the requisite vigorous measures,—it was a matter, you know, of fists and elbows and knees,—and obtained places for the two ladies at the Midnight Mass at the Sistine Chapel. Mrs Waddington was my especial charge, and on coming out we found we had lost sight of our companions in the crowd. We waited awhile in the Colonnade, but they were not among the passers, and we supposed that they had gone home independently, and expected us to do likewise. But on reaching Mrs Waddington's lodging we found they had not come in. As their prolonged absence demanded an explanation, it occurred to me that they had wandered into Saint Peter's, with many others of the attendants at the Mass, and were watching the tapers twinkle in its dusky immensity. It was not perfectly regular that a young lady should be wandering about at three o'clock in the morning with a very "unattractive" young man; but "after all," said Mrs Waddington, "she's almost his cousin." By the time they returned she was much more. I went home, went to bed, and slept as late as the Christmas bells would allow me. On rising, I knocked at Scrope's door to wish him the compliments of the season, but on his coming to open it for me, perceived that such common-place greetings were quite below the mark. He was but half undressed, and had flung himself, on his return, on the outside of his bed. He had gone with Adina, as I supposed, into Saint Peter's, and they had found the twinkling tapers as picturesque as need be. He walked about the room for some time restlessly, and I saw that he had something to say. At last he brought it out. "I say, I'm accepted. I'm engaged. I'm what's called a happy man."

Of course I wished him joy on the news; and could assure him, with ardent conviction, that he had chosen well. Miss Waddington was the loveliest, the purest, the most interesting of young girls. I could see that he was grateful for my sympathy, but he disliked "expansion," and he contented himself, as he shook hands with me, with simply saying—"Oh yes; she's the right thing." He took two or three more turns about the room, and then suddenly stopped before his toilet-table, and pulled out a tray in his dressing-case. There lay the great intaglio; larger even than I should have dared to boast. "That would be a pretty thing to offer one's *fiancée*," he said, after gazing at it for some time. "How could she wear it—how could one have it set?"

"There could be but one way," I said; "as a massive medallion, depending from a necklace. It certainly would light up the world more, on the bosom of a beautiful woman, than thrust away here, among your brushes and razors. But, to my sense, only a beauty of a certain type could properly wear it— a splendid, dusky beauty, with the brow of a Roman Empress, and the shoulders of an antique statue. A fair, slender girl, with blue eyes, and sweet smile, would seem, somehow, to be overweighted by it, and if I were to see it hung, for instance, round Miss Waddington's white neck, I should feel as if it were pulling her down to the ground, and giving her a mysterious pain."

He was a trifle annoyed, I think, by this rather fine-spun objection; but he smiled as he closed the tray. "Adina may not have the shoulders of the Venus of Milo," he said, "but I hope it will take more than a bauble like this to make her stoop."

I don't always go to church on Christmas Day; but I have a life-long habit of taking a solitary walk, in all weathers, and harboring Christian thoughts if they come. This was a Southern Christmas, without snow on the ground, or sleighbells in the air, or the smoke of crowded firesides rising into a cold, blue sky. The day was mild, and almost warm, the sky gray and sunless. If I was disposed toward Christmas thoughts, I confess, I sought them among Pagan memories. I strolled about the forums, and then walked along to the Coliseum. It was empty, save for a single figure, sitting on the steps at the foot of the cross in the center—a young man, apparently, leaning forward, motionless, with his elbows on his knees, and his head buried in his hands. As he neither stirred nor observed me when I passed near him, I said to myself that, brooding there so intensely in the shadow of the sign of redemption, he might pass for an image of youthful remorse. Then, as he never moved, I wondered whether it was not a deeper passion even than repentance. Suddenly he looked up, and I recognized our friend Angelo—not immediately, but in response to a gradual movement of recognition in his own face. But seven weeks had passed since our meeting, and yet he looked three years older. It seemed to me that he had lost flesh, and gained expression. His simple-souled smile was gone; there was no trace of it in the shy mistrust of his greeting. He looked graver, manlier, and very much less rustic. He was equipped in new garments of a pretentious pattern, though they were carelessly worn, and bespattered with mud.

I remember he had a flaming orange necktie, which harmonized admirably with his picturesque coloring. Evidently he was greatly altered; as much altered as if he had made a voyage round the world. I offered him my hand, and asked if he remembered me.

"*Per Dio!*" he cried. "With good reason." Even his voice seemed changed; it was fuller and harsher. He bore us a grudge. I wondered how his eyes had been opened. He fixed them on me with a dumb reproachfulness, which was half appealing and half ominous. He had been brooding and brooding on his meager bargain till the sense of wrong had become a kind of smothered fear. I observed all this with poignant compassion, for it seemed to me that he had parted with something more precious even than his imperial intaglio. He had lost his boyish ignorance—that pastoral piece of mind which had suffered him to doze there so gracefully with his head among the flowers. But even in his resentment he was simple still. "Where is the other one—your friend?" he asked.

"He's at home—he's still in Rome."

"And the stone—what has he done with it?"

"Nothing. He has it still."

He shook his head dolefully. "Will he give it back to me for twenty-five *scudi?*"

"I'm afraid not. He values it."

"I believe so. Will he let me see it?"

"That you must ask him. He shows it to no one."

"He's afraid of being robbed, eh? That proves its value! He hasn't shown it to a jeweler—to a, what do they call them? —a lapidary?"

"To no one. You must believe me."

"But he has cleaned it, and polished it, and discovered what it is?"

"It's very old. It's hard to say."

"Very old! Of course it's old. There are more years in it

than it brought me *scudi*. What does it look like? Is it red, blue, green, yellow?"

"Well, my friend," I said, after a moment's hesitation, "it's yellow."

He gave me a searching stare; then quickly—"It's what's called a topaz," he cried.

"Yes, it's what's called a topaz."

"And it's sculptured—that I could see! It's an intaglio. Oh, I know the names, and I've paid enough for my learning. What's the figure? A king's head—or a Pope's, perhaps, eh? Or the portrait of some beautiful woman that you read about?"

"It is the figure of an Emperor."

"What is his name?"

"Tiberius."

"*Corpo di Cristo!*" his face flushed, and his eyes filled with angry tears.

"Come," I said, "I see you're sorry to have parted with the stone. Some one has been talking to you, and making you discontented."

"Every one, *per Dio!* Like the finished fool I was, I couldn't keep my folly to myself. I went home with my eleven *scudi*, thinking I should never see the end of them. The first thing I did was to buy a gilt hair-pin from a peddler, and give it to the Ninetta—a young girl of my village, with whom I had a friendship. She stuck it into her braids, and looked at herself in the glass, and then asked how I had suddenly got so rich! 'Oh, I'm richer than you suppose,' said I, and showed her my money, and told her the story of the stone. She is a very clever girl, and it would take a knowing fellow to have the last word with her. She laughed in my face, and told me I was an idiot, that the stone was surely worth five hundred *scudi;* that my *forestiere* was a pitiless rascal; that I ought to have brought it away, and shown it to my elders and betters; in fine, that I might take her word for it, I had held a fortune in

my hand, and thrown it to the dogs. And, to wind up this
sweet speech, she took out her hairpin, and tossed it into my
face. She never wished to see me again; she had as lief marry a
blind beggar at a cross-road. What was I to say? She had a
sister who was waiting-maid to a fine lady in Rome,—a
marchesa,—who had a priceless necklace made of fine old
stones picked up on the Campagna. I went away hanging my
head, and cursing my folly: I flung my money down in the
dirt, and spat upon it! At last, to ease my spirit, I went to
drink a *foglietta* at the wine-shop. There I found three or four
young fellows I knew; I treated them all round; I hated my
money, and wanted to get rid of it. Of course they too wanted
to know how I came by my full pockets. I told them the truth.
I hoped they would give me a better account of things than
that vixen of a Ninetta. But they knocked their glasses on the
table, and jeered at me in chorus. Any donkey, out a-grazing,
if he had turned up such a treasure with his nose, would have
taken it in his teeth and brought it home to his master. This
was cold comfort; I drowned my rage in wine. I emptied one
flask after another; for the first time in my life I got drunk.
But I can't speak of that night! The next day I took what was
left of my money to my uncle, and told him to give it to the
poor, to buy new candlesticks for his church, or to say masses
for the redemption of my blaspheming soul. He looked at it
very hard, and hoped I had come by it honestly. I was in for
it; I told *him* too! He listened to me in silence, looking at me
over his spectacles. When I had done, he turned over the
money in his hands, and then sat for three minutes with his
eyes closed. Suddenly he thrust it back into my own hands.
'Keep it—keep it, my son,' he said, 'your wits will never help
you to a supper, make the most of what you've got!' Since
then, do you see, I've been in a fever. I can think of nothing
else but the fortune I've lost."

"Oh, a fortune!" I said, deprecatingly. "You exaggerate."

"It would have been a fortune to me. A voice keeps ringing

in my ear night and day, and telling me I could have got a thousand *scudi* for it."

I'm afraid I blushed; I turned away a moment; when I looked at the young man again, his face had kindled. "Tiberius eh? A Roman emperor sculptured on a big topaz—that's fortune enough for me! Your friend's a rascal—do you know that? I don't say it for you; I like your face, and I believe that, if you can, you'll help me. But your friend is an ugly little monster. I don't know why the devil I trusted him; I saw he wished me no good. Yet, if ever there was a harmless fellow, I was. *Ecco!* it's my fate. That's very well to say; I say it and say it, but it helps me no more than an empty glass helps your thirst. I'm not harmless now. If I meet your friend, and he refuses me justice, I won't answer for these two hands. You see—they're strong; I could easily strangle him! Oh, at first, I shall speak him fair, but if he turns me off, and answers me with English oaths, I shall think only of my *revenge!*" And with a passionate gesture he pulled off his hat, and flung it on the ground, and stood wiping the perspiration from his forehead.

I answered him briefly but kindly enough. I told him to leave his case in my hands, go back to Lariccia and try and find some occupation which would divert him from his grievance. I confess that even as I gave this respectable advice, I but half believed in it. It was none of poor Angelo's mission to arrive at virtue through tribulation. His indolent nature, active only in immediate feeling, would have found my prescription of wholesome labor more intolerable even than his wrong. He stared gloomily and made no answer, but he saw that I had his interests at heart, and he promised me, at least, to leave Rome, and believe that I would fairly plead his cause. If I had good news for him I was to address him at Lariccia. It was thus I learned his full name,—a name, certainly, that ought to have been to its wearer a sort of talisman against trouble,—Angelo Beati.

II

SAM SCROPE looked extremely annoyed when I began to tell
him of my encounter with our friend, and I saw there was still
a cantankerous something in the depths of his heart intensely
hostile to fairness. It was characteristic of his peculiar temper
that his happiness, as an accepted lover, had not disposed him
to graceful concessions. He treated his bliss as his own private
property, and was as little in the humor to diffuse its influence
as he would have been to send out in charity a choice dish from
an unfinished dinner. Nevertheless, I think he might have
stiffly admitted that there was a grain of reason in Angelo's
claim, if I had not been too indiscreetly accurate in my report
of our interview. I had been impressed, indeed, with something picturesquely tragic in the poor boy's condition, and, to
do perfect justice to the picture, I told him he had flung down
his hat on the earth as a gauntlet of defiance and talked about
his *revenge*. Scrope hereupon looked fiercely disgusted and
pronounced him a theatrical jackanapes; but he authorized me
to drop him a line saying that he would speak with him a
couple of days later. I was surprised at Scrope's consenting to
see him, but I perceived that he was making a conscientious
effort to shirk none of the disagreeables of the matter. "I
won't have him stamping and shouting in the house here," he
said. "I'll also meet him at the Coliseum." He named his hour
and I despatched to Lariccia three lines of incorrect but
courteous Italian.

It was better,—far better,—that they should not have met.
What passed between them Scrope requested me on his return
to excuse him from repeating; suffice it that Angelo was an
impudent puppy, and that he hoped never to hear of him
again. Had Angelo, at last, I asked, received any compensation? "Not a farthing!" cried Scrope, and walked out of the

room. Evidently the two young men had been a source of
immitigable offense to each other. Angelo had promised to
speak to him fair, and I inclined to believe had done so; but
the very change in his appearance, by seeming to challenge
my companion's sympathy in too peremptory a fashion, had
had the irritating effect of a menace. Scrope had been con-
temptuous, and his awkward, ungracious Italian had doubtless made him seem more so. One can't handle Italians with
contempt; those who know them have learned what may be
done with a moderate amount of superficial concession.
Angelo had replied in wrath, and, as I afterwards learned, had
demanded, as a right, the restitution of the topaz in exchange
for the sum received for it. Scrope had rejoined that if he took
that tone he should get nothing at all, and the injured youth
had retorted with reckless and insulting threats. What had
prevented them from coming to blows, I know not, no sign
of flinching, certainly, on my companion's part. Face to face,
he had not seemed to Angelo so easy to strangle, and that
saving grain of discretion which mingles with all Italian
passion had whispered to the young man to postpone his
revenge. Without taking a melodramatic view of things, it
seemed to me that Scrope had an evil chance in waiting for
him. I had, perhaps, no definite vision of a cloaked assassin
lurking under a dark archway, but I thought it perfectly
possible that Angelo might make himself intolerably disagreeable. His simply telling his story up and down Rome
to whomsoever would listen to him, might be a grave annoyance; though indeed Scrope had the advantage that most
people might refuse to believe in the existence of a gem of
which its owner was so little inclined to boast. The whole
situation, at all events, made me extremely nervous. I cursed
my companion one day for a hungrier Jew than Shylock, and
pitied him the next as the victim of a moral hallucination. If we
gave him time, he *would* come to his senses; he would repay
poor Angelo with interest. Meanwhile, however, I could do

nothing, for I felt that it was worse than useless to suggest to Scrope that he was in danger. He would have scorned the idea of a ranting Italian making him swerve an inch from his chosen path.

I am unable to say whether Angelo's "imprudence" had seemed to relieve him, generally, from his vow to conceal the intaglio; a few words, at all events, from Miss Waddington, a couple of evenings later, reminded me of the original reservation he had made to the vow. Mrs Waddington was at the piano, deciphering a new piece of music, and Scrope, who was fond of a puzzle, as a puzzle, was pretending, half jocosely, to superintend and correct her. "I've seen it," Adina said to me, with grave, expanded eyes; "I've seen the wonderful topaz. He says you are in the secret. He won't tell me how he came by it. Honestly, I hope."

I tried to laugh. "You mustn't investigate too closely the honesty of hunters for antiquities. It's hardly dishonest in their code to treat loose cameos and snuff-boxes as pickpockets treat purses."

She looked at me in shy surprise, as if I had made a really cruel joke. "He says that I must wear it one of these days as a medallion." she went on. "But I shall not. The stone is beautiful, but I should feel most uncomfortable in carrying the Emperor Tiberius so near my heart. Wasn't he one of the bad Emperors—one of the worst? It is almost a pollution to have a thing that *he* had looked at and touched coming to one in such direct descent. His image almost spoils for me the beauty of the stone and I'm very glad Mr Scrope keeps it out of sight." This seemed a very becoming state of mind in a blonde angel of New England origin.

The days passed by and Angelo's "revenge" still hung fire. Scrope never met his fate at a short turning of one of the dusky Roman streets; he came in punctually every evening at eleven o'clock. I wondered whether our brooding friend had already spent the sinister force of a nature formed to be lazily contented. I hoped so, but I was wrong. We had gone to walk one afternoon,—the ladies, Scrope and I,—in the charming Villa Borghese, and, to escape from the rattle of the fashionable world and its distraction, we had wandered away to an unfrequented corner where the old moldering wall and the slim black cypresses and the untrodden grass made, beneath the splendid Roman sky, the most harmonious of pictures. Of course there was a mossy stone hemicycle not far off, and cracked benches with griffins' feet, where one might sit and gossip and watch the lizards scamper in the sun. We had done so for some half an hour when Adina espied the first violet of the year glimmering at the root of a cypress. She made haste to rise and gather it, and then wandered further, in the hope of giving it a few companions. Scrope sat and watched her as she moved slowly away, trailing her long shadow on the grass and drooping her head from side to side in her charming quest. It was not, I know, that he felt no impulse to join her; but that he was in love, for the moment, with looking at her from where he sat. Her search carried her some distance and at last she passed out of sight behind a bend in the villa wall. Mrs Waddington proposed in a few moments that we should overtake her, and we moved forward. We had not advanced many paces before she re-appeared, glancing over her shoulder as she came towards us with an air of suppressed perturbation. In an instant I saw she was being followed; a man was close behind her—a man in whom my second glance recognized Angelo Beati. Adina was pale; something had evidently passed between them. By the time she had met us, we were also face to face with Angelo. He was pale, as well, and, between these two pallors, Scrope had flushed crimson. I was afraid of an explosion and stepped toward Angelo to avert it. But to my surprise, he was evidently following another line. He turned the cloudy brightness of his eyes upon each of us and poised his hand in the air as if to say, in answer to my unspoken charge—"Leave me alone, I know what I am about." I exchanged a glance with Scrope, urging him to pass on with the ladies and let me deal with the intruder. Miss Waddington stopped; she was gazing at Angelo with soft intentness. Her lover, to lead her away, grasped her arm almost rudely, and as she went with him I saw her faintly flushing. Mrs Waddington, unsuspicious of evil, saw nothing but a very handsome young man. "What a beautiful creature for a sketch!" I heard her exclaim, as she followed her step-daughter.

"I'm not going to make a noise," said Angelo, with a somber smile; "don't be frightened! I know what good manners are. These three weeks now that I've been hanging about Rome, I've learned to play the gentleman. Who is that young lady?"

"My dear young man, it's none of your business. I hope you had not the hardihood to speak to her."

He was silent a moment, looking after her as she retreated on her companion's arm. "Yes, I spoke to her—and she understood me. Keep quiet; I said nothing she mightn't hear. But such as it was, she understood it. She's your friend's *amica*; I know that. I've been watching you for half an hour from behind those trees. She is wonderfully beautiful. Farewell; I wish you no harm, but tell your friend I've not forgotten *him*. I'm only awaiting my chance; I think it will come. I don't want to kill him; I want to give him some hurt that he'll survive and *feel*—forever!" He was turning away, but he paused and watched my companions till they disappeared. At last—"He has more than his share of good luck," he said, with a sort of forced coldness. "A topaz—and a pearl! both at once! Eh, farewell!" And he walked rapidly away, waving his hand. I let him go. I was unsatisfied, but his unexpected sobriety left me nothing to say.

When a startling event comes to pass, we are apt to waste a good deal of time in trying to recollect the correct signs and portents which preceded it, and when they seem fewer than they should be, we don't scruple to imagine them—we invent

them after the fact. Therefore it is that I don't pretend to be
sure that I was particularly struck, from this time forward,
with something strange in our quiet Adina. She had always
seemed to me vaguely, innocently strange; it was part of her
charm that in the daily noiseless movement of her life a
mystic undertone seemed to murmur—"You don't half know
me!" Perhaps we three prosaic mortals were not quite worthy
to know her: yet I believe that if a practised man of the world
had whispered to me, one day, over his wine, after Miss
Waddington had rustled away from the table, that *there* was a
young lady who, sooner or later, would treat her friends to a
first class surprise, I should have laid my finger on his sleeve
and told him with a smile that he phrased my own thought.
Was she more silent than usual, was she preoccupied, was she
melancholy, was she restless? Picturesquely, she ought to
have been all these things; but in fact, she was still to the un-
illumined eye simply a very pretty blonde maiden, who smiled
more than she spoke, and accepted her lover's devotion with
a charming demureness which savored much more of humility
than of condescension. It seemed to me useless to repeat to
Scrope the young Italian's declaration that he had spoken to
her, and poor Sam never intimated to me either that he had
questioned her in suspicion of the fact, or that she had offered
him any account of it. I was sure, however, that something
must have passed between the young girl and her lover in
the way of question and answer, and I privately wondered
what the deuce Angelo had meant by saying she had understood him. What had she understood? Surely not the story of
Scrope's acquisition of the gem; for granting—what was
unlikely—that Angelo had had time to impart it, it was unnatural that Adina should not have frankly demanded an
explanation. At last I broke the ice and asked Scrope if he
supposed Miss Waddington had reason to connect the great
intaglio with the picturesque young man she had met in the
Villa Borghese.

My question caused him visible discomfort. "Picturesque?" he growled. "Did she tell you she thought him picturesque?"

"By no means. But he is! You must at least allow him that."

"He hadn't brushed his hair for a week—if that's what you mean. But it's a charm which I doubt that Adina appreciates. But she has certainly taken," he added in a moment, "an unaccountable dislike to the topaz. She says the Emperor Tiberius spoils it for her. It's carrying historical antipathies rather far: I supposed nothing could spoil a fine gem for a pretty woman. It appears," he finally said, "that that rascal spoke to her."

"What did he say?"

"He asked her if she was engaged to me."

"And what did she answer?"

"Nothing."

"I suppose she was frightened."

"She might have been; but she says she was not. He begged her not to be; he told her he was a poor harmless fellow looking for justice. She left him, without speaking. I told her he was crazy—it's not a lie."

"Possibly!" I rejoined. Then, as a last attempt—"You know it wouldn't be quite a lie," I added, "to say that *you* are not absolutely sane. You're very erratic, about the topaz; obstinacy, pushed under certain circumstances beyond a certain point, bears a dangerous likeness to craziness."

I suppose that if one could reason with a mule it would make him rather more mulish to know one called him stubborn. Scrope gave me a chilling grin. "I deny your circumstances. If I'm mad, I claim the madman's privilege of believing myself peculiarly sane. If you wish to preach to me, you must catch me in a lucid interval."

The breath of early spring in Rome, though magical, as you know, in its visible influence on the dark old city, is often rather trying to the foreign constitution. After a fortnight of uninterrupted sirocco, Mrs Waddington's fine spirits confessed to depression. She was afraid, of course, that she was going to have "the fever," and made haste to consult a physician. He reasssured her, told her she simply needed change of air, and recommended a month at Albano. To Albano, accordingly, the two ladies repaired, under Scrope's escort. Mrs Waddington kindly urged my going with them; but I was detained in Rome by the arrival of some relations of my own, for whom I was obliged to play *cicerone*. I could only promise to make an occasional visit to Albano. My uncle and his three daughters were magnificent sight-seers, and gave me plenty to do; nevertheless, at the end of a week I was able to redeem my promise. I found my friends lodging at the inn, and the two ladies doing their best to merge the sense of dirty stone floors and crumpled yellow table-cloth in ecstatic contemplation, from their windows, of the great misty sea-like level of the Campagna. The view apart, they were passing delightful days. You remember the loveliness of the place and its picturesque neighborhood of strange old mountain towns. The country was blooming with early flowers and foliage, and my friends lived in the open air. Mrs Waddington sketched in water colors. Adina gathered wild nosegays, and Scrope hovered contentedly between them—not without an occasional frank stricture on the elder lady's use of her pigments and Adina's combinations of narcissus and cyclamen. All seemed to me very happy and, without ill-nature, I felt almost tempted to wonder whether the most desirable gift of the gods is not a thick-and-thin conviction of one's own impeccability. Yet even a lover with a bad conscience might be cheated into a disbelief in retribution by the unbargained sweetness of such a presence in his life as Adina Waddington's.

I spent the night at Albano, but as I had pledged myself to go the next morning to a funzione with my fair cousins in Rome,—"fair" is for rhetoric; but they were excellent girls: —I was obliged to rise and start at dawn. Scrope had offered to go with me part of the way, and walk back to the inn before

Q

breakfast; but I declined to accept so onerous a favor, and departed alone, in the early twilight. A rickety diligence made the transit across the Campagna, and I had a five minutes' walk to the post-office, while it stood waiting for its freight. I made my way through the little garden of the inn, as this saved me some steps. At the sound of my tread on the gravel, a figure rose slowly from a bench at the foot of a crippled grim statue, and I found myself staring at Angelo Beati. I greeted him with an exclamation, which was virtually a challenge of his right to be there. He stood and looked at me fixedly, with a strangely defiant, unembarrassed smile, and at last, in answer to my repeated inquiry as to what the deuce he was about, he said he supposed he had a right to take stroll in a neighbor's garden.

"A neighbor?" said I. "How——?"

"Eh, *per Dio!* don't I live at Lariccia?" And he laughed in almost as simple a fashion as when we had awaked him from his dreamless sleep in the meadows.

I had had so many other demands on my attention during my friend's absence that it never occurred to me that Scrope had lodged himself in the very jaws of the enemy. But I began to believe that, after all, the enemy was very harmless. If Angelo confined his machinations to sitting about in damp gardens at malarial hours, Scrope would not be the first to suffer. I had fancied at first that his sense of injury had made a man of him; but there seemed still to hang about him a sort of a romantic ineffectiveness. His painful impulse toward maturity had lasted but a day and he had become again an irresponsible lounger in Arcady. But he must have had an Arcadian constitution to brave the Roman dews at that rate. "And you came here for a purpose," I said. "It ought to be a very good one to warrant your spending your nights out of doors in this silly fashion. If you are not careful you'll get the fever and die, and that will be the end of everything."

He seemed grateful for my interest in his health. "No, no,

Signorino mio, I'll not get the fever. I've a fever here"—and he struck a blow on his breast—"that's a safeguard against the other. I've had a purpose in coming here, but you'll never guess it. Leave me alone; I shan't harm you! But now, that day is beginning, I must go; I must not be seen."

I grasped him by the arm, looked at him hard and tried to penetrate his meaning. He met my eyes frankly and gave a little contented laugh. Whatever his secret was, he was not ashamed of it; I saw with some satisfaction that it was teaching him patience. Something in his face, in the impression it gave me of his nature, reassured me, at the same time, that it contradicted my hypothesis of a moment before. There was no evil in it and no malignity, but a deep, insistent, natural desire which seemed to be slumbering for the time in a mysterious prevision of success. He thought, apparently, that his face was telling too much. He gave another little laugh, and began to whistle softly. "You are meant for something better," I said, "than to skulk about here like a burglar. How would you like to go to America and do some honest work?" I had an absurd momentary vision of helping him on his way, and giving him a letter of introduction to my brother-in-law, who was in the hardware business.

He took off his hat and passed his hand through his hair. "You think, then, I am meant for something good?"

"If you will! If you'll give up your idle idea of 'revenge' and trust to time to right your wrong."

"Give it up?—Impossible!" he said, grimly. "Ask me rather to chop off my arm. This is the same thing. It's part of my life. I *have* trusted to time—I've waited four long months, and yet here I stand as poor and helpless as at the beginning. No, no, I'm not to be treated like a dog. If he had been just, I would have done anything for him. I'm not a bad fellow; I never had an unkind thought. Very likely I was too simple, too stupid, too contented with being poor and shabby. The Lord does with us as he pleases; he thought I needed a little shaking up. I've got it, surely! But did your friend take counsel of the Lord? No, no! He took counsel of his own selfishness, and he thought himself clever enough to steal the sweet and never taste the bitter. But the bitter will come; and it will be my sweet."

"That's fine talk! Tell me in three words what it means."

"*Aspetti!*—If you are going to Rome by the coach, as I suppose, you should be moving. You may lose your place. I have an idea we shall meet again." He walked away, and in a moment I heard the great iron gate of the garden creaking on its iron hinges.

I was puzzled, and for a moment, I had a dozen minds to stop over with my friends. But on the one hand, I saw no definite way in which I could preserve them from annoyance; and on the other, I was confidently expected in Rome. Besides, might not the dusky cloud be the sooner dissipated by letting Angelo's project,—substance or shadow, whatever it was,—play itself out? To Rome accordingly I returned; but for several days I was haunted with a suspicion that something ugly, something sad, something strange, at any rate, was taking place at Albano. At last it became so oppressive that I hired a light carriage and drove back again. I reached the inn toward the close of the afternoon, and but half expected to find my friends at home. They had in fact gone out to walk, and the landlord had not noticed in what direction. I had nothing to do but to stroll about the dirty little town till their return. Do you remember the Capuchin convent at the edge of the Alban lake? I walked up to it and, seeing the door of the church still open, made my way in. The dusk had gathered in the corners, but the altar, for some pious reason, was glowing with an unusual number of candles. They twinkled picturesquely in the gloom; here and there a kneeling figure defined itself vaguely; it was a pretty piece of chiaroscuro, and I sat down to enjoy it. Presently I noticed the look of intense devotion of a young woman sitting near me. Her hands were clasped on her knees, her head thrown back and her eyes fixed in strange expansion on the shining altar. We make out pictures, you know, in the glow of the hearth at home; this young girl seemed to be reading an ecstatic vision in the light of the tapers. Her expression was so peculiar that for some moments it disguised her face and left me to perceive with a sudden shock that I was watching Adina Waddington. I looked round for her companions, but she was evidently alone. It seemed to me then that I had no right to watch her covertly, and yet I was indisposed either to disturb her or to retire and leave her. The evening was approaching; how came it that she was unaccompanied? I concluded that she was waiting for the others; Scrope, perhaps, had gone in to see the sunset from the terrace of the convent garden—a privilege denied to ladies; and Mrs Waddington was lingering outside the church to take memoranda for a sketch. I turned away, walked round the church and approached the young girl on the other side. This time my nearness aroused her. She removed her eyes from the altar, looked at me, let them rest on my face, and yet gave no sign of recognition. But at last she slowly rose and I saw that she knew me. Was she turning Catholic and preparing to give up her heretical friends? I greeted her, but she continued to look at me with intense gravity, as if her thoughts were urging her beyond frivolous civilities. She seemed not in the least flurried—as I had feared she would be—at having been observed; she was preoccupied, excited, in a deeper fashion. In suspecting that something strange was happening at Albano, apparently I was not far wrong—"What are you doing, my dear young lady," I asked brusquely, "in this lonely church?"

"I'm asking for light," she said.

"I hope you've found it!" I answered smiling.

"I think so!" and she moved toward the door. "I'm alone," she added, "will you take me home?" She accepted my arm and we passed out; but in front of the church she paused. "Tell me," she said suddenly, "are you a very intimate friend of Mr Scrope's?"

"You must ask him," I answered, "if he considers me so. I at least aspire to the honor." The intensity of her manner embarrassed me, and I tried to take refuge in jocosity.

"Tell me then this: will he bear a disappointment—a keen disappointment?"

She seemed to appeal to me to say yes! But I felt that she had a project in hand, and I had no warrant to give her a license. I looked at her a moment; her solemn eyes seemed to grow and grow till they made her whole face a mute entreaty.

"No;" I said resolutely, "decidedly not!"

She gave a heavy sigh and we walked on. She seemed buried in her thoughts; she gave no heed to my attempts at conversation, and I had to wait till we reached the inn for an explanation of her solitary visit to Capuccini. Her companions had come in, and from them, after their welcome, I learned that the three had gone out together, but that Adina had presently complained of fatigue, and obtained leave to go home. "If I break down on the way," she had said, "I will go into a church to rest." They had been surprised at not finding her at the inn, and were grateful for my having met her. Evidently, they, too, had discovered that the young girl was in a singular mood. Mrs Waddington had a forced smile, and Scrope had no smile at all. Adina quietly sat down to her needlework, and we confessed, even tacitly, to no suspicion of her being "nervous." Common nervousness it certainly was not; she bent her head calmly over her embroidery, and drew her stitches with a hand innocent of the slightest tremor. At last we had dinner; it passed somewhat oppressively, and I was thankful for Scrope's proposal, afterwards, to go and smoke a cigar in the garden. Poor Scrope was unhappy; I could see that, but I hardly ventured to hope that he would tell me off-hand what was the matter with Adina. It naturally occurred to me that she had shown a disposition to retract her engagement. I gave him a dozen chances to say so, but he evidently could not trust himself to utter his fears. To give

an impetus to our conversation, I reminded him of his nearness to Lariccia, and asked whether he had had a glimpse of
Angelo Beati.

"Several," he said. "He has passed me in the village, or on
the roads, some half a dozen times. He gives me an impudent
stare and goes his way. He takes it out in looking daggers
from his dark eyes; you see how much there is to be feared
from him!"

"He doesn't quite take it out," I presently said, "in looking
daggers. He hangs about the inn at night; he roams about the
garden while you're in bed, as if he thought that he might give
you bad dreams by staring at your windows." And I described our recent interview at dawn.

Scrope stared in great surprise, then slowly flushed in rising
anger. "Curse the meddling idiot!" he cried. "If he doesn't
know where to stop, I'll show him."

"Buy him off!" I said sturdily.

"I'll buy him a horsewhip and give it to him over his
broad back!"

I put my hands in my pockets, I believe, and strolled away,
whistling. Come what might, I washed my hands of media-
tion! But it was not irritation, for I felt a strange, half-
reasoned increase of pity for my friend's want of pliancy. He
stood puffing his cigar gloomily, and by way of showing him
that I didn't altogether give up, I asked him at last whether it
had yet been settled when he should marry. He had told me
shortly before that this was still an open question, and that
Miss Waddington preferred to leave it so.

He made no immediate answer, but looked at me hard,
"Why do you ask—just now?"

"Why, my dear fellow, friendly curiosity—" I began.

He tossed the end of his cigar nervously upon the ground.
"No, no; it's not friendly curiosity!" he cried. "You've
noticed something—you suspect something!"

Since he insisted, I confessed that I did. "That beautiful

girl," I said, "seems to me agitated and preoccupied; I wondered whether you had been having a quarrel."

He seemed relieved at being pressed to speak.

"That beautiful girl is a puzzle. I don't know what's the matter with her; it's all very painful; she's a very strange creature. I never dreamed there was an obstacle to our happiness—to our union. She has never protested and promised; it's not her way, nor her nature; she is always humble, passive, gentle; but always extremely grateful for every sign of tenderness. Till within three or four days ago, she seemed to me more so than ever; her habitual gentleness took the form of a sort of shrinking, almost suffering, deprecation of my attentions, my *petits soins*, my lover's nonsense. It was as if they oppressed and mortified her—and she would have liked me to bear more lightly. I did not see directly that it was not the excess of my devotion, but my devotion itself—the very fact of my love and her engagement that pained her. When I did it was a blow in the face. I don't know what under heaven I've done! Women are fathomless creatures. And yet Adina is not capricious, in the common sense. Mrs Waddington told me that it was a 'girl's mood,' that we must not seem to heed it,—it would pass over. I've been waiting, but the situation don't mend; you've guessed at trouble without a hint. So these are *peines d'amour?*" he went on, after brooding a moment. "I didn't know how fiercely I was in love!"

I don't remember with what well-meaning foolishness I was going to attempt to console him; Mrs Waddington suddenly appeared and drew him aside. After a moment's murmured talk with her, he went rapidly into the house. She remained with me and, as she seemed greatly perplexed, and we had, moreover, often discussed our companion's situation and prospects, I immediately told her that Scrope had just been relating his present troubles. "They are very unexpected," she cried. "It's thunder in a clear sky. Just now Adina laid down her work and told me solemnly that she would like to see Mr

Scrope alone; would I kindly call him? Would she kindly tell me, I inquired, what in common sense was the matter with her, and what she proposed to say to him." She looked at me a moment as if I were a child of five years old interrupting family prayers; then came up gently and kissed me, and said I would know everything in good time. Does she mean to stand there in that same ghostly fashion and tell him that, on the whole, she has decided not to marry him? What has the poor man done?"

"She has ceased to love him," I suggested.

"Why ceased, all of a sudden?"

"Perhaps it's not so sudden as you suppose. Such things have happened, in young women's hearts, as a gradual revision of a first impression."

"Yes, but not without a particular motive—another fancy. Adina is fanciful, that I know; with all respect be it said, it was fanciful to accept poor Sam to begin with. But her choice deliberately made, what has put her out of humor with it?— in a word the only possible explanation would be that our young lady has transferred her affections. But it's impossible!"

"Absolutely so?" I asked.

"Absolutely. Judge for yourself. To whom, pray? She hasn't seen another man in a month. Who could have so mysteriously charmed her? The little hunchback who brings us mandarin oranges every morning? Perhaps she has lost her heart to Prince Doria! I believe he has been staying at his villa yonder."

I found no smile for this mild sarcasm. I was wondering— wondering. "Has she literally seen no one else?" I asked when my wonderings left me breath.

"I can't answer for whom she may have *seen*; she's not blind. But she has spoken to no one else, nor been spoken to; that's very certain. Love at sight—at sight only—used to be common in the novels I devoured when I was fifteen; but I doubt whether it exists anywhere else."

I had a question on my tongue's end, but I hesitated some time to risk it. I debated some time in silence and at last I uttered it, with a prefatory apology. "On which side of the house is Adina's room?"

"Pray, what are you coming to?" said my companion. "On this side."

"It looks into the garden?"

"There it is in the second story."

"Be so good——which one?"

"The third window—the one with the shutters tied back with a handkerchief."

The shutters and the handkerchief suddenly acquired a mysterious fascination for me. I looked at them for some time, and when I glanced back at my companion our eyes met. I don't know what she thought—what she thought I thought. I thought it *might* be out of a novel—such a thing as love at sight; such a thing as an unspoken dialogue, between a handsome young Italian with a "wrong," in a starlit garden, and a fanciful western maid at a window. From her own sudden impression Mrs Waddington seemed slowly to recoil. She gathered her shawl about her, shivered, and turned towards the house. "The thing to do," I said, offering her my arm, "is to leave Albano to-morrow."

On the inner staircase we paused; Mrs Waddington was loth to interrupt Adina's interview with Scrope. While she was hesitating whither to turn, the door of her sitting-room opened, and the young girl passed out. Scrope stood behind her, very pale, his face distorted with an emotion he was determined to repress. She herself was pale, but her eyes were lighted up like two wind-blown torches. Meeting the elder lady, she stopped, stood for a moment, looking down and hesitating, and then took Mrs Waddington's two hands and silently kissed her. She turned to me, put out her hand, and said "Good night!" I shook it, I imagine, with sensible ardor, for somehow, I was deeply impressed. There was a nameless force in the girl, before which one had to stand back. She lingered but an instant and rapidly disappeared towards her room, in the dusky corridor. Mrs Waddington laid her hand kindly upon Scrope's arm and led him back into the parlor. He evidently was not going to be plaintive; his pride was rankling and burning, and it seasoned his self-control.

"Our engagement is at an end," he simply said.

Mrs Waddington folded her hands. "And for what reason?"

"None."

It was cruel, certainly; but what could we say? Mrs Waddington sank upon the sofa and gazed at the poor fellow in mute, motherly compassion. Her large, caressing pity irritated him; he took up a book and sat down with his back to her. I took up another, but I couldn't read; I sat noticing that he never turned his own page. Mrs Waddington at last transferred her gaze uneasily, appealingly, to me; she moved about restlessly in her place; she was trying to shape my vague intimations in the garden into something palpable to common credulity. I could give her now no explanation that would not have been a gratuitous offense to Scrope. But I felt more and more nervous; my own vague previsions oppressed me. I flung down my book at last, and left the room. In the corridor Mrs Waddington overtook me, and requested me to tell her what I meant by my extraordinary allusions to—"in plain English," she said, "to an intrigue."

"It would be needless, and it would be painful," I answered, "to tell you now and here. But promise me to return to Rome to-morrow. There we can take breath and talk."

"Oh, we shall bundle off, I promise!" she cried. And we separated. I mounted the stairs to go to my room; as I did so I heard her dress rustling in the corridor, undecidedly. Then came the sound of a knock; she had stopped at Adina's door. Involuntarily I paused and listened. There was a silence, and then another knock; another silence and a third knock; after this, despairing, apparently, of obtaining admission, she moved away, and I went to my room. It was useless going to bed; I knew I should not sleep. I stood a long time at my open window, wondering whether I had anything to say to Scrope. At the end of half an hour I wandered down into the garden again, and strolled through all the alleys. They were empty, and there was a light in Adina's window. No; it seemed to me that there was nothing I could bring myself to say to Scrope, but that he should leave Albano the next day, and Rome and Italy as soon after as possible, wait a year, and then try his fortune with Miss Waddington again. Towards morning I *did* sleep.

Breakfast was served in Mrs Waddington's parlor, and Scrope appeared punctually, as neatly shaved and brushed as if he were still under tribute to a pair of blue eyes. He really, of course, felt less serene than he looked. It can never be comfortable to meet at breakfast the young lady who has rejected you over night. Mrs Waddington kept us waiting some time, but at last she entered with surprising energy. Her comely face was flushed from brow to chin, and in her hand she clasped a crumpled note. She flung herself upon the sofa and burst into tears; I had only time to turn the grinning *cameriera* out of the room. "She's gone, gone, gone!" she cried, among her sobs. "Oh the crazy, wicked, ungrateful girl!"

Scrope, of course, knew no more than a tea-pot what she meant; but I understood her more promptly—and yet I believe I gave a long whistle. Scrope stood staring at her as she thrust out the crumpled note: that she meant that Adina— that Adina had left us in the night—was too large a horror for his unprepared sense. His dumb amazement was an almost touching sign of the absence of a thought which could have injured the girl. He saw by my face that I knew something, and he let me draw the note from Mrs Waddington's hand and read it aloud:

"Good-bye to everything! Think me crazy if you will. I could never explain. Only forget me and believe that I am happy, happy, happy!   Adina Beati."

I laid my hand on his shoulder; even yet he seemed powerless to apprehend. "Angelo Beati," I said gravely, "has at last taken his revenge!"

"Angelo Beati!" he cried. "An Italian beggar! It's a lie!"

I shook my head and patted his shoulder. "He has insisted on payment. He's a clever fellow!"

He saw that I knew, and slowly, distractedly he answered with a burning blush!

It was a most extraordinary occurrence; we had ample time to say so, and to say so again, and yet never really to understand it. Neither of my companions ever saw the young girl again; Scrope never mentioned her but once. He went about for a week in absolute silence; when at last he spoke I saw that the fold was taken, that he was going to be a professional cynic for the rest of his days. Mrs Waddington was a good-natured woman, as I have said, and, better still, she was a just woman. But I assure you, she never forgave her step-daughter. In after years, as I grew older, I took an increasing satisfaction in having assisted, as they say, at this episode. As mere *action*, it seemed to me really superb, and in judging of human nature I often weighed it mentally against the perpetual spectacle of strong impulses frittered in weakness and perverted by prudence. There has been no prudence here, certainly, but there has been ardent, full-blown, positive passion. We see the one every day, the other once in five years. More than once I ventured to ventilate this heresy before the kindly widow, but she always stopped me short. "The thing was odious," she said; "I thank heaven the girl's father did not live to see it."

We didn't finish that dismal day at Albano, but returned in the evening to Rome. Before our departure I had an interview with the Padre Girolamo of Lariccia, who failed to strike me as the holy man whom his nephew had described. He was a swarthy, snuffy little old priest, with a dishonest eye—quite capable, I believed, of teaching his handsome nephew to play his cards. But I had no reproaches to waste upon him; I simply wished to know whither Angelo had taken the young girl. I obtained the information with difficulty and only after a solemn promise that if Adina should reiterate, *vivâ voce*, to a person delegated by her friends, the statement that she was happy, they would take no steps to recover possession of her. She was in Rome, and in that holy city they should leave her. "Remember," said the Padre, very softly, "that she is of age, and her own mistress, and can do what she likes with her money;—she has a good deal of it, eh?" She had less than he thought, but evidently the Padre knew his ground. It was he, he admitted, who had united the young couple in marriage, the day before; the ceremony had taken place in the little old circular church on the hill, at Albano, at five o'clock in the morning. "You see, Signor," he said, slowly rubbing his yellow hands, "she had taken a great fancy!" I gave him no chance, by any remark of my own, to remind me that Angelo had a grudge to satisfy, but he professed the assurance that his nephew was the sweetest fellow in the world. I heard and departed in silence; my curiosity, at least, had not yet done with Angelo.

Mrs Waddington, also, had more of this sentiment than she confessed to; her kindness wondered, under protest of her indignation, how on earth the young girl was living, and whether the smells on her staircase were very bad indeed. It was, therefore, at her tacit request that I repaired to the lodging of the young pair, in the neighborhood of the Piazza Barberini. The quarters were modest, but they looked into the quaint old gardens of the Capuchin Friars; and in the way of smells, I observed nothing worse than the heavy breath of a great bunch of pinks in a green jug on the window sill. Angelo stood there, pulling one of the pinks to pieces, and looking quite the proper hero of his romance. He eyed me shyly and a trifle coldly at first, as if he were prepared to stand firm against a possible blowing up; but when he saw that I chose to make no allusions whatever to the past, he suffered his dark brow to betray his serene contentment. I was no more disposed than I had been a week before, to call him a bad fellow; but he was a mystery,—his character was as great an enigma as the method of his courtship. That he was in love I don't pretend to say; but I think he had already forgotten how his happiness had come to him, and that he was basking in a sort of primitive natural, sensuous delight in being adored. It was like the warm sunshine, or like plenty of good wine. I don't believe his fortune in the least surprised him; at the bottom of every genuine Roman heart,—even if it beats beneath a beggar's rags,—you'll find an ineradicable belief that we are all barbarians, and made to pay them tribute. He was welcome to all his grotesque superstitions, but what sort of a future did they promise for Adina? I asked leave to speak with her; he shrugged his shoulders, said she was free to choose, and went into an adjoining room with my proposal. Her choice apparently was difficult; I waited some time, wondering how she would look on the other side of the ugly chasm she had so audaciously leaped. She came in at last, and I immediately saw that she was vexed by my visit. She wished to utterly forget her past. She was pale and very grave; she seemed to wear a frigid mask of reserve. If she had seemed to me a singular creature before, it didn't help me to understand her to see her there, beside her extraordinary husband. My eyes went from one to the other and, I suppose, betrayed my reflections; she suddenly begged me to inform her of my errand.

"I have been asked," I said, "to enquire whether you are contented. Mrs Waddington is unwilling to leave Rome while there is a chance of your——" I hesitated for a word, and she interrupted me.

"Of my repentance, is what you mean to say?" She fixed her eyes on the ground for a moment, then suddenly raised them. "Mrs Waddington may leave Rome," she said softly. I turned in silence, but waited a moment for some slight message of farewell. "I only ask to be forgotten!" she added, seeing me stand.

Love is said to be *par excellence* the egotistical passion; if so Adina was far gone. "I can't promise to forget you," I said; "you and my friend here deserve to be remembered!"

She turned away; Angelo seemed relieved at the cessation of our English. He opened the door for me, and stood for a moment with a significant, conscious smile.

"She's happy, eh?" he asked.

"So she says!"

He laid his hand on my arm, "So am I!—She's better than the topaz!"

"You're a queer fellow!" I cried; and, pushing past him, I hurried away.

Mrs Waddington gave her step-daughter another chance to repent, for she lingered in Rome a fortnight more. She was disappointed at my being able to bring her no information as to how Adina had eluded observation—how she had played her game and kept her secret. My own belief was that there had been a very small amount of courtship, and that until she stole out of the house the morning before her flight, to meet the Padre Girolamo and his nephew at the church, she had barely heard the sound of her lover's voice. There had been signs, and glances, and other unspoken vows, two or three notes, perhaps. Exactly who Angelo was, and what had originally secured for us the honor of his attentions, Mrs Waddington never learned; it was enough for her that he was a friendless, picturesque Italian. Where everything was a painful puzzle, a shade or two, more or less, of obscurity hardly mattered. Scrope, of course, never attempted to account for his own blindness, though to his silent thoughts it must have seemed bitterly strange. He spoke of Adina, as I said, but once.

He knew by instinct, by divination,—for I had not told him,—that I had been to see her, and late on the evening following my visit, he proposed to me to take a stroll through the streets. It was a soft, damp night, with vague, scattered cloud masses through which the moon was slowly drifting. A warm south wind had found its way into the dusky heart of the city. "Let us go to St Peter's," he said, "and see the fountains play in the fitful moonshine." When we reached the bridge of St Angelo, he paused and leaned some time on the parapet, looking over into the Tiber. At last, suddenly raising himself—"You've seen her?" he asked.

"Yes."

"What did she say?"

"She said she was happy."

He was silent, and we walked on. Half-way over the bridge he stopped again and gazed at the river. Then he drew a small velvet case from his pocket, opened it, and let something shine in the moonlight. It was the beautiful, the imperial, the baleful topaz. He looked at me and I knew what his look meant. It made my heart beat, but I did not say—no! It had been a curse, the golden gem, with its cruel emblems; let it return to the moldering underworld of the Roman past! I shook his hand firmly, he stretched out the other and, with a great flourish, tossed the glittering jewel into the dusky river. There it lies! Some day, I suppose, they will dredge the Tiber for treasures, and, possibly, disinter our topaz, and recognize it. But who will guess at this passionate human interlude to its burial of centuries?

R

PROFESSOR FARGO

I

THE little town of P—— is off the railway, and reached by a coach drive of twenty-five miles, which the primitive condition of the road makes a trial to the flesh, and the dulness of the landscape a weariness to the spirit. It was therefore not balm to my bruises, physical or intellectual, to find, on my arrival, that the gentleman for whose sake I had undertaken the journey had just posted off in a light buggy for a three days' holiday. After venting my disappointment in a variety of profitless expletives, I decided that the only course worthy of the elastic philosophy of a commercial traveller was to take a room at the local tavern and await his return. P—— was obviously not an exhilarating place of residence, but I had out-weathered darker hours, and I reflected that having, as the phrase is, a bone to pick with my correspondent, a little accumulated irritation would arm me for the combat. Moreover, I had been rattling about for three months by rail; I was mortally tired, and the prospect of spending a few days beyond earshot of the steam whistle was not unwelcome. A certain audible, rural hush seemed to hang over the little town, and there was nothing apparently to prevent my giving it the whole of my attention. I lounged awhile in the tavern porch, but my presence seemed only to deepen the spell of silence on that customary group of jaundiced ruminants who were tilting their chairs hard by. I measured thrice, in its length, the dusty plank sidewalk of the main street, counted the hollyhocks in the front yards, and read the names on the little glass door plates; and finally, in despair, I visited the cemetery. Although we were at the end of September, the day was hot, and this youthful institution boasted but a scanty growth of funereal umbrage. No weeping willow, no dusky cypress offered a friendly shelter to the meditative visitor. The yellow grass and the white tombstones glared in the hot light, and though I felt very little merrier than a graveyard ghost, I staid hardly longer than one who should have mistaken his hour. But I am fond of reading country epitaphs, and I promised myself to come back when the sun was lower. On my way back to the inn I found myself, on a lately opened cross street, face to face with the town hall, and pausing approached its threshold with hopes of entertainment scarcely less ardent than those which, during a journey abroad, had guided my steps toward some old civic palace of France or Italy. There was, of course, no liveried minion to check my advance, and I made my way unchallenged into the large, bare room which occupied the body of the edifice. It was the accustomed theatre of town meetings, caucuses, and other solemn services, but it seemed just now to have been claimed for profaner uses. An itinerant lecturer, of a boisterous type, was unpacking his budget and preparing his *mise en scène*. This seemed to consist simply of a small table and three chairs in a row, and of a dingy specimen of our national standard, to whose awkward festoons, suspended against the blank wall at the rear of the platform, the orator in person was endeavoring to impart a more artistic grace. Another personage on the floor was engaged in scrawling the date of the performance, in red chalk, upon a number of printed handbills. He silently thrust one of these documents at me as I passed, and I saw with some elation that I had a resource for my evening. The latter half of the page consisted of extracts from village newspapers, setting forth the merits of the entertainments. The headings alone, as I remember them, ran somewhat in this fashion:

A MESSAGE FROM THE SPIRIT WORLD

THE HIGHER MATHEMATICS MADE EASY TO LADIES
AND CHILDREN

A New Revelation! A New Science!

Great Moral and Scientific Combination

Professor Fargo, the Infallible Waking Medium and
Magician, Clairvoyant, Prophet, and Seer!

Colonel Gifford, the famous Lightning Calculator
and Mathematical Reformer!

This was the substance of the programme, but there were
a great many incidental *fioriture* which I have forgotten. By
the time I had mastered them, however, for the occasion, the
individual who was repairing the tattered flag, turned round,
perceived me, and showed me a countenance which could
belong only to an "infallible waking medium." It was not,
indeed, that Professor Fargo had the abstracted and emaciated
aspect which tradition attributes to prophets and visionaries.
On the contrary, the fleshly element in his composition
seemed, superficially, to enjoy a luxurious preponderance
over the spiritual. He was tall and corpulent, and wore an
air of aggressive robustness. A mass of reddish hair was
tossed back from his forehead in a leonine fashion, and a
lustrous auburn beard diffused itself complacently over an
expansive but by no means immaculate shirt front. He was
dressed in a black evening suit, of a tarnished elegance, and it
was in keeping with the festal pattern of his garments, that on
the right forefinger of a large, fat hand, he should wear an
immense turquoise ring. His intimate connection with the
conjuring class was stamped upon his whole person; but to a
superficial glance he might have seemed a representative of its
grosser accomplishments. You could have fancied him, in
spangled fleshings, looking down the lion's mouth, or cracking the ring-master's whip at the circus, while Mlle Josephine
jumped through the hoops. It was his eyes, when you fairly
met them, that proved him an artist on a higher line. They
were eyes which had peeped into stranger places than even

lions' mouths. Their pretension, I know, was to pierce the veil of futurity; but if this was founded, I could only say that the vision of Ezekiel and Jeremiah was but another name for consummate Yankee shrewdness. They were, in a single word, the most impudent pair of eyes I ever beheld, and it was the especial sign of their impudence that they seemed somehow to undertake to persuade you of their disinterested benevolence. Being of a fine reddish brown color, it was probable that several young women that evening would pronounce them magnificent. Perceiving, apparently, that I had not the rustic physiognomy of a citizen of P——, Professor Fargo deemed my patronage worth securing. He advanced to the cope of the platform with his hands in his pockets, and gave me a familiar nod.

"Mind you come to-night, young man!" he said, jocosely imperious.

"Very likely I shall," I answered. "Anything in the world to help me through an evening at P——."

"Oh, you won't want your money back," the Professor rejoined. "Mine is a first-class entertainment; none of your shuffling break-downs. We are perfect, my friends and I, in our respective parts. If you are fond of a good, stiff, intellectual problem, we'll give you something to think about." The Professor spoke very slowly and benignantly, and his full, sonorous voice rolled away through the empty hall. He evidently liked to hear it himself; he balanced himself on his toes and surveyed the scene of his impending exploits. "I don't blow my own trumpet," he went on; "I'm a modest man; you'll see for yourself what I can do. But I should like to direct your attention to my friend the Colonel. *He's* a rare old gentleman to find in a travelling show! The most remarkable old gentleman, perhaps, that ever addressed a promiscuous audience. You needn't be afraid of the higher mathematics; it's all made as pretty as a game of billiards. It's his own daughter does the sums. We don't put her down in the bills, for motives of delicacy; but I'll tell you for your private satisfaction that she is an exquisite young creature of seventeen."

It was not every day that I found myself in familiar conversation with a prophet, and the opportunity for obtaining a glimpse of the inner mechanism of the profession was too precious to be neglected. I questioned the Professor about his travels, his expenses, his profits, and the mingled emotions of the itinerant showman's lot; and then, taking the bull by the horns, I asked him whether, between ourselves, an accomplished medium had not to be also a tolerable conjurer? He leaned his head on one side and stood stroking his beard, and looking at me between lids shrewdly half closed. Then he gave a little dry chuckle, which expressed, at my choice, compassion either for my disbelief in his miracles or for my faith in his urbanity.

"I confess frankly," I said, "that I'm a skeptic. I don't believe in messages from the spirit world. I don't believe that even the depressing prospect of immortality is capable of converting people who talked plain sense here on earth into the authors of the inflated platitudes which people of your profession pretend to transmit from them. I don't believe people who have expressed themselves for a lifetime in excellent English can ever be content with conversation by raps on the dinner table. I don't believe that you know anything more about the future world than you do about the penal code of China. My impression is that you don't believe so yourself. I can hardly expect you, of course, to take the wind out of your own sails. What I should vastly like you to do is, to tell me *viva voce*, in so many words, that your intentions are pure and your miracles genuine."

The Professor remained silent, still caressing his prophetic beard. At last, in a benevolent drawl, "Have you got any dear friend in the spirit land?" he asked.

"I don't know what you call the spirit land," I answered. "Several of my friends have died."

"Would you like to see 'em?" the Professor promptly demanded.

"No, I confess I shouldn't!"

The Professor shook his head.

"You've not a rich nature," he rejoined blandly.

"It depends on what you call rich. I possess on some points a wealth of curiosity. It would gratify me peculiarly to have you say outright, standing there on your own platform, that you're an honest man."

It seemed to give him pleasure to trifle with my longing for this sensation. "I'll give you leave," he said, for all answer, "to tie my hands into the tightest knot you can invent—and then I'll make your great-grandfather come in and stop the clock. You know I couldn't stop a clock, perched up on a mantel shelf five feet high, with my heels."

"I don't know," said I. "I fancy you're very clever."

"Cleverness has nothing to do with it. I've great magnetism."

"You'd magnetize my great-grandfather down from heaven?"

"Yes, sir, if I could establish communication. You'll see to-night what I can do. I'll satisfy you. If I don't, I shall be happy to give you a private sitting. I'm also a healing medium. You don't happen to have a toothache? I'd set you down there and pull it right out, as I'd pull off your boot."

In compliment to this possibility, I could only make him my bow. His, at least, was a "rich nature." I bade him farewell, with the assurance that, skeptic as I was, I would applaud him impartially in the evening. I had reached the top of the hall, on my way out, when I heard him give a low, mellifluous whistle. I turned around, and he beckoned to me to return. I walked back, and he leaned forward from the platform, uplifting his stout forefinger. "I simply desire to remark," he said, "that I'm an honest man!"

On my return to the hotel I found that my impatience for

the Professor's further elucidation of his honesty made the
interval look long. Fortune, however, assisted me to traverse
it at an elastic pace. Rummaging idly on a bookshelf in the
tavern parlor, I found, amid a pile of farmers' almanacs and
Methodist tracts, a tattered volume of "Don Quixote." I
repaired to my room, tilted back my chair, and communed
deliciously with the ingenious hidalgo. Here was "magnetism" superior even to that of Professor Fargo. It proved so
effective that I lost all note of time, and, at last on looking at
my watch, perceived that dinner must have been over for an
hour. Of "service" at this unsophisticated hostelry there was
but a rigidly democratic measure, and if I chose to cultivate
a too elegant absence of eagerness for beefsteak pie and huckle-
berry pudding, the young lady in long, tight ringlets and short
sleeves, who administered these delicacies in the dining-room,
was altogether too haughty a spirit to urge them on my
attention. So I sat alone and ate them cold. After dinner I
returned for an hour to La Mancha, and then strolled forth,
according to my morning's vow, to see the headstones in the
cemetery cast longer shadows. I was disappointed in the
epitaphs; they were posterior to the age of theological *naïveté*.
The cemetery covered the two opposed sides of a hill, and on
walking up to the ridge and looking over it, I discovered that
I was not the only visitor. Two persons had chosen the spot
for a quiet talk. One of them was a young girl, dressed in
black, and seated on a headstone, with her face turned toward
me. In spite of her attitude, however, she seemed not to perceive me, wrapt as she was in attention to her companion—a
tall, stout fellow, standing before her, with his back to me.
They were at too great a distance for me to hear their talk,
and indeed in a few minutes I began to fancy they were not
speaking. Nevertheless, the young girl's eyes remained fixed
on the man's face; he was holding her spellbound by an influence best known to himself. She was very pretty. Her hat
was off, and she was holding it in her lap; her lips were parted,

and her eyes fixed intently on her companion's face. Suddenly she gave a bright, quick smile, made a rapid gesture in the air, and laid her forefinger on her lips. The movement, and the manner of it, told her story. She was deaf and dumb, and the man had been talking to her with his fingers. I would willingly have looked at her longer, but I turned away in delicacy, and walked in another direction. As I was leaving the cemetery, however, I saw her advancing with her companion to take the path which led to the gate. The man's face was now turned to me, and I straightway recognized it, in spite of the high peaked white hat which surmounted it. It was natural enough, I suppose, to find Professor Fargo in a graveyard; as the simplest expedient for ascertaining what goes on beyond the tomb might seem to be to get as close as possible to the hither cope of it. Besides, if he was to treat the townsfolk to messages from their buried relatives, it was not amiss to "get up" a few names and dates by the perusal of the local epitaphs. As he passed me, however, and flourished his hand in the air by way of salutation, there was a fine absence in his glance of any admission that he had been caught cheating. This, too, was natural enough; what surprised me was that such a vulgar fellow should be mated with so charming a companion. She gave me as she passed the trustfully unshrinking glance of those poor mortals who are obliged to listen, as one may say, with their eyes. Her dress was scanty and simple, but there was delicacy in her mobile features. Who was she, and how had *he* got hold of her? After all, it was none of my business; but as they passed on, walking rather briskly, and I strolled after them, watching the Professor's ponderous tread and the gliding footfall of the young girl, I began to wonder whether he might not be right—might not, in truth, have that about him which would induce the most venerable of my ancestors to revert from eternity and stop the clock.

II

His handbills had done their office, and the Town Hall, when I entered it that evening, was filled with a solemnly expectant auditory. P—— was evidently for the evening a cluster of empty houses. While my companions scanned the stage for the shadow of coming events, I found ample pastime in perusing the social physiognomy of the town. A shadow presently appeared in the person of a stout young countryman, armed with an accordion, from which he extracted an ingenious variety of lamentable sounds. Soon after this mysterious prelude, the Professor marshalled out his forces. They consisted, first and foremost, of himself, his leonine *chevelure*, his black dress suit, and his turquoise ring, and then of an old gentleman who walked in gravely and stiffly, without the Professor's portentous salaam to the audience, bearing on his arm a young girl in black. The Professor managed somehow, by pushing about the chairs, turning up the lamps, and giving a twist to the patriotic drapery in the background, to make his audience feel his presence very intimately. His assistants rested themselves tranquilly against the wall. It took me but a short time to discover that the young girl was none other than the companion of the Professor's tour of inspection in the cemetery, and then I remembered that he had spoken in the morning of the gentleman who performed the mathematical miracles being assisted by his daughter. The young girl's infirmity, and her pretty face, promised to impart a picturesque interest to this portion of the exhibition; but meanwhile I inferred from certain ill-suppressed murmurs, and a good deal of vigorous pantomime among the female spectators, that she was found wanting in the more immediate picturesqueness demanded of a young lady attached to a show. Her plain black dress found no favor; the admission fee had justified the expectation of a good deal of trimming and several bracelets. She, however, poor girl, sat indifferent in her place, leaning her head back rather wearily against the wall, and looking as if, were she disposed, she might count without trouble all the queer bonnets among her judges. Her father sat upright beside her, with a cane between his knees and his two hands crossed on the knob. He was a man of sixty-five—tall, lean, pale, and serious. The lamp hanging above his head deepened the shadows on his face, and transformed it into a sort of pictorial mask. He was very bald, and his forehead, which was high and handsome, wore in the lamplight the gleam of old ivory. The sockets of his eyes were in deep shadow, and out of them his pupils gazed straight before him, with the glow of smouldering fire. His high-arched nose cast a long shadow over his mouth and chin, and two intensified wrinkles, beside his moustache, made him look strangely tragic. With his tragic look, moreover, he seemed strangely familiar. His daughter and the Professor I regarded as old friends; but where had I met this striking specimen of antique melancholy? Though his gaze seemed fixed, I imagined it was covertly wandering over the audience. At last it appeared to me that it met mine, and that its sombre glow emitted a spark of recognition of my extra-provincial and inferentially more discriminating character. The next moment I identified him—he was Don Quixote in the flesh; Don Quixote, with his sallow Spanish coloring, his high-browed, gentlemanly visage, his wrinkles, his moustache, and his sadness.

Professor Fargo's lecture was very bad. I had expected he would talk a good deal of nonsense, but I had imagined it would be cleverer nonsense. Very possibly there was a deeper cleverness in it than I perceived, and that, in his extreme shrewdness, he was giving his audience exactly what they preferred. It is an ascertained fact, I believe, that rural assemblies have a relish for the respectably ponderous, and an honest pride in the fact that they cannot be bored. The Professor, I suppose, felt the pulse of his listeners, and detected treasures of latent sympathy in their solemn, irresponsive silence. I should have said the performance was falling dead, but the Professor probably would have claimed that this was the rapture of attention and awe. He certainly kept very meagrely the promise of his grandiloquent programme, and gave us a pound of precept to a grain of example. His miracles were exclusively miracles of rhetoric. He discoursed upon the earth life and the summer land, and related surprising anecdotes of his intimacy with the inhabitants of the latter region; but to my disappointment, the evening passed away without his really bringing us face to face with a ghost. A number of "prominent citizens" were induced to step upon the platform and be magnetized, but the sturdy agricultural temperament of P—— showed no great pliancy under the Professor's manual blandishments. The attempt was generally a failure— the only brilliant feature being the fine impudence with which the operator lodged the responsibility of the *fiasco* upon what he called his victim's low development. With three or four young girls the thing was a trifle better. One of them closed her eyes and shivered; another had a fearful access of nervous giggling; another burst into tears, and was restored to her companions with an admonitory wink. As every one knew every one else and every one else's family history, some sensation was probably produced by half a dozen happy guesses as to the Christian names and last maladies of certain defunct town worthies. Another deputation of the prominent citizens ascended the platform and wrote the names of departed friends on small bits of paper, which they threw into a hat. The Professor then folded his arms and clutched his beard, as if he were invoking inspiration. At last he approached the young girl, who sat in the background, took her hand, and led her forward. She picked the papers out of the hat and held them up one by one, for the Professor to look at. "There is no possible collusion," he said with a flourish, as he presented her to the audience. "The young lady is a deaf mute!" On a gesture of her companion she passed the paper to one of the contemplative gray heads who represented the scientific curiosity of P——, and he verified the Professor's guess. The Professor risked an "Abijah" or a "Melinda," and it turned out generally to be an Ezekiel or a Hepzibah. Three several times, however, the performer's genius triumphed; whereupon, the audience not being up to the mark, he gave himself a vigorous round of applause. He concluded with the admission that the spirits were shy before such a crowd, but that he would do much better for the ladies and gentlemen individually, if they would call on him at the hotel.

It was all terribly vulgar rubbish, and I was glad when it was over. While it lasted, the old gentleman behind continued to sit motionless, seeming neither to see, to hear, nor to understand. I wondered what he thought of it, and just what it cost his self-respect to give it the sanction of his presence. It seemed, indeed, as if mentally he were not present; as if by an intense effort he had succeeded in making consciousness a blank, and was awaiting his own turn in a kind of trance. Once only he moved—when the Professor came and took his daughter by the hand. He gave an imperceptible start, controlled himself, then, dropping his hand a little, closed his eyes and kept them closed until she returned to his side. There was an intermission, during which the Professor walked about the platform, shaking his mane and wiping his forehead, and surveying the audience with an air of lofty benevolence, as if, having sown the seed, he was expecting to see it germinate on the spot. At last he rapped on the table and introduced the old gentleman—Colonel Gifford, the Great Mathematical Magician and Lightning Calculator; after which he retreated in turn to the background—if a gentleman with tossing mane and flowing beard, that turquoise ring, and generally expansive and importunate presence, could be said to be, under any circumstances, in the background. The old gentleman came forward and made his bow, and the young girl placed herself beside him, simply, unaffectedly, with her hands hanging and crossed in front of her—with all the childish grace and serenity of Mignon in "Wilhelm Meister," as we see her grouped with the old harper. Colonel Gifford's performance gave me an exquisite pleasure, which I am bound to confess was quite independent of its intrinsic merits. These, I am afraid, were at once too numerous and too scanty to have made it a popular success. It was a very ingenious piece of scientific contrivance, but it was meagrely adapted to tickle the ears of the groundlings. If one had read it—the substance of it—in a handsomely printed pamphlet, under the lamp, of a wet evening when no one was likely to call, one would have been charmed at once with the quaint vivacity of the author's mode of statement, and with the unexpected agility of one's own intellect. But in spite of an obvious effort to commend himself to understandings more familiar with the rule of thumb than with the differential calculus, Colonel Gifford remained benignantly but formidably unintelligible. He had devised—so far as I understood it—an extension of the multiplication table to enormous factors, by which he expected to effect a revolution in the whole science of accounts. There was the theory, which rather lost itself, thanks to his discursive fervor, in the mists of the higher mathematics, and there was the practice, which, thanks to his daughter's coöperation, was much more gracefully concrete. The interesting thing to me was the speaker's personality, not his system. Although evidently a very positive old man, he had a singularly simple, unpretentious tone. His intensity of faith in the supreme importance of his doctrine gave his manner a sort of reverential hush. The echoes of Professor Fargo's windy verbiage increased the charms of his mild sincerity. He spoke in a feeble, tremulous voice, which every now and then quavered upward with excitement, and then subsided into a weary, plaintive cadence. He was an old gentleman of a single idea, but his one idea was a religion. It was impossible not to feel a kindness for him, and imagine that he excited among his auditors something of the vague good will—half pity and half reverence—that uncorrupted souls entertain for those neat, keeneyed, elderly people who are rumored to have strange ways and say strange things—to be "cracked," in short, like a fine bit of porcelain which will hold together only so long as you don't push it about. But it was upon the young girl, when once she had given them a taste of her capacity, that they bestowed their frankest admiration. Now that she stood forward in the bright light, I could observe the character of her prettiness. It was no brilliant beauty, but a sort of meagre, attenuated, angular grace, the delicacy and fragility of the characteristic American type. Her chest was flat, her neck extremely thin, her visage narrow, and her forehead high and prominent. But her fair hair encircled her head in such fleecy tresses, her cheeks had such a pale pink flush, her eyes such an appealing innocence, her attitude such a quaint unconscious felicity, that one watched her with a kind of upstart belief that to such a stainless little spirit the working of miracles might be really possible. A couple of blackboards were hung against the wall, on one of which the old man rapidly chalked a problem—choosing one, of course, on the level of the brighter minds in the audience. The young girl glanced at it, and before we could count ten dashed off a great bold answer on the other tablet. The brighter minds were then invited to verify, and the young lady was invariably found to have hit the mark. She was in fact a little arithmetical fairy, and her father made her perform a series of gymnastics among numbers as brilliant in their way as the vocal flourishes and roulades of an accomplished singer. Communicating with her altogether by the blackboard, he drew from her a host of examples of the beauty of his system of transcendent multiplication. A person present was requested to furnish two enormous numbers, one to multiply the other. The old man wrote them out. After standing an instant meditative and just touching her forehead with her forefinger, she chalked down the prodigious result. Her father then performed rapidly, on the blackboard, the operation according to his own system (which she had employed mentally), and finally satisfied every one by repeating it in the roundabout fashion actually in use. This was all Colonel Gifford's witchcraft. It sounds very ponderous, but it was really very charming, and I had an agreeable sense of titillation in the finer parts of my intellectual mechanism. I felt more like a thinking creature. I had never supposed I was coming to P—— to take a lesson in culture.

It seemed on the morrow as if, at any rate, I was to take a lesson in patience. It was a Sunday, and I awoke to hear the rain pattering against my window panes. A rainy Sunday at P—— was a prospect to depress the most elastic mind. But as I stepped into my slippers, I bethought myself of my unfinished volume of "Don Quixote," and promised myself to borrow from Sancho Panza a philosophic proverb or so applicable to my situation. "Don Quixote" consoled me, as it turned out, in an unexpected fashion. On descending to the dining-room of the inn, while I mentally balanced the contending claims of muddy coffee and sour green tea, I found that my last evening's friends were also enjoying the hospitality of the establishment. It was the only inn in the place, and it would already have occurred to a more investigating mind that we were fellow-lodgers. The Professor, happily, was absent; and it seemed only reasonable that a ghost-seer should lie in bed late of a morning. The melancholy old mathematician was seated at the breakfast table cutting his dry toast into geometrical figures. He gave me a formal bow as I entered, and proceeded to dip his sodden polygons into his tea. The young girl was at the window, leaning her forehead against the pane, and looking out into the sea of yellow mud in the village street. I had not been in the room a couple of minutes when, seeming

S

in spite of her deafness to feel that I was near, she turned straight round and looked at me. She wore no trace of fatigue from her public labors, but was the same clear-eyed, noiseless little sprite as before. I observed that, by daylight, her black dress was very shabby, and her father's frock coat, buttoned with military precision up to his chin, had long since exchanged its original lustre for the melancholy brilliancy imparted by desperate brushing. I was afraid that Professor Fargo was either a niggardly *impresario*, or that the great "moral and scientific combination" was not always as remunerative as it seemed to have been at P——. While I was making these reflections the Professor entered, with an exhilaration of manner which I conceived to be a tribute to unwonted success.

"Well, sir," he cried, as his eyes fell upon me, "what do you say to it now? I hope we did things handsomely, eh? I hope you call that a solid entertainment. This young man, you must know, is one of the scoffers," he went on, turning to the Colonel. "He came yesterday and bearded the lion in his den. He snaps his fingers at spirits, suspects me of foul play, and would like me to admit, in my private character, that you and I are a couple of sharpers. I hope we satisfied you!"

The Colonel went on dipping his toast into his tea, looking grave and saying nothing. "Poor man!" I said to myself; "he despises his colleague—and so do I. I beg your pardon," I cried with warmth; "I would like nothing of the kind. I was extremely interested in this gentleman's exhibition;" and I made the Colonel a bow. "It seemed to me remarkable for its perfect good faith and truthfulness."

"Many thanks for the compliment," said the Professor. "As much as to say the Colonel's an apostle, and I'm a rascal. Have it as you please; if so, I'm a hardened one!" he declared with a great slap on his pocket; "and anyhow, you know, it's all one concern," and the Professor betook himself to the window where Miss Gifford was standing. She had not looked round at him on his entrance, as she had done at me. The Colonel, in response to my compliment, looked across at me with mild benignity, and I assured him afresh of my admiration. He listened silently, stirring his tea; his face betrayed an odd mixture of confidence and deprecation; as if he thought it just possible that I might be laughing at him, but that if I was not, it was extremely delightful. I continued to insist on its being distinctively *his* half of the performance that had pleased me; so that, gradually convinced of my respectful sympathy, he seemed tacitly to intimate that, if we were only alone and he knew me a little better, it would do him a world of good to talk it all over. I determined to give him a chance at the earliest moment. The Professor, meanwhile, waiting for his breakfast, remained at the window experimenting in the deaf and dumb alphabet with the young girl. It took him, as an amateur, a long time to form his sentences, but he went on bravely, brandishing his large, plump knuckles before her face. She seemed very patient of his slowness, and stood watching his gestures with the same intense earnestness I had caught a glimpse of in the cemetery. Most of my female friends enjoy an unimpeded use of their tongues, and I was unable from experience to appreciate his situation; but I could easily fancy what a delightful sense of intimacy there must be in this noiseless exchange of long looks with a pretty creature toward whom all *tendresse* of attitude might be conveniently attributed to compassion. Before long the Colonel pushed away his cup, turned about, folded his arms, and fixed his eyes with a frown on the Professor. It seemed to me that I read in his glance a complete revelation of moral torture. The stress of fortune had made them associates, but the Colonel jealously guarded the limits of their private intimacy. The Professor, with all his audacity, suffered himself to be reminded of them. He suddenly pulled out his watch and clamored for his coffee, and was soon seated at a repast which indicated that the prophetic temperament requires a generous diet. The young girl roamed about the room, looking idly at this and that, as if she were used to doing nothing. When she met my eye, she smiled brightly, after a moment's gravity, as if she were also used to saying to people, mentally, "Yes, I know I'm a strange little creature, but you must not be afraid of me." The Professor had hardly got that array of innumerable little dishes, of the form and dimensions of soap-trays, with which one is served in the rural hostelries of New England, well under contribution, before a young lady was introduced who had come to request him to raise a ghost—a resolute young lady, with several ringlets and a huge ancestral umbrella, whose matutinal appetite for the supernatural had not been quenched by the raw autumnal storm. She produced very frankly a "tin-type" of a florid young man, actually deceased, and demanded to be confronted with his ghost. The day was beginning well for the Professor. He gallantly requested her to be seated, and promised her every satisfaction. While he was hastily despatching his breakfast, the Colonel's daughter made acquaintance with her bereaved sister. She drew the young man's portrait gently out of her hand, examined it, and then shook her head with a little grimace of displeasure. The young woman laughed good-naturedly, and screamed into her ear that she didn't believe she was a bit deaf and dumb. At the announcement the Colonel, who, after eyeing her while she stated her credulous errand with solemn compassion, had turned away to the window, as if to spare himself the spectacle of his colleague's unblushing pretensions, turned back again and eyed her coldly from head to foot. "I recommend you, madam," he said sternly, "to reserve your suspicions for an occasion in which they may be more pertinent."

Later in the morning I found him still in the dining-room with his daughter. Professor Fargo, he said, was in the parlor, raising ghosts by the dozen: and after a little pause he gave an angry laugh, as if his suppressed irritation were causing him more than usual discomfort. He was walking up and down,

2

with slow, restless steps, and smoking a frugal pipe. I took the liberty of offering him a good cigar, and while he puffed it gratefully, the need to justify himself for his odd partnership slowly gathered force. "It would be a satisfaction for me to tell you, sir," he said at last, looking at me with eyes that fairly glittered with the pleasure of hearing himself speak the words, "that my connection with Professor Fargo implies no—no—" and he paused for a moment—"no intellectual approval of his extraordinary pretensions. This, of course, is between ourselves. You're a stranger to me, and it's doubtless the height of indiscretion in me to take you into my confidence. My subsistence depends on my not quarrelling with my companion. If you were to repeat to him that I went about undermining the faith, the extremely retributive faith, as you see" (and he nodded toward the parlor door), "of his audiences, he would of course dissolve our partnership and I should be adrift again, trying to get my heavy boat in tow. I should perhaps feel like an honest man again, but meanwhile, probably, I should starve. Misfortune," he added bitterly, "makes strange bedfellows; and I have been unfortunate!"

There was so much melancholy meaning in this declaration that I asked him frankly who and what he was. He puffed his cigar vigorously for some moments without replying, and at last turned his fine old furrowed visage upon me through a cloud of smoke. "I'm a fanatic. I feed on illusions and cherish ambitions which will never butter my bread. Don't be afraid; I won't buttonhole *you*; but I have a head full of schemes which I believe the world would be the happier for giving a little quiet attention to. I'm an inventor; and like all inventors whose devices are of value, I believe that my particular contrivance would be the salvation of a misguided world. I have looked a good deal into many things, but my latest hobby is the system of computation of which I tried to give a sketch last night. I'm afraid you didn't understand a word of it, but I assure you it's a very beautiful thing. If it could only get a fair hearing and be thoroughly propagated and adopted, it would save our toiling human race a prodigious deal of ungrateful labor. In America alone, I have calculated, it would save the business community about 23,000 hours in the course of ten years. If time is money, they are worth saving. But there I go! You oughtn't to ask me to talk about myself. Myself is my ideas!"

A little judicious questioning, however, drew from him a number of facts of a more immediately personal kind. His colonelship, he intimated, was held by the inglorious tenure of militia service, and was only put forward to help him to make a figure on Professor Fargo's platform. It was part of the general humbuggery of the attempt to *bribe* people to listen to wholesome truths—truths the neglect of which was its own chastisement. "I have always had a passion for scientific research, and I have squandered my substance in experiments which the world called fruitless. They were curious, they were beautiful, they were divine! But they wouldn't turn any one's mill or grind any one's corn, and I was treated like a mediæval alchemist, astray in the modern world. Chemistry, physics, mathematics, philology, medicine—I've dug deep in them all. Each, in turn, has been a passion to which I've given my days and my nights. But apparently I haven't the art of finding favor for my ideas—of sweetening the draught so that people will drink it. So here I am, after all my vigils and ventures, an obscure old man, ruined in fortune, broken down in health and sadly diminished in hope, trying hard to keep afloat by rowing in the same boat as a gentleman who turns tables and raises ghosts. I'm a proud man, sir, and a devotee of the exact sciences. You may imagine what I suffer. I little fancied ten years ago that I was ever going to make capital, on a mountebank's booth, of the pathetic infirmity of my daughter."

The young girl, while her father talked, sat gazing at him in wistful surprise. I inferred from it that this expansive mood was rare; she wondered what long story he was telling. As he mentioned her, I gave her a sudden glance. Perceiving it, she blushed slightly and turned away. The movement seemed at variance with what I had supposed to be her characteristic indifference to observation. "I have a good reason," he said, "for treating her with more than the tenderness which such an infirmity usually commands. At the time of my marriage, and for some time after, I was performing a series of curious chemical researches. My wife was a wonderfully pretty little creature. She used to come tripping and rustling about my laboratory, asking questions of the most comical ignorance, peeping and rummaging everywhere, raising the lids of jars, and making faces at the bad smells. One day while she was in the room I stepped out on the balcony to examine something which I had placed to dry in the sun. Suddenly I heard a terrific explosion; it smashed the window-glass into atoms. Rushing in, I found my wife in a swoon on the floor. A compound which I had placed to heat on a furnace had been left too long; I had underestimated its activity. My wife was not visibly injured, but when she came to her senses again, she found she had lost her hearing. It never returned. Shortly afterwards my daughter was born—born the poor deaf creature you see. I lost my wife and I gave up chemistry. As I advanced in life, I became convinced that my ruling passion was mathematics. I've gone into them very deeply; I consider them the noblest acquisition of the human mind, and I don't hesitate to say that I have profound and original views on the subject. If you have a head for such things, I could open great vistas to you. But I'm afraid you haven't! Ay, it's a desperately weak-witted generation. The world has a horror of concentrated thought; it wants the pill to be sugared; it wants everything to be made easy; it prefers the brazen foolery that you and I sat through last night to the divine harmonies of the infinite science of numbers. That's why I'm a beggar, droning out my dreary petition and pushing forth my little girl to catch the coppers. That's why I've had to strike a partnership with a vulgar charlatan. I was a long time coming to it, but I'm well in for it now. I won't tell you how, from rebuff to rebuff, from failure to failure, through hope deferred and justice denied, I have finally come to this. It would overtax both your sympathy and your credulity. You wouldn't believe the stories I could relate of the impenetrable stupidity of mankind, of the leaden empire of Routine. I squandered my property, I confess it, but not in the vulgar way. It was a carnival of high research, a long debauch of experiment. When I had melted down my last cent in the consuming crucible, I thought the world might be willing to pay me something for my results. The world had better uses for its money than the purchase of sovereign truth! I became a solicitor; I went from door to door, offering people a choice of twenty superb formulated schemes, the paltriest of which contained the germs of a peaceful revolution. The poor unpatented visions are at this hour all in a bundle up stairs in my trunk. In the midst of my troubles I had the ineffable pleasure of finding that my little girl was a genius. I don't know why it should have been a pleasure; her poor father's genius stood there before me as a warning. But it was a delight to find that her little imprisoned soundless mind was not a blank. She had inherited my passion for numbers. My folly had taken a precious faculty from her; it was but just I should give her another. She was in good hands for becoming perfect. Her gift is a rare one among women, but she is not of the common feminine stuff. She's very simple—strangely simple in some ways. She has never been talked to by women about petticoats, nor by men about love. She doesn't reason; her skill at figures is a kind of intuition. One day it came into my head that I might lecture for a livelihood. I had listened to windy orators, in crowded halls, who had less to say than I. So I lectured, sometimes to twenty people, sometimes to five, once to no one at all. One morning, some six months ago, I was waited upon by my friend there. He told me frankly that he had a show which didn't draw as powerfully as it deserved, and proposed that, as I also seemed unable to catch the public ear, we should combine our forces and carry popularity by storm. His entertainment, alone, was rather thin; mine also seemed to lack the desirable consistency; but a mixture of the two might produce an effective compound. I had but five dollars in my pocket. I disliked the man, and I believe in spiritualism about as much as I believe that the sun goes round the earth. But we must live, and I made a bargain. It was a very poor bargain, but it keeps us alive. I took a few hints from the Professor, and brightened up my lucky formulas a little. Still, we had terribly thin houses. I couldn't play the mountebank; it's a faculty I lack. At last the Professor bethought himself that I possessed the golden goose. From the mountebank's point of view a pretty little deaf and dumb daughter, who could work miracles on the blackboard, was a treasure to a practical mind. The idea of dragging my poor child and her pathetic idiosyncrasies before the world was extremely repulsive to me; but the Professor laid the case before the little maid herself, and at the end of a fortnight she informed him that she was ready to make her curtsey on the platform as a 'lightning calculator.' I consented to let her try, and you see that she succeeded. She draws, not powerfully, but sufficiently, and we manage to keep afloat."

Half an hour later the Professor returned from his morning's labors—flushed, dishevelled, rubbing his hands, evidently in high good humor. The Colonel immediately became silent and grave, asked no questions, and, when dinner was served shortly afterwards, refused everything and sat with a melancholy frown and his eyes fixed on his plate. His comrade was plainly a terrible thorn in his side. I was curious, on the other hand, to know how the Colonel affected the Professor, and I soon discovered that the latter was by no means his exuberant impudent self within the radius of his colleague's pregnant silence. If there was little love lost between them, the ranting charlatan was at least held in check by an indefinable respect for his companion's probity. He was a fool, doubt-less, with his careful statements and his incapacity to take a humorous view of human credulity; but, somehow, he was a venerable fool, and the Professor, as a social personage, with-out the inspiration of a lecture-room more or less irritatingly interspaced, and with that pale, grave old mathematician sit-ting by like a marble monument to Veracity, lacked the courage to ventilate his peculiar pretensions. On this occa-sion, however, he swallowed the Colonel's tacit protest with a wry face. I don't know what he had brought to pass in the darkened parlor; whatever it was, it had agreeably stimulated his confidence in his resources. We had been joined, moreover, at dinner by half a dozen travellers of less oppressively skep-tical mould than the Colonel, and under these circumstances it was peculiarly trying to have to veil one's brighter genius. There was undischarged thunder in the air.

The rain ceased in the afternoon, and the sun leaped out and set the thousand puddles of the village street a-flashing. I found the Colonel sitting under the tavern porch with a village urchin between his knees, to whom he seemed to be imparting the rudiments of mathematical science. The little boy had a bulging forehead, a prodigious number of freckles, and the general aspect of a juvenile Newton. Being present at the Colonel's lecture, he had been fired with a laudable curiosity to know more, and learning that Professor Fargo imparted information *à domicile*, had ventured to believe that his col-league did likewise. The child's father, a great, gaunt, brown-faced farmer, with a yellow tuft on his chin, stood by, blush-ing at the audacity of his son and heir, but grinning delightedly at his brightness. The poor Colonel, whose meed of recog-nition had as yet been so meagre, was vastly tickled by this expression of infantine sympathy, and discoursed to the little prodigy with the most condescending benevolence. Certainly, as the boy grows up, the most vivid of his childish memories will be that of the old man with glowing eyes and a softened voice coming from under his white moustache—the voice which held him stock-still for a whole half hour, and assured him afterwards that he was a little Trojan. When the lesson was over, I proposed a walk to the Colonel, and we wandered away out of the village. The afternoon, as it waned, became glorious; the heavy clouds, broken and dispersed, sailed through the glowing sky like high-prowed galleys, draped in purple and silver. I, on my side, shall never forget the Colonel's excited talk, nor how at last, as we sat on a rocky ridge looking off to the sunset, he fairly unburdened his conscience.

"Yes, sir!" he said; "it's a base concession to the ignoble need of keeping body and soul together. Sometimes I feel as if I couldn't stand it another hour—as if it were better to break with the impudent rascal and sink or swim as fate decrees, than get a hearing for the truth at such a cost. It's all very well holding my tongue and insisting that I, at least, make no claims for the man's vile frauds; my connection with him is itself a sanction, and my presence at his damnable mummeries an outrage to the purity of truth. You see I have the misfortune to believe in something, to *know* something, and to think it makes a difference whether people feed, intellectually, on poisoned garbage or on the ripe, sweet fruit of true science! I shut my eyes every night, and lock my jaws, and clench my teeth, but I can't help hearing the man's windy rubbish. It's a tissue of scandalous lies, from beginning to end. I know them all by heart by this time, and I verily believe I could stand up and rattle them off myself. They ring in my ears all day, and I have horrible dreams at night of crouching under a table with a long cloth, and tapping on the top of it. The Professor stands outside swearing to the audience that it's the ghost of Archimedes. Then I begin to suffocate, and overturn the table, and appear before a thousand people as the accomplice of the impostor. There are times when the value of my own unheeded message to mankind seems so vast, so immeasurable, that I am ready to believe that any means are lawful which may enable me to utter it; that if one's ship is to set sail for the golden islands, even a flaunting buccaneer may tow it into the open sea. In such moods, when I sit there against the wall, in the shade, closing my eyes and trying not to hear—I really *don't* hear! My mind is a myriad miles away—floating, soaring on the wings of invention. But all of a sudden the odiousness of my position comes over me, and I can't believe my senses that it's verily I who sit there—I to whom a grain of scientific truth is more precious than a mountain of gold!"

He was silent a long time, and I myself hardly knew what consolation to offer him. The most friendly part was simply to let him expend his bitterness to the last drop. "But that's not the worst," he resumed after a while. "The worst is that I hate the greasy rascal to come near my daughter, and that, living and travelling together as we do, he's never far off. At first he used to engage a small child beforehand to hold up his little folded papers for him; but a few weeks ago it came into his head that it would give the affair an even greater air of innocence, if he could make use of my poor girl. It does, I believe, and it tells, and I've been brought so low that I sit by night after night and endure it. She, on her side, dreams of no harm, and takes the Professor for an oracle and his lecture for a masterpiece. I have never undeceived her, for I have no desire to teach her that there are such things as falsity and impurity. Except that our perpetual railway journeys give her bad headaches, she supposes that we lead a life of pure felicity. But some fine day our enterprising friend will be wanting to put her into a pink dress and a garland of artificial flowers, and then, with God's help, we shall part company!"

My silence, in reply to this last burst of confidence, implied the most deferential assent; but I was privately wondering whether "the little maid" was so perfectly ignorant of evil as the old man supposed. I remembered the episode at the cemetery the day before, and doubted greatly whether her father had countenanced it. With his sentiments touching the

Professor, this was most unlikely. The young girl, then, had a secret, and it gave me real discomfort to think this coarse fellow should keep the key of it. I feared that the poor Colonel was yoked to his colleague more cruelly than he knew. On our return to the inn this impression was vividly confirmed. Dusk had fallen when we entered the public room, and in the gray light which pervaded it two figures at one of the windows escaped immediate recognition. But in a moment one of them advanced, and in the sonorous accents of Professor Fargo hoped that we had enjoyed our expedition. The Colonel started and stared, and left me to answer. He sat down heavily on the sofa; in a moment his daughter came over and sat beside him, placing her hand gently on his knee. But he let it lie, and remained motionless, resting his hot head on his cane. The Professor withdrew promptly, but with a swagger which suggested to my sense that he could now afford to treat his vanity to a dose of revenge for the old man's contempt.

Late in the evening I came down stairs again, and as I passed along the hall heard Professor Fargo perorating vigorously in the bar-room. Evidently he had an audience, and the scene was probably curious. Drawing near, I found this gifted man erect on the floor, addressing an assemblage of the convivial spirits of P——. In an extended hand he brandished a glass of smoking whiskey and water; with the other he caressed his rounded periods. He had evidently been drinking freely, and I perceived that even the prophetic vision was liable to obfuscation. It had been a brilliant day for him; fortune smiled, and he felt strong. A dozen rustic loafers, of various degrees of inveteracy, were listening to him with a speechless solemnity, which may have been partly faith, but was certainly partly rum. In a corner, out of the way, sat the Colonel, with an unfinished glass before him. The Professor waved his hand as I appeared, with magnificent hospitality, and resumed his discourse.

"Let me say, gentlemen," he cried, "that's it's not my peculiar influence with the departed that I chiefly value; for, after all, you know, a ghost is but a ghost. It can't do much any way. You can't touch it, half the time you can't see it. If it happens to be the spirit of a pretty girl, you know, this makes you kind of mad. The great thing now is to be able to exercise a mysterious influence over living organisms. You can do it with your eye, you can do it with your voice, you can do it with certain motions of your hand—as thus, you perceive; you can do it with nothing at all by just setting your mind on it. That is, of course, some people can do it; not very many—certain rich, powerful, sympathetic natures that you now and then come across. It's called magnetism. Various works have been written on the subject, and various explanations offered, but they don't amount to much. All you can say is that it's just magnetism, and that you've either got it or you haven't got it. Now the Lord has seen fit to bestow it on me. It's a great responsibility, but I try to make a noble use of it. I can do all sorts of things. I can find out things. I can make people confess. I can make 'em sick and I can make 'em well. I can make 'em in love—what do you say to that? I can take 'em out of love again, and make 'em swear they wouldn't marry the loved object, not if they were paid for it. How it is I do it I confess I can't tell you. I just say to myself, 'Come now, Professor, we'll fix this one or that one.' It's a free gift. It's magnetism, in short. Some folks call it animal magnetism, but I call it spiritual magnetism."

There was a profound silence; the air seemed charged with that whimsical retention of speech which is such a common form of American sociability. I looked askance at the Colonel; it seemed to me that he was paler than usual, and that his eyes were really fierce. Professor Fargo turned about to the bar to replenish his glass, and the old man slowly rose and came out into the middle of the room. He looked round at the company; he evidently meant to say something. He stood silent for some moments, and I saw that he was in a tremor of excitement. "You've listened to what this gentleman has been saying?" he began. "I won't say, Have you understood it? It's not to be understood. Some of you, perhaps, saw me last night sitting on the platform while Professor Fargo said his say. You know that we are partners—that for convenience' sake we work together. I wish to say that you are not therefore to believe that I assent to the doctrines he has just promulgated. 'Doctrines' is a flattering name for them. I speak in the name of science. Science recognizes no such thing as 'spiritual magnetism'; no such thing as mysterious fascinations; no such thing as spirit-rappings and ghost-raisings. I owe it to my conscience to say so. I can't remain there and see you all sit mum when this gentleman concludes such a monstrous piece of talk. I have it on my conscience to assure you that no intelligent man, woman, or child need fear to be made to do anything against his own will by the supernatural operation of the will of Professor Fargo."

If there had been silence on the conclusion of Professor Fargo's harangue, what shall I say of the audible absence of commentary which followed the Colonel's remarks? There was an intense curiosity—I felt it myself—to see what a clever fellow like the Professor would do. The Colonel stood there wiping his forehead, as if, having thrown down the gauntlet, he were prepared to defend it. The Professor looked at him with his head on one side, and a smile which was an excellent imitation of genial tolerance. "My dear sir," he cried, "I'm glad you've eased your mind. I knew you wanted to; I hope you feel better. With your leave, we won't go into the philosophy of the dispute. It was George Washington, I believe, who said that people should wash their dirty linen at home. You don't endorse my views—you're welcome. If you weren't a very polite old gentleman, I know you'd like to say that, in a single word, they're the views of a quack. Now, in a single word, I deny it. You deny the existence of the magnetic power; I reply that I personally possess it, and that if you'll give me a little more time, I'll force you to say that there's something in it. I'll force you to say I can do something. These gentlemen here can't witness the consummation, but at least they can hear my promise. I promise you evidence. You go by facts: I'll give you facts. I'd like just to have you remark before our friends here, that you'll take account of them!"

The Colonel stood still, wiping his forehead. He had even less prevision than I of the character of the Professor's projected facts, but of course he could make but one answer. He bowed gravely to the Professor and to the company. "I shall never refuse," he said, "to examine serious evidence. Whatever," he added, after a moment, "it might cost my prejudices."

III

THE Colonel's incorruptible conservatism had done me good mentally, and his personal situation had deeply interested me. As I bade him farewell the next day—the "Combination" had been heralded in a neighboring town—I wished him heartily that what was so painfully crooked in the latter might be straightened out in time. He shook his head sadly, and answered that his time was up.

He was often in my thoughts for the next six weeks, but I got no tidings of him. Meanwhile I too was leading an ambulant life, and travelling from town to town in a cause which demanded a good deal of ready-made eloquence. I didn't exactly pretend that the regeneration of society depended on its acceptance of my wares, but I devoted a good deal of fellow feeling to the Colonel's experience as an uncredited solicitor. At the beginning of the winter I found myself in New York. One evening, as I wandered along a certain

avenue, undedicated to gentility, I perceived, in the flare of
a gas-lamp, on a placard beside a doorway, the name and
attributes of Professor Fargo. I immediately stopped and read
the manifesto. It was even more grandiloquent than the yellow hand-bill at P——; for to overtop concurrence in the
metropolis one must mount upon very high stilts indeed. The
"Combination" still subsisted, and Colonel Gifford brought
up the rear. I observed with interest that his daughter now
figured in an independent and extremely ornamental para-
graph. Above the door was a blue lamp, and beneath the lamp
the inscription "Excelsior Hall." No one was going in, but as
I stood there a young man in a white overcoat, with his hat
on his nose, came out and planted himself viciously, with
a tell-tale yawn, in the doorway. The poor Colonel had lost
an auditor; I was determined he should have a substitute.
Paying my fee and making my way into the room, I found
that the situation was indeed one in which units rated high.
There were not more than twenty people present, and the
appearance of this meagre group was not in striking harmony
with the statement on the placard without, that Professor
Fargo's entertainment was thronged with the intellect and
fashion of the metropolis. The Professor was on the platform,
unfolding his budget of miracles; behind him, as at P——,
sat the Colonel and his daughter. The Professor was evidently
depressed by the preponderance of empty benches, and carried
off his revelations with an indifferent grace. Disappointment
made him brutal. He was heavy, vulgar, slipshod; he stumbled
in his periods, and bungled more than once in his guesses
when the folded papers with the names were put into the hat.
His brow wore a vicious, sullen look, which seemed to deepen
the expression of melancholy patience in his companions. I
trembled for my friends. The Colonel had told me that his
bargain with his impresario was a poor one, and I was sure
that if, when the "Combination" was in a run of luck, as it
had been at P——, his dividend was scanty, he was paying a

T

heavy share of the penalty for the present eclipse of fortune. I sat down near the door, where the hall was shrouded in a thrifty dimness, so that I had no fear of being recognized. The Professor evidently was reckless—a fact which rather puzzled me in so shrewd a man. When he had brought his own performance to an unapplauded close, instead of making his customary speech on behalf of his coadjutor, he dropped into a chair and gaped in the face of his audience. But the Colonel, after a pause, threw himself into the breach—or rather lowered himself into it with stately gravity—and addressed his humble listeners (half of whom were asleep) as if they had been the flower of the Intellect and Fashion. But if his manner was the old one, his discourse was new. He had too many ideas to repeat himself, and, although those which he now attempted to expound were still above the level of my frivolous apprehension, this unbargained abundance of inspiration half convinced me that his claim to original genius was just. If there had been something grotesquely sad in his appeal to the irresponsive intellect of P——, it was almost intolerably dismal to sit there and see him grappling with the dusky void of Excelsior Hall. The sleepers waked up, or turned over, at least, when Miss Gifford came forward. She wore, as yet, neither a pink dress nor an artificial garland, but it seemed to me that I detected here and there an embryonic hint of these ornaments—a ruffle round her neck, a colored sash over her black dress, a curl or two more in her hair. But her manner was as childish, as simple and serene as ever; the empty benches had no weary meaning for her.

I confess that in spite of my personal interest in my friend, the entertainment seemed wofully long; more than once I was on the point of departing, and awaiting the conclusion in the street. But I had not the heart to inflict upon the poor Colonel the sight of a retreating spectator. When at last my twenty companions had shuffled away, I made my way to the platform and renewed acquaintance with the trio. The Professor nodded with uncompromising familiarity, the Colonel seemed cordially glad to see me, and his daughter, as I made her my bow, gazed at me with even more than usual of her clear-eyed frankness. She seemed to wonder what my reappearance meant for them. It meant, to begin with, that I went the next day to see the Colonel at his lodging. It was a terribly modest little lodging, but he did me the honors with a grace which showed that he had an old habit of hospitality. He admitted frankly that the "Combination" had lately been doing a very poor business, but he made the admission with a gloomy stoicism which showed me that he had been looking the event full in the face, and had assented to it helplessly. They had gone their round in the country, with varying success. They had the misfortune to have a circus keeping just in advance of them, and beside the gorgeous pictorial placards of this establishment, their own superior promises, even when swimming in a deluge of exclamation points, seemed pitifully vague. "What are my daughter and I," said the Colonel, "after the educated elephant and the female trapezist? What even is the Professor, after the great American clown?" Their profits, however, had been kept fairly above the minimum, and victory would still have hovered about their banners if they had been content to invoke her in the smaller towns. The Professor, however, in spite of remonstrance, had suddenly steered for New York, and what New York was doing for them I had seen the night before. The last half dozen performances had not paid for the room and the gas. The Colonel told me that he was bound by contract for five more lectures, but that when these were delivered he would dissolve the partnership. The Professor, in insisting on coming to the city, had shown a signal want of shrewdness; and when his shrewdness failed him, what had you left? What to attempt himself, the Colonel couldn't imagine. "At the worst," he said, "my daughter can go into an asylum, and I can go into the poorhouse." On my asking him whether his colleague had yet established, according to his vow, the verities of "spiritual magnetism," he stared in surprise and seemed quite to have forgotten the Professor's engagement to convert him. "Oh, I've let him off," he said, shaking his head. "He was tipsy when he made the promise, and I expect to hear no more about it."

I was very busy, and the pensive old man was gloomy company; but his character and his fortunes had such a melancholy interest that I found time to pay him several visits. He evidently was thankful to be diverted from his sombre self-consciousness and his paternal anxiety, and, when once he was aroused from the dogged resignation in which he seemed plunged, enjoyed vastly the chance to expatiate on his multitudinous and irrealizable theories. Most of the time his meaning was a cloud bank to me, but I listened, assented, applauded; I felt the charm of pure intellectual passion. I incline to believe that he had excogitated some extremely valuable ideas. We took long walks through the crowded streets. The Colonel was indefatigable, in spite of his leanness and pallor. He strode along with great steps, talking so loud, half the time, in his high, quavering voice, that even the eager pedestrians in the lower latitudes of Broadway slackened pace to glance back at him. He declared that the crowded streets gave him a strange exhilaration, and the mighty human hum of the great city quickened his heart-beats almost to pain. More than once he stopped short, on the edge of a curbstone or in the middle of a crossing, and laying his hand on my arm, with a deeper glow beneath his white eyebrows, broke into a kind of rhapsody of transcendental thought. "It's for all these millions I would work, if they would let me!" he cried. "It's to the life of great cities my schemes are addressed. It's to make millions wiser and better that I stand pleading my cause so long after I have earned my rest." One day he seemed taciturn and preoccupied. He talked much less than usual, noticed nothing, and walked with his eyes on the pavement. I imagined that, in a phrase with which he had made me familiar, he had caught the tail of an idea and was holding it fast, in spite of its slippery contortions. As we neared his lodging at the end of our walk, he stopped abruptly in the middle of the street, and I had to give him a violent pull to rescue him from a rattling butcher's cart. When we reached the pavement he stopped again, grasped me by the hand, and fixed his eyes on me with a very extraordinary exaltation. We were at the top of the shabby cross-street in which he had found a shelter. A row of squalid tenements faced us, and half a dozen little Irish ragamuffins were sprawling beneath our feet, between their doorways and the gutter. "Eureka! Eureka!" he cried. "I've found it—I've found it!" And on my asking him what he had found, "Something science has groped for, for ages—the solution of the incalculable! Perhaps, too, my fortune; certainly my immortality! Quick, quick! Before it vanishes I must get at my pen." And he hurried me along to his dingy little dwelling. On the doorstep he paused. "I can't tell you now," he cried. "I must fling it down in black and white. But for heaven's sake, come to-night to the lecture, and in the first flush of apprehension I think I can knock off a statement!" To the lecture I promised to come. At the same moment I raised my eyes and beheld in the window of the Colonel's apartment the ominous visage of Professor Fargo. I had been kindled by the Colonel's ardor, but somehow I was suddenly chilled by the presence of the Professor. I feared that, be the brilliancy of my friend's sudden illumination what it might, the shock of meeting his unloved *confrère* under his own roof would loosen his grasp of his idea. I found a pretext for keeping him standing a moment, and observed that the Professor disappeared. The next moment the door opened and he stepped forth. He had put on his hat, I suppose, hastily; it was cocked toward one side with a jauntiness which seemed the climax of his habitual swagger. He was evidently in better spirits than when I listened to him at Excelsior Hall; but neither the Professor's smiles nor his frowns were those of an honest man. He bestowed on my companion and me one of the most expansive of the former, gave his hat a cock in the opposite direction, and was about to pass on. But suddenly bethinking himself, he paused and drew from his pocket a small yellow ticket, which he presented to me. It was admission to Excelsior Hall.

"If you can use this to-night," he said, "I think you'll see something out of the common." This intimation, accompanied with a wink of extreme suggestiveness, seemed to indicate that the Professor also, by a singular coincidence, had had a flash of artistic inspiration. But giving me no further clue, he rapidly went his way. As I shook hands in farewell with the Colonel, I saw that the light of the old man's new inspiration had gone out in angry wonderment over the Professor's errand with his daughter.

I can hardly define the vague apprehensiveness which led me to make that evening a peculiarly prompt appearance at Excelsior Hall. There was no one there when I arrived, and for half an hour the solitude remained unbroken. At last a shabby little man came in and sat down on the last bench, in the shade. We remained a while staring at the white wall behind the three empty chairs of the performers and listening to the gas-burners, which were hissing with an expressiveness which, under the circumstances, was most distressing. At last my companion left his place and strolled down the aisle. He stopped before the platform, turned about, surveyed the capacity of the room, and muttered something between a groan and an imprecation. Then he came back toward me and stopped. He had a dirty shirt-front, a scrubby beard, a small, wrathful black eye, and a nose unmistakably Judaic.

"If you don't want to sit and be lectured at all alone," he said, "I guess you'd better go."

I expressed a hope that some one would turn up yet, and said that I preferred to remain, in any event, as I had a particular interest in the performance.

"A particular interest?" he cried; "that's about what I've got. I've got the rent of my room to collect. This thing has been going on here for three weeks now, and I haven't seen the first dollar of *my* profits. It's been going down hill steady, and I think the Professor, and the Colonel, and the deaf and dumb young woman had better shut up shop. They ain't appreciated; they'd better try some other line. There's mighty little to this thing, anyway; it ain't what I call an attractive exhibition. I've got an offer for the premises for a month from the Canadian Giantess, and I mean to ask the present company to pay me down and vacate."

It looked, certainly, as if the "Combination" would have some difficulty in meeting its engagements. The Professor's head emerged inquiringly from a door behind the stage and disappeared, after a brief communion with the vacuity of the scene. In a few minutes, however, the customary trio came forth and seated itself gravely on the platform. The Professor thrust his thumbs into his waistcoat and drummed on the floor with his toes, as if it cost his shrewdness a painful effort to play any longer at expectation. The Colonel sat stiff and solemn, with his eyes on the ground. The young girl gazed forth upon the ungrateful void with her characteristically irresponsible tranquillity. For myself, after listening some ten minutes more for an advancing tread, I leaned my elbows on the back of the bench before me and buried my head; I couldn't bear any longer to look at the Colonel. At last I heard a scramble behind me, and looking round, saw my little Jew erecting himself on his feet on a bench.

"Gentlemen!" he cried out, "I don't address the young woman; I'm told she can't hear. I suppose the man with the biggest audience has a right to speak. The amount of money in this hall to-night is just thirty cents—unless, indeed, my friend here is on the free list. Now it stands to reason that you can't pay your night's expenses out of thirty cents. I think we might as well turn down some of this gas; we can still see to settle our little account. To have it paid will gratify me considerably more than anything you can do there. I don't judge your entertainment; I've no doubt it's a very smart thing. But it's very evident it don't suit this city. It's too intellectual. I've got something else in view—I don't mind telling you it's the Canadian Giantess. It is going to open tomorrow with a matinée, and I want to put some props under that platform. So you'd better pay this young man his money back, and go home to supper. But before you leave, I'll trouble you for the sum of ninety-three dollars and eighty-seven cents."

The Professor stroked his beard; the Colonel didn't move. The little Jew descended from his perch and approached the platform with his bill in his hand. In a moment I followed him.

"We're a failure," said the Professor, at last. "Very well! I'm not discouraged; I'm a practical man. I've got an idea in my head by which, six months hence, I expect to fill the Academy of Music." Then, after a pause, turning to his companion, "Colonel, do you happen to have ninety-three dollars and eighty-seven cents?"

The Colonel slowly raised his eyes and looked at him; I shall never forget the look.

"Seriously speaking," the Professor went on, daunted but for an instant, "you're liable for half the debt. But I'll assume your share on a certain condition. I have in my head the plan of another entertainment. Our friend here is right; we have been too intellectual. Very good!" and he nodded at the empty benches. "I've learned the lesson. Henceforth I'm going to be sensational. My great sensation"—and he paused a moment to engage again the eye of the Colonel, who presently looked vaguely up at him—"is this young lady!" and he thrust out a hand toward Miss Gifford. "Allow me to exhibit your daughter for a month, in my own way and according to my own notions, and I assume your debt."

The young girl dropped her eyes on the ground, but kept

her place. She had evidently been schooled. The Colonel
slowly got up, glaring and trembling with indignation. I
wished to cut the knot, and I interrupted his answer. "Your
inducement is null," I said to the Professor. "I assume the
Colonel's debt. It shall be paid this moment."

Professor Fargo gave an honestly gleeful grin; this was
better even than the Colonel's assent. "You refuse your consent then," he demanded of the old man, "to your daughter's
appearance under my exclusive management."

"Utterly!" cried the Colonel.

"You are aware, I suppose, that she's of age?"

The Colonel stared at me with a groan. "What under
heaven is the fellow coming to?"

"To this!" responded the Professor; and he fixed his eye
for a moment on the young girl. She immediately looked up
at him, rose, advanced, and stood before him. Her face
betrayed no painful consciousness of what she was doing, and
I have often wondered how far, in her strangely simple mood
and nature, her consciousness on this occasion was a guilty
one. I never ascertained. This was the most unerring stroke I
had seen the Professor perform. The poor child fixed her
charming eyes on his gross, flushed face, and awaited his
commands. She was fascinated; she had no will of her own.
"You'll be so good as to choose," the Professor went on,
addressing her in spite of her deafness, "between your father
and me. He says we're to part. I say you're to follow me.
What do you say?"

For all answer, after caressing him a moment with her
gentle gaze, she dropped before him on her knees. The
Colonel sprang toward her with a sort of howl of rage and
grief, but she jumped up, retreated, and tripped down the
steps of the platform into the room. She rapidly made her
way to the door. There she paused and looked back at us. Her
father stood staring after her in helpless bewilderment. The
Professor disappeared into the little ante-room behind the

stage, and came back in a moment jamming his hat over his eyes and carrying the young girl's shawl. He reached the edge of the platform, and then, stopping, shook the forefinger with the turquoise ring at the Colonel.

"What do you say now?" he cried. "Is spiritual magnetism a humbug?"

The little Jew rushed after him, shrieking and brandishing the unpaid bill; but the Professor cleared at half a dozen strides the interval which divided him from the door, caught the young girl round the waist, and made a triumphant escape. Half an hour later the Colonel and I left the little Jew staring distractedly at his unretributed gas-burners.

I walked home with the old man, and, having led him into his shabby refuge, suffered him to make his way alone, with groans, and tears, and imprecations, into his daughter's empty room. At last he came tottering out again; it seemed as if he were going mad. I brought him away by force, and he passed the night in my own quarters. He had spoken shortly before of the prospect of an asylum for his daughter, but it became evident that the asylum would have to be for him.

I sometimes go to see him. He spends his days covering little square sheets of paper with algebraic signs, but I am assured by his superintendent, who understands the matter, that they represent no coherent mathematical operation. I never treated myself to the "sensation" of attending Professor Fargo's new entertainment.

EUGENE PICKERING

I

It was at Homburg, several years ago, before the gaming had been suppressed. The evening was very warm, and all the world was gathered on the terrace of the Kursaal and the esplanade below it, to listen to the excellent orchestra; or half the world, rather, for the crowd was equally dense in the gaming-rooms, around the tables. Everywhere the crowd was great. The night was perfect, the season was at its height, the open windows of the Kursaal sent long shafts of unnatural light into the dusky woods, and now and then, in the intervals of the music, one might almost hear the clink of the napoleons and the metallic call of the croupiers rise above the watching silence of the saloons. I had been strolling with a friend, and we at last prepared to sit down. Chairs, however, were scarce. I had captured one, but it seemed no easy matter to find a mate for it. I was on the point of giving up in despair and proposing an adjournment to the damask divans of the Kursaal, when I observed a young man lounging back on one of the objects of my quest, with his feet supported on the rounds of another. This was more than his share of luxury, and I promptly approached him. He evidently belonged to the race which has the credit of knowing best, at home and abroad, how to make itself comfortable; but something in his appearance suggested that his present attitude was the result of inadvertence rather than egotism. He was staring at the conductor of the orchestra and listening intently to the music. His hands were locked round his long legs, and his mouth was half open, with rather a foolish air. "There are so few chairs," I said, "that I must beg you to surrender this second one." He started, stared, blushed, pushed the chair away with awkward alacrity, and murmured something about not having noticed that he had it.

"What an odd-looking youth!" said my companion, who had watched me, as I seated myself beside her.

"Yes, he's odd-looking; but what is odder still is that I've seen him before, that his face is familiar to me, and yet that I can't place him." The orchestra was playing the Prayer from Der Freischütz, but Weber's lovely music only deepened the blank of memory. Who the deuce was he? where, when, how, had I known him? It seemed extraordinary that a face should be at once so familiar and so strange. We had our backs turned to him, so that I could not look at him again. When the music ceased, we left our places and I went to consign my friend to her mamma on the terrace. In passing, I saw that my young man had departed; I concluded that he only strikingly re-sembled some one I knew. But who in the world was it he resembled? The ladies went off to their lodgings, which were near by, and I turned into the gaming-rooms and hovered about the circle at roulette. Gradually, I filtered through to the inner edge, near the table, and, looking round, saw my puzzling friend stationed opposite to me. He was watching the game, with his hands in his pockets; but, singularly enough, now that I observed him at my leisure, the look of familiarity quite faded from his face. What had made us call his appear-ance odd was his great length and leanness of limb, his long, white neck, his blue, prominent eyes, and his ingenuous, unconscious absorption in the scene before him. He was not handsome, certainly, but he looked peculiarly amiable; and if his overt wonderment savored a trifle of rurality, it was an agreeable contrast to the hard, inexpressive masks about him. He was the verdant offshoot, I said to myself, of some ancient, rigid stem; he had been brought up in the quietest of homes, and was having his first glimpse of life. I was curious to see whether he would put anything on the table; he evidently felt the temptation, but he seemed paralyzed by chronic embarrassment. He stood gazing at the rattling cross-fire of losses and gains, shaking his loose gold in his pocket, and every now and then passing his hand nervously over his eyes.

Most of the spectators were too attentive to the play to have many thoughts for each other; but before long I noticed a lady who evidently had an eye for her neighbors as well as for the table. She was seated about half-way between my friend and me, and I presently observed that she was trying to catch his eye. Though at Homburg, as people said, "one could never be sure," I yet doubted whether this lady was one of those whose especial vocation it was to catch a gentleman's eye. She was youthful rather than elderly, and pretty rather than plain; indeed, a few minutes later, when I saw her smile, I thought her wonderfully pretty. She had a charming gray eye and a good deal of blond hair, disposed in picturesque disorder; and though her features were meagre and her complexion faded, she gave one a sense of sentimental, artificial gracefulness. She was dressed in white muslin very much puffed and frilled, but a trifle the worse for wear, relieved here and there by a pale blue ribbon. I used to flatter myself on guessing at people's nationality by their faces, and, as a rule, I guessed aright. This faded, crumpled, vaporous beauty, I conceived, was a German,—such a German, somehow, as I had seen imaged in literature. Was she not a friend of poets, a correspondent of philosophers, a muse, a priestess of æsthetics,—something in the way of a Bettina, a Rahel? My conjectures, however, were speedily merged in wonderment as to what my diffident friend was making of her. She caught his eye at last, and raising an ungloved hand, covered altogether with blue-gemmed rings, —turquoises, sapphires, and lapis,—she beckoned him to come to her. The gesture was executed with a sort of practised coolness and accompanied with an appealing smile. He stared a moment, rather blankly, unable to suppose that the invitation was addressed to him; then, as it was immediately repeated, with a good deal of intensity, he blushed to the roots of his hair, wavered awkwardly, and at last made his way to the lady's chair. By the time he reached it he was crimson and wiping his forehead with his pocket-handkerchief. She tilted back, looked up at him with the same smile, laid two fingers on his sleeve, and said something, interrogatively, to which he replied by a shake of the head. She was asking him, evidently, if he had ever played, and he was saying no. Old players have a fancy that when luck has turned her back on them, they can put her into good-humor again by having their stakes placed by an absolute novice. Our young man's physiognomy had seemed to his new acquaintance to express the perfection of inexperience, and, like a practical woman, she had determined to make him serve her turn. Unlike most of her neighbors, she had no little pile of gold before her, but she drew from her pocket a double napoleon, put it into his hand, and bade him place it on a number of his own choosing. He was evidently filled with a sort of delightful trouble; he enjoyed the adventure, but he shrank from the hazard. I would have staked the coin on its being his companion's last; for, although she still smiled intently as she watched his hesitation, there was anything but indifference in her pale, pretty face. Suddenly, in desperation, he reached over and laid the piece on the table. My attention was diverted at this moment by my having to make way for a lady with a great many flounces, before me, to give up her chair to a rustling friend to whom she had promised it; when I again looked across at the lady in white muslin, she was drawing in a very goodly pile of gold with her little blue-gemmed claw. Good luck and bad, at the Homburg tables, were equally undemonstrative, and this fair adventuress rewarded her young friend for the sacrifice of his innocence with a single, rapid, upward smile. He had innocence enough left, however, to look round the table with a gleeful, conscious laugh, in the midst of which his eyes encountered my own. Then, suddenly, the familiar look which had vanished from his face flickered up unmistakably; it was the boyish laugh of a boyhood's friend. Stupid fellow that I was, I had been looking at Eugene Pickering!

Though I lingered on for some time longer, he failed to recognize me. Recognition, I think, had kindled a smile in my own face; but, less fortunate than he, I suppose my smile had ceased to be boyish. Now that luck had faced about again, his companion played for herself,—played and won hand over hand. At last she seemed disposed to rest on her gains, and proceeded to bury them in the folds of her muslin. Pickering had staked nothing for himself, but as he saw her prepare to withdraw, he offered her a double napoleon and begged her to place it. She shook her head with great decision, and seemed to bid him put it up again; but he, still blushing a good deal, urged her with awkward ardor, and she at last took it from him, looked at him a moment fixedly, and laid it on a number. A moment later the croupier was raking it in. She gave the young man a little nod which seemed to say, "I told you so"; he glanced round the table again and laughed; she left her chair, and he made a way for her through the crowd. Before going home I took a turn on the terrace and looked down on the esplanade. The lamps were out, but the warm starlight vaguely illumined a dozen figures scattered in couples. One of these figures, I thought, was a lady in a white dress.

I had no intention of letting Pickering go without reminding him of our old acquaintance. He had been a very droll boy, and I was curious to see what had become of his drollery. I looked for him the next morning at two or three of the hotels, and at last discovered his whereabouts. But he was out, the waiter said; he had gone to walk an hour before. I went my way, confident that I should meet him in the evening. It was the rule with the Homburg world to spend its evenings at the Kursaal, and Pickering, apparently, had already discovered a good reason for not being an exception. One of the charms of Homburg is the fact that of a hot day you may walk about for a whole afternoon in unbroken shade. The umbrageous gardens of the Kursaal mingle with the charming Hardtwald, which, in turn, melts away into the wooded slopes of the Taunus Mountains. To the Hardtwald I bent my steps, and strolled for an hour through mossy glades and the still, perpendicular gloom of the fir woods. Suddenly, on the grassy margin of a by-path, I came upon a young man stretched at his length in the sun-checkered shade and kicking his heels toward a patch of blue sky. My step was so noiseless on the turf, that before he saw me, I had time to recognize Pickering again. He looked as if he had been lounging there for some time; his hair was tossed about as if he had been sleeping; on the grass near him, beside his hat and stick, lay a sealed letter. When he perceived me he jerked himself forward, and I stood looking at him without elucidating,—purposely, to give him a chance to recognize me. He put on his glasses, being awkwardly near-sighted, and stared up at me with an air of general trustfulness, but without a sign of knowing me. So at last I introduced myself. Then he jumped up and grasped my hands and stared and blushed and laughed and began a dozen random questions, ending with a demand as to how in the world I had known him.

"Why, you're not changed so utterly," I said, "and, after all, it's but fifteen years since you used to do my Latin exercises for me."

"Not changed, eh?" he answered, still smiling, and yet speaking with a sort of ingenuous dismay.

Then I remembered that poor Pickering had been in those Latin days a victim of juvenile irony. He used to bring a bottle of medicine to school and take a dose in a glass of water before lunch; and every day at two o'clock, half an hour before the rest of us were liberated, an old nurse with bushy eyebrows came and fetched him away in a carriage. His extremely fair complexion, his nurse, and his bottle of medicine, which suggested a vague analogy with the phial of poison in the tragedy, caused him to be called Juliet. Certainly, Romeo's sweetheart hardly suffered more; she was not, at least, a standing joke in Verona. Remembering these things, I hastened to say to Pickering that I hoped he was still the same good fellow who used to do my Latin for me. "We were capital friends, you know," I went on, "then and afterwards."

"Yes, we were very good friends," he said, "and that makes it the stranger I shouldn't have known you. For you know as a boy I never had many friends, nor as a man either. You see," he added, passing his hand over his eyes, "I'm dazed and bewildered at finding myself for the first time—alone." And he jerked back his shoulders nervously and threw up his head, as if to settle himself in an unwonted position. I wondered whether the old nurse with the bushy eyebrows had remained attached to his person up to a recent period, and discovered presently that, virtually at least, she had. We had the whole summer day before us, and we sat down on the grass together and overhauled our old memories. It was as if we had stumbled upon an ancient cupboard in some dusky corner, and rummaged out a heap of childish playthings,—tin soldiers and torn story-books, jack-knives and Chinese puzzles. This is what we remembered, between us.

He had made but a short stay at school,—not because he was tormented, for he thought it so fine to be at school at all that he held his tongue at home about the sufferings incurred through the medicine bottle; but because his father thought he was learning bad manners. This he imparted to me in confidence at the time, and I remember how it increased my oppressive awe of Mr Pickering, who had appeared to me, in glimpses, as a sort of high-priest of the proprieties. Mr Pickering was a widower,—a fact which seemed to produce in him a sort of preternatural concentration of parental dignity. He was a majestic man, with a hooked nose, a keen, dark eye, very large whiskers, and notions of his own as to how a boy—or his boy, at any rate—should be brought up. First and foremost,

U

he was to be a "gentleman"; which seemed to mean, chiefly, that he was always to wear a muffler and gloves, and be sent to bed, after a supper of bread and milk, at eight o'clock. School-life, on experiment, seemed hostile to these observances, and Eugene was taken home again, to be moulded into urbanity beneath the parental eye. A tutor was provided for him, and a single select companion was pre-scribed. The choice, mysteriously, fell upon me, born as I was under quite another star; my parents were appealed to, and I was allowed for a few months to have my lessons with Eugene. The tutor, I think, must have been rather a snob, for Eugene was treated like a prince, while I got all the questions and the raps with the ruler. And yet I remember never being jealous of my happier comrade, and striking up, for the time, a huge boyish friendship. He had a watch and a pony and a great store of picture-books, but my envy of these luxuries was tempered by a vague compassion, which left me free to be generous. I could go out to play alone, I could button my jacket myself, and sit up till I was sleepy. Poor Pickering could never take a step without a prior petition, or spend half an hour in the garden without a formal report of it when he came in. My parents, who had no desire to see me inoculated with importunate virtues, sent me back to school at the end of six months. After that I never saw Eugene. His father went to live in the country, to protect the lad's morals, and Eugene faded, in reminiscence, into a pale image of the depressing effects of education. I think I vaguely supposed that he would melt into thin air, and indeed began gradually to doubt of his existence and to regard him as one of the foolish things one ceased to believe in as one grew older. It seemed natural that I should have no more news of him. Our present meeting was my first assurance that he had really survived all that muffling and coddling.

I observed him now with a good deal of interest, for he was a rare phenomenon,—the fruit of a system persistently and uninterruptedly applied. He struck me, in a fashion, like certain young monks I had seen in Italy; he had the same candid, unsophisticated cloister-face. His education had been really almost monastic. It had found him, evidently, a very compliant, yielding subject; his gentle, affectionate spirit was not one of those that need to be broken. It had bequeathed him, now that he stood on the threshold of the great world, an extraordinary freshness of impression and alertness of desire, and I confess that, as I looked at him and met his transparent blue eye, I trembled for the unwarned innocence of such a soul. I became aware, gradually, that the world had already wrought a certain work upon him and roused him to a restless, troubled, self-consciousness. Everything about him pointed to an experience from which he had been debarred; his whole organism trembled with a dawning sense of unsuspected possibilities of feeling. This appealing tremor was indeed outwardly visible. He kept shifting himself about on the grass, thrusting his hands through his hair, wiping a light perspiration from his forehead, breaking out to say something and rushing off to something else. Our sudden meeting had greatly excited him, and I saw that I was likely to profit by a certain overflow of sentimental fermentation. I could do so with a good conscience, for all this trepidation filled me with a great friendliness.

"It's nearly fifteen years, as you say," he began, "since you used to call me 'butter-fingers' for always missing the ball. That's a long time to give an account of, and yet they have been, for me, such eventless, monotonous years that I could almost tell their history in ten words. You, I suppose, have had all kinds of adventures and travelled over half the world. I remember you had a turn for deeds of daring; I used to think you a little Captain Cook in roundabouts, for climbing the garden fence to get the ball, when I had let it fly over. I climbed no fences then or since. You remember my father, I suppose, and the great care he took of me? I lost him some five months ago. From those boyish days up to his death we were always together. I don't think that in fifteen years we spent half a dozen hours apart. We lived in the country, winter and summer, seeing but three or four people. I had a succession of tutors, and a library to browse about in; I assure you I'm a tremendous scholar. It was a dull life for a growing boy, and a duller life for a young man grown, but I never knew it. I was perfectly happy." He spoke of his father at some length and with a respect which I privately declined to emulate. Mr Pickering had been, to my sense, a cold egotist, unable to conceive of any larger vocation for his son than to become a mechanical reflection of himself. "I know I've been strangely brought up," said my friend, "and that the result is something grotesque; but my education, piece by piece, in detail, became one of my father's personal habits, as it were. He took a fancy to it at first through his intense affection for my mother and the sort of worship he paid her memory. She died at my birth, and as I grew up, it seems that I bore an extraordinary likeness to her. Besides, my father had a great many theories; he prided himself on his conservative opinions; he thought the usual American *laissez aller* in education was a very vulgar practice, and that children were not to grow up like dusty thorns by the wayside. So you see," Pickering went on, smiling and blushing, and yet with something of the irony of vain regret, "I'm a regular garden plant. I've been watched and watered and pruned, and, if there is any virtue in tending, I ought to take the prize at a flower-show. Some three years ago my father's health broke down and he was kept very much within doors. So, although I was a man grown, I lived altogether at home. If I was out of his sight for a quarter of an hour he sent for me. He had severe attacks of neuralgia, and he used to sit at his window, basking in the sun. He kept an opera-glass at hand, and when I was out in the garden he used to watch me with it. A few days before his death, I was twenty-seven years old, and the most innocent youth, I suppose, on the continent. After he died I missed him greatly," Pickering continued, evidently with no intention of making an epigram. "I stayed at home, in a sort of dull stupor. It seemed as if life offered itself to me for the first time, and yet as if I didn't know how to take hold of it."

He uttered all this with a frank eagerness which increased as he talked, and there was a singular contrast between the meagre experience he described and a certain radiant intelligence which I seemed to perceive in his glance and tone. Evidently, he was a clever fellow, and his natural faculties were excellent. I imagined he had read a great deal, and recovered, in some degree, in restless intellectual conjecture, the freedom he was condemned to ignore in practice. Opportunity was now offering a meaning to the empty forms with which his imagination was stored, but it appeared to him dimly, through the veil of his personal diffidence.

"I've not sailed round the world, as you suppose," I said, "but I confess I envy you the novelties you are going to behold. Coming to Homburg, you have plunged *in medias res*."

He glanced at me to see if my remark contained an allusion, and hesitated a moment. "Yes, I know it. I came to Bremen in the steamer with a very friendly German, who undertook to initiate me into the glories and mysteries of the fatherland. At this season, he said, I must begin with Homburg. I landed but a fortnight ago, and here I am." Again he hesitated, as if he were going to add something about the scene at the Kursaal; but suddenly, nervously, he took up the letter which was lying beside him, looked hard at the seal with a troubled frown, and then flung it back on the grass with a sigh.

"How long do you expect to be in Europe?" I asked.

"Six months, I supposed when I came. But not so long— now!" And he let his eyes wander to the letter again.

"And where shall you go—what shall you do?"

"Everywhere, everything, I should have said yesterday. But now it is different."

I glanced at the letter interrogatively, and he gravely picked it up and put it into his pocket. We talked for a while longer, but I saw that he had suddenly become preoccupied; that he was apparently weighing an impulse to break some last barrier of reserve. At last he suddenly laid his hand on my arm, looked at me a moment appealingly, and cried, "Upon my word, I should like to tell you everything."

"Tell me everything, by all means," I answered, smiling, "I desire nothing better than to lie here in the shade and hear everything."

"Ah, but the question is, will you understand it? No matter; you think me a queer fellow already. It's not easy, either, to tell you what I feel,—not easy for so queer a fellow as I to tell you in how many ways he's queer!" He got up and walked away a moment, passing his hand over his eyes, then came back rapidly and flung himself on the grass again. "I said just now I always supposed I was happy; it's true; but now that my eyes are open, I see I was only stultified. I was like a poodle-dog, led about by a blue ribbon, and scoured and combed and fed on slops. It was not life; life is learning to know one's self, and in that sense I've lived more in the past six weeks than in all the years that preceded them. I'm filled with this feverish sense of liberation; it keeps rising to my head like the fumes of strong wine. I find I'm an active, sentient, intelligent creature, with desires, with passions, with possible convictions,—even with what I never dreamed of, a possible will of my own! I find there is a world to know, a life to lead, men and women to form a thousand relations with. It all lies there like a great surging sea, where we must plunge and dive and feel the breeze and breast the waves. I stand shivering here on the brink, staring, longing, wondering, charmed by the smell of the brine and yet afraid of the water. The world beckons and smiles and calls, but a nameless influence from the past, that I can neither wholly obey nor wholly resist, seems to hold me back. I'm full of impulses, but, somehow, I'm not full of strength. Life seems inspiring at certain moments, but it seems terrible and unsafe; and I ask myself why I should wantonly measure myself with merciless forces, when I have learned so well how to stand aside and let them pass. Why shouldn't I turn my back upon it all and go home to—what awaits me?—to that sightless, soundless country life, and long days spent among old books? But if a man *is* weak, he doesn't want to assent beforehand to his weakness; he wants to taste whatever sweetness there may be in paying for the knowledge. So it is there comes and comes again this irresistible impulse to take my plunge, to let myself swing, to go where liberty leads me." He paused a moment, fixing me with his excited eyes, and perhaps perceived in my own an irrepressible smile at his intensity. " 'Swing ahead, in heaven's name,' you want to say, 'and much good may it do you.' I don't know whether you are laughing at my trepidation or at what possibly strikes you as my depravity. I doubt," he went on gravely, "whether I have an inclination toward wrong-doing; if I have, I'm sure I sha'n't prosper in it. I honestly believe I may safely take out a license to amuse myself. But it isn't that I think of, any more than I dream of playing with suffering. Pleasure and pain are empty words to me; what I long for is knowledge,—some other knowledge than comes to us in formal, colorless, impersonal precept. You would understand all this better if you could breathe for an hour the musty indoor atmosphere in which I have always lived. To break a window and let in light and air,—I feel as if at last I must *act!*"

"Act, by all means, now and always, when you have a chance," I answered. "But don't take things too hard, now or ever. Your long seclusion makes you think the world better worth knowing than you're likely to find it. A man with as good a head and heart as yours has a very ample world within himself, and I'm no believer in art for art, nor in what's called 'life' for life's sake. Nevertheless, take your plunge, and

come and tell me whether you've found the pearl of wisdom."
He frowned a little, as if he thought my sympathy a trifle
meagre. I shook him by the hand and laughed. "The pearl of
wisdom," I cried, "is love; honest love in the most convenient
concentration of experience! I advise you to fall in love." He
gave me no smile in response, but drew from his pocket the
letter of which I've spoken, held it up, and shook it solemnly.
"What is it?" I asked.

"It's my sentence!"

"Not of death, I hope!"

"Of marriage."

"With whom?"

"With a person I don't love."

This was serious. I stopped smiling and begged him to
explain.

"It's the singular part of my story," he said at last. "It will
remind you of an old-fashioned romance. Such as I sit here,
talking in this wild way, and tossing off invitations to destiny,
my destiny is settled and sealed. I'm engaged,—I'm given in
marriage. It's a bequest of the past,—the past I never said nay
to! The marriage was arranged by my father, years ago, when
I was a boy. The young girl's father was his particular friend;
he was also a widower, and was bringing up his daughter, on
his side, in the same rigid seclusion in which I was spending
my days. To this day, I'm unacquainted with the origin of the
bond of union between our respective progenitors. Mr Vernor was largely engaged in business, and I imagine that once
upon a time he found himself in a financial strait and was
helped through it by my father's coming forward with a heavy
loan, on which, in his situation, he could offer no security but
his word. Of this my father was quite capable. He was a man
of dogmas, and he was sure to have a precept adapted to the
conduct of a gentleman toward a friend in pecuniary embarrassment. What's more, he was sure to adhere to it. Mr Vernor, I believe, got on his feet, paid his debt, and owed my

father an eternal gratitude. His little daughter was the apple of his eye, and he pledged himself to bring her up to be the wife of his benefactor's son. So our fate was fixed, parentally, and we have been educated for each other. I've not seen my betrothed since she was a very plain-faced little girl in a sticky pinafore, hugging a one-armed doll—of the male sex, I believe—as big as herself. Mr Vernor is in what's called the Eastern trade, and has been living these many years at Smyrna. Isabel has grown up there in a white-walled garden, in an orange grove, between her father and her governess. She is a good deal my junior; six months ago she was seventeen; when she is eighteen we're to marry!"

He related all this calmly enough, without the accent of complaint, dryly rather and doggedly, as if he were weary of thinking of it. "It's a romance indeed," I said, "for these dull days, and I heartily congratulate you. It's not every young man who finds, on reaching the marrying age, a wife kept in cotton for him. A thousand to one Miss Vernor is charming; I wonder you don't post off to Smyrna."

"You're joking," he answered, with a wounded air, "and I am terribly serious. Let me tell you the rest. I never suspected this tender conspiracy till something less than a year ago. My father, wishing to provide against his death, informed me of it, solemnly. I was neither elated nor depressed; I received it, as I remember, with a sort of emotion which varied only in degree from that with which I could have hailed the announcement that he had ordered me a dozen new shirts. I supposed that it was under some such punctual, superterrestrial dispensation as this that all young men were married. Novels and poems indeed said otherwise; but novels and poems were one thing and life was another. A short time afterwards he introduced me to a photograph of my predestined, who has a pretty, but an extremely inanimate face. After this his health failed rapidly. One night I was sitting, as I habitually sat for hours, in his dimly lighted room, near his bed, to which he had been confined for a week. He had not spoken for some time, and I supposed he was asleep, but happening to look at him I saw his eyes wide open and fixed on me strangely. He was smiling benignantly, intensely, and in a moment he beckoned to me. Then, on my going to him—'I feel that I sha'n't last long,' he said, 'but I am willing to die when I think how comfortably I have arranged your future.' He was talking of death, and anything but grief at that moment was doubtless impious and monstrous; but there came into my heart for the first time a throbbing sense of being over-governed. I said nothing, and he thought my silence was all sorrow. 'I sha'n't live to see you married,' he went on, 'but since the foundation is laid, that little signifies; it would be a selfish pleasure, and I have never had a thought but for your own personal advantage. To fore-see your future, in its main outline, to know to a certainty that you'll be safely domiciled here, with a wife approved by my judgment, cultivating the moral fruit of which I have sown the seed,—this will content me. But, my son, I wish to clear this bright vision from the shadow of a doubt. I believe in your docility; I believe I may trust the salutary force of your respect for my memory. But I must remember that when I am removed, you will stand here alone, face to face with a myriad nameless temptations to perversity. The fumes of unrighteous pride may rise into your brain and tempt you, in the interest of a vain delusion which it will call your independence, to shatter the edifice I have so laboriously constructed. So I must ask you for a promise,—the solemn promise you owe my condition.' And he grasped my hand. 'You will follow the path I have marked; you will be faithful to the young girl whom an influence as devoted as that which has governed your own young life has moulded into everything amiable; you will marry Isabel Vernor.' There was something porten-tous in this rigid summons. I was frightened. I drew away my hand and asked to be trusted without any such terrible vow. My reluctance startled my father into a suspicion that the vain delusion of independence had already been whispering to me. He sat up in his bed and looked at me with eyes which seemed to foresee a lifetime of odious ingratitude. I felt the reproach; I feel it now. I promised! And even now I don't regret my promise nor complain of my father's tenacity. I feel, some-how, as if the seeds of ultimate rest had been sown in those unsuspecting years,—as if after many days I might gather the mellow fruit. But after many days! I'll keep my promise, I'll obey; but I want to *live* first!"

"My dear fellow, you're living now. All this passionate consciousness of your situation is a very ardent life. I wish I could say as much for my own."

"I want to forget my situation. I want to spend three months without thinking of the past or the future, grasping whatever the present offers me. Yesterday, I thought I was in a fair way to sail with the tide. But this morning comes this memento!" And he held up his letter again.

"What is it?"

"A letter from Smyrna."

"I see you have not yet broken the seal."

"No, nor do I mean to, for the present. It contains bad news."

"What do you call bad news?"

"News that I'm expected in Smyrna in three weeks. News that Mr Vernor disapproves of my roving about the world. News that his daughter is standing expectant at the altar."

"Isn't this pure conjecture?"

"Conjecture, possibly, but safe conjecture. As soon as I looked at the letter, something smote me at the heart. Look at the device on the seal, and I'm sure you'll find it's *Tarry not!*" And he flung the letter on the grass.

"Upon my word, you had better open it," I said.

"If I were to open it and read my summons, do you know what I should do? I should march home and ask the Ober-kellner how one gets to Smyrna, pack my trunk, take my ticket, and not stop till I arrived. I know I should; it would be the fascination of habit. The only way, therefore, to wander to my rope's end is to leave the letter unread."

"In your place," I said, "curiosity would make me open it."

He shook his head. "I have no curiosity! For these many weeks the idea of my marriage has ceased to be a novelty, and I have contemplated it mentally in every possible light. I fear nothing from that side, but I do fear something from conscience. I want my hands tied. Will you do me a favor? Pick up the letter, put it into your pocket, and keep it till I ask you for it. When I do, you may know that I am at my rope's end."

I took the letter, smiling. "And how long is your rope to be? The Homburg season doesn't last for ever."

"Does it last a month? Let that be my season! A month hence you'll give it back to me."

"To-morrow, if you say so. Meanwhile, let it rest in peace!" And I consigned it to the most sacred interstice of my pocket-book. To say that I was disposed to humor the poor fellow would seem to be saying that I thought his demand fantastic. It was his situation, by no fault of his own, that was fantastic, and he was only trying to be natural. He watched me put away the letter, and when it had disappeared gave a soft sigh of relief. The sigh was natural, and yet it set me thinking. His general recoil from an immediate responsibility imposed by others might be wholesome enough; but if there was an old grievance on one side, was there not possibly a new-born delusion on the other? It would be unkind to withhold a reflection that might serve as a warning; so I told him, abruptly, that I had been an undiscovered spectator, the night before, of his exploits at roulette.

He blushed deeply, but he met my eyes with the same radiant frankness.

"Ah, you saw then," he cried, "that wonderful lady?"

"Wonderful she was indeed. I saw her afterwards, too, sitting on the terrace in the starlight. I imagine she was not alone."

"No, indeed, I was with her—for nearly an hour. Then I walked home with her."

"Verily! And did you go in?"

"No, she said it was too late to ask me; though in a general way, she declared she did not stand upon ceremony."

"She did herself injustice. When it came to losing your money for you, she made you insist."

"Ah, you noticed that too?" cried Pickering, still quite unconfused. "I felt as if the whole table was staring at me; but her manner was so gracious and reassuring that I concluded she was doing nothing unusual. She confessed, however, afterwards, that she is very eccentric. The world began to call her so, she said, before she ever dreamed of it, and at last finding that she had the reputation, in spite of herself, she resolved to enjoy its privileges. Now, she does what she chooses."

"In other words, she is a lady with no reputation to lose?"

Pickering seemed puzzled, and smiled a little. "Isn't that what you say of bad women?"

"Of some—of those who are found out."

"Well," he said, still smiling, "I haven't yet found out Madame Blumenthal."

"If that's her name, I suppose she's German."

"Yes; but she speaks English so well that you might almost doubt it. She is very clever. Her husband's dead."

I laughed, involuntarily, at the conjunction of these facts, and Pickering's clear glance seemed to question my mirth. "You have been so bluntly frank with me," I said, "that I too must be frank. Tell me, if you can, whether this clever Madame Blumenthal, whose husband is dead, has given an edge to your desire for a suspension of communication with Smyrna."

He seemed to ponder my question, unshrinkingly. "I think

not," he said, at last. "I've had the desire for three months; I've known Madame Blumenthal for less than twenty-four hours."

"Very true. But when you found this letter of yours on your plate at breakfast, did you seem for a moment to see Madame Blumenthal sitting opposite?"

"Opposite?" he repeated, frowning gently.

"Opposite, my dear fellow, or anywhere in the neighborhood. In a word, does she interest you?"

"Very much!" he cried, with his frown clearing away.

"Amen!" I answered, jumping up with a laugh. "And now, if we are to see the world in a month, there is no time to lose. Let us begin with the Hardtwald."

Pickering rose, and we strolled away into the forest, talking of lighter things. At last we reached the edge of the wood, sat down on a fallen log, and looked out across an interval of meadow at the long wooded waves of the Taunus. What my friend was thinking of, I can't say; I was revolving his quaint history and letting my wonderment wander away to Smyrna. Suddenly I remembered that he possessed a portrait of the young girl who was waiting for him there in a white-walled garden. I asked him if he had it with him. He said nothing, but gravely took out his pocket-book and drew forth a small photograph. It represented, as the poet says, a simple maiden in her flower,—a slight young girl, with a certain childish roundness of contour. There was no ease in her posture; she was standing, stiffly and shyly, for her likeness; she wore a short-waisted white dress; her arms hung at her sides and her hands were clasped in front; her head was bent downward a little, and her dark eyes fixed. But her awkwardness was as pretty as that of some angular seraph in a mediæval carving, and in her sober gaze there seemed to lurk the questioning gleam of childhood. "What is this for?" her charming eyes appeared to ask; "why have I been decked, for this ceremony, in a white frock and amber beads?"

"Gracious powers!" I said to myself; "what an enchanting thing is innocence!"

"That portrait was taken a year and a half ago," said Pickering, as if with an effort to be perfectly just. "By this time, I suppose, she looks a little wiser."

"Not much, I hope," I said, as I gave it back. "She's lovely!"

"Yes, poor girl, she's lovely—no doubt!" And he put the thing away without looking at it.

We were silent for some moments. At last, abruptly: "My dear fellow," I said, "I should take some satisfaction in seeing you immediately leave Homburg."

"Immediately?"

"To-day—as soon as you can get ready."

He looked at me, surprised, and little by little he blushed. "There's something I've not told you." he said; "something that your saying that Madame Blumenthal has no reputation to lose has made me half afraid to tell you."

"I think I can guess it. Madame Blumenthal has asked you to come and check her numbers for her at roulette again."

"Not at all!" cried Pickering, with a smile of triumph. "She says that she plays no more, for the present. She has asked me to come and take tea with her this evening."

"Ah, then," I said, very gravely, "of course you can't leave Homburg."

He answered nothing, but looked askance at me, as if he were expecting me to laugh. "Urge it strongly," he said in a moment. "Say it's my duty,—command me."

I didn't quite understand him, but, feathering the shaft with a harmless expletive, I told him that unless he followed my advice, I would never speak to him again.

He got up, stood before me, and struck the ground with his stick. "Good!" he cried. "I wanted an occasion to break a rule,—to leap an obstacle. Here it is! I stay!"

I made him a mock bow for his energy. "That's very fine,"

I said; "but now, to put you in a proper mood for Madame Blumenthal's tea, we'll go and listen to the band play Schubert under the lindens." And we walked back through the woods.

I went to see Pickering the next day, at his inn, and on knocking, as directed, at his door, was surprised to hear the sound of a loud voice within. My knock remained unnoticed, so I presently introduced myself. I found no company, but I discovered my friend walking up and down the room and apparently declaiming to himself from a little volume bound in white vellum. He greeted me heartily, threw his book on the table, and said that he was taking a German lesson.

"And who is your teacher?" I asked, glancing at the book.

He rather avoided meeting my eye, as he answered, after an instant's delay, "Madame Blumenthal."

"Indeed! Has she written a grammar?" I inquired.

"It's not a grammar; it's a tragedy." And he handed me the book.

I opened it, and beheld, in delicate type, in a very large margin, a *Trauerspiel* in five acts, entitled Cleopatra. There were a great many marginal corrections and annotations, apparently from the author's hand; the speeches were very long, and there was an inordinate number of soliloquies by the heroine. One of them, I remember, toward the end of the play, began in this fashion:—

"What, after all, is life but sensation, and sensation but deception?—reality that pales before the light of one's dreams, as Octavia's dull beauty fades beside mine? But let me believe in some intenser bliss and seek it in the arms of death!"

"It seems decidedly passionate," I said. "Has the tragedy ever been acted?"

"Never in public; but Madame Blumenthal tells me that she had it played at her own house in Berlin, and that she herself undertook the part of the heroine."

Pickering's unworldly life had not been of a sort to sharpen his perception of the ridiculous, but it seemed to me an unmistakable sign of his being under the charm, that this information was very soberly offered. He was preoccupied, and irresponsive to my experimental observations on vulgar topics,—the hot weather, the inn, the advent of Adelina Patti. At last he uttered his thoughts, and announced that Madame Blumenthal had turned out an extraordinarily interesting woman. He seemed to have quite forgotten our long talk in the Hardtwald, and betrayed no sense of this being a confession that he had taken his plunge and was floating with the current. He only remembered that I had spoken slightingly of the lady and hinted that it behooved me to amend my opinion. I had received the day before so strong an impression of a sort of spiritual fastidiousness in my friend's nature, that on hearing now the striking of a new hour, as it were, in his consciousness, and observing how the echoes of the past were immediately quenched in its music, I said to myself that it had certainly taken a delicate hand to regulate that fine machinery. No doubt Madame Blumenthal was a clever woman. It is a good German custom, at Homburg, to spend the hour preceding dinner in listening to the orchestra in the Kurgarten; Mozart and Beethoven, for organisms in which the interfusion of soul and sense is peculiarly mysterious, are a vigorous stimulus to the appetite. Pickering and I conformed, as we had done the day before, to the fashion, and when we were seated under the trees, he began to expatiate on his friend's merits.

"I don't know whether she is eccentric or not," he said; "to me every one seems eccentric, and it's not for me, yet awhile, to measure people by my narrow precedents. I never saw a gaming-table in my life before, and supposed that a gamester was, of necessity, some dusky villain with an evil eye. In Germany, says Madame Blumenthal, people play at roulette as they play at billiards, and her own venerable mother originally taught her the rules of the game. It is a recognized source of subsistence for decent people with small means. But I confess

x

Madame Blumenthal might do worse things than play roulette, and yet make them harmonious and beautiful. I have never been in the habit of thinking positive beauty the most excellent thing in a woman. I have always said to myself that if my heart was ever to be captured it would be by a sort of general grace,—a sweetness of motion and tone,—on which one could count for soothing impressions, as one counts on a musical instrument that is perfectly in tune. Madame Blumenthal has it,—this grace that soothes and satisfies; and it seems the more perfect that it keeps order and harmony in a character really passionately ardent and active. With her multifarious impulses and accomplishments nothing would be easier than that she should seem restless and over-eager and importunate. You will know her, and I leave you to judge whether she does. She has every gift, and culture has done everything for each. What goes on in her mind, I of course can't say; what reaches the observer—the admirer—is simply a penetrating perfume of intelligence, mingled with a penetrating perfume of sympathy."

"Madame Blumenthal," I said, smiling, "might be the loveliest woman in the world, and you the object of her choicest favors, and yet what I should most envy you would be, not your peerless friend, but your beautiful imagination."

"That's a polite way of calling me a fool," said Pickering. "You're a sceptic, a cynic, a satirist! I hope I shall be a long time coming to that."

"You'll make the journey fast if you travel by express trains. But pray tell me, have you ventured to intimate to Madame Blumenthal your high opinion of her?"

"I don't know what I may have said. She listens even better than she talks, and I think it possible I may have made her listen to a great deal of nonsense. For after the first few words I exchanged with her I was conscious of an extraordinary evaporation of all my old diffidence. I have, in truth, I suppose," he added, in a moment, "owing to my peculiar circumstances, a great accumulated fund of unuttered things of all sorts to get rid of. Last evening, sitting there before that lovely woman, they came swarming to my lips. Very likely I poured them all out. I have a sense of having enshrouded myself in a sort of mist of talk, and of seeing her lovely eyes shining through it opposite to me, like stars above a miasmatic frog-pond." And here, if I remember rightly, Pickering broke off into an ardent parenthesis, and declared that Madame Blumenthal's eyes had something in them that he had never seen in any others. "It was a jumble of crudities and inanities," he went on, "which must have seemed to her terribly farcical; but I feel the wiser and the stronger, somehow, for having poured them out before her; and I imagine I might have gone far without finding another woman in whom such an exhibition would have provoked so little of mere cold amusement."

"Madame Blumenthal, on the contrary," I surmised, "entered into your situation with warmth."

"Exactly so,—the greatest! She's wise, she knows, she has felt, she has suffered, and now she understands!"

"She told you, I imagine, that she understood you to a *t*, and she offered to be your guide, philosopher, and friend."

"She spoke to me," Pickering answered, after a pause, "as I had never been spoken to before, and she offered me, in effect, formally, all the offices of a woman's friendship."

"Which you as formally accepted?"

"To you the scene sounds absurd, I suppose, but allow me to say I don't care!" Pickering cried, with an air of genial aggression which was the most inoffensive thing in the world. "I was very much moved; I was, in fact, very much excited. I tried to say something, but I couldn't; I had had plenty to say before, but now I stammered and bungled, and at last I took refuge in an abrupt retreat."

"Meanwhile she had dropped her tragedy into your pocket!"

"Not at all. I had seen it on the table before she came in. Afterwards she kindly offered to read German aloud with me, for the accent, two or three times a week. 'What shall we begin with?' she asked. 'With this!' I said, and held up the book. And she let me take it to look it over."

I was neither a cynic nor a satirist, but even if I had been, I might have had my claws clipped by Pickering's assurance, before we parted, that Madame Blumenthal wished to know me and expected him to introduce me. Among the foolish things which, according to his own account, he had uttered, were some generous words in my praise, to which she had civilly replied. I confess I was curious to see her, but I begged that the introduction should not be immediate. I wished, on the one hand, to let Pickering work out his destiny without temptation, on my part, to play providence; and, on the other hand, I had at Homburg a group of friends with whom for another week I had promised to spend my leisure hours. For some days I saw little of Pickering, though we met at the Kursaal and strolled occasionally in the park. I watched, in spite of my desire to let him alone, for the signs and portents of the world's action upon him,—of that portion of the world, in especial, which Madame Blumenthal had gathered up into her comprehensive soul. He seemed very happy, and gave me in a dozen ways an impression of increased self-confidence and maturity. His mind was admirably active, and always, after a quarter of an hour's talk with him, I asked myself what experience could really do, that seclusion had not, to make it bright and fine. Every now and then I was struck with his deep enjoyment of some new spectacle,—often trifling enough,—something foreign, local, picturesque, some detail of manner, some accident of scenery; and of the infinite freedom with which he felt he could go and come and rove and linger and observe it all. It was an expansion, an awakening, a coming to manhood in a graver fashion; as one might arrive somewhere, after delays, in some quiet after-hour which

should transmute disappointment into gratitude for the preternatural vividness of first impressions. Each time I met him
he spoke a little less of Madame Blumenthal, but let me know
generally that he saw her often, and continued to admire her
—tremendously! I was forced to admit to myself, in spite of
preconceptions, that if she was really the ruling star of this
serene efflorescence, she must be a very fine woman. Pickering
had the air of an ingenuous young philosopher sitting at the
feet of an austere muse, and not of a sentimental spendthrift
dangling about some supreme incarnation of levity.

II

MADAME BLUMENTHAL seemed, for the time, to have
abjured the Kursaal, and I never caught a glimpse of her. Her
young friend, apparently, was an interesting study; she wished
to pursue it undiverted.

She reappeared, however, at last, one evening at the opera,
where from my chair I perceived her in a box, looking extremely
pretty. Adelina Patti was singing, and after the rising of the
curtain I was occupied with the stage; but on looking round
when it fell for the *entr' acte*, I saw that the authoress of Cleopatra had been joined by her young admirer. He was sitting a
little behind her, leaning forward, looking over her shoulder,
and listening, while she, slowly moving her fan to and fro
and letting her eye wander over the house, was apparently
talking of this person and that. No doubt she was saying
sharp things; but Pickering was not laughing; his eyes were
following her covert indications; his mouth was half open, as
it always was when he was interested; he looked intensely
serious. I was glad that, having her back to him, she was
unable to see how he looked. It seemed the proper moment to
present myself and make her my bow; but just as I was about

to leave my place, a gentleman, whom in a moment I perceived to be an old acquaintance, came to occupy the next chair. Recognition and mutual greetings followed, and I was forced to postpone my visit to Madame Blumenthal. I was not sorry, for it very soon occurred to me that Niedermeyer would be just the man to give me a fair prose version of Pickering's lyrical tributes to his friend. He was an Austrian by birth, and had formerly lived about Europe a great deal, in a series of small diplomatic posts. England especially he had often visited, and he spoke the language almost without accent. I had once spent three rainy days with him in the house of an English friend in the country. He was a sharp observer and a good deal of a gossip; he knew a little something about every one, and about some people everything. His knowledge on social matters generally had the flavor of all German science; it was copious, minute, exhaustive. "Do tell me," I said, as we stood looking round the house, "who and what is the lady in white, with the young man sitting behind her."

"Who?" he answered, dropping his glass. "Madame Blumenthal! What? It would take long to say. Be introduced; it's easily done; you'll find her charming. Then, after a week, you'll tell me what she is."

"Perhaps I shouldn't. My friend there has known her a week, and I don't think he is yet able to give an accurate account of her."

He raised his glass again, and after looking awhile, "I'm afraid your friend is a little—what do you call it?—a little 'soft.' Poor fellow! he's not the first. I've never known this lady that she had not some eligible youth hovering about in some such attitude as that, undergoing the softening process. She looks wonderfully well, from here. It's extraordinary how those women last!"

"You don't mean, I take it, when you talk about 'those women,' that Madame Blumenthal is not embalmed, for duration, in a certain dilution of respectability?"

"Yes and no. The sort of atmosphere that surrounds her is entirely of her own making. There is no reason, in her antecedents, that people should lower their voice when they speak of her. But some women are never at their ease till they have given some odd twist or other to their position before the world. The attitude of upright virtue is unbecoming, like sitting too straight in a fauteuil. Don't ask me for opinions, however; content yourself with a few facts, and an anecdote. Madame Blumenthal is Prussian, and very well born. I remember her mother, an old Westphalian Gräfin, with principles marshalled out like Frederick the Great's grenadiers. She was poor, however, and her principles were an insufficient dowry for Anastasia, who was married very young to a shabby Jew, twice her own age. He was supposed to have money, but I'm afraid he had less than was nominated in the bond, or else that his pretty young wife spent it very fast. She has been a widow these six or eight years, and living, I imagine, in rather a hand-to-mouth fashion. I suppose she is some thirty-four or five years old. In winter one hears of her in Berlin, giving little suppers to the artistic rabble there; in summer one often sees her across the green table at Ems and Wiesbaden. She's very clever, and her cleverness has spoiled her. A year after her marriage she published a novel, with her views on matrimony, in the George Sand manner, but really out-Heroding Herod. No doubt she was very unhappy; Blumenthal was an old beast. Since then she has published a lot of stuff,—novels and poems and pamphlets on every conceivable theme, from the conversion of Lola Montez, to the Hegelian philosophy. Her talk is much better than her writing. Her radical theories on matrimony made people think lightly of her at a time when her rebellion against it was probably only theoretic. She had a taste for spinning fine phrases, she drove her shuttle, and when she came to the end of her yarn, she found that society had turned its back. She tossed her head, declared that at last she could breathe the air of freedom, and formally announced her adhesion to an 'intellectual' life. This meant unlimited *camaraderie* with scribblers and daubers, Hegelian philosophers and Hungarian pianists waiting for engagements. But she has been admired also by a great many really clever men; there was a time, in fact, when she turned a head as well set on its shoulders as this one!" And Niedermeyer tapped his forehead. "She has a great charm, and, literally, I know no harm of her. Yet for all that, I'm not going to speak to her; I'm not going near her box. I'm going to leave her to say, if she does me the honor to observe the omission, that I too have gone over to the Philistines. It's not that; it is that there is something sinister about the woman. I'm too old to have it frighten me, but I'm good-natured enough to have it pain me. Her quarrel with society has brought her no happiness, and her outward charm is only the mask of a dangerous discontent. Her imagination is lodged where her heart should be! So long as you amuse it, well and good; she's radiant. But the moment you let it flag, she's capable of dropping you without a pang. If you land on your feet, you're so much the wiser, simply; but there have been two or three, I believe, who have almost broken their necks in the fall."

"You're reversing your promise," I said, "and giving me an opinion, but not an anecdote."

"This is my anecdote. A year ago a friend of mine made her acquaintance in Berlin, and though he was no longer a young man and had never been what's called a susceptible one, he took a great fancy to Madame Blumenthal. He's a major in the Prussian artillery,—grizzled, grave, a trifle severe, a man every way firm in the faith of his fathers. It's a proof of Anastasia's charm that such a man should have got into the way of calling on her every day for a month. But the major was in love, or next door to it! Every day that he called he found her scribbling away at a little ormolu table on a lot of half-sheets of note-paper. She used to bid him sit down and hold his tongue for a quarter of an hour, till she had finished her chapter; she was writing a novel, and it was promised to a publisher. Clorinda, she confided to him, was the name of the injured heroine. The major, I imagine, had never read a work of fiction in his life, but he knew by hearsay that Madame Blumenthal's literature, when put forth in pink covers, was subversive of several respectable institutions. Besides, he didn't believe in women knowing how to write at all, and it irritated him to see this inky goddess scribbling away under his nose for the press; irritated him the more that, as I say, he was in love with her and that he ventured to believe she had a kindness for his years and his honors. And yet she was not such a woman as he could easily ask to marry him. The result of all this was that he fell into the way of railing at her intellectual pursuits and saying he should like to run his sword through her pile of papers. A woman was clever enough when she could guess her husband's wishes, and learned enough when she could spell out her prayer-book. At last, one day, Madame Blumenthal flung down her pen and announced in triumph that she had finished her novel. Clorinda had danced her dance. The major, by way of congratulating her, declared that her novel was coquetry and vanity and that she propagated vicious paradoxes on purpose to make a noise in the world and look picturesque and passionate. He added, however, that he loved her in spite of her follies, and that if she would formally abjure them he would as formally offer her his hand. They say that in certain cases women like being frightened and snubbed. I don't know, I'm sure; I don't know how much pleasure, on this occasion, was mingled with Anastasia's wrath. But her wrath was very quiet, and the major assured me it made her look terribly handsome. 'I have told you before,' she says, 'that I write from an inner need. I write to unburden my heart, to satisfy my conscience. You call my poor efforts coquetry, vanity, the desire to produce a sensation. I can prove to you that it is the quiet labor itself I care for, and not the world's more or less flattering attention to it!' And seizing the manuscript of Clorinda she thrust it into the fire. The major stands staring, and the first thing he knows she is sweeping him a great courtesy and bidding him farewell forever. Left alone and recovering his wits, he fishes out Clorinda from the embers and then proceeds to thump vigorously at the lady's door. But it never opened, and from that day to the day three months ago when he told me the tale, he had not beheld her again.

"By Jove, it's a striking story," I said. "But the question is, what does it prove?"

"Several things. First (what I was careful not to tell my friend), that Madame Blumenthal cared for him a trifle more than he supposed; second, that he cares for her more than ever; third, that the performance was a master stroke, and that her allowing him to force an interview upon her again is only a question of time."

"And last?" I asked.

"This is another anecdote. The other day, Unter den Linden, I saw on a bookseller's counter a little pink-covered romance: Sophronia, by Madame Blumenthal. Glancing through it, I observed an extraordinary abuse of asterisks; every two or three pages the narrative was adorned with a portentous blank, crossed with a row of stars."

"Well, but poor Clorinda?" I objected, as Niedermeyer paused.

"Sophronia, my dear fellow, is simply Clorinda renamed by the baptism of fire. The fair author comes back, of course, and finds Clorinda tumbled upon the floor, a good deal scorched, but on the whole more frightened than hurt. She picks her up, brushes her off, and sends her to the printer. Wherever the flames had burnt a hole, she swings a constellation! But if the major is prepared to drop a penitent tear over the ashes of Clorinda, I shan't whisper to him that the urn is empty."

Even Adelina Patti's singing, for the next half-hour, but

half availed to divert me from my quickened curiosity to
behold Madame Blumenthal face to face. As soon as the curtain had fallen again, I repaired to her box and was ushered in
by Pickering with zealous hospitality. His glowing smile
seemed to say to me, "Ay, look for yourself, and adore!"
Nothing could have been more gracious than the lady's greeting, and I found, somewhat to my surprise, that her prettiness
lost nothing on a nearer view. Her eyes indeed were the finest
I have ever seen,—the softest, the deepest, the most intensely
responsive. In spite of something faded and jaded in her physiognomy, her movements, her smile, and the tone of her voice,
especially when she laughed, had an almost girlish frankness
and spontaneity. She looked at you very hard with her radiant
gray eyes, and she indulged in talking in a superabundance of
restless, zealous gestures, as if to make you take her meaning
in a certain very particular and rather superfine sense. I wondered whether after a while this might not fatigue one's
attention; then, meeting her charming eyes, I said, No! not
for ages, at least. She was very clever, and, as Pickering had
said, she spoke English admirably. I told her, as I took my
seat beside her, of the fine things I had heard about her from
my friend, and she listened, letting me run on some time, and
exaggerate a little, with her fine eyes fixed full upon me.
"Really?" she suddenly said, turning short round upon
Pickering, who stood behind us, and looking at him in the
same way, "is that the way you talk about me?"

He blushed to his eyes, and I repented. She suddenly began
to laugh; it was then I observed how sweet her voice was in
laughter. We talked after this of various matters, and in a
little while I complimented her on her excellent English, and
asked if she had learned it in England.

"Heaven forbid!" she cried. "I've never been there and
wish never to go. I should never get on with the—" I wondered what she was going to say; the fogs, the smoke, or whist
with six-penny stakes?—"I should never get on," she said,

"with the Aristocracy! I'm a fierce democrat, I'm not ashamed of it. I hold opinions which would make my ancestors turn in their graves. I was born in the lap of feudalism. I'm a daughter of the crusaders. But I'm a revolutionist! I have a passion for freedom,—boundless, infinite, ineffable freedom. It's to your great country I should like to go. I should like to see the wonderful spectacle of a great people free to do everything it chooses, and yet never doing anything wrong!"

I replied, modestly, that, after all, both our freedom and our virtue had their limits, and she turned quickly about and shook her fan with a dramatic gesture at Pickering. "No matter, no matter!" she cried, "I should like to see the country which produced that wonderful young man. I think of it as a sort of Arcadia,—a land of the golden age. He's so delightfully innocent! In this stupid old Germany, if a young man is innocent, he's a fool; he has no brains; he's not a bit interesting. But Mr Pickering says the most naïf things, and after I have laughed five minutes at their simplicity, it suddenly occurs to me that they are very wise, and I think them over for a week. True!" she went on, nodding at him. "I call them inspired solecisms, and I treasure them up. Remember that when I next laugh at you!"

Glancing at Pickering, I was prompted to believe that he was in a state of beatific exaltation which weighed Madame Blumenthal's smiles and frowns in an equal balance. They were equally hers; they were links alike in the golden chain. He looked at me with eyes that seemed to say, "Did you ever hear such wit? Did you ever see such grace?" I imagine he was but vaguely conscious of the meaning of her words; her gestures, her voice and glance, made an irresistible harmony. There is something painful in the spectacle of absolute inthralment, even to an excellent cause. I gave no response to Pickering's challenge, but embarked upon some formal tribute to the merits of Adelina Patti's singing. Madame Blumenthal, as became a "revolutionist," was obliged to confess that she could see no charm in it; it was meagre, it was trivial, it lacked soul. "You must know that in music, too," she said, "I think for myself!" And she began with a great many flourishes of her fan to expound what it was she thought. Remarkable things, doubtless; but I cannot answer for it, for in the midst of the exposition, the curtain rose again. "You can't be a great artist without a great passion!" Madame Blumenthal was affirming. Before I had time to assent, Madame Patti's voice rose wheeling like a skylark, and rained down its silver notes. "Ah, give me that art," I whispered, "and I'll leave you your passion!" And I departed for my own place in the orchestra. I wondered afterwards whether the speech had seemed rude, and inferred that it had not, on receiving a friendly nod from the lady, in the lobby, as the theatre was emptying itself. She was on Pickering's arm, and he was taking her to her carriage. Distances are short in Homburg, but the night was rainy, and Madame Blumenthal exhibited a very pretty satin-shod foot as a reason why, though but a penniless creature, she should not walk home. Pickering left us together a moment while he went to hail the vehicle, and my companion seized the opportunity, as she said, to beg me to be so very kind as to come and see her. It was for a particular reason! It was reason enough for me, of course I answered, that I could grasp at the shadow of a permission. She looked at me a moment with that extraordinary gaze of hers, which seemed so absolutely audacious in its candor, and answered that I paid more compliments than our young friend there, but that she was sure I was not half so sincere. "But it's about him I want to talk," she said. "I want to ask you many things: I want you to tell me all about him. He interests me, but you see my sympathies are so intense, my imagination is so lively, that I don't trust my own impressions. They have misled me more than once!" And she gave a little tragic shudder.

I promised to come and compare notes with her, and we bade her farewell at her carriage door. Pickering and I

remained awhile, walking up and down the long glazed gallery
of the Kursaal. I had not taken many steps before I became
aware that I was beside a man in the very extremity of love.
"Isn't she wonderful?" he asked, with an implicit confidence
in my sympathy which it cost me some ingenuity to elude.
If he was really in love, well and good! For although, now
that I had seen her, I stood ready to confess to large possibilities of fascination on Madame Blumenthal's part, and even
to certain possibilities of sincerity of which I reserved the
precise admeasurement, yet it seemed to me less ominous to
have him give the reins to his imagination than it would have
been to see him stand off and cultivate an "admiration" which
should pique itself on being discriminating. It was on his
fundamental simplicity that I counted for a happy termination
of his experiment, and the former of these alternatives seemed
to me to prove most in its favor. I resolved to hold my tongue
and let him run his course. He had a great deal to say about
his happiness, about the days passing like hours, the hours
like minutes, and about Madame Blumenthal being a "revelation." "She was nothing to-night!" he said; "nothing to
what she sometimes is in the way of brilliancy,—in the way
of repartee. If you could only hear her when she tells her
adventures!"

"Adventures?" I inquired. "Has she had adventures?"

"Of the most wonderful sort!" cried Pickering, with rapture. "She hasn't vegetated, like me! She has lived in the
tumult of life. When I listen to her reminiscences, it's like
hearing the opening tumult of one of Beethoven's symphonies,
as it loses itself in a triumphant harmony of beauty and faith!"

I could only bow, but I desired to know before we separated
what he had done with that troublesome conscience of his.
"I suppose you know, my dear fellow," I said, "that you're
simply in love. That's what they call your state of mind."

He replied with a brightening eye, as if he were delighted
to hear it. "So Madame Blumenthal told me," he cried, "only

this morning!" And seeing, I suppose, that I was slightly puzzled, "I went to drive with her," he continued; "we drove to Königstein, to see the old castle. We scrambled up into the heart of the ruin and sat for an hour in one of the crumbling old courts. Something in the solemn stillness of the place unloosed my tongue; and while she sat on an ivied stone, on the edge of the plunging wall, I stood there and made a speech. She listened to me, looking at me, breaking off little bits of stone and letting them drop down into the valley. At last she got up and nodded at me two or three times silently, with a smile, as if she were applauding me for a solo on the violin. 'You're in love,' she said. 'It's a perfect case!' And for some time she said nothing more. But before we left the place she told me that she owed me an answer to my speech. She thanked me heartily, but she was afraid that if she took me at my word she would be taking advantage of my inexperience. I had known few women, I was too easily pleased, I thought her better than she really was. She had great faults; I must know her longer and find them out; I must compare her with other women,—women younger, simpler, more innocent, more ignorant; and then if I still did her the honor to think well of her, she would listen to me again. I told her that I was not afraid of preferring any woman in the world to her, and then she repeated, 'Happy man, happy man! you're in love, you're in love!'"

I called upon Madame Blumenthal a couple of days later, in some agitation of thought. It has been proved that there are, here and there, in the world, such people as sincere attitudinizers; certain characters cultivate fictitious emotions in perfect good faith. Even if this clever lady enjoyed poor Pickering's bedazzlement, it was conceivable that, taking vanity and charity together, she should care more for his welfare than for her own entertainment; and her offer to abide by the result of hazardous comparison with other women was a finer stroke than her fame—and indeed than probability—had seemed to foreshadow. She received me in a shabby little sitting-room, littered with uncut books and newspapers, many of which I saw at a glance were French. One side of it was occupied by an open piano, surmounted by a jar full of white roses. They perfumed the air; they seemed to me to exhale the pure aroma of Pickering's devotion. Buried in an arm-chair, the object of this devotion was reading the Revue des Deux Mondes. The purpose of my visit was not to admire Madame Blumenthal on my own account, but to ascertain how far I might safely leave her to work her will upon my friend. She had impugned my sincerity the evening of the opera, and I was careful on this occasion to abstain from compliments and not to place her on her guard against my penetration. It is needless to narrate our interview in detail; indeed, to tell the perfect truth, I was punished for my ambition to read her too clearly by a temporary eclipse of my own perspicacity. She sat there so questioning, so perceptive, so genial, so generous, and so pretty withal, that I was quite ready at the end of half an hour to shake hands with Pickering on her being a wonderful woman. I have never liked to linger, in memory, on that half-hour. The result of it was to prove that there were many more things in the composition of a woman who, as Niedermeyer said, had lodged her imagination in the place of her heart, than were dreamt of in my philosophy. Yet, as I sat there stroking my hat and balancing the account between nature and art in my affable hostess, I felt like a very competent philosopher. She had said she wished me to tell her everything about our friend, and she questioned me, categorically, as to his family, his fortune, his antecedents, and his character. All this was natural in a woman who had received a passionate declaration of love, and it was expressed with an air of charmed solicitude, a radiant confidence that there was really no mistake about his being a supremely fine fellow, and that if I chose to be explicit, I might deepen her conviction to disinterested ecstasy, which might have almost inspired me to invent a good opinion, if I had not had one at hand. I told her that she really knew Pickering better than I did, and that until we met at Homburg, I had not seen him since he was a boy.

"But he talks to you freely," she answered; "I know you're his confidant. He has told me certainly a great many things, but I always feel as if he were keeping something back; as if he were holding something behind him, and showing me only one hand at once. He seems often to be hovering on the edge of a secret. I have had several friendships in my life,—thank Heaven! but I have had none more dear to me than this one. Yet in the midst of it I have the painful sense of my friend being half afraid of me; of his thinking me terrible, strange, perhaps a trifle out of my wits. Poor me! If he only knew what a plain good soul I am, and how I only want to know him and befriend him!"

These words were full of a plaintive magnanimity which made mistrust seem cruel. How much better I might play providence over Pickering's experiments with life, if I could engage the fine instincts of this charming woman on the providential side! Pickering's secret was, of course, his engagement to Miss Vernor; it was natural enough that he should have been unable to bring himself to talk of it to Madame Blumenthal. The simple sweetness of this young girl's face had not faded from my memory; I couldn't rid myself of the fancy that in going further Pickering might fare much worse. Madame Blumenthal's professions seemed a virtual promise to agree with me, and after a momentary hesitation I said that my friend had, in fact, a substantial secret, and that it appeared to me enlightened friendship to put her into possession of it. In as few words as possible I told her that Pickering stood pledged by filial piety to marry a young lady at Smyrna. She listened intently to my story; when I had finished it there was a faint flush of excitement in each of her cheeks. She broke out into a dozen exclamations of admiration and compassion. "What a wonderful tale—what a romantic situation! No wonder poor Mr Pickering seemed restless and unsatisfied; no wonder he wished to put off the day of submission. And the poor little girl at Smyrna, waiting there for the young Western prince like the heroine of an Eastern tale! She would give the world to see her photograph; did I think Mr Pickering would show it to her? But never fear; she would ask nothing indiscreet! Yes, it was a marvellous story, and if she had invented it herself, people would have said it was absurdly improbable." She left her seat and took several turns about the room, smiling to herself and uttering little German cries of wonderment. Suddenly she stopped before the piano and broke into a little laugh; the next moment she buried her face in the great bouquet of roses. It was time I should go, but I was indisposed to leave her without obtaining some definite assurance that, as far as pity was concerned, she pitied the young girl at Smyrna more than the young man at Homburg. "Of course you appreciate," I said, rising, "my hopes in telling you all this."

She had taken one of the roses from the vase and was arranging it in the front of her dress. Suddenly, looking up, "Leave it to me, leave it to me!" she cried. "I'm interested!" And with her little blue-gemmed hand she tapped her forehead. "I'm interested,—don't interfere!"

And with this I had to content myself. But more than once, for the day following, I repented of my zeal, and wondered whether a providence with a white rose in her bosom might not turn out a trifle too human. In the evening, at the Kursaal, I looked for Pickering, but he was not visible, and I reflected that my revelation had not as yet, at any rate, seemed to Madame Blumenthal a reason for prescribing a cooling-term to his passion. Very late, as I was turning away, I saw him arrive,—with no small satisfaction, for I had determined to let him know immediately in what way I had attempted to serve him. But he straightway passed his arm through my own and led me off toward the gardens. I saw that he was too excited to allow me prior speech.

"I've burnt my ships!" he cried, when we were out of earshot of the crowd. "I've told her everything. I've insisted that it's simple torture for me to wait, with this idle view of loving her less. It's well enough for her to ask it, but I feel strong enough now to override her reluctance. I've cast off the millstone from round my neck. I care for nothing, I know nothing but that I love her with every pulse of my being,— and that everything else has been a hideous dream, from which she may wake me into blissful morning with a single word!"

I held him off at arm's-length and looked at him gravely. "You have told her, you mean, of your engagement to Miss Vernor?"

"The whole story! I've given it up,—I've thrown it to the winds. I've broken utterly with the past. It may rise in its grave and give me its curse, but it can't frighten me now. I've a right to be happy. I've a right to be free, I've a right not to bury myself alive. It wasn't *I* who promised! I wasn't born then. I myself, my soul, my mind, my option,—all this is but a month old! Ah," he went on, "if you knew the difference it makes,—this having chosen and broken and spoken! I'm twice the man I was yesterday! Yesterday I was afraid of her; there was a kind of mocking mystery of knowledge and clever-ness about her, which oppressed me in the midst of my love. But now I'm afraid of nothing but of being too happy."

I stood silent, to let him spend his eloquence. But he paused a moment, and took off his hat and fanned himself. "Let me perfectly understand," I said at last. "You've asked Madame Blumenthal to be your wife?"

"The wife of my intelligent choice."

"And does she consent?"

"She asks three days to decide."

"Call it four! She has known your secret since this morn-ing. I'm bound to let you know I told her."

"So much the better!" cried Pickering, without apparent resentment or surprise. "It's not a brilliant offer for such a woman, and in spite of what I have at stake I feel that it would be brutal to press her."

"What does she say," I asked in a moment, "to your breaking your promise?"

Pickering was too much in love for false shame. "She tells me," he answered bravely, "that she loves me too much to find courage to condemn me. She agrees with me that I have a right to be happy. I ask no exemption from the common law. What I claim is simply freedom to try to be!"

Of course I was puzzled; it was not in that fashion that I had expected Madame Blumenthal to make use of my information. But the matter now was quite out of my hands, and all I could do was to bid my companion not work himself into a fever over either fortune.

The next day I had a visit from Niedermeyer, on whom, after our talk at the opera, I had left a card. We gossiped awhile, and at last he said suddenly: "By the way, I have a sequel to the history of Clorinda. The major is in Homburg!"

"Indeed!" said I. "Since when?"

"These three days."

"And what is he doing?"

"He seems," said Niedermeyer with a laugh, "to be chiefly occupied in sending flowers to Madame Blumenthal. That is, I went with him the morning of his arrival to choose a nose-gay, and nothing would suit him but a small haystack of white roses. I hope it was received."

"I can assure you it was," I cried. "I saw the lady fairly nestling her head in it. But I advise the major not to build upon that. He has a rival."

"Do you mean the soft young man of the other night?"

"Pickering is soft, if you will, but his softness seems to have served him. He has offered her everything, and she has not yet refused it." I had handed my visitor a cigar and he was puffing it in silence. At last he abruptly asked if I had been introduced to Madame Blumenthal; and, on my affirmative, inquired what I thought of her. "I'll not tell you," I said, "or you'll call *me* soft."

He knocked away his ashes, eying me askance. "I've noticed your friend about," he said, "and even if you had not told me, I should have known he was in love. After he has left his adored, his face wears for the rest of the day the expression with which he has risen from her feet, and more than once I've felt like touching his elbow, as you would that of a man who has inadvertently come into a drawing-room in his overshoes. You say he has offered our friend everything; but, my dear fellow, he hasn't everything to offer her. He's as amiable, evidently, as the morning, but madame has no taste for daylight."

"I assure you," said I, "Pickering is a very interesting fellow."

"Ah, there it is! Hasn't he some story or other? isn't he an orphan, or natural child, or consumptive, or contingent heir to great estates? She'll read his little story to the end, and close the book very tenderly and smooth down the cover, and then, when he least expects it, she'll toss it into the dusty limbo of all her old romances. She'll let him dangle, but she'll let him drop!"

"Upon my word," I cried with heat, "if she does, she'll be a very unprincipled little creature!"

Niedermeyer shrugged his shoulders. "I never said she was a saint!"

Shrewd as I felt Niedermeyer to be, I was not prepared to take his simple word for this consummation, and in the evening I received a communication which fortified my doubts. It was a note from Pickering, and it ran as follows:—

"My dear Friend,—I have every hope of being happy, but I am to go to Wiesbaden to learn my fate. Madame Blumenthal goes thither this afternoon to spend a few days, and she allows me to accompany her. Give me your good wishes; you shall hear of the event.   "E.P."

One of the diversions of Homburg for new-comers is to dine in rotation at the different *tables d'hôtes*. It so happened that, a couple of days later, Niedermeyer took pot-luck at my hotel and secured a seat beside my own. As we took our places I found a letter on my plate, and, as it was postmarked Wiesbaden, I lost no time in opening it. It contained but three lines:—

"I'm happy—I'm accepted—an hour ago. I can hardly believe it's your poor old   "E.P."

I placed the note before Niedermeyer: not exactly in triumph, but with the alacrity of all privileged confutation. He looked at it much longer than was needful to read it, stroking down his beard gravely, and I felt it was not so easy to confute a pupil of the school of Metternich. At last, folding the note and handing it back, "Has your friend mentioned," he asked, "Madame Blumenthal's errand at Wiesbaden?"

"You look very wise. I give it up!" said I.

"She's gone there to make the major follow her. He went by the next train."

"And has the major, on his side, dropped you a line?"

"He's not a letter-writer."

"Well," said I, pocketing my letter, "with this document in my hand I'm bound to reserve my judgment. We'll have a bottle of Johannisberg, and drink to the triumph of virtue."

For a whole week more I heard nothing from Pickering,—somewhat to my surprise, and, as the days went by, not a little to my discomposure. I had expected that his bliss would continue to overflow in an occasional brief bulletin, and his silence was possibly an indication that it had been clouded. At last I wrote to his hotel at Wiesbaden, but received no answer; whereupon, as my next resource, I repaired to his former lodging at Homburg, where I thought it possible he had left property which he would sooner or later send for. There I learned that he had indeed just telegraphed from Cologne for his baggage. To Cologne I immediately despatched a line of inquiry as to his prosperity and the cause of his silence. The next day I received three words in answer,—a simple, un-commented request that I would come to him. I lost no time, and reached him in the course of a few hours. It was dark when I arrived, and the city was sheeted in a cold, autumnal rain. Pickering had stumbled, with an indifference which was itself a symptom of distress, on a certain musty old Mainzer-hof, and I found him sitting over a smouldering fire in a vast dingy chamber, which looked as if it had grown gray with watching the ennui of ten generations of travellers. Looking at him, as he rose on my entrance, I saw that he was in extreme tribulation. He was pale and haggard; his face was five years older. Now, at least, in all conscience, he had tasted of the cup of life. I was anxious to know what had turned it so suddenly to bitterness; but I spared him all importunate curiosity, and let him take his time. I assented, tacitly, to the symptoms of his trouble, and we made for a while a feeble effort to discuss the picturesqueness of Cologne. At last he rose and stood a long time looking into the fire, while I slowly paced the length of the dusky room.

"Well!" he said as I came back; "I wanted knowledge, and I certainly know something I didn't a month ago." And here-with, calmly and succinctly enough, as if dismay had worn itself out, he related the history of the foregoing days. He touched lightly on details; he evidently never was to gush as freely again as he had done during the prosperity of his suit. He had been accepted one evening, as explicitly as his imagina-tion could desire, and had gone forth in his rapture and roamed about till nearly morning in the gardens of the Conversation House, taking the stars and the perfumes of the summer night into his confidence. "It's worth it all, almost," he said, "to have been wound up for an hour to that celestial pitch. No man, I'm sure, can ever know it but once." The next morning he had repaired to Madame Blumenthal's lodging and had been met, to his amazement, by a naked refusal to see him. He had strode about for a couple of hours—in another mood—and then had returned to the charge. The servant handed him a three-cornered note; it contained these words: "Leave me alone to-day; I'll give you ten minutes to-morrow evening." Of the next thirty-six hours he could give no coherent account, but at the appointed time Madame Blumenthal had received him. Almost before she spoke there had come to him a sense of the depth of his folly in supposing he knew her. "One has heard all one's days," he said, "of people removing the mask; it's one of the stock phrases of romance. Well, there she stood with her mask in her hand. Her face," he went on gravely, after a pause,—"her face was horrible!" "I give you ten minutes," she had said, pointing to the clock. "Make your scene, tear your hair, brandish your dagger!" And she had sat down and folded her arms. "It's not a joke," she cried, "it's dead earnest; let's get through with it. You're dismissed! Have you nothing to say?" He had stammered some frantic demand for an explanation; and she had risen and come near him, looking at him from head to feet, very pale, and evidently more excited than she wished to have him see. "I've done with you!" she said with a smile; "you ought to have done with me! It has all been delightful, but there are excellent reasons why it should come to an end." "You've been playing a part, then," he had gasped out; "you never cared for me?" "Yes; till I knew you; till I saw how far you'd go. But now the story's finished; we've reached the dénouement. We'll close the book and be good friends." "To see how far I would go?" he had repeated. "You led me on, meaning all the while to do *this?*" "I led you on, if you will. I received your visits in season and out! Sometimes they were very entertaining; sometimes they bored me fearfully. But you were such a very curious case of—what shall I call it?—of enthusiasm, that I determined to take good and bad together. I wanted to make you commit yourself unmistakably. I should have preferred not to bring you to this place: but that too was necessary. Of course I can't marry you; I can do better. Thank your fate for it. You've thought wonders of me for a month, but your good-humor wouldn't last. I'm too old and too wise; you're too young and too foolish. It seems to me that I've been very good to you; I've entertained you to the top of your bent, and, except perhaps that I'm a little brusque just now, you've nothing to complain of. I would have let you down more gently if I could have taken another month to it; but circumstances have forced my hand. Abuse me, revile me, if you like. I'll make every allowance!" Pickering listened to all this intently enough to perceive that, as if by some sudden natural cataclysm, the ground had broken away at his feet, and that he must recoil. He turned away in dumb amazement. "I don't know how I seemed to be taking it," he said, "but she seemed really to desire—I don't know why —something in the way of reproach and vituperation. But I couldn't, in that way, have uttered a syllable. I was sickened; I wanted to get away into the air,—to shake her off and come to my senses. 'Have you nothing, nothing, nothing to say?' she cried, as I stood with my hand on the door. 'Haven't I treated you to talk enough?' I believe I answered. 'You'll write to me then, when you get home?' 'I think not,' said I. 'Six months hence, I fancy, you'll come and see me!' 'Never!' said I. 'That's a confession of stupidity,' she answered. 'It means that, even on reflection, you'll never understand the philosophy of my conduct.' The word 'philosophy' seemed so strange that I verily believe I smiled. 'I've given you,' she went on, 'all that you gave me. Your passion was an affair of the head.' 'I only wish you had told me sooner,' I exclaimed, 'that you considered it so!' And I went my way. The next day I came down the Rhine. I sat all day on the boat, not knowing where I was going, where to get off. I was in a kind of ague of terror; it seemed to me I had seen something infernal. At last I saw the cathedral towers here looming over the city. They seemed to say something to me, and when the boat stopped, I came ashore. I've been here a week: I haven't slept at night,—and yet it has been a week of rest!"

It seemed to me that he was in a fair way to recover, and that his own philosophy, if left to take its time, was adequate to the occasion. After his story was told I recurred to his grievance but once,—that evening, later, as we were about to separate for the night. "Suffer me to say," I said, "that there was some truth in *her* account of your relations. You were using her, intellectually, and all the while, without your knowing it, she was using you. It was diamond cut diamond. Her needs were the more superficial and she came to an end first." He frowned and turned uneasily away, but he offered no denial. I waited a few moments, to see if he would remember, before we parted, that he had a claim to make upon me. But he seemed to have forgotten it.

The next day we strolled about the picturesque old city, and of course, before long, went into the cathedral. Pickering said little; he seemed intent upon his own thoughts. He sat down beside a pillar near a chapel, in front of a gorgeous window, and, leaving him to his meditations, I wandered through the church. When I came back I saw he had something to say. But before he had spoken, I laid my hand on his shoulder and looked at him with a significant smile. He slowly bent his head and dropped his eyes, with a mixture of assent and humility. I drew forth his letter from where it had lain untouched for a month, placed it silently on his knee, and left him to deal with it alone.

Half an hour later I returned to the same place, but he had gone, and one of the sacristans, hovering about and seeing me looking for Pickering, said he thought he had left the church. I found him in his gloomy chamber at the inn, pacing slowly up and down. I should doubtless have been at a loss to say just what effect I expected his letter to produce; but his actual aspect surprised me. He was flushed, excited, a trifle irritated.

"Evidently," I said, "you've read your letter."

"I owe you a report of it," he answered. "When I gave it to you a month ago, I did my friends injustice."

"You called it a 'summons,' I remember."

"I was a great fool! It's a release!"

"From your engagement?"

"From everything! The letter, of course, is from Mr Vernor. He desires to let me know at the earliest moment, that his daughter, informed for the first time a week before of what was expected of her, positively refuses to be bound by by the contract or to assent to my being bound. She had been given a week to reflect and had spent it in inconsolable tears. She had resisted every form of persuasion; from compulsion, writes Mr Vernor, he naturally shrinks. The young lady considers the arrangement 'horrible.' After accepting her duties cut and dried all her life, she presumes at last to have a taste of her own. I confess I'm surprised; I had been given to believe that she was idiotically passive and would remain so to the end of the chapter. Not a bit! She has insisted on my being formally dismissed, and her father intimates that in case of non-compliance she threatens him with an attack of brain fever. Mr Vernor condoles with me handsomely, and lets me know that the young lady's attitude has been a great shock to his own nerves. He adds that he will not aggravate such regret as I may do him the honor to entertain, by any allusion to his daughter's charms and to the magnitude of my loss, and he concludes with the hope that, for the comfort of all concerned, I may already have amused my fancy with other 'views.' He reminds me in a postscript that, in spite of this painful occurrence, the son of his most valued friend will always be a welcome visitor at his house. I am free, he observes; I have my life before me; he recommends an extensive course of travel. Should my wanderings lead me to the East, he hopes that no false embarrassment will deter me from presenting myself at Smyrna. He will insure me at least a friendly reception. It's a very polite letter."

Polite as the letter was, Pickering seemed to find no great exhilaration in having this famous burden so handsomely lifted from his conscience. He fell a-brooding over his liberation in a manner which you might have deemed proper to a renewed sense of bondage. "Bad news," he had called his letter originally; and yet, now that its contents proved to be in flat contradiction to his foreboding, there was no impulsive voice to reverse the formula and declare the news was good. The wings of impulse in the poor fellow had of late been terribly clipped. It was an obvious reflection, of course, that if he had not been so doggedly sure of the matter a month before, and had gone through the form of breaking Mr Vernor's seal, he might have escaped the purgatory of Madame Blumenthal's blandishments. But I left him to moralize in private; I had no desire, as the phrase is, to rub it in. My thoughts, moreover, were following another train; I was saying to myself that if to those gentle graces of which her young visage had offered to my fancy the blooming promise, Miss Vernor added in this striking measure the capacity for magnanimous action, the amendment to my friend's career had been less happy than the rough draught. Presently, turning about, I saw him looking at the young lady's photograph. "Of course, now," he said, "I have no right to keep it!" And before I could ask for another glimpse of it, he had thrust it into the fire.

"I am sorry to be saying it just now," I observed after a while, "but I shouldn't wonder if Miss Vernor were a lovely creature."

"Go and find out," he answered gloomily. "The coast is clear. My part," he presently added, "is to forget her. It oughtn't to be hard. But don't you think," he went on suddenly, "that for a poor fellow who asked nothing of fortune but leave to sit down in a quiet corner, it has been rather a cruel pushing about?"

Cruel indeed, I declared, and he certainly had the right to demand a clean page on the book of fate, and a fresh start. Mr

Vernor's advice was sound; he should seek diversion in the grand tour of Europe. If he would allow it to the zeal of my sympathy, I would go with him on his way. Pickering assented without enthusiasm; he had the discomfited look of a man who, having gone to some cost to make a good appearance in a drawing-room, should find the door suddenly slammed in his face. We started on our journey, however, and little by little his enthusiasm returned. He was too capable of enjoying fine things to remain permanently irresponsive, and after a fortnight spent among pictures and monuments and antiquities, I felt that I was seeing him for the first time in his best and healthiest mood. He had had a fever and then he had had a chill; the pendulum had swung right and left in a manner rather trying to the machine; but now, at last, it was working back to an even, natural beat. He recovered in a measure the generous eloquence with which he had fanned his flame at Homburg, and talked about things with something of the same passionate freshness. One day when I was laid up at the inn at Bruges with a lame foot, he came home and treated me to a rhapsody about a certain meek-faced virgin of Hans Memling, which seemed to me sounder sense than his compliments to Madame Blumenthal. He had his dull days and his sombre moods,—hours of irresistible retrospect; but I let them come and go without remonstrance, because I fancied they always left him a trifle more alert and resolute. One evening, however, he sat hanging his head in so doleful a fashion that I took the bull by the horns and told him he had by this time surely paid his debt to penitence, and owed it to himself to banish that woman forever from his thoughts.

He looked up, staring; and then with a deep blush: "That woman?" he said. "I was not thinking of Madame Blumenthal!"

After this I gave another construction to his melancholy. Taking him with his hopes and fears, at the end of six weeks of active observation and keen sensation, Pickering was as fine a fellow as need be. We made our way down to Italy and spent a fortnight at Venice. There something happened which I had been confidently expecting; I had said to myself that it was merely a question of time. We had passed the day at Torcello, and came floating back in the glow of the sunset, with measured oar-strokes. "I'm well on the way," Pickering said; "I think I'll go!"

We had not spoken for an hour, and I naturally asked him, Where? His answer was delayed by our getting in to the Piazzetta. I stepped ashore first and then turned to help him. As he took my hand he met my eyes, consciously, and it came: "To Smyrna!"

A couple of days later he started. I had risked the conjecture that Miss Vernor was a lovely creature, and six months afterwards he wrote me that I was right.

BENVOLIO

I

ONCE upon a time (as if he had lived in a fairy-tale) there was a very interesting young man. This is not a fairy-tale, and yet our young man was in some respects as pretty a fellow as any fairy prince. I call him interesting because his type of character is one I have always found it profitable to observe. If you fail to consider him so, I shall be willing to confess that the fault is mine and not his; I shall have told my story with too little skill.

His name was Benvolio; that is, it was not; but we shall call him so for the sake both of convenience and of picturesqueness. He was about to enter upon the third decade of our mortal span; he had a little property, and he followed no regular profession. His personal appearance was in the highest degree prepossessing. Having said this, it were perhaps well that I should let you—you especially, madam—suppose that he exactly corresponded to your ideal of manly beauty; but I am bound to explain definitely wherein it was that he resembled a fairy prince, and I need furthermore to make a record of certain little peculiarities and anomalies in which it is probable that your brilliant conception would be deficient. Benvolio was slim and fair, with clustering locks, remarkably fine eyes, and such a frank, expressive smile that on the journey through life it was almost as serviceable to its owner as the magic key, or the enchanted ring, or the wishing-cap, or any other bauble of necromantic properties. Unfortunately this charming smile was not always at his command, and its place was sometimes occupied by a very perverse and dusky frown, which rendered the young man no service whatever—

not even that of frightening people; for though it expressed extreme irritation and impatience, it was characterized by the brevity of contempt, and the only revenge upon disagreeable things and offensive people that it seemed to express a desire for on Benvolio's part was that of forgetting and ignoring them with the utmost possible celerity. It never made any one tremble, though now and then it perhaps made irritable people murmur an imprecation or two. You might have supposed from Benvolio's manner, when he was in good humour (which was the greater part of the time), from his brilliant, intelligent glance, from his easy, irresponsible step, and in especial from the sweet, clear, lingering, caressing tone of his voice—the voice as it were of a man whose fortune has been made for him, and who assumes, a trifle egotistically, that the rest of the world is equally at leisure to share with him the sweets of life, to pluck the wayside flowers, and chase the butterflies afield— you might have supposed, I say, from all this luxurious assurance of demeanour, that our hero really had the wishing-cap sitting invisible on his handsome brow, or was obliged only to close his knuckles together a moment to exert an effective pressure upon the magic ring. The young man, I have said, was a mixture of inconsistencies; I may say more exactly that he was a tissue of contradictions. He did possess the magic ring, in a certain fashion; he possessed in other words the poetic imagination. Everything that fancy could do for him was done in perfection. It gave him immense satisfactions; it transfigured the world; it made very common objects sometimes seem radiantly beautiful, and it converted beautiful ones into infinite sources of intoxication. Benvolio had what is called the poetic temperament. It is rather out of fashion to describe a man in these terms; but I believe, in spite of much evidence to the contrary, that there are poets still; and if we may call a spade a spade, why should we not call such a person as Benvolio a poet?

These contradictions that I speak of ran through his whole

nature, and they were perfectly apparent in his habits, in his manners, in his conversation, and even in his physiognomy. It was as if the souls of two very different men had been placed together to make the voyage of life in the same boat, and had agreed for convenience' sake to take the helm in alternation. The helm, with Benvolio, was always the imagination; but in his different moods it worked very differently. To an acute observer his face itself would have betrayed these variations; and it is certain that his dress, his talk, his way of spending his time, one day and another, abundantly indicated them. Sometimes he looked very young—rosy, radiant, blooming, younger than his years. Then suddenly, as the light struck his head in a particular manner, you would see that his golden locks contained a surprising number of silver threads; and with your attention quickened by this discovery, you would proceed to detect something grave and discreet in his smile— something vague and ghostly, like the dim adumbration of the darker half of the lunar disk. You might have met Benvolio, in certain states of mind, dressed like a man of the highest fashion—wearing his hat on his ear, a rose in his button-hole, a wonderful intaglio or an antique Syracusan coin, by way of a pin, in his cravat. Then, on the morrow, you would have espied him braving the sunshine in a rusty scholar's coat, with his hat pulled over his brow—a costume wholly at odds with flowers and gems. It was all a matter of fancy; but his fancy was a weather-cock, and faced east or west as the wind blew. His conversation matched his coat and breeches; he talked one day the talk of the town; he chattered, he gossipped, he asked questions and told stories; you would have said that he was a charming fellow for a dinner-party or the pauses of a cotillon. The next he either talked philosophy or politics, or said nothing at all; he was absent and indifferent; he was thinking his own thoughts; he had a book in his pocket, and evidently he was composing one in his head. At home he lived in two chambers. One was an immense room, hung with pictures,

z

lined with books, draped with rugs and tapestries, decorated with a multitude of ingenious devices (for of all these things he was very fond); the other, his sleeping-room, was almost as bare as a monastic cell. It had a meagre little strip of carpet on the floor, and a dozen well-thumbed volumes of classic poets and sages on the mantelshelf. On the wall hung three or four coarsely-engraved portraits of the most exemplary of these worthies; these were the only ornaments. But the room had the charm of a great window, in a deep embrasure, looking out upon a tangled, silent, moss-grown garden, and in the embrasure stood the little ink-blotted table at which Benvolio did most of his poetic scribbling. The windows of his sumptuous sitting-room commanded a wide public square, where people were always passing and lounging, where military music used to play on vernal nights, and half the life of the great town went forward. At the risk of your thinking our hero a sad idler, I will say that he spent an inordinate amount of time in gazing out of these windows (in either direction) with his elbows on the sill. The garden did not belong to the house which he inhabited, but to a neighbouring one, and the proprietor, a graceless old miser, was very chary of permits to visit his domain. But Benvolio's fancy used to wander through the alleys without stirring the long arms of the untended plants, and to bend over the heavy-headed flowers without leaving a footprint on their beds. It was here that his happiest thoughts came to him—that inspiration (as we may say, speaking of a man of the poetic temperament), descended upon him in silence, and for certain divine, appreciable moments stood poised along the course of his scratching quill. It was not, however, that he had not spent some very charming hours in the larger, richer apartment. He used to receive his friends there—sometimes in great numbers, sometimes at boisterous, many-voiced suppers, which lasted far into the night. When these entertainments were over he never made a direct transition to his little scholar's cell. He went out and wandered for an hour through the dark, sleeping streets of the town, ridding himself of the fumes of wine, and feeling not at all tipsy, but intensely, portentously sober. More than once, when he had come back and prepared to go to bed, he saw the first faint glow of dawn trembling upward over the tree-tops of his garden. His friends, coming to see him, often found the greater room empty, and advancing, rapped at the door of his chamber. But he frequently kept quiet, not desiring in the least to see them, knowing exactly what they were going to say, and not thinking it worth hearing. Then, hearing them stride away, and the outer door close behind them, he would come forth and take a turn in his slippers, over his Persian carpets, and glance out of the window and see his defeated visitant stand scratching his chin in the sunny square. After this he would laugh lightly to himself—as is said to be the habit of the scribbling tribe in moments of production.

Although he had many relatives he enjoyed extreme liberty. His family was so large, his brothers and sisters were so numerous, that he could absent himself and be little missed. Sometimes he used this privilege freely; he tired of people whom he had seen very often, and he had seen, of course, a great deal of his family. At other moments he was extremely domestic; he suddenly found solitude depressing, and it seemed to him that if one sought society as a refuge, one needed to be on familiar terms with it, and that with no one was familiarity so natural as among people who had grown up at a common fireside. Nevertheless it frequently occurred to him—for sooner or later everything occurred to him—that he was too independent and irresponsible; that he would be happier if he had a little golden ball and chain tied to his ankle. His curiosity about all things—life and love and art and truth —was great, and his theory was to satisfy it as freely as might be; but as the years went by this pursuit of impartial science appeared to produce a singular result. He became conscious of an intellectual condition similar to that of a palate which has lost its relish. To a man with a disordered appetite all things taste alike, and so it seemed to Benvolio that the gustatory faculty of his mind was losing its keenness. It had still its savoury moments, its feasts and its holidays; but, on the whole, the spectacle of human life was growing flat and stale. This is simply a wordy way of expressing that comprehensive fact—Benvolio was *blasé*. He knew it, he knew it betimes, and he regretted it acutely. He believed that the mind can keep its freshness to the last, and that it is only fools that are over-bored. There was a way of never being bored, and the wise man's duty was to find it out. One of its rudiments, he believed, was that one grows tired of one's self sooner than of anything else in the world. Idleness, every one admitted, was the greatest of follies; but idleness was subtle, and exacted tribute under a hundred plausible disguises. One was often idle when one seemed to be ardently occupied; one was always idle when one's occupation had not a high aim. One was idle therefore when one was working simply for one's self. Curiosity for curiosity's sake, art for art's sake, these were essentially broken-winded steeds. Ennui was at the end of everything that did not multiply our relations with life. To multiply his relations, therefore, Benvolio reflected, should be the wise man's aim. Poor Benvolio had to reflect on this, because, as I say, he was a poet and not a man of action. A fine fellow of the latter stamp would have solved the problem without knowing it, and bequeathed to his fellow men not frigid formulas but vivid examples. But Benvolio had often said to himself that he was born to imagine great things—not to do them; and he had said this by no means sadly, for on the whole he was very well content with his portion. Imagine them he determined he would, and on a magnificent scale. He would multiply his labours at least, and they should be very serious ones. He would cultivate great ideas, he would enunciate great truths, he would write immortal verses. In all this there was a large amount of talent and a liberal share of

ambition. I will not say that Benvolio was a man of genius; it
may seem to make the distinction too cheap; but he was at any
rate a man with an intellectual passion; and if, being near him,
you had been able to listen intently enough, he would, like
the great people of his craft, have seemed to emit something
of that vague magical murmur—the voice of the infinite—
which lurks in the involutions of a sea-shell. He himself, by
the way, had once made use of this little simile, and had
written a poem in which it was melodiously set forth that the
poetic minds scattered about the world correspond to the little
shells one picks up on the beach, all resonant with the echo of
ocean. The whole thing was of course rounded off with the
sands of time, the waves of history, and other harmonious
conceits.

II

But (as you are naturally expecting to hear), Benvolio knew
perfectly well that there is one relation with life which is a
better antidote to ennui than any other—the relation established with a charming woman. Benvolio was of course in
love. Who was his mistress, you ask (I flatter myself with
some impatience), and was she pretty, was she kind, was he
successful? Hereby hangs my tale, which I must relate in due
form.

Benvolio's mistress was a lady whom (as I cannot tell you
her real name) it will be quite in keeping to speak of as the
Countess. The Countess was a young widow, who had some
time since divested herself of her mourning weeds—which
indeed she had never worn but very lightly. She was rich,
extremely pretty, and free to do as she listed. She was passionately fond of pleasure and admiration, and they gushed forth
at her feet in unceasing streams. Her beauty was not of the

conventional type, but it was dazzlingly brilliant; few faces were more expressive, more fascinating. Hers was never the same for two days together; it reflected her momentary circumstances with extraordinary vividness, and in knowing her you had the advantage of knowing a dozen different women. She was clever and accomplished, and had the credit of being perfectly amiable; indeed it was difficult to imagine a person combining a greater number of the precious gifts of nature and fortune. She represented felicity, gaiety, success; she was made to charm, to play a part, to exert a sway. She lived in a great house, behind high verdure-muffled walls, where other Countesses, in other years, had played a part no less brilliant. It was an antiquated quarter, into which the tide of commerce had lately begun to roll heavily; but the turbid wave of trade broke in vain against the Countess's enclosure, and if in her garden and her drawing-room you heard the deep uproar of the city, it was only as a vague undertone to sweeter things— to music, and witty talk, and tender colloquy. There was something very striking in this little oasis of luxury and privacy, in the midst of common toil and traffic.

Benvolio was a great deal at this lady's house; he rarely desired better entertainment. I spoke just now of privacy; but privacy was not what he found there, nor what he wished to find. He went there when he wished to learn with the least trouble what was going on in the world; for the talk of the people the Countess generally had about her was an epitome of the gossip, the rumours, the interests, the hopes and fears, of polite society. She was a thoroughly liberal hostess; all she asked was to be entertained; if you would contribute to the common fund of amusement, of discussion, you were a welcome guest. Sooner or later, among your fellow-guests, you encountered every one of consequence. There were frivolous people and wise people; people whose fortune was in their pockets and people whose fortune was in their brains; people deeply concerned in public affairs and people concerned only with the fit of their garments or with the effect upon the company of the announcement of their names. Benvolio, with his taste for a large and various social spectacle, appreciated all this; but he was best pleased, as a general thing, when he found the Countess alone. This was often his fortune, for the simple reason that when the Countess expected him she invariably caused herself to be refused to every one else. This is almost an answer to your inquiry whether Benvolio was successful in his suit. As yet, strictly speaking, there was no suit; Benvolio had never made love to the Countess. This sounds very strange, but it is nevertheless true. He was in love with her; he thought her the most charming creature conceivable; he spent hours with her alone by her own orders; he had had opportunity—he had been up to his neck in opportunity— and yet he had never said to her, as would have seemed so natural, "Dear Countess, I beseech you to be my wife." If you are surprised, I may also confide to you that the Countess was; and surprise under the circumstances very easily became displeasure. It is by no means certain that if Benvolio had made the little speech we have just imagined, the Countess would have fallen into his arms, confessed to an answering flame, and rung in *finis* to our tale, with the wedding-bells. But she nevertheless expected him in civility to pay her this supreme compliment. Her answer would be—what it might be; but his silence was a permanent offence. Every man, roughly speaking, had asked the Countess to marry him, and every man had been told that she was much obliged, but had not been thinking of changing her condition. But here, with the one man who failed to ask her, she was perpetually thinking of it, and this negative quality in Benvolio was more present to her mind, gave her more to think about, than all the positiveness of her other suitors. The truth was she liked Benvolio extremely, and his independence rendered him excellent service. The Countess had a very lively fancy, and she had fingered, nimbly enough, the volume of the young man's merits. She was by nature a trifle cold; she rarely lost her head; she measured each step as she took it; she had had little fancies and incipient passions; but on the whole she had thought much more about love than felt it. She had often tried to form an image of the sort of man it would be well for her to love—for so it was she expressed it. She had succeeded but indifferently, and her imagination had never found a pair of wings until the day she met Benvolio. Then it seemed to her that her quest was ended—her prize gained. This nervous, ardent, deep-eyed youth struck her as the harmonious counterpart of her own facile personality. This conviction rested with the Countess on a fine sense of propriety which it would be vain to attempt to analyze; he was different from herself and from the other men who surrounded her, and she valued him as a specimen of a rare and distinguished type. In the old days she would have appointed him to be her minstrel or her jester—it is to be feared that poor Benvolio would have figured rather dismally in the latter capacity; and at present a woman who was in her own right a considerable social figure, might give such a man a place in her train as an illustrious husband. I don't know how good a judge the Countess was of such matters, but she believed that the world would hear of Benvolio. She had beauty, ancestry, money, luxury, but she had not genius; and if genius was to be had, why not secure it, and complete the list? This is doubtless a rather coarse statement of the Countess's argument; but you have it thrown in gratis, as it were; for all I am bound to tell you is that this charming young woman took a fancy to this clever young man, and that she used to cry sometimes for a quarter of a minute when she imagined he was indifferent to her. Her tears were wasted, because he really cared for her—more even than she would have imagined if she had taken a favourable view of the case. But Benvolio, I cannot too much repeat, was an exceedingly complex character, and there was many a lapse in the logic of his conduct. The Countess charmed him,

excited him, interested him; he did her abundant justice—
more than justice; but at the end of all he felt that she failed
to satisfy him. If a man could have half a dozen wives—and
Benvolio had once maintained, poetically, that he ought to
have—the Countess would do very well for one of them—
possibly even for the best of them. But she would not serve
for all seasons and all moods; she needed a complement, an
alternative—what the French call a *repoussoir*. One day he
was going to see her, knowing that he was expected. There
was to be a number of other people—in fact, a very brilliant
assembly; but Benvolio knew that a certain touch of the hand,
a certain glance of the eye, a certain caress of the voice, would
be reserved for him alone. Happy Benvolio, you will say, to
be going about the world with such charming secrets as this
locked up in his young heart! Happy Benvolio indeed; but
mark how he trifled with his happiness. He went to the
Countess's gate, but he went no further; he stopped, stood
there a moment, frowning intensely, and biting the finger of
his glove; then suddenly he turned and strode away in the
opposite direction. He walked and walked and left the town
behind him. He went his way till he reached the country, and
here he bent his steps toward a little wood which he knew
very well, and whither indeed, on a spring afternoon, when
she had taken a fancy to play at shepherd and shepherdess, he
had once come with the Countess. He flung himself on the
grass, on the edge of the wood—not in the same place where
he had lain at the Countess's feet, pulling sonnets out of his
pocket and reading them one by one; a little stream flowed
beside him; opposite, the sun was declining; the distant city
lay before him, lifting its towers and chimneys against the red-
dening western sky. The twilight fell and deepened and the
stars came out. Benvolio lay there thinking that he preferred
them to the Countess's wax candles. He went back to town in
a farmer's wagon, talking with the honest rustic who drove
it.

Very much in this way, when he had been on the point of knocking at the gate of the Countess's heart and asking ardently to be admitted, he had paused, stood frowning, and then turned short and rambled away into solitude. She never knew how near, two or three times, he had come. Two or three times she had accused him of being rude, and this was nothing but the backward swing of the pendulum. One day it seemed to her that he was altogether too vexatious, and she reproached herself with her good nature. She had made herself too cheap; such conduct was beneath her dignity; she would take another tone. She closed her door to him, and bade her people say, whenever he came, that she was engaged. At first Benvolio only wondered. Oddly enough, he was not what is commonly called sensitive; he never supposed you meant to offend him; not being at all impertinent himself, he was not on the watch for impertinence in others. Only, when he fairly caught you in the act he was immensely disgusted. Therefore, as I say, he simply wondered what had suddenly made the Countess so busy; then he remembered certain other charming persons whom he knew, and went to see how the world wagged with them. But they rendered the Countess eminent service; she gained by comparison, and Benvolio began to miss her. All that other charming women were who led the life of the world (as it is called) the Countess was in a superior, in a perfect degree; she was the ripest fruit of a high civilization; her companions and rivals, beside her, had but a pallid bloom, an acrid savour. Benvolio had a relish in all things for the best, and he found himself breathing sighs under the Countess's darkened windows. He wrote to her, asking why in the world she treated him so cruelly, and then she knew that her charm was working. She was careful not to answer his letter, and to see that he was refused at her gate as inexorably as ever. It is an ill wind that blows nobody good, and Benvolio, one night after his dismissal, wandered about the moonlit streets till nearly morning, composing the finest verses he had ever produced. The subscribers to the magazine to which he sent them were at least the gainers. But unlike many poets, Benvolio did not on this occasion bury his passion in his poem; or if he did, its ghost was stalking abroad the very next night. He went again to the Countess's gate, and again it was closed in his face. So, after a very moderate amount of hesitation, he bravely (and with a dexterity which surprised him), scaled her garden wall and dropped down in the moonshine, upon her lawn. I don't know whether she was expecting him, but if she had been, the matter could not have been better arranged. She was sitting in a little niche of shrubbery, with no protector, but a microscopic lap-dog. She pretended to be scandalised at his audacity, but his audacity carried the hour. "This time certainly," thought the Countess, "he will make his declaration. He didn't jump that wall, at the risk of his neck, simply to ask me for a cup of tea." Not a bit of it; Benvolio was devoted, but he was not more explicit than before. He declared that this was the happiest hour of his life; that there was a charming air of romance in his position; that, honestly, he thanked the Countess for having made him desperate; that he would never come to see her again but by the garden wall; that something, to-night—what was it?—was vastly becoming to her; that he devoutly hoped she would receive no one else; that his admiration for her was unbounded; that the stars, finally, had a curious pink light! He looked at her, through the flower-scented dusk, with admiring eyes; but he looked at the stars as well; he threw back his head and folded his arms, and let the conversation flag while he examined the firmament. He observed also the long shafts of light proceeding from the windows of the house, as they fell upon the lawn and played among the shrubbery. The Countess had always thought him a singular man, but to-night she thought him more singular than ever. She became satirical, and the point of her satire was that he was after all but a dull fellow; that his admiration was a poor compliment; that he would do well to turn his attention to astronomy! In answer to this he came perhaps (to the Countess's sense) as near as he had ever come to making a declaration.

"Dear lady," he said, "you don't begin to know how much I admire you!"

She left her place at this, and walked about her lawn, looking at him askance while he talked, trailing her embroidered robe over the grass and fingering the folded petals of her flowers. He made a sort of sentimental profession of faith; he assured her that she represented his ideal of a certain sort of woman. This last phrase made her pause a moment and stare at him wide-eyed. "Oh, I mean the finest sort," he cried— "the sort that exerts the widest sway! You represent the world and everything that the world can give, and you represent them at their best—in their most generous, most graceful, most inspiring form. If a man were a revolutionist, you would reconcile him to society. You are a divine embodiment of all the amenities, the refinements, the complexities of life! You are the flower of urbanity, of culture, of tradition! You are the product of so many influences that it widens one's horizon to know you; of you too it is true that to admire you is a liberal education! Your charm is irresistible; I assure you I don't resist it!"

Compliments agreed with the Countess, as we may say; they not only made her happier, but they made her better. It became a matter of conscience with her to deserve them. These were magnificent ones, and she was by no means indifferent to them. Her cheek faintly flushed, her eyes vaguely glowed, and though her beauty, in the literal sense, was questionable, all that Benvolio said of her had never seemed more true. He said more in the same strain, and she listened without interrupting him. But at last she suddenly became impatient; it seemed to her that this was after all a tolerably inexpensive sort of wooing. But she did not betray her impatience with any petulance; she simply shook her finger a moment, to enjoin silence, and then she said, in a voice of extreme gentleness— "You have too much imagination!" He answered that, to do her perfect justice, he had too little. To this she replied that it was not of her any longer he was talking; he had left her far behind. He was spinning fancies about some highly subtilized figment of his brain. The best answer to this, it seemed to Benvolio, was to seize her hand and kiss it. I don't know what the Countess thought of this form of argument; I incline to think it both pleased and vexed her; it was at once too much and too little. She snatched her hand away and went rapidly into the house. Although Benvolio immediately followed her, he was unable to overtake her; she had retired into impenetrable seclusion. A short time afterwards she left town and went for the summer to an estate which she possessed in a distant part of the country.

III

BENVOLIO was extremely fond of the country, but he remained in town after all his friends had departed. Many of them made him promise that he would come and see them. He promised, or half promised, but when he reflected that in almost every case he would find a house full of fellow-guests, to whose pursuits he would have to conform, and that if he rambled away with a valued duodecimo in his pocket to spend the morning alone in the woods, he would be denounced as a marplot and a selfish brute, he felt no great desire to pay visits. He had, as we know, his moods of expansion and of contraction; he had been tolerably inflated for many months past, and now he had begun to take in sail. And then I suspect the foolish fellow had no money to travel withal. He had lately put all his available funds into the purchase of a picture—an estimable work of the Venetian school, which had been suddenly thrown into the market. It was offered for a moderate sum, and Benvolio, who was one of the first to see it, secured it, and hung it triumphantly in his room. It had all the classic Venetian glow, and he used to lie on his divan by the hour, gazing at it. It had, indeed, a peculiar property, of which I have known no other example. Most pictures that are remarkable for their colour (especially if they have been painted for a couple of centuries), need a flood of sunshine on the canvas to bring it out. But this remarkable work seemed to have a hidden radiance of its own, which showed brightest when the room was half darkened. When Benvolio wished especially to enjoy his treasure he dropped his Venetian blinds, and the picture bloomed out into the cool dusk with enchanting effect. It represented, in a fantastic way, the story of Perseus and Andromeda—the beautiful naked maiden chained to a rock, on which, with picturesque incongruity, a wild fig-tree was growing; the green Adriatic tumbling at her feet, and a splendid brown-limbed youth in a curious helmet hovering near her on a winged horse. The journey his fancy made as he lay and looked at his picture Benvolio preferred to any journey he might make by the public conveyances.

But he resorted for entertainment, as he had often done before, to the windows overlooking the old garden behind his house. As the summer deepened, of course the charm of the garden increased. It grew more tangled and bosky and mossy, and sent forth sweeter and heavier odours into the neighbouring air. It was a perfect solitude; Benvolio had never seen a visitor there. One day, therefore, at this time, it puzzled him most agreeably to perceive a young girl sitting under one of the trees. She sat there a long time, and though she was at a distance, he managed, by looking long enough, to make out that she was pretty. She was dressed in black, and when she left her place her step had a kind of nun-like gentleness and demureness. Although she was alone, there was something timid and tentative in her movements. She wandered away and disappeared from sight, save that here and there he saw her white parasol gleaming in the gaps of the foliage. Then she came back to her seat under the great tree, and remained there for some time, arranging in her lap certain flowers that she had gathered. Then she rose again and vanished, and Benvolio waited in vain for her return. She had evidently gone into the house. The next day he saw her again, and the next, and the next. On these occasions she had a book in her hand, and she sat in her former place a long time, and read it with an air of great attention. Now and then she raised her head and glanced toward the house, as if to keep something in sight which divided her care; and once or twice she laid down her book and tripped away to her hidden duties with a lighter step than she had shown the first day. Benvolio formed a theory that she had an invalid parent, or a relation of some kind, who was unable to walk, and had been moved into a window overlooking the garden. She always took up her book again when she came back, and bent her pretty head over it with charming earnestness. Benvolio had already discovered that her head was pretty. He fancied it resembled a certain exquisite little head on a Greek silver coin which lay, with several others, in an agate cup on his table. You see he had also already taken to fancying, and I offer this as the excuse for his staring at his modest neighbour by the hour. But he was not during these hours idle, because he was—I can't say falling in love with her; he knew her too little for that, and besides, he was in love with the Countess—but because he was at any rate cudgelling his brains about her. Who was she? what was she? why had he never seen her before? The house in which she apparently lived was in another street from Benvolio's own, but he went out of his way on purpose to look at it. It was an ancient grizzled, sad-faced structure, with grated windows on the ground floor; it looked like a convent or a prison. Over a wall, beside it, there tumbled into the street some stray tendrils of a wild creeper from Benvolio's garden. Suddenly Benvolio began to suspect that the book the young girl in the garden was reading was none other than a volume of his own, put forth some six months before. His volume had a white cover and so had this; white covers are rather rare, and there was nothing impossible either in this young lady's reading his book or in her finding it interesting. Very many other women had done the same. Benvolio's neighbour had a pencil in her pocket, which she every now and then drew forth, to make with it a little mark on her page. This quiet gesture gave the young man an exquisite pleasure.

I am ashamed to say how much time he spent, for a week, at his window. Every day the young girl came into the garden. At last there occurred a rainy day—a long, warm summer's rain—and she staid within doors. He missed her quite acutely, and wondered, half-smiling, half-frowning, that her absence should make such a difference for him. He actually depended upon her. He was ignorant of her name; he knew neither the colour of her eyes nor the shade of her hair, nor the sound of her voice; it was very likely that if he were to meet her face to face, elsewhere, he would not recognise her. But she interested him; he liked her; he found her little indefinite, black-dressed figure sympathetic. He used to find the Countess sympathetic, and certainly the Countess was as unlike this quiet garden-nymph as she could very well be and be yet a charming woman. Benvolio's sympathies, as we know, were large. After the rain the young girl came out again, and now she had another book, having apparently finished Benvolio's. He was gratified to observe that she bestowed upon this one a much more wandering attention. Sometimes she let it drop listlessly at her side, and seemed to lose herself in maidenly reverie. Was she thinking how much more beautiful Benvolio's verses were than others of the day? Was she perhaps repeating them to herself? It charmed Benvolio to suppose she might be; for he was not spoiled in this respect. The

Countess knew none of his poetry by heart; she was nothing of a reader. She had his book on her table, but he once noticed that half the leaves were uncut.

After a couple of days of sunshine the rain came back again, to our hero's infinite annoyance, and this time it lasted several days. The garden lay dripping and desolate; its charm had quite departed. These days passed gloomily for Benvolio; he decided that rainy weather, in summer, in town, was intolerable. He began to think of the Countess again—he was sure that over her broad lands the summer sun was shining. He saw them, in envious fancy, studded with joyous Watteau-groups, feasting and making music under the shade of ancestral beeches. What a charming life! he thought—what brilliant, enchanted, memorable days! He had said the very reverse of all this, as you remember, three weeks before. I don't know that he had ever devoted a formula to the idea that men of imagination are not bound to be consistent, but he certainly conformed to its spirit. We are not, however, by any means at the end of his inconsistencies. He immediately wrote a letter to the Countess, asking her if he might pay her a visit.

Shortly after he had sent his letter the weather mended, and he went out for walk. The sun was near setting; the streets were all ruddy and golden with its light, and the scattered rain-clouds, broken into a thousand little particles, were flecking the sky like a shower of opals and amethysts. Benvolio stopped, as he sauntered along, to gossip a while with his friend the bookseller. The bookseller was a foreigner and a man of taste; his shop was in the arcade of the great square. When Benvolio went in he was serving a lady, and the lady was dressed in black. Benvolio just now found it natural to notice a lady who was dressed in black, and the fact that this lady's face was averted made observation at once more easy and more fruitless. But at last her errand was finished; she had been ordering several books, and the bookseller was writing down their names. Then she turned round, and Benvolio saw her face. He stood staring at her most inconsiderately, for he felt an immediate certainty that she was the bookish damsel of the garden. She gave a glance round the shop, at the books on the walls, at the prints and busts, the apparatus of learning, in various forms, that it contained, and then, with the soundless, half-furtive step which Benvolio now knew so well, she took her departure. Benvolio seized the startled bookseller by the two hands and besieged him with questions. The bookseller, however, was able to answer but few of them. The young girl had been in his shop but once before, and had simply left an address, without any name. It was the address of which Benvolio had assured himself. The books she had ordered were all learned works—disquisitions on philosophy, on history, on the natural sciences, matters, all of them, in which she seemed an expert. For some of the volumes that she had just bespoken the bookseller was to send to foreign countries; the others were to be despatched that evening to the address which the young girl had left. As Benvolio stood there the old bibliophile gathered these latter together, and while he was so engaged he uttered a little cry of distress: one of the volumes of a set was missing. The work was a rare one, and it would be hard to repair the loss. Benvolio on the instant had an inspiration; he demanded leave of his friend to act as messenger: he himself would carry the books, as if he came from the shop, and he would explain the absence of the lost volume, and the bookseller's views about replacing it, far better than one of the hirelings. He asked leave, I say, but he did not wait till it was given; he snatched up the pile of books and strode triumphantly away!

IV

As there was no name on the parcel, Benvolio, on reaching the old gray house over the wall of whose court an adventurous tendril stretched its long arm into the street, found himself wondering in what terms he should ask to have speech of the person for whom the books were intended. At any hazard he was determined not to retreat until he had caught a glimpse of the interior and its inhabitants; for this was the same man, you must remember, who had scaled the moonlit wall of the Countess's garden. An old serving woman in a quaint cap answered his summons, and stood blinking out at the fading daylight from a little wrinkled white face, as if she had never been compelled to take so direct a look at it before. He informed her that he had come from the bookseller's, and that he had been charged with a personal message for the venerable gentleman who had bespoken the parcel. Might he crave license to speak with him? This obsequious phrase was an improvisation of the moment—he had shaped it on the chance. But Benvolio had an indefinable conviction that it would fit the case; the only thing that surprised him was the quiet complaisance of the old woman.

"If it's on a bookish errand you come, sir," she said, with a little wheezy sigh, "I suppose I only do my duty in admitting you!"

She led him into the house, through various dusky chambers, and at last ushered him into an apartment of which the side opposite to the door was occupied by a broad, low casement. Through its small old panes there came a green dim light—the light of the low western sun shining through the wet trees of the famous garden. Everything else was ancient and brown; the walls were covered with tiers upon tiers of books. Near the window, in the still twilight, sat two persons, one of whom rose as Benvolio came in. This was the young girl of the garden—the young girl who had been an hour since at the bookseller's. The other was an old man, who turned his head, but otherwise sat motionless.

Both his movement and his stillness immediately announced to Benvolio's quick perception that he was blind. In his quality of poet Benvolio was inventive; a brain that is constantly tapped for rhymes is tolerably alert. In a few moments, therefore, he had given a vigorous push to the wheel of fortune. Various things had happened. He had made a soft, respectful speech, he hardly knew about what; and the old man had told him he had a delectable voice—a voice that seemed to belong rather to a person of education than to a tradesman's porter. Benvolio confessed to having picked up an education, and the old man had thereupon bidden the young girl offer him a seat. Benvolio chose his seat where he could see her, as she sat at the low-browed casement. The bookseller in the square thought it likely Benvolio would come back that evening and give him an account of his errand, and before he closed his shop he looked up and down the street, to see whether the young man was approaching. Benvolio came, but the shop was closed. This he never noticed, however; he walked three times round all the arcades, without noticing it. He was thinking of something else. He had sat all the evening with the blind old scholar and his daughter, and he was thinking intently, ardently of them. When I say of them, of course I mean of the daughter.

A few days afterwards he got a note from the Countess, saying it would give her pleasure to receive his visit. He immediately wrote to her that, with a thousand regrets, he found himself urgently occupied in town and must beg leave to defer his departure for a day or two. The regrets were perfectly sincere, but the plea was none the less valid. Benvolio had become deeply interested in his tranquil neighbours, and, for the moment, a certain way the young girl had of looking at him—fixing her eyes, first, with a little vague, half-absent smile, on an imaginary point above his head, and then slowly dropping them till they met his own—was quite sufficient to make him happy. He had called once more on her father, and once more, and yet once more, and he had a vivid prevision that he should often call again. He had been in the garden and found its mild mouldiness even more delightful on a nearer view. He had pulled off his very ill-fitting mask, and let his neighbours know that his trade was not to carry parcels, but to scribble verses. The old man had never heard of his verses; he read nothing that had been published later than the sixth century; and nowadays he could read only with his daughter's eyes. Benvolio had seen the little white volume on the table, and assured himself it was his own; and he noted the fact that in spite of its well-thumbed air, the young girl had never given her father a hint of its contents. I said just now that several things had happened in the first half hour of Benvolio's first visit. One of them was that this modest maiden fell in love with our young man. What happened when she learned that he was the author of the little white volume, I hardly know how to express; her innocent passion began to throb and flutter. Benvolio possessed an old quarto volume bound in Russia leather, about which there clung an agreeable pungent odour. In this old quarto he kept a sort of diary—if that can be called a diary in which a whole year had sometimes been allowed to pass without an entry. On the other hand, there were some interminable records of a single day. Turning it over you would have chanced, not infrequently, upon the name of the Countess; and at this time you would have observed on every page some mention of "the Professor" and of a certain person named Scholastica. Scholastica, you will immediately guess, was the Professor's daughter. Probably this was not her own name, but it was the name by which Benvolio preferred to know her, and we need not be more exact than he. By this time of course he knew a great deal about her, and about her venerable sire. The Professor, before the loss of his eyesight and his health, had been one of the stateliest pillars of the University. He was now an old man; he had married late in life. When his infirmities came upon him he gave up his chair and his classes and buried himself in his library. He made his daughter his reader and his secretary, and his prodigious memory assisted her clear young voice and her softly-moving pen. He was held in great honour in the scholastic world; learned men came from afar to consult the blind sage and to appeal to his wisdom as to the ultimate law. The University settled a pension upon him, and he dwelt in a dusky corner, among the academic shades. The pension was small, but the old scholar and the young girl lived with conventual simplicity. It so happened, however, that he had a brother, or rather a half-brother, who was not a bookish man, save as regarded his ledger and day-book. This personage had made money in trade, and had retired, wifeless and childless, into the old gray house attached to Benvolio's garden. He had the reputation of a skinflint, a curmudgeon, a bloodless old miser who spent his days in shuffling about his mouldy mansion, making his pockets jingle, and his nights in lifting his money-bags out of trapdoors and counting over his hoard. He was nothing but a chilling shadow, an evil name, a pretext for a curse; no one had ever seen him, much less crossed his threshold. But it seemed that he had a soft spot in his heart. He wrote one day to his brother, whom he had not seen for years, that the rumour had come to him that he was blind, infirm, and poor; that he himself had a large house with a garden behind it; and that if the Professor were not too proud, he was welcome to come and lodge there. The Professor had come, in this way, a few weeks before, and though it would seem that to a sightless old ascetic all lodgings might be the same, he took a great satisfaction in his new abode. His daughter found it a paradise, compared with their two narrow chambers under the old gable of the University, where, amid the constant coming and going of students, a young girl was compelled to lead a cloistered life.

Benvolio had assigned as his motive for intrusion, when he had been obliged to acknowledge his real character, an irresistible desire to ask the old man's opinion on certain knotty points of philosophy. This was a pardonable fiction, for the event, at any rate, justified it. Benvolio, when he was fairly launched in a philosophical discussion, was capable of forgetting that there was anything in the world but metaphysics; he revelled in transcendent abstractions and became unconscious of all concrete things—even of that most brilliant of concrete things, the Countess. He longed to embark on a voyage of discovery on the great sea of pure reason. He knew that from such voyages the deep-browed adventurer rarely returns; but if he were to find an El Dorado of thought, why should he regret the dusky world of fact? Benvolio had high colloquies with the Professor, who was a devout Neo-Platonist, and whose venerable wit had spun to subtler tenuity the ethereal speculations of the Alexandrian school. Benvolio at this season declared that study and science were the only game in life worth the candle, and wondered how he could ever for an instant have cared for more vulgar exercises. He turned off a little poem in the style of Milton's *Penseroso*, which, if it had not quite the merit of that famous effusion, was at least the young man's own happiest performance. When Benvolio liked a thing he liked it as a whole—it appealed to all his senses. He relished its accidents, its accessories, its material envelope. In the satisfaction he took in his visits to the Professor it would have been hard to say where the charm of philosophy began or ended. If it began with a glimpse of the old man's mild, sightless blue eyes, sitting fixed beneath his shaggy white brows like patches of pale winter sky under a high-piled cloud, it hardly ended before it reached the little black bow on Scholastica's slipper; and certainly it had taken a comprehensive sweep in the interval. There was nothing in his friends that had not a charm, an interest, a character, for his appreciative mind. Their seclusion, their stillness, their super-simple notions of the world and the world's ways, the faint, musty perfume of the University which hovered about them, their brown old apartment, impenetrable to the rumours of the town—all these things were part of his entertainment. Then the essence of it perhaps was that in this silent, simple life the intellectual key, if you touched it, was so finely resonant. In the way of thought there was nothing into which his friends were not initiated—nothing they could not understand. The mellow light of their low-browed room, streaked with the moted rays that slanted past the dusky book-shelves, was the atmosphere of intelligence. All this made them, humble folk as they were, not so simple as they at first appeared. They, too, in their own fashion, knew the world; they were not people to be patronized; to visit them was not a condescension, but a privilege.

In the Professor this was not surprising. He had passed fifty years in arduous study, and it was proper to his character and his office that he should be erudite and venerable. But his devoted little daughter seemed to Benvolio at first almost grotesquely wise. She was an anomaly, a prodigy, a charming monstrosity. Charming, at any rate, she was, and as pretty, I must lose no more time in saying, as had seemed likely to Benvolio at his window. And yet, even on a nearer view, her prettiness shone forth slowly. It was as if it had been covered with a series of film-like veils, which had to be successively drawn aside. And then it was such a homely, shrinking, subtle prettiness, that Benvolio, in the private record I have mentioned, never thought of calling it by the arrogant name of beauty. He called it by no name at all; he contented himself with enjoying it—with looking into the young girl's mild gray eyes and saying things, on purpose, that caused her candid smile to deepen until (like the broadening ripple of a lake) it reached a particular dimple in her left cheek. This was its maximum; no smile could do more, and Benvolio desired nothing better. Yet I cannot say he was in love with the young girl; he only liked her. But he liked her, no doubt, as a man likes a thing but once in his life. As he knew her better, the oddity of her great learning quite faded away; it seemed delightfully natural, and he only wondered why there were not more women of the same pattern. Scholastica had imbibed the wine of science instead of her mother's milk. Her mother had died in her infancy, leaving her cradled in an old folio, three-quarters opened, like a wide V. Her father had been her nurse, her playmate, her teacher, her life-long companion, her only friend. He taught her the Greek alphabet before she knew her own, and fed her with crumbs from his scholastic revels. She had taken submissively what was given her, and, without knowing it, she grew up a little handmaid of science.

Benvolio perceived that she was not in the least a woman of genius. The passion for knowledge, of its own motion, would never have carried her far. But she had a perfect understanding—a mind as clear and still and natural as a woodland pool, giving back an exact and definite image of everything that was presented to it. And then she was so teachable, so diligent, so indefatigable. Slender and meagre as she was, and rather pale too, with being much within doors, she was never tired, she never had a headache, she never closed her book or laid down a pen with a sigh. Benvolio said to himself that she was exquisitely constituted for helping a man. What a work he might do on summer mornings and winter nights, with that brightly demure little creature at his side, transcribing, recollecting, sympathising! He wondered how much she cared for these things herself; whether a woman could care for them without being dry and harsh. It was in a great measure for information on this point that he used to question her eyes with the frequency that I have mentioned. But they never gave him a perfectly direct answer, and this was why he came and came again. They seemed to him to say, "If you could lead a student's life for my sake, I could be a life-long household scribe for yours." Was it divine philosophy that made Scholastica charming, or was it she that made philosophy divine? I cannot relate everything that came to pass between these young people, and I must leave a great deal to your imagination. The summer waned, and when the autumn afternoons began to grow vague, the quiet couple in the old gray house had expanded to a talkative trio. For Benvolio the days had passed very fast; the trio had talked of so many things. He had spent many an hour in the garden with the young girl, strolling in the weedy paths, or resting on a moss-grown bench. She was a delightful listener, because she not only attended, but she followed. Benvolio had known women to fix very beautiful eyes upon him, and watch with an air of ecstasy the movement of his lips, and yet had found them three minutes afterwards quite incapable of saying what he was talking about. Scholastica gazed at him, but she understood him too.

V

You will say that my description of Benvolio has done him injustice, and that, far from being the sentimental weathercock I have depicted, he is proving himself a model of constancy. But mark the sequel! It was at this moment precisely, that, one morning, having gone to bed the night before singing pæans to divine philosophy, he woke up with a headache, and in the worst of humours with abstract science. He remembered Scholastica telling him that she never had headaches, and the memory quite annoyed him. He suddenly found himself thinking of her as a neat little mechanical toy, wound up to turn pages and write a pretty hand, but with neither a head nor a heart that was capable of human ailments. He fell asleep again, and in one of those brief but vivid dreams that sometimes occur in the morning hours, he had a brilliant vision of the Countess. *She* was human beyond a doubt, and duly familiar with headaches and heartaches. He felt an irresistible desire to see her and to tell her that he adored her. This satisfaction was not unattainable, and before the day was over he was well on his way toward enjoying it. He left town and made his pilgrimage to her estate, where he found her holding her usual court and leading a merry life. He had meant to stay with her a week; he staid two months—the most entertaining months he had ever known. I cannot pretend of course to enumerate the diversions of this fortunate circle, or to say just how Benvolio spent every hour of his time. But if the summer had passed quickly with him, the autumn moved with a tread as light. He thought once in a while of Scholastica and her father—once in a while, I say, when present occupations suffered his thoughts to wander. This was not often, for the Countess had always, as the phrase is, a hundred arrows in her quiver. You see, the negative, with Benvolio, always implied as distinct a positive, and his excuse for being inconstant on one side was that he was at such a time very assiduous on another. He developed at this period a talent as yet untried and unsuspected; he proved himself capable of writing brilliant dramatic poetry. The long autumn evenings, in a great country house, were a natural occasion for the much-abused pastime known as private theatricals. The Countess had a theatre, and abundant material for a troupe of amateur players; all that was lacking was a play exactly adapted to her resources. She proposed to Benvolio to write one; the idea took his fancy; he shut himself up in the library, and in a week produced a masterpiece. He had found the subject, one day when he was pulling over the Countess's books, in an old MS. chronicle written by the chaplain of one of her late husband's ancestors. It was the

germ of an admirable drama, and Benvolio greatly enjoyed
his attempt to make a work of art of it. All his genius, all his
imagination went into it. This was the proper mission of his
faculties, he cried to himself—the study of warm human
passions, the painting of rich dramatic pictures, not the dry
chopping of logic. His play was acted with brilliant success,
the Countess herself representing the heroine. Benvolio had
never seen her don the buskin, and had no idea of her aptitude
for the stage; but she was inimitable, she was a natural artist.
What gives charm to life, Benvolio hereupon said to himself,
is the element of the unexpected; and this one finds only in
women of the Countess's type. And I should do wrong to
imply that he here made an invidious comparison, for he did
not even think of Scholastica. His play was repeated several
times, and people were invited to see it from all the country
round. There was a great bivouac of servants in the castle-
court; in the cold November nights a bonfire was lighted to
keep the servants warm. It was a great triumph for Benvolio,
and he frankly enjoyed it. He knew he enjoyed it, and how
great a triumph it was, and he felt every disposition to drain
the cup to the last drop. He relished his own elation, and found
himself excellent company. He began immediately another
drama—a comedy this time—and he was greatly interested to
observe that when his work was on the stocks he found himself regarding all the people about him as types and available
figures. Everything he saw or heard was grist to his mill;
everything presented itself as possible material. Life on these
terms became really very interesting, and for several nights
the laurels of Molière kept Benvolio awake.

Delightful as this was, however, it could not last for ever.
When the winter nights had begun, the Countess returned to
town, and Benvolio came back with her, his unfinished comedy in his pocket. During much of the journey he was silent
and abstracted, and the Countess supposed he was thinking
of how he should make the most of that capital situation in

his third act. The Countess's perspicacity was just sufficient to carry her so far—to lead her, in other words, into plausible mistakes. Benvolio was really wondering what in the name of mystery had suddenly become of his inspiration, and why the witticisms in his play and his comedy had begun to seem as mechanical as the cracking of the post-boy's whip. He looked out at the scrubby fields, the rusty woods, the sullen sky, and asked himself whether *that* was the world to which it had been but yesterday his high ambition to hold up the mirror. The Countess's *dame de compagnie* sat opposite to him in the carriage. Yesterday he thought her, with her pale, discreet face, and her eager movements that pretended to be indifferent, a finished specimen of an entertaining genus. To-day he could only say that if there was a whole genus it was a thousand pities, for the poor lady struck him as miserably false and servile. The real seemed hideous; he felt home-sick for his dear familiar rooms between the garden and the square, and he longed to get into them and bolt his door and bury himself in his old arm-chair and cultivate idealism for evermore. The first thing he actually did on getting into them was to go to the window and look out into the garden. It had greatly changed in his absence, and the old maimed statues, which all the summer had been comfortably muffled in verdure, were now, by an odd contradiction of propriety, standing white and naked in the cold. I don't exactly know how soon it was that Benvolio went back to see his neighbours. It was after no great interval, and yet it was not immediately. He had a bad conscience, and he was wondering what he should say to them. It seemed to him now (though he had not thought of it sooner), that they might accuse him of neglecting them. He had appealed to their friendship, he had professed the highest esteem for them, and then he had turned his back on them without farewell, and without a word of explanation. He had not written to them; in truth during his sojourn with the Countess, it would not have been hard for him to persuade himself that they were people he had only dreamed about, or read about, at most, in some old volume of memoirs. People of their value, he could now imagine them saying, were not to be taken up and dropped for a fancy; and if friendship was not to be friendship as they themselves understood it, it was better that he should forget them at once and for ever. It is perhaps too much to affirm that he imagined them saying all this; they were too mild and civil, too unused to acting in self-defence. But they might easily receive him in a way that would imply a delicate resentment. Benvolio felt profaned, dishonoured, almost contaminated; so that perhaps when he did at last return to his friends, it was because that was the simplest way to be purified. How did they receive him? I told you a good way back that Scholastica was in love with him, and you may arrange the scene in any manner that best accords with this circumstance. Her forgiveness, of course, when once that chord was touched, was proportionate to her displeasure. But Benvolio took refuge both from his own compunction and from the young girl's reproaches, in whatever form these were conveyed, in making a full confession of what he was pleased to call his frivolity. As he walked through the naked garden with Scholastica, kicking the wrinkled leaves, he told her the whole story of his sojourn with the Countess. The young girl listened with bright intentness, as she would have listened to some thrilling passage in a romance; but she neither sighed, nor looked wistful, nor seemed to envy the Countess or to repine at her own ignorance of the great world. It was all too remote for comparison; it was not, for Scholastica, among the things that might have been. Benvolio talked to her very freely about the Countess. If she liked it, he found on his side that it eased his mind; and as he said nothing that the Countess would not have been flattered by, there was no harm done. Although, however, Benvolio uttered nothing but praise of this distinguished lady, he was very frank in saying that she and her way of life always left him at the end in a worse humour than when they found him. They were very well in their way, he said, but their way was not his way —it only seemed so at moments. For him, he was convinced, the only real felicity was in the pleasures of study! Scholastica answered that it gave her high satisfaction to hear this, for it was her father's belief that Benvolio had a great aptitude for philosophical research, and that it was a sacred duty to cultivate so rare a faculty.

"And what is your belief?" Benvolio asked, remembering that the young girl knew several of his poems by heart.

Her answer was very simple. "I believe you are a poet."

"And a poet oughtn't to run the risk of turning pedant?"

"No," she answered; "a poet ought to run all risks—even that one which for a poet is perhaps most cruel. But he ought to escape them all!"

Benvolio took great satisfaction in hearing that the Professor deemed that he had in him the making of a philosopher, and it gave an impetus to the zeal with which he returned to work.

VI

OF course even the most zealous student cannot work always, and often, after a very philosophic day, Benvolio spent with the Countess a very sentimental evening. It is my duty as a veracious historian not to conceal the fact that he discoursed to the Countess about Scholastica. He gave such a puzzling description of her that the Countess declared that she must be a delightfully quaint creature and that it would be vastly amusing to know her. She hardly supposed Benvolio was in love with this little bookworm in petticoats, but to make sure —if that might be called making sure—she deliberately asked him. He said No; he hardly saw how he could be, since he

was in love with the Countess herself! For a while this
answer satisfied her, but as the winter went by she began to
wonder whether there were not such a thing as a man being
in love with two women at once. During many months that
followed, Benvolio led a kind of double life. Sometimes it
charmed him and gave him an inspiring sense of personal
power. He haunted the domicile of his gentle neighbours, and
drank deep of the garnered wisdom of the ages; and he made
appearances as frequent in the Countess's drawing-room,
where he played his part with magnificent zest and ardour. It
was a life of alternation and contrast, and it really demanded
a vigorous and elastic temperament. Sometimes his own
seemed to him quite inadequate to the occasion—he felt
fevered, bewildered, exhausted. But when it came to the point
of choosing one thing or the other, it was impossible to give
up either his worldly habits or his studious aspirations.
Benvolio raged inwardly at the cruel limitations of the human
mind, and declared it was a great outrage that a man should
not be personally able to do everything he could imagine
doing. I hardly know how she contrived it, but the Countess
was at this time a more engaging woman than she had ever
been. Her beauty acquired an ampler and richer cast, and she
had a manner of looking at you as she slowly turned away
with a vague reproachfulness that was at the same time an
encouragement, which had lighted a hopeless flame in many a
youthful breast. Benvolio one day felt in the mood for finishing his comedy, and the Countess and her friends acted it. Its
success was no less brilliant than that of its predecessor, and
the manager of the theatre immediately demanded the privilege of producing it. You will hardly believe me, however,
when I tell you that on the night that his comedy was introduced to the public, its eccentric author sat discussing the
absolute and the relative with the Professor and his daughter.
Benvolio had all winter been observing that Scholastica never
looked so pretty as when she sat, of a winter's night, plying

a quiet needle in the mellow circle of a certain antique brass lamp. On the night in question he happened to fall a-thinking of this picture, and he tramped out across the snow for the express purpose of looking at it. It was sweeter even than his memory promised, and it banished every thought of his theatrical honours from his head. Scholastica gave him some tea, and her tea, for mysterious reasons, was delicious; better, strange to say, than that of the Countess, who, however, it must be added, recovered her ground in coffee. The Professor's parsimonious brother owned a ship which made voyages to China and brought him goodly chests of the incomparable plant. He sold the cargo for great sums, but he kept a chest for himself. It was always the best one, and he had at this time carefully measured out a part of his annual dole, made it into a little parcel, and presented it to Scholastica. This is the secret history of Benvolio's fragrant cups. While he was drinking them on the night I speak of—I am ashamed to say how many he drank—his name, at the theatre, was being tossed across the footlights to a brilliant, clamorous multitude, who hailed him as the redeemer of the national stage. But I am not sure that he even told his friends that his play was being acted. Indeed, this was hardly possible, for I meant to say just now that he had forgotten it.

It is very certain, however, that he enjoyed the criticisms the next day in the newspapers. Radiant and jubilant, he went to see the Countess, with half a dozen of them in his pocket. He found her looking terribly dark. She had been at the theatre, prepared to revel in his triumph—to place on his head with her own hand, as it were, the laurel awarded by the public; and his absence had seemed to her a sort of personal slight. Yet his triumph had nevertheless given her an exceeding pleasure, for it had been the seal of her secret hopes of him. Decidedly he was to be a great man, and this was not the moment for letting him go! At the same time there was something noble in his indifference, his want of eagerness, his

2B

finding it so easy to forget his honours. It was only an intellectual Crœsus, the Countess said to herself, who could afford
to keep so loose an account with fame. But she insisted on
knowing where he had been, and he told her he had been
discussing philosophy and tea with the Professor.

"And was not the daughter there?" the Countess demanded.

"Most sensibly!" he cried. And then he added in a moment
—"I don't know whether I ever told you, but she's almost as
pretty as you."

The Countess resented the compliment to Scholastica
much more than she enjoyed the compliment to herself. She
felt an extreme curiosity to see this inky-fingered syren, and
as she seldom failed, sooner or later, to compass her desires,
she succeeded at last in catching a glimpse of her innocent
rival. To do so she was obliged to set a great deal of machinery
in motion. She induced Benvolio to give a lunch, in his rooms,
to some ladies who professed a desire to see his works of art,
and of whom she constituted herself the chaperon. She took
care that he threw open a certain vestibule that looked into the
garden, and here, at the window, she spent much of her time.
There was but a chance that Scholastica would come forth
into the garden, but it was a chance worth staking something
upon. The Countess gave to it time and temper, and she was
finally rewarded. Scholastica came out. The poor girl strolled
about for half an hour, in profound unconsciousness that the
Countess's fine eyes were devouring her. The impression she
made was singular. The Countess found her both pretty and
ugly: she did not admire her herself, but she understood that
Benvolio might. For herself, personally, she detested her, and
when Scholastica went in and she turned away from the window, her first movement was to pass before a mirror, which
showed her something that, impartially considered, seemed to
her a thousand times more beautiful. The Countess made no
comments, and took good care Benvolio did not suspect the
trick she had played him. There was something more she

promised herself to do, and she impatiently awaited her opportunity.

In the middle of the winter she announced to him that she was going to spend ten days in the country; she had received the most attractive accounts of the state of things on her domain. There had been great snow-falls, and the sleighing was magnificent; the lakes and streams were solidly frozen, there was an unclouded moon, and the resident gentry were skating, half the night, by torch-light. The Countess was passionately fond both of sleighing and skating, and she found this picture irresistible. And then she was charitable, and observed that it would be a kindness to the poor resident gentry, whose usual pleasures were of a frugal sort, to throw open her house and give a ball or two, with the village fiddlers. Perhaps even they might organize a bear-hunt—an entertainment at which, if properly conducted, a lady might be present as spectator. The Countess told Benvolio all this one day as he sat with her in her boudoir, in the fire-light, during the hour that precedes dinner. She had said more than once that he must decamp—that she must go and dress; but neither of them had moved. She did not invite him to go with her to the country; she only watched him as he sat gazing with a frown at the fire-light—the crackling blaze of the great logs which had been cut in the Countess's bear-haunted forests. At last she rose impatiently, and fairly turned him out. After he had gone she stood for a moment looking at the fire, with the tip of her foot on the fender. She had not to wait long; he came back within the minute—came back and begged her leave to go with her to the country—to skate with her in the crystal moonlight and dance with her to the sound of the village violins. It hardly matters in what terms his request was granted; the notable point is that he made it. He was her only companion, and when they were established in the castle the hospitality extended to the resident gentry was less abundant than had been promised. Benvolio, however, did not

2B*

complain of the absence of it, because, for the week or so, he was passionately in love with his hostess. They took long sleigh-rides and drank deep of the poetry of winter. The blue shadows on the snow, the cold amber lights in the west, the leafless twigs against the snow-charged sky, all gave them extraordinary pleasure. The nights were even better, when the great silver stars, before the moonrise, glittered on the polished ice, and the young Countess and her lover, firmly joining hands, launched themselves into motion and into the darkness and went skimming for miles with their winged steps. On their return, before the great chimney-place in the old library, they lingered a while and drank little cups of wine heated with spices. It was perhaps here, cup in hand—this point is uncertain—that Benvolio broke through the last bond of his reserve, and told the Countess that he loved her, in a manner to satisfy her. To be his in all solemnity, his only and his for ever—this he explicitly, passionately, imperiously demanded of her. After this she gave her ball to her country neighbours, and Benvolio danced, to a boisterous, swinging measure, with a dozen ruddy beauties dressed in the fashions of the year before last. The Countess danced with the lusty male counterparts of these damsels, but she found plenty of chances to watch Benvolio. Toward the end of the evening she saw him looking grave and bored, with very much such a frown in his forehead as when he had sat staring at the fire that last day in her boudoir. She said to herself for the hundredth time that he was the strangest of mortals.

On their return to the city she had frequent occasions to say it again. He looked at moments as if he had repented of his bargain—as if it did not at all suit him that his being the Countess's only lover should involve her being his only mistress. She deemed now that she had acquired the right to make him give an account of his time, and he did not conceal the fact that the first thing he had done on reaching town was to go to see his eccentric neighbours. She treated him here-

upon to a passionate outburst of jealousy; called Scholastica
a dozen harsh names—a little dingy blue-stocking, a little
underhand, hypocritical Puritan; demanded he should promise never to speak to her again, and summoned him to make
a choice once for all. Would he belong to her, or to that odious
little schoolmistress? It must be one thing or the other; he
must take her or leave her; it was impossible she should have
a lover who was so little to be depended upon. The Countess
did not say this made her unhappy, but she repeated a dozen
times that it made her ridiculous. Benvolio turned very pale;
she had never seen him so before; a great struggle was evidently taking place within him. A terrible scene was the consequence. He broke out into reproaches and imprecations; he
accused the Countess of being his bad angel, of making him
neglect his best faculties, mutilate his genius, squander his life;
and yet he confessed that he was committed to her, that she
fascinated him beyond resistance, and that, at any sacrifice, he
must still be her slave. This confession gave the Countess un-
common satisfaction, and made up in a measure for the unflattering remarks that accompanied it. She on her side confessed—what she had always been too proud to acknowledge
hitherto—that she cared vastly for him, and that she had
waited for long months for him to say something of this kind.
They parted on terms which it would be hard to define—full
of mutual resentment and devotion, at once adoring and hat-
ing each other. All this was deep and stirring emotion, and
Benvolio, as an artist, always in one way or another found his
profit in emotion, even when it lacerated or suffocated him.
There was, moreover, a sort of elation in having burnt his
ships behind him, and vowed to seek his fortune, his intellectual fortune, in the tumult of life and action. He did no work;
his power of work, for the time at least, was paralyzed. Sometimes this frightened him; it seemed as if his genius were dead,
his career cut short; at other moments his faith soared
supreme; he heard, in broken murmurs, the voice of the muse,

and said to himself that he was only resting, waiting, storing up knowledge. Before long he felt tolerably tranquil again; ideas began to come to him, and the world to seem entertaining. He demanded of the Countess that, without further delay, their union should be solemnized. But the Countess, at that interview I have just related, had, in spite of her high spirit, received a great fright. Benvolio, stalking up and down with clenched hands and angry eyes, had seemed to her a terrible man to marry; and though she was conscious of a strong will of her own, as well as of robust nerves, she had shuddered at the thought that such scenes might often occur. She had hitherto seen little but the mild and genial, or at most the joyous and fantastic side of her friend's disposition; but it now appeared that there was another side to be taken into account, and that if Benvolio had talked of sacrifices, these were not all to be made by him. They say the world likes its master—that a horse of high spirit likes being well ridden. This may be true in the long run; but the Countess, who was essentially a woman of the world, was not yet prepared to pay our young man the tribute of her luxurious liberty. She admired him more, now that she was afraid of him, but at the same time she liked him a trifle less. She answered that marriage was a very serious matter; that they had lately had a taste of each other's tempers; that they had better wait a while longer; that she had made up her mind to travel for a year, and that she strongly recommended him to come with her, for travelling was notoriously an excellent test of friendship.

VII

She went to Italy, and Benvolio went with her; but before he went he paid a visit to his other mistress. He flattered himself that he had burned his ships behind him, but the fire was still visibly smouldering. It is true, nevertheless, that he passed a very strange half-hour with Scholastica and her father. The young girl had greatly changed; she barely greeted him; she looked at him coldly. He had no idea her face could wear that look; it vexed him to find it there. He had not been to see her for many weeks, and he now came to tell her that he was going away for a year; it is true these were not conciliatory facts. But she had taught him to think that she possessed in perfection the art of trustful resignation, of unprotesting, cheerful patience—virtues that sat so gracefully on her bended brow that the thought of their being at any rate supremely becoming took the edge from his remorse at making them necessary. But now Scholastica looked older as well as sadder, and decidedly not so pretty. Her figure was meagre, her movements were angular, her charming eye was dull. After the first minute he avoided this charming eye; it made him uncomfortable. Her voice she scarcely allowed him to hear. The Professor, as usual, was serene and frigid, impartial and transcendental. There was a chill in the air, a shadow between them. Benvolio went so far as to wonder that he had ever found a great attraction in the young girl, and his present disillusionment gave him even more anger than pain. He took leave abruptly and coldly, and puzzled his brain for a long time afterward over the mystery of Scholastica's reserve.

The Countess had said that travelling was a test of friendship; in this case friendship (or whatever the passion was to be called) promised for some time to resist the test. Benvolio passed six months of the liveliest felicity. The world has nothing better to offer to a man of sensibility than a first visit to Italy during those years of life when perception is at its keenest, when knowledge has arrived, and yet youth has not departed. He made with the Countess a long, slow progress through the lovely land, from the Alps to the Sicilian sea; and it seemed to him that his imagination, his intellect, his genius, expanded with every breath and rejoiced in every glance. The

Countess was in an almost equal ecstasy, and their sympathy
was perfect in all points save the lady's somewhat indiscrimin-
ate predilection for assemblies and receptions. She had a
thousand letters of introduction to deliver, which entailed a
vast deal of social exertion. Often, on balmy nights when he
would have preferred to meditate among the ruins of the
Forum, or to listen to the moonlit ripple of the Adriatic,
Benvolio found himself dragged away to kiss the hand of a
decayed princess, or to take a pinch from the snuff-box of an
epicurean cardinal. But the cardinals, the princesses, the ruins,
the warm southern tides which seemed the voice of history
itself—these and a thousand other things resolved themselves
into an immense pictorial spectacle—the very stuff that inspiration is made of. Everything Benvolio had written before
coming to Italy now appeared to him worthless; this was the
needful stamp, the consecration of talent. One day, however,
his felicity was clouded; by a trifle you will say, possibly; but
you must remember that in men of Benvolio's disposition
primary impulses are almost always produced by small accidents. The Countess, speaking of the tone of voice of some
one they had met, happened to say that it reminded her of the
voice of that queer little woman at home—the daughter of the
blind professor. Was this pure inadvertence, or was it malicious design? Benvolio never knew, though he immediately
demanded of her, in surprise, when and where she had heard
Scholastica's voice. His whole attention was aroused; the
Countess perceived it, and for a moment she hesitated. Then
she bravely replied that she had seen the young girl in the
musty old book-room where she spent her dreary life. At
these words, uttered in a profoundly mocking tone, Benvolio
had an extraordinary sensation. He was walking with the
Countess in the garden of a palace, and they had just approached the low balustrade of a terrace which commanded
a magnificent view. On one side were violet Apennines,
dotted here and there with a gleaming castle or convent; on

the other stood the great palace through whose galleries the two had just been strolling, with its walls incrusted with medallions and its cornice charged with statues. But Benvolio's heart began to beat; the tears sprang to his eyes; the perfect landscape around him faded away and turned to blankness, and there rose before him, distinctly, vividly present, the old brown room that looked into the dull northern garden, tenanted by the quiet figures he had once told himself that he loved. He had a choking sensation and a sudden overwhelming desire to return to his own country.

The Countess would say nothing more than that the fancy had taken her one day to go and see Scholastica. "I suppose I may go where I please!" she cried in the tone of the great lady who is accustomed to believe that her glance confers honour wherever it falls. "I am sure I did her no harm. She's a good little creature, and it's not her fault if she's so ridiculously plain." Benvolio looked at her intently, but he saw that he should learn nothing from her that she did not choose to tell. As he stood there he was amazed to find how natural, or at least how easy, it was to disbelieve her. She had been with the young girl; that accounted for anything; it accounted abundantly for Scholastica's painful constraint. What had the Countess said and done? what infernal trick had she played upon the poor girl's simplicity? He helplessly wondered, but he felt that she could be trusted to hit her mark. She had done him the honour to be jealous, and in order to alienate Scholastica she had invented some ingenious calumny against himself. He felt sick and angry, and for a week he treated his companion with grim indifference. The charm was broken, the cup of pleasure was drained. This remained no secret to the Countess, who was furious at the mistake she had made. At last she abruptly told Benvolio that the test had failed; they must separate; he would gratify her by taking his leave. He asked no second permission, but bade her farewell in the midst of her little retinue, and went journeying out of Italy with no other company than his thick-swarming memories and projects.

The first thing he did on reaching home was to repair to the Professor's abode. The old man's chair, for the first time, was empty, and Scholastica was not in the room. He went out into the garden, where, after wandering hither and thither, he found the young girl seated in a dusky arbour. She was dressed, as usual, in black; but her head was drooping, her empty hands were folded, and her sweet face was more joyless even than when he had last seen it. If she had been changed then, she was doubly changed now. Benvolio looked round, and as the Professor was nowhere visible, he immediately guessed the cause of her mourning aspect. The good old man had gone to join his immortal brothers, the classic sages, and Scholastica was utterly alone. She seemed frightened at seeing him, but he took her hand, and she let him sit down beside her. "Whatever you were once told that made you think ill of me is detestably false," he said. "I have the tenderest friendship for you, and now more than ever I should like to show it." She slowly gathered courage to meet his eyes; she found them reassuring, and at last, though she never told him in what way her mind had been poisoned, she suffered him to believe that her old confidence had come back. She told him how her father had died, and how, in spite of the philosophic maxims he had bequeathed to her for her consolation, she felt very lonely and helpless. Her uncle had offered her a maintenance, meagre but sufficient; she had the old serving-woman to keep her company, and she meant to live in her present abode and occupy herself with collecting her father's papers and giving them to the world according to a plan for which he had left particular directions. She seemed irrestibly tender and touching, and yet full of dignity and self-support. Benvolio fell in love with her again on the spot, and only abstained from telling her so because he remembered just in time that he had an engagement to be married to the Countess, and that this

understanding had not yet been formally rescinded. He paid
Scholastica a long visit, and they went in together and rummaged over her father's books and papers. The old scholar's
literary memoranda proved to be extremely valuable; it would
be a useful and interesting task to give them to the world.
When Scholastica heard Benvolio's high estimate of them her
cheek began to glow and her spirit to revive. The present
then was secure, she seemed to say to herself, and she would
have occupation for many a month. He offered to give her
every assistance in his power, and in consequence he came
daily to see her. Scholastica lived so much out of the world
that she was not obliged to trouble herself about vulgar
gossip. Whatever jests were aimed at the young man for his
visible devotion to a mysterious charmer, he was very sure
that her ear was never wounded by base insinuations. The old
serving-woman sat in a corner, nodding over her distaff, and
the two friends held long confabulations over yellow manuscripts in which the commentary, it must be confessed, did not
always adhere very closely to the text. Six months elapsed,
and Benvolio found an ineffable charm in this mild mixture of
sentiment and study. He had never in his life been so long of
the same mind; it really seemed as if, as the phrase is, the fold
were taken for ever—as if he had done with the world and
were ready to live henceforth in the closet. He hardly thought
of the Countess, and they had no correspondence. She was in
Italy, in Greece, in the East, in the Holy Land, in places and
situations that taxed the imagination.

One day, in the darkness of the vestibule, after he had left
Scholastica, he was arrested by a little old man of sordid
aspect, of whom he could make out hardly more than a pair
of sharply-glowing eyes and an immense bald head, polished
like a ball of ivory. He was a quite terrible little figure in his
way, and Benvolio at first was frightened. "Mr Poet," said the
old man, "let me say a single word. I give my niece a maintenance. She may do what she likes. But she forfeits every

penny of her allowance and her expectations if she is fool enough to marry a fellow who scribbles rhymes. I am told they are sometimes an hour finding two that will match! Good evening, Mr Poet!" Benvolio heard a sound like the faint jingle of loose coin in a breeches pocket, and the old man abruptly retreated into his domiciliary gloom. Benvolio had never seen him before, and he had no wish ever to see him again. He had not proposed to himself to marry Scholastica, and even if he had, I am pretty sure he would now have taken the modest view of the matter and decided that his hand and heart were an insufficient compensation for the relinquishment of a miser's fortune. The young girl never spoke of her uncle; he lived quite alone, apparently, haunting his upper chambers like a restless ghost, and sending her, by the old serving-woman, her slender monthly allowance, wrapped up in a piece of old newspaper. It was shortly after this that the Countess at last came back. Benvolio had been taking one of those long walks to which he had always been addicted, and passing through the public gardens on his way home, he had sat down on a bench to rest. In a few moments a carriage came rolling by; in it sat the Countess—beautiful, sombre, solitary. He rose with a ceremonious salute, and she went her way. But in five minutes she passed back again, and this time her carriage stopped. She gave him a single glance, and he got in. For a week afterward Scholastica vainly awaited him. What had happened? It had happened that though she had proved herself both false and cruel, the Countess again asserted her charm, and our precious hero again succumbed to it. But he resumed his visits to Scholastica after an interval of neglect not long enough to be unpardonable; the only difference was that now they were not so frequent.

My story draws to a close, for I am afraid you have already lost patience with the history of this amiable weathercock. Another year ran its course, and the Professor's manuscripts were arranged in great piles and almost ready for the printer.

Benvolio had had a constant hand in the work, and had found it exceedingly interesting; it involved inquiries and researches of the most stimulating and profitable kind. Scholastica was very happy. Her friend was often absent for many days, during which she knew he was leading the great world's life; but she had learned that if she patiently waited, the pendulum would swing back, and he would reappear and bury himself in their books and papers and talk. And their talk, you may be sure, was not all technical; they touched on everything that came into their heads, and Benvolio by no means felt obliged to be silent about those mundane matters as to which a vow of personal ignorance had been taken for his companion. He took her into his poetic confidence, and read her everything he had written since his return from Italy. The more he worked the more he desired to work; and so, at this time, occupied as he was with editing the Professor's manuscripts, he had never been so productive on his own account. He wrote another drama, on an Italian subject, which was performed with magnificent success; and this production he discussed with Scholastica scene by scene and speech by speech. He proposed to her to come and see it acted from a covered box, where her seclusion would be complete. She seemed for an instant to feel the force of the temptation; then she shook her head with a frank smile, and said it was better not. The play was dedicated to the Countess, who had suggested the subject to him in Italy, where it had been imparted to her, as a family anecdote, by one of her old princesses. This easy, fruitful, complex life might have lasted for ever, but for two most regrettable events. *Might* have lasted I say; you observe I do not affirm it positively. Scholastica lost her peace of mind; she was suffering a secret annoyance. She concealed it as far as she might from her friend, and with some success; for although he suspected something and questioned her, she persuaded him that it was his own fancy. In reality it was no fancy at all, but the very uncomfortable fact that her shabby

old uncle, the miser, was a terrible thorn in her side. He had
told Benvolio that she might do as she liked, but he had
recently revoked this amiable concession. He informed her
one day, by means of an illegible note, scrawled with a blunt
pencil, on the back of an old letter, that her beggarly friend
the Poet came to see her altogether too often; that he was
determined she never should marry a crack-brained rhyme-
ster; and that he requested that before the sacrifice became too
painful she would be so good as to dismiss Mr Benvolio.
This was accompanied by an intimation, more explicit than
gracious, that he opened his money-bags only for those who
deferred to his incomparable wisdom. Scholastica was poor,
and simple, and lonely; but she was proud, for all that, with
a shrinking and unexpressed pride of her own, and her uncle's
charity, proffered on these terms, became intolerably bitter to
her soul. She sent him word that she thanked him for his past
liberality, but she would no longer be a charge upon him.
She said to herself that she could work; she had a superior
education; many women, she knew, supported themselves.
She even found something inspiring in the idea of going out
into the world of which she knew so little, to seek her fortune.
Her great desire, however, was to keep her situation a secret
from Benvolio, and to prevent his knowing the sacrifice she
was making for him. This it is especially that proves she was
proud. It so happened that circumstances made secrecy
possible. I don't know whether the Countess had always an
idea of marrying Benvolio, but her imperious vanity still
suffered from the spectacle of his divided allegiance, and it
suggested to her a truly malignant revenge. A brilliant political mission, to treat of a special question, was about to be
despatched to a neighbouring government, and half a dozen
young men of eminence were to be attached to it. The Countess had influence at Court, and without saying anything to
Benvolio, she immediately urged his claim to a post on the
ground of his distinguished services to literature. She pulled

her wires so cleverly that in a very short time she had the pleasure of presenting him his appointment on a great sheet of parchment, from which the royal seal dangled by a blue ribbon. It involved an exile of but a few weeks, and to this with her eye on the sequel of her project, she was able to resign herself. Benvolio's imagination took fire at the thought of spending a month at a foreign court, in the very hotbed of consummate diplomacy; this was a phase of experience with which he was as yet unacquainted. He departed, and no sooner had he gone than the Countess, at a venture, waited upon Scholastica. She knew the girl was poor, and she believed that in spite of her homely virtues she would not, if the opportunity were placed before her in a certain light, prove implacably indisposed to better her fortunes. She knew nothing of the young girl's contingent expectations from her uncle, and her interference at this juncture was simply a remarkable coincidence. She laid before her a proposal from a certain great lady, whose husband, an eminent general, had just been dubbed governor of an island on the other side of the globe. This lady desired a preceptress for her children; she had heard of Scholastica's merit, and she ventured to hope that she might persuade her to accompany her to the Antipodes and reside in her family. The offer was brilliant; to Scholastica it seemed mysteriously and providentially opportune. Nevertheless she hesitated, and demanded time for reflection; without telling herself why, she wished to wait till Benvolio should return. He wrote her two or three letters, full of the echoes of his brilliant actual life, and without a word about the things that were nearer her own experience. The month elapsed, but he was still absent. Scholastica, who was in correspondence with the governor's wife, delayed her decision from week to week. She had sold her father's manuscripts to a publisher, for a very small sum, and gone, meanwhile, to live in a convent. At last the governor's lady demanded her ultimatum. The poor girl scanned the horizon, and saw no rescuing friend;

Benvolio was still at the court of Illyria! What she saw was the Countess's fine eyes eagerly watching her over the top of her fan. They seemed to contain a horrible menace, and to hold somehow her happiness at their mercy. Her heart sank; she gathered up her few possessions and set sail, with her illustrious protectors, for the Antipodes. Shortly after her departure Benvolio returned. He felt a terrible pang of rage and grief when he learned that she had gone; he went to the Countess, prepared to accuse her of the basest treachery. But she checked his reproaches by arts that she had never gone so far as to use before, and promised him that, if he would trust her, he should never miss that pale-eyed little governess. It can hardly be supposed that he believed her; but be appears to have been guilty of letting himself be persuaded without belief. For some time after this he almost lived with the Countess. He had, with infinite pains, purchased from his neighbour, the miser, the right of occupancy of the late Professor's apartment. This repulsive proprietor, in spite of his constitutional aversion to rhymesters, had not resisted the financial argument, and seemed greatly amazed that a poet should have a dollar to spend. Scholastica had left all things in their old places, but Benvolio, for the present, never went into the room. He turned the key in the door, and kept it in his waistcoat-pocket, where, while he was with the Countess, his fingers fumbled with it. Several months rolled by, and the Countess's promise was not verified. He missed Scholastica wofully, and missed her more as time elapsed. He began at last to go to the old brown room and to try to do some work there. He only half succeeded in a fashion; it seemed dark and empty; doubly empty when he remembered what it might have been. Suddenly he ceased to visit the Countess; a long time passed without her seeing him. She met him at another house, and had some remarkable words with him. She covered him with reproaches that were doubtless deserved, but he made her an answer that caused her to open her eyes and flush, and admit afterward that, for a clever woman, she had been a great fool. "Don't you see," he said, "can't you imagine, that I cared for you only by contrast? You took the trouble to kill the contrast, and with it you killed everything else. For a constancy I prefer *this!*" And he tapped his poetic brow. He never saw the Countess again.

I rather regret now that I said at the beginning of my story that it was not to be a fairy-tale; otherwise I should be at liberty to relate, with harmonious geniality, that if Benvolio missed Scholastica, he missed the Countess also, and led an extremely fretful and unproductive life, until one day he sailed for the Antipodes and brought Scholastica home. After this he began to produce again; only, many people said that his poetry had become dismally dull. But excuse me; I am writing as if it *were* a fairy-tale!

A NOTE ON THE TEXT

In preparing these tales for publication, the editor had to choose between James's original magazine texts, those published in book form soon afterwards and those revised and rewritten for the New York Edition. The obvious choice, it seemed to him, was the original book form of the story where there was one. In that form it had the benefit of revision from magazine to volume; and in that form it was best known to James's generation. It seemed to the editor that in a chronological edition of James's shorter fictions, the New York Edition texts had no relevance. They belong exclusively to the edition for which they were designed; particularly since the revisions were often made several decades after the original publication.

The original magazine publications of the tales in this volume were as follows:

"The Madonna of the Future," *Atlantic Monthly*, March 1873.

"The Sweetheart of M. Briseux," *Galaxy*, June 1873.

"The Last of the Valerii," *Atlantic Monthly*, January 1874.

"Madame de Mauves," *Galaxy*, February–March 1874.

"Adina," *Scribner's Monthly*, May–June 1874.

"Professor Fargo," *Galaxy*, August 1874.

"Eugene Pickering," *Atlantic Monthly*, October–November 1874.

"Benvolio," *Galaxy*, August 1875.

James included "The Madonna of the Future," "The Last of the Valerii," "Madame de Mauves," and "Eugene Pickering" in his first book, *A Passionate Pilgrim*, in 1875. He reprinted all but the second of these four tales, and also "Benvolio", in *The Madonna of the Future* in 1879. The text used here is that of the first book publication. The rest of the tales follow the original magazine texts which have never before appeared in England.

For the complete bibliography of the tales the reader is referred to *A Bibliography of the Writings of Henry James* by Leon Edel and Dan H. Laurence (second edition, revised, London, 1961) in the Soho Bibliographies published by Rupert Hart-Davis.